"YOU WILL NOT FALL. I PROMISE."

Faith let go, and in the next moment strong arms came around her waist from behind. She waited for him to set her feet on the ground, but he held her tight for a moment, in a grip that told her she'd be helpless if he decided to do anything more. She grasped the hard rock of his forearms that were wrapped around her from behind. "You can put me down now."

"I am well aware of that."

Faith frowned. "Then why don't you?"

He lifted her a little higher, and in the next moment she felt his lips at the side of her neck. He kissed and licked her there, sending a fiery tingle through her blood, but also shocking her.

"Gabe—"

His lips were at her cheek. Why was she turning her face toward him? "Gabe, don't—"

His lips were on her mouth, and her own lips parted. His kiss burned deep, and one strong hand moved to grasp her breast.

It had been so long . . . so long since she had truly wanted a man . . .

Bantam Books by Rosanne Bittner

MONTANA WOMAN

EMBERS OF THE HEART

IN THE SHADOW OF THE MOUTAINS

OUTLAW HEARTS

SONG OF THE WOLF

THUNDER ON THE PLAINS

TENDER BETRAYAL

WILDEST DREAMS

THE FOREVER TREE

CHASE THE SUN

Rosanne Bittner

Tame the Wild Wind

BANTAM BOOKS
New York Toronto London Sydney Auckland

TAME THE WILD WIND

A Bantam Book / October 1996

All rights reserved.

ISBN 0-553-56996-1

Published simultaneously in the United States and Canada

Bantam Books are published by Bantam Books, a division of Bantam
Doubleday Dell Publishing Group, Inc. Its trademark, consisting of the
words "Bantam Books" and the portrayal of a rooster, is Registered in
U.S. Patent and Trademark Office and in other countries. Marca Regis-
trada. Bantam Books, 1540 Broadway, New York, New York 10036.

PRINTED IN THE UNITED STATES OF AMERICA

RAD   0 9 8 7 6 5 4 3 2 1

Free spirits,
That was what they shared.
Wild hearts and courageous daring
Brought them to Wyoming . . .
And into each other's arms.

Part One

Chapter One

1846 . . .

"*Gardez ceci pour vous, mon fils.*" Alexander Beaumont handed the bear-claw necklace to his ten-year-old son, Gabriel.

"*Merci, mon père.*" Delight shined in Gabriel's green eyes as he took the necklace and studied it. The steam whistle of the riverboat on which they traveled filled the air just then, its cry echoing against the muddy waters of the Mississippi.

"It was a gift from your grandfather," Alexander said. "Your mother's people have always been my good friends."

Gabriel fingered the necklace in wonder. He had met his grandfather only twice. His mother's people lived in the Upper Missouri River country, and they moved their camps often to follow the game. It was not always easy to find them when Alexander hunted and trapped there, and now they had moved west of the river country because of increased white settlement. For two years now Gabriel and his mother had not seen their Sioux relatives.

"I will treasure the necklace always, father." Gabriel's words carried the French accent he'd learned from growing up with Alexander Beaumont. The boy spoke both French and English, and through his mother he even knew a good deal of the Sioux tongue.

"Your grandfather, Two Moccasins, is an honored man among his people," Alex told his son. "I paid many horses and guns and much tobacco for your mother. Her people did not want her to go to a white man, but they knew I was their good friend and have the heart of an Indian, *oui*?"

Gabe smiled. *"Oui, père."* He wondered if he would ever be as big and strong and skilled as his father, who lived off the land almost the same as the Sioux most of the time. Hunting and trapping was the only life Gabe himself had ever known, and usually they lived in a tepee in the deep woods, except when they made these excursions to St. Louis by riverboat to sell their bounty.

Gabriel found the trips thrilling, enjoyed the wonders of the white man's life. His mother did not like the steaming, noisy riverboats, and she did not trust the "white-eyes" they encountered there. She always balked at staying in any of the rooming houses in St. Louis, claiming the closed roof kept the Great Spirit from hearing her prayers. Besides that, fancy white women in colorful dresses and odd hats often stared at her and whispered, and sometimes men made crude remarks. Fortunately, most did not care to tangle with Alexander Beaumont, who could be fierce as a bear when angered or insulted.

"I was waiting until you were old enough to understand how special that necklace is, *mon fils,* before I would give it to you," Alex was saying. "Two Moccasins killed that bear with only a knife. He was badly hurt, but he lived, and only a year later he killed another bear with his bow and arrow. He worships the bear spirit, is grateful those bears gave themselves to him, for the meat and their large warm robes, and for the honor they brought him. You have seen me thank the spirits of the animals I kill for meat and furs.

That is a custom of your mother's people. They believe all things have a soul and spirit, as humans do. I promised Two Moccasins when I took your mother for a wife that I would be sure to teach our children about the Sioux way, that I would make sure they always remembered their mother's people."

Gabe leaned back against the railing of the upper deck of the *Glory Girl,* which was churning its way back upriver to the "big woods." This trip to St. Louis had been profitable, according to Alex, but he had worked hard over the winter to trap enough beaver and fox, as well as kill enough deer to make it so. Gabriel was aware that prices for beaver pelts had fallen, and his father was worried. Alex was a wandering man who knew only one way to make a living, and he had talked about heading farther west to find more deer and perhaps begin hunting buffalo. Alex claimed that there was a growing interest among whites for buffalo hides. The buyer in St. Louis had told him so. The only reason he had put off going farther west was because Gabriel's mother had wept over the thought of leaving the country she knew best, moving even farther away from her people's homeland.

Gabriel wished his mother would not always be so sad. He knew she missed her family. She talked about them often, had taught him many things about their language and customs. Since he was born, Yellow Beaver had given birth to two more babies, but both had died only weeks after their birth. Gabriel could clearly remember his mother's wailing when each had been buried. He was her only child, and he knew he was very special to her, as she was special to him.

He put the necklace over his head, and it felt heavy on his still-slender neck. His mother was always saying how tall he was for his age, that he would someday have his father's build. He wanted to be like his father, but right now he only had Alex's green eyes. As he watched his father light a pipe, he wondered what it would be like to be a white man, to live as a white man, instead of being half one thing and half another. Alex was a grand mixture of tame and wild, a white man who lived like an Indian, and Gabriel idolized him.

"Can we try to find Two Moccasins when we reach Fort Snelling?" Gabriel asked.

Alex shrugged. "Perhaps. I think maybe your mother's people have gone farther west themselves, and that is where we must go to find the buffalo. The supplier told me winter is the best time to hunt the great beast. That is when his hide is thickest with fur. Your mother should not be so sad about going farther west. I told her that is where we might find Two Moccasins, but I think it is her mother she misses most."

Gabe frowned, thinking. "I would miss *my* mother if I had to be away from her."

Alex gave out a throaty laugh. "*Oui,* I suppose that you would. Yellow Beaver is a fine woman, a good mother. I greatly honor her, but I fear I do not make her so happy as being with her own people. After all the trips we have made on steamboats to forts and cities, it seems she never learns to enjoy it. Always she hides in a corner belowdecks, staying with our supplies, no?"

Gabe grinned. "I will go down and stay with her for a while. I want to show her my necklace." He lost his smile then. "Do you think it will make her cry?"

Alex studied his son thoughtfully. His boy had a good heart. "Your mother cries too much. Perhaps if she had not lost her babies . . ." His own heart often ached over the losses, and he blamed himself. Perhaps it was because he'd kept his wife always on the move, living such a difficult, unsettled life, that the babies had not survived. But Gabriel had always been a strong, healthy boy, and for that he was grateful.

"This time if she cries, it will be because she is happy I have given you your grandfather's necklace," he told Gabriel. "That will mean very much to her. She will tell you more about Two Moccasins, and that will make her happy, so go and show her the necklace."

After Gabriel ran off, Alex turned to lean on the ship's railing. He knew it was getting to be time for him to settle in one place. He was getting older, and every year it seemed harder and harder to rough it through the winters, hunting for their food, hauling wood, struggling to hunt and trap in the bitter cold. He knew no other way to live, but Yellow Beaver had put up with it for years. Perhaps it was time to let her live the way *she* wanted to live.

Sadie Kelley had wanted her husband with her for the birth of their first child, but it was forbidden. A man should not be witness to such an intimate event in a woman's life, or so she'd been told by Matthew, and by the females who attended her now. But Sadie had never thought the same as most other women, and it seemed ironic to her that Matthew Kelley could invade her private parts in the night and plant his seed in her, yet he could not witness the lovely miracle of what that seed had become.

Sadie had always felt restless living among Quakers, wondered if she had truly made the right decision joining them in order to marry Matthew; but she did love him so, and a woman had to do what was required once she was a wife. These were her husband's people, and they were kind. She had made many good friends among them, and the Quakers were a deeply religious group who sometimes risked their lives fighting for human rights. She had no disagreement with their love for humankind, but the stringent religious life that came with the sect sometimes made her feel suffocated.

Now the daughter to whom she had just given birth would be raised in the sect, taught to dress plainly, to be quiet and prayerful, that most pleasures in life were sinful. She would be expected to feel the Holy Spirit within her, to search for that Spirit, spend many quiet hours waiting for the Spirit to speak to her and guide her ways.

I only want you to laugh and play and be free, Sadie thought, as Mary Jane Withrow laid her new little girl in her arms.

"You are washed and fully covered now. I'll get Matthew for you," Mary Jane told her. "She is a beautiful little girl, Sadie. She has your red hair and blue eyes. What will you name her?"

"I don't know," Sadie answered. "I've left that up to Matthew."

"Of course. That's the proper thing to do."

After Mary Jane and the other women who had tended the birth left the room, Sadie studied her baby. She *was* pretty. She remembered how she used to study herself in the mirror, wondering if others thought she was as pretty as she thought she was. Her hair was thick and long, "as red as a sunset," her father used to say. Her bosom was full and her waist slender . . . or at least it had been until she'd become large with child. She remembered when she used to wear a little color on her cheeks and lips, when she wore pretty dresses and attended dances where boys would woo her.

Then had come Matthew Kelley, a Quaker man, very handsome but always so very serious. She'd met him when her family had moved to Pennsylvania. No one knew her father had come there from New York because he'd faced debtors' prison. They were penniless when they arrived, and the whole family had gone to work as helpers on Quaker farms. Matthew was the son of one of the wealthier Quaker farming families, and she had been young and foolish and in love.

Now she was a Quaker wife, and there was no changing that. Matthew was good to her, but deep inside she ached to feel pretty again, to wear a fancy dress and color on her cheeks, to laugh, dance, travel. Those things could never be now. Maybe her daughter would one day know that kind of freedom.

"Sadie!"

Matthew walked into the room, a big man, strong, dark hair and eyes. He had taken the day off from working in the fields to wait for the birth, and now it pleased Sadie to see him grin, a rare sight on a man usually quite sober. He leaned over the bed and studied his daughter.

"Isn't she pretty?" Sadie asked. "She's healthy and strong, Matthew."

The man nodded, touching the baby's cheek with a finger. "And how are you?"

"I'm all right." Sadie felt resentment at the fact that he

had no idea what she'd been through. A man planted his seed, then walked away and went about his work while his wife suffered hours of black pain to give forth the life he'd fathered. Then the man walked in to see everything tidy, his new child magically produced as though there were nothing to it. "What name do you want to give her?" she asked.

Matthew straightened, folding his arms thoughtfully. He walked around to the foot of the bed. "I've been thinking, Sadie. You have a free spirit, and I know you struggle with that. Let's pray that our daughter does not have the same struggle. Let's pray that she is a quiet, faithful child who will look to God for guidance all her life, and who will help your own faith. Every time you speak her name, you will be reminded of that faith, for that is what we will call her . . . Faith. Faith Irene Kelley. Irene for my deceased mother. Is that agreeable with you?"

Would it matter if it wasn't? Sadie wanted to ask. But such a remark would sound critical, and a wife did not criticize her husband. "I like it just fine. Faith it is."

Matthew nodded. "Fine." He walked around the bed and leaned down to kiss her cheek. "Thank you for my daughter, Sadie. We will have to begin trying for a son as soon as possible."

Getting pregnant again anytime soon was the last thing Sadie wanted. "Yes, we will," she answered.

Matthew patted her cheek. "I'll go tell the elders about my new daughter."

After he left the room, Sadie closed her eyes, a tear slipping down one side of her face.

Gabe sat in the cargo section of the steamboat, watching his mother patiently sew a beaded design on a new pair of moccasins for his father. She used a lantern for light, as it was dark outside now, pitch-black down here where all the baggage was. He thought how pretty his mother looked by the soft glow of the lantern. If only the white people would treat her better. So what if she was Indian? They acted as though that was something to be ashamed of. It seemed to him that being part Indian was even more shameful in their

eyes. Some called him "breed" or "half-breed bastard."
Before leaving St. Louis, his father had gotten into a brutal
fistfight with a man over that word, along with "scummy"
and "lice infected."

"Father says we will probably find Two Moccasins if we
go farther west to hunt the buffalo," Gabriel said to his
mother, hoping to make her feel happier.

"I hope that he is right," she answered, keeping her eyes
on her beadwork. "You have much faith in your father,
Gabriel."

"Of course."

Yellow Beaver looked at her son and smiled. "Of
course," she mimicked. "And he is a good man. I married
him knowing I might never see my father and mother
again, but it is hard for me." With a longing look in her
eyes, she studied the bear-claw necklace he wore. "Not
many men can boast of killing a bear with only a knife, but
my father can. He was a great man. Perhaps one day you
will be a fine warrior like Two Moccasins."

At that moment someone shouted, "There they are!"
and Gabriel turned.

Three men approached, wearing the dark-blue uniforms
that designated they worked for the boat's captain. They
carried a brightly lit lantern to find their way. A few other
passengers who slept belowdecks because they could not
afford cabins cursed and grumbled at the intrusion.

"You there, boy!" one of the workers called out, coming
closer. "You're Alexander Beaumont's half-breed son,
aren't you? I've seen you up top with the man."

Gabriel rose, frowning. "Yes. I am Gabriel Beaumont."
His mother's eyes were wide with fright.

"I'm sorry, boy, but I have some bad news."

Gabriel's heart pounded harder. Where was his father?
"What is it?"

The man leaned closer, his mustache so wide, it reached
past the sides of his face. "Your father's dead, boy. He's
been killed—by robbers, I suppose. Lord knows they're
probably still on this boat, but how the hell are we supposed to know who it was?"

Gabriel heard little after the words "Your father's

dead." Nothing was making sense. Stunned, he looked at his mother, who was staring wide-eyed at the worker.

"Tell me you lie!" she cried out.

"Sorry, ma'am. The body is up on deck. We need the two of you to come identify it for sure. Then we'll put him in a pine box. I don't know if you have any money besides what was stole off him, but somebody's got to bury him next stop. You're paid up to go to Fort Snelling, so we'll take you that far. It's only another three days."

Still, nothing was making sense. His big, strong father—killed? Alex was such a skilled man. Gabriel had never seen him lose a fight with anyone, even if the other person was armed. Never had he even imagined anyone could kill Alexander Beaumont! Now these men had come to tell him his father was dead, with no more feeling than if they were telling him it was raining outside! Did they think he and his mother had no feelings? "I will go and see the body," he told his mother. "You stay here."

Suddenly he felt older. He left with the crewmen, bewildered by their casual manner, hoping they had made some kind of mistake. It was true that it was not like Alex to stay up top away from Yellow Beaver so long after dark. Blindly he stumbled over other passengers, followed the men to the upper deck to where a crowd had gathered. The men ordered others out of the way, then held the lantern over someone who lay on his back, his green eyes still open.

"Found him near the stairwell going belowdecks, lying facedown, stabbed in the back," one of the men told Gabe. "I remember he wore a money belt. It's gone. Could be the robbers swam away with it. That *is* him, ain't it? Your pa?"

Gabe wondered if the pain in his chest would kill him, too. The tears came suddenly and uncontrollably. He fell to his knees, leaning down and weeping at his father's chest, where there was no longer a heartbeat. This couldn't be happening. Only this morning Alex had given him the treasured bear-claw necklace.

Someone pulled him off the body. "Well, we know who he is now. Take him back down to the hole and get this body into a coffin before it begins to stink. Is Haley working on the damn box?"

"It will be ready shortly," came another voice.

Gabriel was dragged toward the stairs leading down to the lower decks. He tried to fight off the hands, angry, hurt, confused, full of grief. He didn't want to leave his father lying there dead like that. And who had done this? He needed to find the killer.

But they took him back to his mother. At the sight of Gabriel's face, Yellow Beaver broke out in the keening wail, the way she'd wept when she'd lost her little babies, and quickly others belowdecks began shouting for her to shut up so they could sleep. She continued her crying mixed with a song of mourning, until a man came over and grabbed her arm.

"Shut up, squaw, the rest of us are trying to sleep."

Young Gabriel, who had sobbed quietly beside his mother, kicked at the man's arm. "You leave my mother alone!" he growled.

The man let go, grabbing Gabriel around the throat and pushing him against a stack of flour sacks. "Then you make her shut up!" he ordered. "You ain't got your pa here to protect you now, so don't be mouthin' off, boy!"

Finally the man left him alone and Gabriel's thin shoulders jerked in deep sobs. The reality of how right the man was hit him then. He no longer had his father to protect him and teach him. There was only he and his mother now. He knelt beside Yellow Beaver, putting an arm around her. "You have to be quiet, *mère*. We will take our things off the boat at the next stop and sell what we need to sell to bury father. Then we can mourn. For now we must be strong. I promise that as soon as father is buried, we will go find Two Moccasins. Somehow we will do this. Perhaps we can find a scout, or a hunter, someone who can take us to them. We will go back to the Sioux."

Yellow Beaver began to weep quietly.

Gabriel wanted to pray, but he was not sure to what God he should pray—the white people's God or the God of his mother's people. Suddenly, he hated the whites. They had killed his father, and they were treating him and Yellow Beaver as though their loss meant nothing. Now he wanted desperately to find his mother's people. He would become a Sioux warrior and leave behind the white man's world.

Fiercely, Gabriel began to pray to *Wakan-Tanka*.

Chapter Two

1855 . . .

Faith wanted to cry with frustration. She simply could not understand why she had to sit for so long without uttering a word, without even raising her eyes and looking around. The latter command was impossible to keep, and she carefully cast sly, sidelong glances at those around her, all of whom had their heads bowed in silence.

This was the time for quiet waiting, the time during worship when all those assembled closed their eyes and prayed to the Holy Spirit, asking for guidance, asking for whatever divine revelation the Spirit might wish to grant them, asking the Spirit to speak through them. It was a time of waiting, but she was not sure herself just what a child her age should be waiting for. She was only nine years old, and she did not understand who this Holy Spirit was, or what she should do if He spoke to her. So far she neither felt nor heard a thing, and the desire to squirm, to talk, to laugh and play, was next to unbearable.

Then she heard it. Someone's stomach growled fiercely.

It was all she needed to give in to a need to giggle. She tried to stifle it at first, but to no avail. A muffled snicker turned into a louder giggle, and she was soon joined by her five-year-old brother, Benny. Faith's laughter was cut off when her father grabbed her thigh and squeezed painfully. She knew the signal. She had behaved sinfully, and she would be reprimanded, which meant a paddling in the woodshed. Her mother quickly jerked Benny from where he'd been sitting to Faith's right, and she plopped the boy to her own right, moving next to Faith.

Faith felt the desire to laugh change quickly to a need to cry. It seemed every natural feeling she had was wrong, so that she hardly knew how she should behave anymore. Sometimes she felt like running away, but where would she go? She knew nothing about the world outside the little Quaker settlement where she lived, and she loved her mother and father. It would break their hearts if she left them. But sometimes she deeply resented all the rules they set for her.

Finally a man began to speak, loudly proclaiming that the faithful must see that all men are treated equally. "We must speak out against the sinful practice of slavery," he proclaimed.

"Amen," most replied in unison.

"No man can own another. No man can treat another like cattle, breed another race like animals."

"Amen," came the resounding reply again.

"We must send our own people forth, bring Christianity to the Negroes and those who own them and persecute them."

Faith looked over at the man who spoke, and he seemed to have a kind of glow on his face, in his eyes. Was that a sign that the mysterious Holy Spirit had come into the man? Was it truly the Holy Spirit who was speaking now? That was what these others thought, for whenever someone spoke in these prayer meetings, it was the Quaker belief that the Holy Spirit was using him or her to give direction to the others.

"By bringing Christianity to slave masters and the Negroes kept in bondage, we will be doing Christ's bidding and perhaps save this country from war and strife. God surely will bring his wrath against this land if we allow slavery to continue."

"Hallelujah!" another man shouted.

Now others began speaking. Faith listened curiously, wondering if the fact that the Holy Spirit had never spoken to her meant she was bad. Maybe because she had giggled during prayer, the Holy Spirit would never come to her. One thing was certain. Her father would punish her once the meeting was over. Benny would probably get away with a good scolding, because he was younger and still not of an age to truly understand. Her parents would say it was her fault Benny had erred. She had started laughing first, and she was a "big girl" now and should know better.

Benny never got spanked for anything. He was the favored one. Something had "gone wrong" when he was born, and a real doctor had been brought in from nearby Johnstown. Her mother had cried at being told she would have no more children. Not only was Benny the last baby she would have, but he was a boy, a son for Matthew Kelley. Her father adored the boy, and sometimes Faith hated her brother. But she knew it really wasn't his fault for being born. It was really her father she resented more than her brother, for showing his son more love and attention than he did to her.

Her mother treated both of them equally, and Faith felt sorry for the fact that her mother would have no more children. She'd often caught her crying about it, and sometimes the woman would cry for reasons unknown. Faith had no idea where babies came from, and she wondered what had happened that her mother could have no more. Had she sinned in some way? Was she being punished by the Holy Spirit? She was not sure she even liked this Being called the Holy Spirit. It seemed to have considerable control over people's lives, and she was frightened by it.

The spoken revelations went on for nearly two more hours in the rising heat of the day. The meeting was held outside, as usual, and flies bit at Faith's neck and ankles, but she was afraid to swat at them for fear that, too, would be considered sinful. She had to relieve herself so badly that she was afraid she would wet herself before reaching the privy once they could leave. She wished there was a way to avoid a spanking, but she knew she'd not get out of it. Maybe her mother could help. Her mother seemed to be the only one who understood her energy, her desire to laugh and run and play. Just the other day they'd even swum naked together in a pond, something terribly forbidden, but it had felt so wonderful to be so totally free and cool and happy, to splash and laugh together. She would treasure the memory forever.

Finally the service ended. Faith jumped up from the crate she'd used for a chair, in a hurry to get to the privy, but her father grabbed her arm. "You are coming straight to the woodshed, Faith Kelley!"

"But, Father—"

"No buts about it!"

To Faith's embarrassment the man half dragged her past the others, many of whom scowled at her. She could remember remarks she'd heard at other meetings.

The child has too much spirit. She should be chastised for it.

You must tame that girl, Sadie.

Faith needs to learn respect for others and for the Holy Spirit, Mr. Kelley.

Such a lovely child she is. You will have to be careful of that one. Do not let her become vain, and keep the young men away from her.

Faith had no idea what "vain" meant, and she was certainly too young for anyone to be worrying about young men being interested in her. Nor did she have any interest in boys, except to hate most of them.

All of this and more swam through her head as her father dragged her to the woodshed. "I couldn't help it," she tried to explain. "It's hard to sit so long without talking or giggling, Father. I heard a woman's stomach growl."

"For all you know, it was the Holy Spirit beginning to move within her," he answered angrily.

"In her *belly*? Why would it do that?"

Matthew squeezed his daughter's arm more tightly, knowing he was hurting her, yet unable to control his anger. "You are being insulting now. One must *never* joke about the Holy Spirit, Faith! And one must certainly never laugh during such a serious time as silent prayer!"

Their own home was only several yards from the church, and already they were in the woodshed.

"But, Father, I have to—"

"Be still! Can't you *ever* keep quiet when you're told?"

Faith blinked back tears. How could she explain that she had to pee?

"I'm sorry, Faith, but you force me to do this. If you would just obey the rules, I would never have to give you these thrashings. Now, bend over!"

Faith pressed her lips tight together, silent tears running down her cheeks. She turned and bent over to grasp a sawhorse, and her father took a flat wooden paddle from the wall. He threw her dress up across her back, exposing her plain white cotton drawers, material too thin to be much of a buffer for the paddle. She jerked when she felt the first smack against her bottom. Then came another, three, four, five, six. Her bottom stung fearfully, and she could feel it getting hot. Seven, eight. She wondered if a paddle could break a bone.

Her dress was jerked down. "Now maybe you will think twice about giggling during prayer service," her father told her. "Remember that I love you, Faith Kelley. That is the only reason I do this. I want you to grow up to be a good and faithful woman, a woman of honor and respect. Fight the free spirit inside of you that causes you to do foolish things. Pray about it, Faith."

After he left, Faith heard her mother outside, protesting. "She's just being a child," Sadie was saying.

"She is nine years old! That's old enough to know right from wrong! And don't you dare go in there and console her, Sadie Kelley. You'll just encourage her to go against the rules again. She must know that we are together on this! And you'd best be praying for your own soul, woman! It's your free spirit she's got. Do you think I don't know how you struggle to remain faithful and quiet? *Pray*, woman! Pray for yourself and for your daughter!"

Faith peeked through a crack in the woodshed. She saw

her father take Benny's hand and walk off with the boy, watched her mother cover her face with her hands and weep. Her own tears came again, and she wondered how she was going to explain the fact that she had just wet herself. The beating had forced it out of her. Maybe she would get another spanking for it.

One thing she knew for sure. When she was big enough to fend for herself, she was going to run away from this place and never come back.

Gabriel lay awake. He was not sure of the time, since the Sioux did not use clocks and timepieces to keep track of such things. He remembered how to read a clock, still had a pocket watch that had belonged to his beloved father. He could even still remember some French and English, and for that he had become of value to the Minniconjou tribe with whom he and his mother had lived for the past nine years. His mother had remarried, a Sioux warrior called Five Crows. Gabriel was glad. She had even had another child three years ago, a little girl who had lived. His half sister's name was Many Flowers.

Many Crows had taught him the warrior way, but his beloved grandfather, Two Moccasins, had taught Gabriel the deep, spiritual side of the People. He had experienced the sweat lodge, and later this summer he would suffer his first Sun Dance sacrifice, something he considered a great honor. His grandfather would be very proud of him that day, and so would Alexander Beaumont if he could be there to see it. He would never forget his real father, and often he felt the man's presence, especially in the night.

He breathed deeply with pride, staring at the awakening sky through the smoke hole at the top of the tepee, his thoughts turning to the pretty girl called Little Otter. He was a man now, nineteen. Little Otter was only fourteen summers, not quite old enough to become a wife, but soon, very soon . . . He had been watching her for two years already, wanting her more as he grew older.

Little Otter was Santee. Gabriel saw her only at the gathering of tribes for a buffalo hunt, or for the Sun Dance and other special occasions. Her father was a prominent

Santee warrior, and Gabriel knew it would take many horses and proof of bravery to win her hand. His own sacrifice at the Sun Dance this summer would make a great impression. It was at this dance he expected to receive a vision from the Great Spirit that would show him what animal should guide him, and from which he would take his Indian name. He must have an Indian name before he asked for Little Otter's hand.

He had already decided he would suffer the Sun Dance every year until Little Otter was old enough to marry, just to prove himself to her father. He would not cry out with the pain. Already he had captured many horses, both wild and tame, horses he would present to Little Otter's father to try to make the man promise not to let her go to anyone else. He also had two very fine buffalo hides and his father's hunting knife to give as a gift. He hated to give up the knife. It was special to him. But Alexander Beaumont would understand.

He felt an urgency deep in his loins for Little Otter. He knew what a man and woman did to get babies, and he was very anxious to plant himself between Little Otter's legs, to see her naked and make her his woman once she was old enough. Last year, during the women's blanket dance at the huge Sun Dance gathering, Little Otter had been allowed to dance, and she had thrown her blanket over him to show that she favored him. They had sat under the blanket for several minutes, talking about their families, enjoying being close. He had kissed her cheek. She didn't know about kissing. That was a white man's practice, but she had enjoyed the kiss, especially when he had kissed her on the lips. She had let him touch her still-small breasts, and ever since then he had been on fire for her.

He no longer thought so much about whether he should be white or Indian. He had no qualms about stealing horses from white settlers, but so far he had not killed any of them. He could not quite bring himself to do that, for he had known some good white people as he'd grown up, mostly other hunters who had been friends with his father. Alex would not want him killing innocent whites. His father's best friend had been a crusty, often smelly, but honest and friendly trapper named Jess Willett, who had saved Alex's life once. Gabriel remembered him most vividly, but he had not seen the man since Alex's death.

It ate at him to realize the day was coming when he would have to make a decision over killing whites, for settlers encroached more and more into precious Sioux hunting grounds. Just last year a camp of Brule Sioux was wrongfully attacked by bluecoat soldiers. It had all started over a cow shot by a Minniconjou, a man from his mother's own tribe. From what they could figure, the owner of the cow had reported it, and soldiers had been sent out to try to bring in all Minniconjou men and find the culprit. But the stupid leader of the soldiers didn't know one Indian from another, and he had attacked the Brule camp, none of whom had had anything to do with shooting the cow. The soldiers had fired one of those big guns that sent exploding metal in a shower of injurious horror into the middle of the camp, killing and injuring innocent women and children. The Brule had retaliated by killing every one of those soldiers, to the last man.

Now all Minniconjou were worried about what would happen because of the massacre. But Gabriel's only personal concern was how long he would have to wait to marry Little Otter. He would then become a member of the Santee tribe, since by custom the wife was always allowed to remain with her family's tribe. He would have to leave his precious mother, but she had Five Crows now, and her father and little daughter. He was himself a grown man, and it was time to become a husband and a provider . . . and have sons of his own.

He stretched, thinking what a quiet morning it was there at Blue Water Creek. They were camped with Chief Little Thunder's tribe, preparing for a hunt. He listened to morning birdcalls, then frowned when he thought he heard something different, a sound that did not fit with birds or the wind. It was an odd clanking sound.

A horse whinnied, and he sat up, his keen senses coming alert. He pulled on a pair of deerskin leggings, walked to where his mother and Five Crows slept. He nudged Five Crows, who at forty summers of age was still quite strong and alert, a good hunter. The man opened his eyes and sat up.

"I hear something strange," Gabriel told him quietly in the Sioux tongue. "We should look."

Both knew the Minniconjou were in danger of a soldier attack, yet they had hoped the incident over the cow was forgotten. As far as the massacre of the soldiers by Brule Sioux, it was the Brule who should be punished, not the Minniconjou.

Five Crows quickly dressed. Yellow Beaver awoke and Gabriel turned away while she dressed. He grabbed his rifle and left the tepee with Five Crows to alert some of the others. They heard voices then and turned to see soldiers lined on a hillside in the distance. "Bluecoats!" Five Crows yelled. "Alert the others!" The man ran off shouting into other tepees for the men to get the women to safety and prepare to fight.

"Run for cover!" Gabriel yelled to his own mother. He hurried to another tepee, just as the dreaded booming sound filled his ears. They were using the big guns! The injustice of it enraged him. This was a peaceful camp.

There came an explosion directly behind him then, and he turned to see that the first howitzer shell had destroyed the tepee he had just exited. He ducked as debris flew everywhere, turned again to see that the tepee was in smoldering ruins. "Mother!" he screamed. "Many Flowers!"

By then the camp was alive with screaming, running women and children, men shouting orders, trying to get to their horses, one man running about completely naked. There were more explosions, shrapnel flying everywhere, but Gabriel saw none of it. All he was aware of was the ruins of the tepee where only moments earlier he had been quietly sleeping, dreaming about the Sun Dance and about Little Otter. All feeling had deserted his legs, and they had to carry him to the tepee, where his mother and Many Flowers lay dead, their bodies covered with blood from massive shrapnel wounds.

Cinders burned his still-bare feet as he ran into the embers, but he felt no pain. He rose, holding up his rifle and letting out a long scream: "Nooooo!"

Hatred burned in his soul, hotter than the embers that burned his feet.

Numbly he ran to help some other women and children get to safety, joined in shooting at the oncoming soldiers. It had all happened so swiftly, there was not even time to get to the horses, and many men had not had time to take up their weapons. This was not a battle that could be won. . . .

It was a slaughter, not a battle. This was the soldiers' revenge for what had happened to their own kind.

The bluecoats came on, while those Indians who could save themselves retreated into the underbrush and ravines. The camp was destroyed, Indian horses taken. Women and children who could not get away quickly enough were rounded up and taken prisoner, and through it all Gabriel saw countless friends and fellow warriors shot down. Five Crows was one of them . . . and his precious grandfather, Two Moccasins, a man who had taught him so much, had loved him, helped raise him. He was an old man now, no threat to the soldiers. But he was shot down anyway.

In minutes everyone important to his life was gone, all except Little Otter, who did not live among this tribe.

He wanted to cry, *needed* to cry. But a stubborn fury would not let him . . . not yet.

He retreated farther into the hills, helping an old woman and a little girl, both of whom were quietly weeping. When they reached the top of a hill, he looked back. From this vantage point he could see the village burning, wondered if the soldiers would bother to bury the dead.

Mother. His precious mother was down there. Silent tears began to spill down his cheeks. If only his father were there to tell him what to do.

His skin was dark, and he'd grown his black hair nearly to his waist. His eyes were green, but as far as he was concerned, that was all there was about him that was white. He knew for certain now that he wanted no part of the white world.

He would become a Santee warrior.

Chapter Three

October 1860 . . .

Fourteen-year-old Faith shivered, but it was not from the Holy Spirit, and not because it was cold. In fact, a few days of what her parents called Indian summer had arrived, and by that late afternoon it had grown so warm, she did not even need a sweater. The chill she felt was a pleasant experience, and it came from a simple touch. Johnny Sommers had casually touched her hand during prayer.

She did not know much about Johnny, except that he was seventeen and the best-looking young man she had ever seen. This was only the second time she'd been around him. Her father had met Johnny's father when selling some of his produce in Johnstown. Herbert and Gertrude Sommers, who owned a farm-supply store, had become interested in the Quakers' beliefs and had started attending meetings.

The Sommerses did not believe in violence. There had been so much bloodshed in Kansas—now called bleeding Kansas because of border wars with Missouri over slavery—that they had left, bringing Johnny and his four younger siblings back to Pennsylvania to be near Mrs. Sommers's parents.

Faith's father feared a civil war could not be avoided. That was nearly all that was discussed at the Quaker meetings these days—war, and how they should avoid getting involved. Already several Southern states had seceded from the Union. Men in Congress were arguing. There had even been physical fights. Several Federal forts had been seized by Southern states. Kansas would soon vote on statehood, claiming it would be a free state.

Faith knew these things because she'd heard her father talk about them constantly. There had been several visits between him and Johnny's father, both men agreeing war was folly. Faith was not sure what was right. Her heart was too full of what she was sure were the beginnings of love for Johnny Sommers. Her heart had pounded so hard that it almost hurt when Johnny not only came to this second gathering, but sat down beside her! The group of faithful Quakers met in a barn outside Johnstown, where many new and interested outsiders had come to listen and learn.

After several minutes of quiet prayer a leader named Simon Webster announced that "These will be trying times."

"We must be strong against war," another put in.

"War will be at our doorstep. We must not get involved," Faith's father spoke out.

A moment of silence followed, the elders all waiting for the Holy Spirit to speak through them. Faith dared to turn her head and glance sidelong at Johnny. He returned the look, his brown eyes dancing with a kind of mischief only someone like Faith understood. She knew in that look that he hated these meetings just as much as she did. He was there only because his parents were there, just as she was there because of Matthew and Sadie Kelley. She could not help a smile, and Johnny smiled in return, his eyes dropping to her chest. She felt as though her budding breasts were suddenly huge, and for the first time she was proud of the signs of becoming a woman.

The meeting seemed to last forever. When it finally

ended, Johnny leaned close and whispered in her ear. "Behind the barn. Try to get away."

Faith felt suddenly clammy instead of cold. Johnny wanted to meet alone with her! Her parents would be furious if they knew, but she would meet him anyway and take the chance. She still longed to be her own person and laugh and dance and be free, which made her do and say things that got her chastised. She decided she would never please her father, so why should she keep trying? Besides, ten-year-old Benny had become her father's whole world, and the boy was always able to remain surprisingly quiet during meetings, even when he was little, which greatly impressed Matthew. He was convinced his son was destined to become a leader among the Quakers, and he often told Faith she could take lessons in obedience and faith from her brother. Somehow everything she did was wrong, and everything Benny did was right. He was the perfect son.

After the meeting ended, the men and women began visiting, the possibility of war still the main topic of conversation. Matthew was deep in conversation with three other men, Benny standing beside him and listening intently, while her mother shared recipes with some of the other women.

Johnny had already slipped away. Faith told her mother she was going to find a privy, then hurried out and walked around the barn, glad that dusk was already turning to darkness. It was finally getting cooler, and she rubbed the backs of her arms, wondering where her next breath would come from, she was so excited. Was she crazy to be doing this? Maybe Johnny had only been teasing her. She reached the corner of the barn, peeked around.

There he was! He was leaning against the barn, and he was smoking a pipe. Excitement made it difficult for her even to move her legs, but she managed to get around the corner. When Johnny saw her, there was that handsome smile again! He had good teeth, surrounded by full lips set in a handsome face. His sandy hair was thick and wavy, and the way a piece of it hung over one eye made him even better looking. It gave him a rather wild look, and she suspected he was a daring young man, adored him for being well traveled. After all, he'd lived in Kansas, had seen war and violence. He'd traveled through Missouri, Illinois, Indiana, Ohio, had met different people, seen other cities.

"Hi, Faith. I was afraid you wouldn't come."

"I . . . I wasn't sure you really meant it."

"Sure I meant it." He again glanced at her breasts, then studied her face adoringly. "I'd be crazy not to want to get to know the prettiest girl in Pennsylvania a little better."

Faith felt herself blushing, and she turned away. "I don't know about that, Johnny, but . . . thank you."

"Heck, you know you're pretty. How old are you? Fourteen?"

She nodded.

"That's pretty near a woman. I'm glad my folks got to know yours, Faith, but I wanted you to know I'm not so sure about all this Quaker stuff. I'm only here because of my parents. I'm not much on religion, and I'm not so sure there's anything wrong with war. Fact is, if we do have one, I just might join up with the Union side. Might be right exciting, being a soldier and all. What do you think of it?"

Faith turned, studying him again. "I . . . I'd hate to see you go away. You could be hurt or killed."

He puffed on the pipe, strutting closer to her. "Would you care?"

Faith wondered if her cheeks would catch fire. "Of course I'd care. I mean . . . you're nice, and . . . and we've just met, and . . ."

"I like knowing you'd care." Johnny took the pipe from his mouth and laid it on a flat rock beside him. "Would you wait for me, Faith, if I went off to war?"

"Wait for you?"

"You know. I mean, in a couple years you'd be sixteen. It could be that long I'd be away if I joined the army. I'd like to know you'd be here waiting, that you'd write to me and all."

Faith frowned. "Why?"

"I'm not sure." Johnny shrugged. "I don't hardly know you, but you're real pretty. Heck, pretty soon lots of boys will be coming after you, asking you to dances, hay rides, things like that. I'd like to know you won't go and marry one of them before I come home, and I'd like to see more of you before there's a war. I'd like to be good friends before I go." He reached out and touched her arm. "Maybe more than just friends. I was thinking we could . . . you know . . . get together and talk. We'll find ways. Your pa probably thinks you're too young for somebody like me, being a man and all. But I don't think you're too young, and I know you already like me, Faith." He folded his arms. "And I'll bet you hate those prayer meetings as much as I do."

She smiled, finally meeting his gaze again. "I do! How did you know?"

"I could tell. Don't you sometimes just want to jump up and shout? Sing? Dance? Run? Hear music? Be kind of wild and do something you've never done before?"

Her heart pounded harder. "Yes!" She clasped her hands. "Oh, Johnny, you don't know how happy I am to hear you say that! Nobody ever understood me before! I just . . . I want to see things, go places, laugh. Father is always scolding me for being too wild. But it's just in me, and it's so hard to sit through the meetings. It isn't that I don't believe in God or that I don't pray. I just can't sit there for that long, waiting for . . . I don't even know for sure what I'm waiting for. The Holy Spirit must not want to use me, because He's never spoken to me. Has He ever spoken to you?"

Johnny laughed. "Heck, I don't think so. I've been waiting for Him to tell me I should go to war. Then I could tell my father I'm going because the Holy Spirit says I should go."

They both laughed then, and Johnny clasped her hand. "They're having another meeting here in three days. Let's meet back here again then, and I'll make excuses to come see your family. My pa makes me work long hours at his store, but I'll get away as often as I can."

"I'd like that," she answered joyfully.

"You'd best get back to your folks before they start looking for you," Johnny told her.

She studied his slender build, for the first time beginning

to wonder about men, how they were made, what it might feel like to be held in a man's arms, kissed by a man. "Yes, I should," she answered. "I just . . . I don't understand why you chose me. You hardly know me, Johnny."

"I don't need to. I can see in those pretty blue eyes we think a lot alike. And a man would be crazy not to try to get to know such a pretty girl a lot better. Nothing strange about that."

She rubbed at her arms again. "I guess not." She heard her mother calling for her then, and she lost her smile. "I'd better go! 'Bye, Johnny."

" 'Bye, Faith. I'll see you right here three days from now."

Faith nodded and ran off. Johnny watched her, wondering if she'd ever been kissed. He'd had a good roll in the hay with a girl back in Kansas, and he'd damn well liked it. He'd like to do that to Faith Kelley, but she was pretty young, and she was probably one of those good girls who would have to be married first. That might not be so bad, but it would be better if he could get under her skirts without that kind of responsibility. He'd just have to wait and see what happened. He supposed it wouldn't be so bad taking on the responsibilities of a husband. At least he'd have the prettiest wife in all of Pennsylvania.

But right now she was too young, and there was a war to think about. He hoped it *would* come. He liked experiencing new things, and being a soldier sounded exciting. Having somebody like Faith Kelley waiting for him would just make it all the sweeter.

He was no longer called Gabriel. He was Tall Bear, and he belonged to an honored warrior society of the Santee, to which only proven warriors could belong. He had suffered the Sun Dance bravely more than once over the past five years. As was custom, he had fasted for several days beforehand, had not cried out when his flesh had been pierced, had danced around the Sun Dance pole until the skewers were torn from his flesh. Little Otter had been there each time to watch, and she had been proud.

During his last sacrifice Tall Bear had had a vision, of a

bear with green eyes that could walk in the sky. A crow
had come and told him he must decide whether he wanted
to be white or brown, that if he was brown, he could
belong to the proud warrior society and would be highly
respected. If the bear chose white, he must leave the Santee
and live in the world of the Wasicu. There he would also be
respected, but he would not be able to live among the great
Sioux Nation.

When Tall Bear had told a priest of his vision, it had
been explained he must make a final choice between the
white and Indian world, that if he stayed among the Sioux,
he should be called Tall Bear. He had no doubt what his
choice would be, and he had married Little Otter, then
sixteen. Lying with her had indeed been an exquisite pleasure. She had given him a son, now two years old, and
Gabriel Beaumont was never more sure he was where he
belonged, never so happy. He had a family again. He belonged. He still sometimes had trouble deep inside with his
conscience over raiding white settlements. He would never
forget his father, or some of his father's friends, as well as
traders and merchants he had met on their trips to the
cities. Still, greedy white men had killed Alex, white
soldiers had killed his mother, sister, and grandfather.
More white settlers were moving into Sioux hunting
grounds, flagrantly ignoring boundaries, shooting at the
Sioux as though they were wild animals to be chased off.

These whites who came now were not there to trade.
They wanted nothing to do with the Sioux, seemed to be
not just afraid of them, but also horrified at associating
with them, as though they were vermin. He returned the
insults by stealing their horses, killing their cattle, killing
the men who dared come to this land and call it their own.

He was happy here among the Santee, proud of his little
son, Running Fox. Since he had learned to walk, the boy
seemed never to toddle anyplace slowly. He liked to run,
and he especially liked to run and hide. Sly like a fox, Tall
Bear thought, and thus he had given the boy his new name.
When he was born, he had been called Kicker, but among
the Sioux a child's name was often changed as he or she
grew, until a final name was decided based on dreams and

visions. Sometimes Tall Bear worried over what the future held for his little boy, and for other children he and Little Otter might have.

"I have made a stew, Tall Bear," came Little Otter's voice behind him now. "The weather is very cold. It is a time for a man to eat plenty, for warmth and strength."

Tall Bear had been standing outside their tepee, watching the surrounding hills, wondering what to do about yet another white settlement that had sprung up only eight miles away. He turned to his wife, held open the heavy buffalo robe he wore against the bitter January cold. Little Otter had stepped outside without putting on a robe of her own. She smiled and wrapped her arms around his waist while Tall Bear in turn wrapped her into the robe. "I draw my warmth and strength from you," he told her in the Sioux tongue.

As she looked up at him, he leaned down and covered her mouth with his own in a deep kiss. She ran her hands down over his hips, bringing one around to caress his man part teasingly. Tall Bear laughed in a groan, kissing her harder.

"I will want to do more than eat if you keep doing that."

"I would not mind, my husband. There is little else to do when the snows are deep. It is a good way to keep warm."

He pressed himself against her belly. "I agree."

His friend, Buffalo Bull, shouted to him from where he'd left his tepee to tend his horses. "Tall Bear! I see what you are doing. Enjoy your woman now, before spring comes and we must go out and hunt and make war!" Tall Bear laughed, whisking Little Otter into their tepee.

Running Fox sat inside playing with a tin cup, banging it against a rock. He paid little heed when his mother and father lay down on their mat together near the fire, where the stew cooked slowly in an iron pot hanging over the coals. Little Otter began making strange noises as she and Tall Bear moved beneath the robes that covered them, and Running Fox was not sure if his mother was in pain or feeling some kind of happiness. He knew his father would never hurt her. Tall Bear was on top of her, moving back and forth, tasting her mouth. Running Fox only grinned and banged at the rock again, sensing his parents were quite happy.

Tall Bear had learned that the Sioux saw nothing wrong with making love in front of their children. It was a natural part of life. Little Otter seldom wore anything under her tunic. He had simply to push it up and slide himself into her after unlacing his own leggings. He liked these quiet days of winter, this time spent alone with his wife and son. Sometimes they visited with others, and men and women alike shared stories, sometimes a little exaggerated, about hunting adventures, particularly brave feats in battle. Sometimes they told ghost stories, or just talked about earlier days, before the white man came. In spite of his own white blood, Tall Bear had been fully accepted into the tribe, and he was honored by them because he knew the white man's tongue. He'd forced himself to remember it, was teaching it to Running Fox, so that his son could never be tricked by the whites.

For several minutes he enjoyed the exquisite pleasure of being inside his wife. He unlaced her tunic, pulling down the front and tasting her breasts, where a little milk still lingered from feeding Running Fox. It was the custom of Sioux women to nurse their children well into their third year. For this moment, though, she would nurse her husband instead. He met her mouth again in a deep, hungry kiss that climaxed with his life spilling into her belly. They both lay still then for several minutes, until Running Fox came over and banged the tin cup on his father's head.

"Hey!" Tall Bear objected. He laughed, moving off Little Otter and lacing up his leggings. "You count coup on your own father!" he told his son. He picked up a little kindling stick and held it up. "Now I count coup on you!"

Running Fox laughed and ran, heading straight out of the tepee. Tall Bear chased after him, tapping him on the head and bringing him back inside. "You will get sick running out in that cold with no robe around you," he told the boy, carrying a giggling Running Fox to the fire. "Sit there and we will eat. It is time for you to begin eating more meat and drinking less milk." He ruffled his son's long black hair. Then he turned back to Little Otter, who stood with her back to him, washing herself. He studied her slender thighs and firm hips, the milky brown color of her smooth skin. He had made a good choice with this woman. She was beautiful, her dark eyes full of love for him. She was a loyal, devoted wife. "Now I am ready for that stew," he told her.

Little Otter turned, lowering her tunic over her legs. "You cannot stop your little son from feeding at my breast when his father does the same," she said jokingly.

"My reasons are far different from his," Tall Bear replied with a grin.

Little Otter scooped some stew into a gourd using a spoon made of buffalo bone and handed the food to her husband. "You are an honored warrior, strong and brave, my husband. But under the robe you are at this woman's mercy." She smiled slyly.

Tall Bear laughed. "You are right. Just do not tell others." He ate the stew quickly, finding it delicious. He wished life could always be this way for them, peaceful, plenty of food. But spring would come, along with more whites, who killed off the game and brought more danger and unrest. He would not think about that now.

Chapter Four

1861 . . .

Fifteen-year-old Faith Kelley was sure she was in love with Johnny Sommers, fully a man now at eighteen. Her parents still thought she was too young to be seeing any boys, let alone a grown man like Johnny. She had met him in secret, which gave her a feeling of freedom she had never known. Johnny made her feel important, and she was sure he loved her more than her own father did. He most certainly understood her better.

Together they dreamed big dreams. Johnny had promised to marry her. He was going to go west some day, settle on free land. He was tired of working for his father, doing more than he felt he should have to do, and getting only a small allowance for it. She understood that. Her father had mentioned he thought Johnny was rather lazy, said Johnny's father had trouble getting him to work as he should. Faith did not believe that.

It had been difficult not to defend Johnny, but that might give away her true feelings for him, and she didn't want her parents to know yet. They could not know until she and Johnny were ready to marry and had enough money saved to run away together, start life new someplace else, somewhere in that wonderous, romantic land west of the Mississippi. Johnny remembered Kansas, had liked it there. He wanted to go even farther than that, see the Rocky Mountains, maybe discover gold!

She was sure Johnny could do anything he set out to do. He seemed so confident and sure, and, after all, he was already well traveled. In her eyes he was brave and daring, and she liked that. The excitement he'd brought to her life made daily chores and daily prayer meetings more bearable.

Now she waited for him at a creek in the woods behind her parents' house, where they met on specific days at two o'clock. Johnny always managed to find an excuse to come there, usually telling his father he wanted to go pray alone to wait for the Holy Spirit to bring him a message. They both knew it was wrong to lie, but surely God understood how much they loved each other and needed to be together. Someday, when they married, all the lies would be made right.

She heard the horse then, pushed back a strand of red hair that had fallen across her cheek. Her stomach tightened, and her heart pounded harder. She wished she could meet with him more often than once a week. At first they could manage to meet only about once a month, but over this past year they had gradually managed to find more ways to be together secretly. She was old enough now to have a little more freedom. She did not have to account for her every move, but her parents were still watchful. To keep them appeased, she had forced herself to be quiet at prayer meetings. They thought she was finally "settling down," as they put it, finally "growing more mature."

She most certainly was—mature enough to share these moments with the young man she loved. Mature enough to let him hold her, kiss her, even touch her breasts. Part of her wanted to do even more, but that also frightened her. Johnny had wanted much more. He'd moved his hands under her skirts the last time they'd met, and their kisses had become much deeper, to the point where she had become afraid of that "unknown" thing that happened between man and woman. Surely it was bad. Her mother had explained to her once how babies were made and had also explained that it was something a woman did only with her husband, and only in order to give him children. It must never be for pleasure. That was a sin.

Johnny walked through the trees, leading his horse through the underbrush. Whenever Faith laid eyes on him, saw his bright smile, his dancing brown eyes, she could not help wondering again if she should be brave and allow him to have his way with her. Surely, though, he might not want her anymore after that. He might think she was a terribly wicked woman. It was so hard to know what to do, and she couldn't talk to anyone about it, certainly not her friends, who might tell on her, and not her mother, who would be furious with her.

She ran to Johnny, flung her arms around his neck. "I missed you, Johnny!"

"I missed you, too."

Their lips met in a hungry kiss. She felt on fire. The kiss lingered, until finally he picked her up and carried her to a place near the creek where the grass was thick and soft. He knelt down and laid her back, kissing her again, his hand moving over her breasts, making her want to let him do that one forbidden thing, out of pure curiosity and in answer to an almost painful ache deep within. If being with a man that way was supposed to be so wrong, why did she feel only pleasure when he touched her breasts, and when his hand moved down to her skirt, pushing it up so he could run his hand over her thigh? Why did she like it, even though she was terrified of what it would be like?

"I want to be with you, Faith," he groaned, touching her between the legs. "I'm going away, maybe never to come back," he added between kisses. "We have to be together once first, so forever I'll have been your first man."

Alarm began to invade her soul, beginning to override the fiery desire his touch created in her. Faith pulled away, sitting up. "Going away? Where? What do you mean, you might never come back?"

"Faith—" He reached up, tried to pull her back down. His face was flushed, his eyes gleaming with desire. "Please, honey—"

Faith jumped up. "Johnny, if you're going away, we can't do this! If you didn't come back, I'd be a shamed woman, perhaps—" She turned away, embarrassed. "Perhaps carrying a baby . . ."

She heard him sigh deeply. "Faith, I don't think a woman gets in a bad way after being with a man just once."

She turned to face him. "We could just go ahead and get married, Johnny. And you don't have to go away. You never said why you had to." Her eyes widened. "Oh, Johnny, you aren't *really* going to join the army, are you? I heard father talking about a battle or something at a place called Fort Sumter. He said the country will be at war now."

Johnny rose, lifting his chin proudly. "And I'm going to join the Union Army." He saw the fallen look on her freckled face. He'd hoped that his leaving would be just the incentive she needed to allow him to have his way with her. The last thing he wanted to do was get married at eighteen, but he wasn't sure how long he could wait to have his way with her. He'd been torn between staying there so he could be close to Faith, and experiencing the adventure of being a soldier.

"Johnny, your parents would never approve—"

"All the more reason to go off to war! You should understand that better than anyone. I'll bet if women could be soldiers, you'd join up, too, just for the excitement of it!"

Faith had to admit she would probably do just that. "Johnny, don't you love me? I'll go crazy staying here doing chores and attending prayer meetings, all the while missing you terribly, worrying about you. Don't leave me here, Johnny. I'll be miserable."

He shook his head, stepping closer and grasping her arms. "I do love you, Faith, and I want to marry you and go west like we talked about. There are a lot of things I want to do. But right now there's a war going on, and volunteers are needed. I've always wanted to be free of my pa and all his rules. I'm a man now. I can do whatever I want. But I've got to see more of what's out there before I take a wife. And we'll need money. I can make some this way. Rumor is the government will even pay some of us in land if we want. It's a chance for me to go do something on my own, out from under my pa, without needing any money at first. Food, uniforms, weapons, everything will be given to us. I'll come back more of a man, more experienced, older, ready to really settle. You'll be older, ready to be a wife, and I'll have some money saved."

Faith could not help the tears that burned her eyes. Something did not seem quite right. Why hadn't he told her all this before he'd laid her down in the grass and tried to talk her into letting him do bad things with her? Still, he *did* love her. He'd said so many times. Surely he just loved her so much, he wanted to make her his own before he went away. What if he was killed? This might be their only chance to unite in true love.

She reminded herself that Johnny Sommers was the sweetest, most honest young man around. No one else could possibly understand her restless heart the way Johnny did. And she understood his. She couldn't blame him for wanting to have her that way before he went off to war, no more than she could blame him for wanting to go in the first place. "I think I understand, Johnny, why you have to go. You'll write to me, won't you? You won't go away and forget me?"

"Forget you?" He pulled her close. "Never, Faith! I'd never forget you. Sure I'll write. I'll make you proud of me. I'll come back a captain or something. You'll see. Maybe if I can be some kind of officer, I'd just stay in the army and we could get married and live on army posts. It would be a good way to travel and get paid for it. They've got forts all over out west."

Faith felt a little confused. It seemed every time they met, he had another plan for their future, how he would make money, where they would go. Still, he was young. Maybe the army would help him decide what he wanted to do with his life. As long as she was a part of it, she didn't care. "It doesn't matter what you do or where you go, as long as we're together, Johnny."

He grinned, meeting her mouth in another fiery kiss. She suddenly realized it might be important, after all, to allow him to do that mysterious thing to her before he left. Maybe he'd remember her better, be more sure to come back. Maybe he was right that a woman didn't always end up with a child every time she lay with a man. After all, he was older. He should know about those things. In fact, maybe he'd been with some other girl, some wild, naughty thing in Johnstown or back in Kansas. That made her feel very jealous, and wanting to prove she was all he needed.

He laid her back down in the grass, his hands roaming over her body again. "Oh, Johnny," she whispered. "I want to make you feel good before you go. I want you to remember me that way, to show you what it would be like to have me for a wife."

Quickly he pushed up her skirts again, pushing his hand inside her drawers. She felt lost in excitement and indecision, love and confusion, desire and fear. Yes, she had to do this. She had to—

"Faith Kelley!"

Quickly Johnny jumped away from her. She briefly caught a glimpse of a swollen lump at the front of his pants, and she realized only then that a man must get big like a male horse. She'd seen horses mate, and it shocked her to think a man had to get like that, too. For the moment, though, that was the last thing to be considered. Their fathers stood only a few yards away, both men redfaced with rage. Quickly Faith pulled down her skirts and also got to her feet. Johnny had turned away, probably embarrassed about that lump in his pants.

"Father! What . . . why are you here? How did you find us?" Faith wanted to crawl into a hole and cover herself. Her cheeks burned, and her eyes teared.

"You know good and well *why* I'm here!" her father replied, stepping closer with clenched fists. "To keep my daughter from soiling herself, shaming herself and her family! It's a good thing your little brother followed you here once and saw you meeting with Johnny! I just hope we've gotten here in time to keep you from behaving no better than a harlot!"

Benny! He'd turned into such a brat, was always looking for ways to impress their father. How could her own brother betray her this way? Her father considered him practically a saint . . . and now she would be the sinner.

"She hasn't done anything wrong, Mr. Kelley," Johnny spoke up for her, turning to face the two men. "I've never done more than kiss her."

"And you will be horsewhipped for this, young man!" his own father bellowed.

"You're never going to lay a whip to me again," Johnny answered. "I'm going away, Pa. I'm going to join the Union Army, be a soldier. I'm eighteen now. You can't tell me what to do anymore."

He ran past all of them and jumped on his horse.

"Johnny!" Faith called out, more tears coming. "I love you!"

"I'll come back for you," he answered, turning the horse to face her. "Wait for me!"

After he rode off, Faith felt sick inside. It had all happened so quickly. One moment she'd been considering allowing him to do that most intimate thing with her, and the next he was riding out of her life. Shivering with sobs, she looked at her father, feeling ashamed, confused. *Was* she bad?

"I love him, Father. He . . . promised to marry me."

"My son changes his mind every day about what he wants to do with his life!" Herbert Sommers told her. "He's always been headstrong, disobedient, lazy, and not very bright. I would not be so sure he'll be back for you, Miss Kelley. If he goes off to join the army, I suspect he'll never come back here, not for you or any other reason."

"He will!" Faith felt sorry for Johnny. He'd shown her bruises and cuts from beatings by a stringent, commanding father. It was part of the reason she loved him. He *needed* that love, just as she needed *his* love.

"You've put your trust in a young man who has no idea what he wants out of life," Sommers repeated. "I am ashamed for my son." He looked at Faith's father. "I am sorry for this, Matthew. Even if my son decides not to join the army, something he's doing only because he knows I am against violence, he will never be welcome in our home again!"

"Against violence?" Faith spoke up, anger rising above her shame. "If you are against violence, Mr. Sommers, then how can you beat Johnny the way you do?"

"That is enough, Faith!" her own father roared. "How dare you speak to Mr. Sommers that way! A man does what he must do to discipline his children and steer them in the right path. Your own chores will be doubled, young lady, and you will spend many hours in prayer! And speaking of discipline, a belt to your own legs might take the foolishness out of you. We thought that restless spirit in you had finally left you, but you were only fooling us so that you could have more freedom to see Johnny." He stepped closer. "Your freedom is ended. I'll not let you out of my sight for quite some time, young lady. Now, get home with you!"

Faith sniffed, wiping at her cheeks. "Johnny's coming back," she swore, "and when he does, I'm going to marry him and go away with him. You should be *glad*, because then you'll be rid of me." She turned and ran off, thinking how wonderful it would be if women *could* join the army. And if Johnny didn't come back for her, once she was a little older, she'd run away and find a new life anyway.

It was a pretty day in June, and Tall Bear carried Running Fox on his shoulders as they walked through the wild prairieland. He and Little Otter, who was again with child, had decided to take a day alone, enjoy the freedom that could so easily be taken from them. The white men were at war now, and many soldiers had been taken away from the Dakotas. That meant there was less danger of being attacked by the bluecoats, at least for a while. Maybe the whites would become so involved in their war that they would forget all about the Indian.

The absence of soldiers also meant they did not have to abide by any treaties, something Makhpiya-sha, Red

Cloud, had already decided need not be done. The great Oglala chief was waging a very successful campaign in Powder River country to chase out more soldiers farther west, and some of the forts had been burned. Tall Bear had not become involved in Red Cloud's war yet, but he had considered it many times.

"Come and pick some of these flowers and put them in your hair," he called to Little Otter, who lagged behind. She smiled and walked a little faster to catch up. She led Tall Bear's spotted horse, which was tied to two more horses, pack animals for their two-week venture of hunting and freedom.

"Take the horses so that I can pick the flowers," she told her husband.

Tall Bear reached up and grabbed hold of his three-year-old son, turning and plopping him atop the first horse. "Hang on, Running Fox," he warned.

The boy laughed with delight, grasping the horse's mane while Tall Bear took the leather reins from Little Otter. "I think perhaps before the summer is over we should go join Red Cloud's Oglala," he told his wife.

Little Otter gathered daisies and began sticking them in her hair and tunic. "That would mean leaving my own family here in the Dakotas." Her heart was sad at the thought. "And more danger for you. You only say this because you want to make war with Red Cloud."

Tall Bear grinned. "Maybe. But it would not be so dangerous. Already Red Cloud has chased away many soldiers, burned forts. Many white men try to go through that country to find gold in the place the whites call Montana Territory. Now maybe they will think twice about coming, with no soldier protection. Maybe there we can enjoy peace and freedom a little longer. We could take your family with us. After all, Red Cloud's Oglala are their relatives. Wouldn't you like to go to that new country?"

She shrugged. "I suppose. I just do not want you to have to go into battle." She walked closer, touching his bare chest. The day was warm, and Tall Bear wore only a loincloth, a beaded leather band around his head, and his grandfather's bear-claw necklace hung around his neck.

"And I am not so sure you should go where my people raid the white settlers so often. Do not forget that part of you is white, my husband. I thinks perhaps that sometimes when you steal horses, make war against them, it is hard for you inside. You still sometimes think of them as your people. You know that they are not the same as the bluecoat leaders who attack us with their big guns because the Great Father in the East tells them to."

He touched her cheek. "I will admit that often I am torn. But it is these new whites I have no use for, those who come not to trade with us, but to steal our land."

She kissed his chest. "If it is making war you want, there is enough of that here, Tall Bear, enough trouble with the settlers in the Dakotas, Minnesota. You must truly know your heart before you take all of us on such a long journey farther west."

"I know my heart only enough to know how much I love you," he said, touching her face. "For now we will just enjoy this time together alone, just the three of us. I will hunt. We will take deer meat home to the others. I will begin teaching Running Fox—"

His words were cut off by the startling report of gunfire, a loud boom that was not like anything Tall Bear had ever heard. In almost the same instant, Running Fox fell from the horse. Little Otter screamed, and Tall Bear turned to see his son lying on the ground, his head seemingly shattered. Tall Bear's breath seemed to leave him as stunned shock took over.

He dropped down into the grass, reaching up to pull Little Otter down with him, but she stood frozen in place, staring in horror at her little boy. Before she ducked down, another shot rang out, again a loud boom that told of a very dangerous weapon. Little Otter jerked forward and landed near Tall Bear in the grass, a large hole in her back.

"Come on and get up, Indian!" someone yelled. "We're here to hunt buffalo and take their hides, but while we're at it, we might as well get rid of some of the smaller varmints in these parts."

Tall Bear heard laughter. He felt vomit coming to his

throat at the realization that his wife and son had just been shot down as though they were skunks.

Buffalo hunters! He'd heard men had come there to kill buffalo, that they used some kind of special rifle, a big gun that made big holes and hit targets many more yards away than any average rifle. That awful weapon had surely just been used on his innocent little boy and his gentle, harmless wife.

"Let's get it over with, Indian!" one of the men shouted.

Tall Bear, reeling with the horror of what had just happened, lay motionless in the tall grass.

"Mighty fine-lookin' horses you got there. We'll help ourselves to them and your supplies once you're done for," came another shout.

Tall Bear peered through tall grass at a distant cluster of rocks from where the voices came. He could not bear to think about Little Otter and Running Fox. No, not yet. First these men had to die, and for that he had to stay calm, rational. He had to get to his own rifle. He had to kill those men.

"Come and get me, you child-killing bastards!" he shouted, unsure just how many there were.

At first there was no reply, and he knew he had surprised them by calling out to them in English. "All you did was kill a squaw and her kid," he yelled. "I am dressed as an Indian, but I am half-white, and this woman was just a squaw to me. There are plenty more where she came from. I have no wish to kill the men who have rid me of a nagging woman!"

He heard a little laughter.

"It is not necessary to kill me. I am just a hunter like you, who took a squaw. I can show you where there are many buffalo, and I can take you to my village, where you can buy many furs for tobacco."

His heart beat faster when one of them rose. "That true? You're half-white?"

"Do I sound like an Indian? I even speak French!" He rattled off a few words, calling them names in French, sure they wouldn't know the difference.

Another one stood up. "I'll be damned," he said.

"I am also wearing no weapons," Tall Bear told them, putting up his hands and slowly rising. This was the only answer. He had to draw them out. He was caught out there in wide-open prairie. They were behind rocks. He could not make a move without getting them out from behind shelter and winning their confidence. He stood and waited cautiously, watching a third man emerge from the rocks. Slowly all three men, wearing soiled buckskins and sporting beards, moved away from the rocks and walked toward him.

"Hell, we didn't know you was a breed, mister," one of them said. "You sure as hell *look* all Indian."

"My mother was Sioux, but my father was a white trapper. When I hunt, I dress and behave like an Indian. The best way to find good buffalo herds is to befriend the Indians first. They will share plenty of information for whiskey and tobacco. They will sometimes even help with the hunt. You take the hide, they get the meat and bones." He stepped closer to his horse, where his rifle hung in its boot. He would have to be steady. Those big rifles they carried looked as though they would be difficult to raise and shoot with the kind of speed a man could shoot a lighter repeating rifle. He had traded some good furs and robes for his rifle, and he'd practiced with it often. His Sioux friends admired the speed and accuracy with which he used the gun, and if he could get to it now . . .

"I never heard of Indians helpin' white men hunt buffalo," one of them called out to him as all three men came even closer.

Tall Bear gauged each one. One was downright fat. He'd be the slowest, so he'd be the one to shoot last. The other two were of average build, and they held their rifles lazily now. One wore a huge knife at his belt. He would have to go first. Casually, he stepped closer to his horse, waited for what he felt was the right moment. Today all these men would die . . . or he himself would die. Without Running Fox and Little Otter, he did not want to live anyway. How could the morning be so calm and beautiful only moments ago, and so full of horror now?

"You just do not know how to deal with Indians," he

answered the last wary statement. The three men came even closer, still watching him carefully. *It is a good day to die,* he thought. In one quick movement he yanked his rifle out of its boot and leveled it at all three men. "But I know how to deal with stinking white murderers!" he shouted.

One . . . two . . . three. He fired the rifle, retracted it, fired again, retracted it, fired again. The gods were with him that day. All three fell, astonished looks on their faces. Two writhed in pain, one reaching for his big buffalo gun. Tall Bear walked up to them, calmly aimed his rifle at first one—shooting him in the head—then the other, who begged for mercy.

"I will show you the same mercy you showed my wife and son," he answered. He pulled the trigger again, putting a hole between the man's eyes. His breathing quickened then, and he knew he must do something he'd never done before. He would take white men's scalps. He looked around to be sure there were only these three, then tossed the rifle aside and knelt down, taking a hunting knife from one of the men and using it to slice off each man's hair near the forehead.

He held up the bloody scalps, giving out a long, eerie cry of mourning. He turned, shoving the scalps through some leather ties on the gear of one of the packhorses. It was only then he could allow the horror of his loss to become real to him. He looked down at Running Fox, his precious son, who was always smiling and full of energy. He would not hear his laughter again, nor would he hold Little Otter in his arms again. Their second child would die in her belly. He would have to wrap their bodies and take them back to the village for proper burial. . . .

His heart shattered, he fell to his knees, Little Otter's body on one side of him, Running Fox's on the other. He tossed the white man's hunting knife aside. He did not want their evil blood to touch his own. He took his own hunting knife from where it was tied at his ankle, and, as was the custom, he slashed his arms, letting blood in mourning for his lost family. His cries of sorrow echoed throughout the nearby hills and valleys.

Chapter Five

1862 . . .

Faith approached Sommers Farm Supply, glad her father was at a meeting of Quakers and had allowed her and her mother to come shopping alone. A proud and arrogant Benny was with his father, the two of them practically inseparable. Faith had given up trying to please her father, was only biding her time until she could find a way to get away from Pennsylvania altogether. She had thought she would leave with Johnny, but there had been no letters as he'd promised. It broke her heart to think he'd probably already forgotten about her, after all his promises of love, promises to write, to come back for her.

She had never seen Johnny again after that day in the woods a year ago, and her father had strictly forbidden her to see any other young men. She had been forced to spend many hours praying, attending meetings, and some looked at her as though she were a shamed woman.

Didn't they understand she had simply been a young girl in love, and that her lover was going off to war? What had been so wrong about what she had done? Her mother seemed to quietly understand. She could see it in the woman's eyes. Sadie had never chastised her personally for what had happened, and she had never asked her about it. When Faith had daringly asked the woman if she could go to Sommers Supply and talk to Mrs. Sommers about Johnny, find out what they had heard from him, Sadie had agreed it was all right to do so. She had even offered to come with her.

They walked inside, where Sadie greeted Gertrude, talking about the daily things all women talked about. Faith suspected they enjoyed the days when only the men went to meeting. For those few hours the women experienced a tiny taste of freedom just to be themselves. When Faith's father scolded her, he would say she had her mother's "wild spirit." It made Faith wonder just how happy her mother really was leading this life. She sometimes felt sorry for the woman. Sadie never complained, but Faith was sure her mother was not happy.

"Where are the children?" Sadie was asking Gertrude now, referring to Johnny's brothers and sisters, who sometimes worked in the store.

"Oh, they are all at home doing chores," Gertrude replied. "I would be there, too, but I have to run the store while Herbert is at the meeting. I just wish this hideous war was over with. There are other young men of our faith who also want to join the army now, and it is getting more and more difficult to discourage them."

Faith walked to an area where spices were displayed in barrels. She glanced into a mirror that hung on a wall behind the barrels, seeing a pretty redheaded, blue-eyed young woman there. They had one small mirror at home, which her father allowed to be used only for his shaving and for her mother to fix her hair. It was not to be used for any other form of vanity. Faith had stolen moments to stare into it, studying herself, wondering if she really was as pretty as her mother had told her many times when they were alone. She thought her mother was very pretty, too.

She put a hand to her nose, which still showed a few freckles. She wondered what Johnny would think of her now at sixteen. She had changed a lot in this one year, was taller, felt more mature. Her breasts had grown much fuller, but she was forced to wear bindings meant to flatten them so that they did not show too obviously. She hated the binding, especially on these hot summer days.

She nervously made her way to the counter where her mother talked with Johnny's mother. Did she dare ask? Would Mrs. Sommers tell her husband Faith had asked about Johnny? Before she could even say anything herself, her mother did the talking for her.

"I know my husband has forbidden you to speak of Johnny around our daughter," she was telling Gertrude, "but Faith has been very anxious to know if he is all right. I wonder if you could tell me if he has written, if he is well. Of course we don't want your husband or mine to know that we inquired. My daughter did care very much for Johnny, you know."

Gertrude glanced at Faith. The woman was more stern than her own mother, certainly more plain in the face and in her dress, but she was kind, and she and Sadie had become fast friends. Faith saw a hint of understanding in Gertrude's eyes. "Johnny is fine, as far as we know," she responded. "He didn't write for a long time, he was so angry about what happened in the woods that day."

Faith felt her face turning crimson. "We were just—saying good-bye," she said. "Johnny promised to write me, but he never did. He'll probably never come back here, and I . . ." She felt the sting of tears. "I thought he loved me. I don't know why he never wrote." A tear slipped down her cheek. She had not expected to be so overpowered by emotion. She supposed it was because it was such a relief just to be able to talk about Johnny, to admit she'd loved him.

"Never wrote?" Gertrude Sommers frowned, glancing at Sadie, folding her arms over the front of her plain gray dress. "Sadie, since this is just between us, there is apparently something you don't know, something your Mr. Kelley has been keeping from you."

Sadie put a hand on Faith's shoulder. "I don't understand."

The door opened, and another woman came inside.

Gertrude walked from behind the counter, talking low to Sadie. "Come into the back with me for a moment." She told the new customer she would be with her shortly, and she led Sadie and Faith to the back of the store into a small room that held a desk and a few extra supplies. She closed the door. "You have not received any of Johnny's letters?" she asked Faith.

Faith shook her head.

Sadie blinked in confusion. "I have never seen any letters," she answered. "My husband picks up the mail every day, and there has never—" Her face reddened with anger. "My goodness! If Johnny wrote to Faith, Matthew must have seen the letters and never given them to Faith! But . . . Faith asked him many times if there were any letters from Johnny, and he always told her no. She even risked whippings for asking, since she's been forbidden to talk about him at all. I just . . . I never expected Matthew to lie like that!"

Gertrude sighed and shook her head. "I don't know how many there have been. I only know that in the four letters we have received from Johnny, he always asked why he had not heard from Faith. He wrote that he had sent her several letters but had never received a reply. I never asked you about it because I knew your husband did not want us talking to you or Faith about Johnny, and because my own husband forbade me to. For all we know, my own husband knows Mr. Kelley has been destroying Johnny's letters."

Faith burst into tears, and her mother put an arm around her shoulder. Gertrude began pacing, looking pensive. "I will try to get a letter to Johnny and explain," she offered. "Or if Faith wants to write him, you can sneak the letter to me and I will mail it off. I have his address. That's all I can do."

Faith reached out and hugged the woman. "Thank you, Mrs. Sommers," she wept.

Gertrude patted her shoulder, sharing an understanding look with Sadie. "I must warn you, Faith, that although my son has a good heart, he has never been very dependable, and he is always changing his mind about what he wants to do." She pulled away and grasped Faith's shoulders. "I know you think you love him, but I fear he would not make a good husband. You should take this time while he is gone to think about that, and the fact that you are very young. Perhaps if he truly loves you, he will settle down." She brushed at tears on Faith's cheeks. "I can't think of a sweeter young woman for my son." She glanced at Sadie again. "I just hope there are no big problems over this when Johnny returns. We both know how stubborn our husbands can be."

"Yes, we certainly do," Sadie said. "Thank you so much for telling us about the letters, Gertrude. You didn't have to do that."

The woman folded her arms again. "Well, I don't always agree with my husband's decisions."

"Johnny would be a good husband," Faith insisted. "He loves me, and I love him. We understand each other." She sniffed, wiping away more tears. "*I* want to write the letter, Mrs. Sommers. Somehow mother will find a way to get it to you. Thank you for offering to mail it for me."

The woman nodded with a sad smile. She remembered what young love was like, remembered how it had felt to love her own young man once, many years ago. She had never forgotten him. Her parents had forbidden them to be together, and one day he had simply gone away and never returned. She never knew why. She had then married Herbert, a young man of her parents' choosing, but she had never known the passion and happiness she'd known with that first love. It was a secret she'd kept all these years. "God be with you, Faith, and with my Johnny."

"Thank you again, Mrs. Sommers." Faith turned and hugged her mother. "And thank you, too, Mother."

"We had better let Gertrude get back to work," Sadie told her, leading her out a back door. "And you must be careful not to appear too happy and lighthearted in front of your father now about writing to Johnny," she warned. "Matthew might suspect."

"Yes, Mother. Thank you again for helping me find out about the letters."

Sadie stopped and faced her daughter. She had told no one how she'd been feeling lately, strange pains that seemed to have no explanation. An odd foreboding had crept into her deepest thoughts of late. "Faith, whatever you do with your life, always remember to believe in God and to pray, but also . . . enjoy your free spirit, as long as you are living a good and proper life. Do not let others live your life for you, or tell you what you must do, whom you must marry, or that it is wrong to laugh and dance. Happiness is never wrong. Love whomever you wish to love and enjoy life. You are very strong and very beautiful. You can have a wonderful life."

Faith wondered at the way the words were spoken, with a sort of finality to them. "You wanted that kind of life, didn't you, Mother?"

The woman turned. "What's past is past, and I made a vow years ago before God. Once a woman makes her choice, she must live with it, Faith. Remember that. Your father is a good man. The times he's been strict with you, he truly thought it was for your own good. You're young and on fire for life, so be careful, especially in choosing a husband."

"I will, Mother. Right now I just—I'm sure I love Johnny and that he loves me. You'll understand if we go away and get married, won't you?"

Sadie began walking again. "Take one day at a time, Faith. I hope I will have you with me for a while longer."

"You will, Mother."

Sadie nodded, praying God would watch out for this high-spirited daughter of hers once her mother was gone from this world.

Tall Bear let out a scream of fiery revenge, charging down the slope to yet another farm, trampling through crops, tearing down a line of clothes, landing a tomahawk into a small chicken house and sending hens and eggs scattering. He tore open a fence and let pigs run loose.

The Sioux rampage in Minnesota had begun over a simple thing—chicken eggs stolen by a young warrior hot for mischief. It had grown into all-out war, and Tall Bear, his heart still screaming with sorrow, his hatred still bitter in his mouth, needed no prompting to join in the raids against these settlers, even though deep inside a voice continued to tell him it was wrong. Some of these people were just as innocent as Running Fox and Little Otter had been. His father would not want him to do this, but he knew no other way to vent his grief.

He whirled his horse and rode toward the farmhouse, where a woman knelt over a man, most likely her husband. Tall Bear had shot a farmer at the last spread he and the band of warriors had attacked. He wasn't sure if he'd killed the man, but his arm still carried a bloody bandage from wrapping a wound where the farmer had shot at him first.

Someone else had shot this man he saw there. Perhaps he should now kill the woman. Other warriors had killed women, fiercely angry over so much white intrusion into their hunting grounds. This was a good time to get rid of the settlers, when most bluecoat soldiers were off fighting their own war farther south.

He charged past the woman, letting out a war whoop. He could not bring himself to kill her, in spite of what had happened to Little Otter. He supposed it was the white blood in his veins that stopped him, and that only made him more angry. He rode his horse through flowers, trampling them, then whacked at a brace that held an iron pot of something cooking over an open fire. Just as the contents of the pot spilled across the dirt, he heard the crack of a rifle, and a bullet skimmed across his horse's neck. The animal reared, but Tall Bear hung on, charging back and forth in front of the house again, yipping and screaming in deeper anger that his horse had been wounded. Someone was still inside the house. That was where the shot had come from. He would find the man and kill him! Maybe he would also take his scalp.

He charged to the porch, and the woman crawled up the steps, screaming "No! No! No!" Tall Bear knew she thought he would kill her, too, and he enjoyed the terror in her eyes.

All around him crops and buildings were being destroyed, a barn on fire, some of the warriors riding off with stolen cattle and horses. He leaped from his horse and pulled a pistol from the waistband of his leggings, one he'd stolen from another farmer. The woman stumbled through the doorway and tried to close the door, but Tall Bear slammed his body against it, charging inside. At first he saw only the screaming, cringing woman. Then came the movement to his right. He whirled and shot.

A little boy! He was perhaps only seven or eight, and he held a big rifle, which went sprawling one way as the child's body flew backward against a wall. The woman let out a chilling wail and ran to the child, who was bleeding badly at the top left area of his chest. Tall Bear could not move at first. He only stood staring as the woman hunched over the child, pulling him into her arms.

Tall Bear felt as though all the blood was suddenly draining from his body. Things were quieting outside as the warriors rode on to yet another settlement to wreak more havoc. Tall Bear just stood staring, his pistol in his hand. "I did not know it was a child," he tried to explain.

The woman, her dress bloody, her hair hanging in strings and her face dirty and tearstained, looked at him in astonishment. "You . . . speak English!" Her body jerked in a sob. "Your eyes! You're not a full-blood Indian. Why are you doing this to your own kind!"

"Mommy . . . ," the little boy sobbed.

Tall Bear felt a glimmer of hope. The boy was not dead. He did not answer the woman. He only turned away, hardly feeling his legs as he walked outside, stepping over the body of the dead man, probably the boy's father. He climbed onto his horse, a sturdy black gelding with bear claws painted on his rump with white paint. Blood stained the horse's neck.

Another horse charged toward him from the burning barn. Its rider was Dark Owl, who let out a delighted war whoop as he approached Tall Bear. The other warriors had ridden off, but Dark Owl was Tall Bear's good friend. He had stayed behind to be sure he was all right. "I was going into the house to find you!" he shouted in the Sioux tongue. "Who is inside? Did you kill them?"

"No," Tall Bear answered. "There is only a woman and

little boy inside. I shot the boy by mistake, and I pray he does not die. It is bad luck to kill children."

Dark Owl nodded. "*Aye*. We could take the woman and child prisoner."

Tall Bear shook his head. "You go with the others."

"You are not coming?" Dark Owl frowned. He suddenly broke into a grin. "I know! You wish to stay here and have your way with the woman!"

Tall Bear nodded. "Go on with the others."

Dark Owl nodded, then let out another war whoop as he rode off.

So much misunderstanding. So many broken promises. So much hatred and intolerance. Tall Bear felt lost, sick inside. He both loved and hated his Indian self, and loved and hated his white self. He belonged nowhere now. He dismounted again, walked back into the cabin to see the woman frantically wrapping strips of cloth around her son's shoulder. The boy was lying on a cot and crying with pain. The woman turned, her dark hair hanging in strands around her tearstained face, part of it still caught up in a prim bun on top of her head. "What do you want now!" she screamed at him. "Haven't you done enough?"

"Come with me," he told her. "I will take you and the boy to Fort Snelling. There is a doctor there."

"What!" she sneered. "You expect me to believe you won't take us someplace as captives?"

"I only want to help the boy. The others have gone. You will come to no harm if you are with me. I promise you that."

She sat down on the cot where her son lay and pulled the boy into her arms. "How in God's name do you expect me to trust you? My husband is lying *dead* out there. He was a good man. Everything he worked for is destroyed, and now you've shot my son. Get out! Just get out!"

"Let me take you to the fort. Do you not want to get help for your son?"

"They would arrest and hang you. Why would you risk that?"

"I will leave you close to the fort and ride away. They would not catch me."

She looked him over, and Tall Bear could understand the skepticism in her tired eyes. "Why would you do this?"

He moved closer, a sneer moving across his lips. "*I* had a son once. I wanted *him* to live also, but white buffalo hunters would not give him that chance. They murdered him *and* my wife, who was with child."

He turned and walked out, waited. The woman finally appeared at the doorway, carrying her son. "I have no choice but to go with you. I want my son to live."

Tall Bear nodded. "Bring him here."

The woman came closer, stepping over the dead man still lying on the steps. "My husband," she wept. "He has to be buried."

"There is no time. The boy could bleed to death." He mounted his horse in one swift movement. "Give him to me."

Reluctantly the woman handed him up. Tall Bear took the child in his right arm, his own bandaged left arm too sore for holding him. Still, he held out that arm for the woman to grab hold, and he helped hoist her onto the horse behind him. With his left hand then he took hold of the reins. "It will be close to dark when we get there."

The woman grabbed hold of his waist, and Tall Bear rode off in the direction of the fort. Deep inside he knew he was not just riding away from a burning homestead. He was also riding away from the life he'd known since coming there with his mother after his father was murdered. It was time to move on again, to explore his own soul even deeper. Perhaps he would head farther west, join in Red Cloud's war. At least there he could fight only soldiers and intruding miners and buffalo hunters. There were not so many settlers farther west. Here in Minnesota there were too many to fight, and many of those were women and children.

This raiding was not going to stop them. That was a false hope. He looked down at the little boy. He had blond hair, and his fair skin showed freckles. So different he was from Running Fox, yet not so different at all. He would pray to Wakan Tanka that the boy would live.

Chapter Six

1863 . . .

Faith hauled another bushel of corn over to her father's wagon, setting it beside the wheel and picking up an empty basket. The morning was hot and still, and she swatted at a fly that landed against her cheek. Farther over in the field she could hear her father and brother talking, their conversation muffled by the muggy air and several rows of tall corn.

It was harvest time, a time she dreaded, especially when the heat of summer hung on into fall as it was doing this year. She was beginning to fear she'd start looking like an old woman long before she really was one, from all this hard, dirty work, too many hours spent in the sun, although she did wear a slat bonnet to protect her face. She dearly hoped that Johnny had something better in mind than farming when they went west.

She walked back into the deep rows of corn where her father could not see her dallying, and she turned the basket upside down and sat on it, wondering if she was silly to

think Johnny was still coming. She'd written him over a
year ago, promised to wait for him. Now that promise had
more meaning than ever, for she had even less reason to
stay in Pennsylvania. For her mother's sake she might have
considered not running off with Johnny, but now her
mother was gone. To think of it hurt so bad, she couldn't
eat sometimes. It had been only four months since her slow
and painful death, and in the end she had not even recognized her family.

Oh, the pain of it! Her dear mother's grave lay behind
the house beside the children she had lost. What hurt the
most was knowing how unhappy her mother truly had
been. She'd been a woman with so much spirit, who
wanted to laugh and dance but had never been able to.
Faith resented her father more than ever now for not having allowed her mother to be herself.

That was not going to happen to her. She was determined not to live against her deepest desires the way her
mother had. Here she was, picking corn, wearing a plain
blue calico dress, her long red hair tied and pinned into a
bun under a common slat bonnet. She would not allow this
to be all there was in life. Work and prayer meetings.

The trouble was, she was seventeen now. It was 1863,
and Johnny had been gone two years. He had to come
home soon. No seventeen-year-old girl should still be un-
married. She should at least be *engaged* to be married.
Most of her friends were already wives or had an understanding with someone, but she had stubbornly refused to
see other young men, even though her father now said that
she could. In fact, he had been angry with her for turning
down one older man, Henry Bartel, who he thought would
be an ideal husband because he was settled, a widower
with two small children. He was also a farmer and one of
the leaders of their Quaker sect.

Faith cringed at the thought of marrying Bartel. He was
at least forty and was a very stern man who seldom smiled.
Her father did not seem to care whether or not marrying
the man was something she wanted, and she was growing
more and more worried he would find a way to force her
into marrying him. She suspected he wanted to marry her

off before Johnny came home, and she was determined she would run away by herself if she had to in order to avoid such a despicable union.

She got up and began picking more corn, throwing the ears into the bushel. She missed her mother fiercely, and without her she felt unprotected from her father's edicts. Her mother had truly understood her, had accepted her passion for life and adventure and happiness. Her only hope now was Johnny. He was her only chance of getting away from there and away from Henry Bartel.

She caught a movement to her left then, down at the end of the long row. Someone was moving toward her. She squinted her eyes, realizing it was neither her father nor Benny. Her heart began to leap with joy when she began to realize who it was. *Johnny!* As he walked closer, he put a finger to his lips, warning her to keep quiet. He began running then, and he swept her into his arms. They both quietly squealed with delight. "Johnny! Johnny!" she whispered. "I was wondering if you would ever really come!"

"I'm here, all right," he whispered in reply, glad for the cover of the tall cornstalks. "Just got here this morning. I haven't even been to see my own folks yet. I was afraid my pa would come running to yours to let him know, and I had to see you first." He pulled away. "I had to look into your eyes and ask if you still want to go away with me."

"Oh, Johnny, you know I do! Did you get my letter last year?"

"I got it. I'm so mad at my pa for helping your pa keep my letters from you. I didn't bother writing back because I knew you wouldn't get the letter, and I was afraid I'd get you in trouble anyway. Then I got wounded and I couldn't write."

"Wounded!" Faith stepped back, looked him over. "Your parents never said a word!"

"I never told them—didn't want to worry my ma." He frowned. "Faith, my ma's last letter said your ma died a couple months ago. I'm real sorry to hear that."

Her eyes teared. "It was a terrible, painful death. The doctor called it cancer, but they don't know much about it.

Oh, Johnny, I missed you even more after she died. Besides you, Mama understood me best."

He grasped her hands. "Well, I'm out of the army now for good. I saw and learned so much, Faith. I have so much to tell you. And I got some money when I mustered out, enough to get us on a train out of here. There's no time now to talk about where we're going and all that. I just wanted to see you right away and make sure you didn't go and marry somebody else!"

Faith looked him over. He looked thinner, but he was as handsome as ever. There was so much to learn about where he'd been, how he'd been wounded, what his plans were for them. Here she was agreeing to go off and marry him, and this was the first time they had even touched or talked for over two years! Little pinpoints of doubt suddenly stabbed at her, but she told herself it was just nervousness from his sudden appearance, the excitement at just the thought of finally being able to leave home.

"I haven't even dated anyone else, Johnny," she whispered. "Father wants me to marry that old Henry Bartel. I'm afraid he'll force the marriage if I don't get away from here."

"Bartel! He's a mean old codger with two kids! You can't marry somebody like that, not my pretty Faith."

She smiled nervously, putting a hand to her face. "I must look terrible. I've been picking corn all morning."

Johnny looked her over. She was only fifteen when he had left. Now she was seventeen, a full woman, and beautiful. She didn't need to know he'd been wounded running away from a battle. It was best she thought his wound was from some heroic deed. After all, he *had* joined the army, hadn't he? He *had* fought in other battles. He'd done his proper duty and shown his courage. It had been an exciting adventure, but no promotions had come of it. He went in a private and came out a private. It was time to find some new adventure, and if he could get Faith to go with him, all the more fun. Once they were away from their families, they could finally make love, go wherever they pleased. Life would be one big adventure, and he'd heard that just about everybody who went west ended up rich—so why shouldn't they?

"You look just fine to me," he told her. "Don't you tell anybody you already saw me. I'll go home, do a little visiting, maybe even come to tonight's prayer meeting. You act like it's the first time you've seen me, and act like I don't mean that much to you anymore. Then tomorrow when you're out here picking corn, you can try to find a way to sneak back to the house while your pa and Benny can't see you. This corn gives you good cover. Have some things packed and I'll pick you up at your house—nine o'clock. We'll ride together on my horse, stick to the woods and camp out till we reach Pittsburgh. We'll take a train from there as far as we can go. What do you think of that?"

Her blood rushed with excitement and trepidation. "Johnny, I don't know—I mean—it's all so quick! We have so much to talk about! And—don't we need a wagon or something?"

He shrugged. "We'll figure it out. We'll have all the time in the world to decide what to do once we're away from here."

She smiled, not wanting to appear too doubtful. What if he left without her? Oh, but he wouldn't do that, would he? And Johnny was her friend and now an experienced soldier. She'd certainly be safe with him.

Still, this didn't seem like the right time to head west. She'd always heard that when people went west they always left in the spring, not in the fall. Something about getting over mountains in winter. Maybe they would have to spend their winter someplace like Chicago or St. Louis—but, then, she wouldn't mind spending time in a big city like that. She would be seeing places she'd only dreamed of seeing until now, and Johnny would make it all real for her. Henry Bartel could certainly never do that for her. If she stayed there much longer, she would go crazy or end up married to Henry.

"All right, Johnny. I'll meet you at nine o'clock tomorrow morning. Just be sure pa doesn't see us. He always picks till noon. He won't notice I'm gone until then, and by that time we can be far enough away that he can't stop us."

Johnny nodded. His eyes danced with eagerness, and Faith thought he was more handsome than ever, in spite of being so thin. "He'll not stop us, Faith. Nobody will." He leaned down and kissed her cheek. "We'll soon be husband and wife, Faith Kelley, and we'll be free to do whatever we want."

"You do love me, don't you, Johnny?"

"Course I love you. Why else would I be here offering to take you away?"

She quickly hugged him, wishing this sudden, unexpected feeling of doubt had not invaded her happiness. If only it hadn't been so quick. But better now than never, and one thing was sure—her father and Benny wouldn't really miss her much. Her father would want her back only so she could cook and clean for him, and so he could marry her off then to Henry Bartel for some land Bartel had offered him for her hand. "You'd better go now, Johnny," she told him, "before my pa hears or sees us."

He nodded. "Remember, act surprised tonight when you see me at prayer meeting, and don't act too excited."

"I'll remember."

He turned and ran off, stopping at the end of the long row and waving. She waved in return, hardly able to believe this was all really happening. Finally! Finally she could leave this place and experience some of the wonderful world beyond this little settlement. She would do this not just for herself but for her mother.

Tall Bear drew his buffalo robe close around his neck, his heart sick at what he saw. Thirty-eight proud warriors, including Dark Owl, all lined up on a specially built gallows, condemned to be hanged. Hanging was the worst way for an Indian to die. A man's spirit was choked off when he died that way. He could never reach the peaceful hunting grounds of the world beyond, where there were no white men except the good ones like his own father.

He was glad his mother was not here to see this, or his old grandfather. In moments like this he was even glad his little son was already dead. What kind of a future lay ahead for the remaining Santee? Reservation life. Boredom. Begging. Government handouts. There would be no more hunting from Canada to Kansas. There would be no more war against the Crow and Shoshone, no more ways for a man to prove himself. They would not even be able to go beyond the reservation to hunt for wild horses. The Oglala still enjoyed some freedom in the Powder River country, and many other tribes had joined Red Cloud, rallying under new leaders called Sitting Bull and Crazy Horse.

He would join them, but deep inside he knew their days also were numbered. They wanted to believe there was still hope, and who was he to tell them there was none? An Indian without hope was a sorry thing indeed. Already many of the Santee were turning to the white man's firewater to make them feel more courageous, happier, to help ease the hurt inside. But the firewater was destroying them. Some had died from too much of it, some had shot themselves in the despondence that often followed a drinking binge. Some did crazy things that only got them into more trouble.

His eyes teared as the thirty-eight condemned men were led to the platform. Originally the army had condemned 307 Indian men to death! All simply because they were Sioux, and it was Sioux who had committed the Minnesota Massacre. Before it was ended and the Indians surrendered, over 450 settlers had been killed, or so Tall Bear had heard at the trials. He knew firsthand that many of them were innocent, and he also knew the raiding had been wrong. But the white settlers simply did not understand how deeply the Santee had been affected years earlier when they had ceded twenty-four million acres of precious hunting grounds for white man's money. Money meant nothing to them, and much of that money had never arrived. Even those twenty-four million acres had not been enough. Settlers had begun moving into land that supposedly still belonged only to the Sioux, and many of them held no regard for an Indian's life—man, woman, or child.

He damn well knew that firsthand, too. Visions of Little Otter's and Running Fox's bloodied bodies would haunt him forever, and that was what created the dilemma in his soul today. He would also be haunted by the memory of shooting that little white boy, a brave child only trying to defend his mother. He'd managed to get that mother and child to the fort and escape. He had no idea whether the boy had lived or died.

He stood around with a few other Indians, their souls sick, their hearts broken. Thank God one good white man, Episcopal bishop Henry Whipple, had interceded for the Sioux, petitioning President Lincoln himself not to allow the hanging of all 307 condemned warriors. Certainly they were not all responsible for the slaughter. Now it was down to these thirty-eight men. Some of them had wives watching, many of them already weeping.

The sentence was read, the nooses positioned, hoods pulled over their heads. A few of them protested against the hoods, and their request was honored. One man began chanting his death song, but before he could finish, one by one the trapdoors that held them were dropped, and body after body snapped to its death. Tall Bear felt a flash of pain at every thud. Women began wailing louder. Soldiers and settlers watched with obvious satisfaction, glad to see so many of their enemy dying.

Tall Bear was not sure himself how many of those being hanged were actually guilty. After shooting the little boy, he'd gone back to the village, trying to convince others the raiding was wrong, urging them to realize it would only bring the wrath of the white man's government down on them. In spite of fighting a war in the east, soldiers had been sent to Minnesota to hunt down the Sioux. They came in big numbers and brought their big guns, and the Sioux had finally surrendered.

Tall Bear had not been arrested, and he wondered if it was only because of his green eyes. Twice he had escaped the noose. He could have been hanged for killing the buffalo hunters, and this time just for living among the Santee. Still, he vowed his days of making war were not over. The tragedy and meaningless deaths of his wife and son still were not fully avenged, not in his heart; but he could not avenge them by killing innocent settlers. He would go west and fight soldiers and miners with Red Cloud. He would steal horses and supplies from the miners, make life miserable for them. He would find and kill more buffalo hunters. It was too late to stop the flow of whites there in Minnesota, but maybe there was hope west of the Black Hills.

Dark Owl! His body jerked as the platform fell from beneath his feet. Such a good friend he had been. They had hunted together so many times, and Dark Owl had enjoyed his stories about the white man's world. Once they had both participated in the Sun Dance together.

The air was filled with *oooh*'s and gasps, curses and weeping. This was indeed a sad day. Tall Bear turned away, determined to wait and try to be allowed to take Dark Owl's body with him for a proper burial. Many of those hanged would be shoved into a mass grave with no honor. Tall Bear shivered. It was the day after Christmas, the white man's celebration of the birth of the one they called their Savior.

He started for his horse, then stopped short when he saw them—the white woman and the little boy! The child stepped closer, stared at him with big blue eyes. "I remember you," he told Tall Bear. "I remember your green eyes."

Tall Bear looked around. Was the child or his mother going to accuse him, too? Try to get him hanged? "I am glad you lived," he told him. "And sorry for your pain."

The boy blinked, his lips puckered, his eyes watery. "You killed my father."

Tall Bear shook his head. "No. I did not. Someone else had already killed him when I got there."

"It's all right, Danny," the woman said, putting a hand on the boy's shoulder. "This one probably saved your life. He could have killed both of us, but he didn't." She stepped closer. "I think down deep inside you know you really belong with the white man."

Tall Bear stiffened. "I belong nowhere," he answered. "That is how it is for those like me who are neither Indian nor white."

The woman glanced at the gallows and grimaced before looking back at Tall Bear. "We never spoke when you brought us here that day you shot my boy. I never thanked you."

"Why should you? I am the one who shot him."

"It was an accident. I knew that by the look on your face when it first happened, and because you found help for him. I wish to know your name so that I can pray for you."

"My name is Tall Bear, but I do not need your prayers. I have my own Great Spirit to pray to."

"I don't want to know your Indian name. I want to know your white name."

He could not help thinking of the irony of the moment. "My white father was French. He told me once my name is like that of an angel from your white man's religion. My white name is Gabriel. Gabriel Beaumont. My father was killed by his own kind. My grandfather, Indian mother, and sister were killed by white soldiers. My wife and son were killed by white buffalo hunters, and now your white government has hanged my best friend. Do not tell me I belong in the white world. I will never belong there!"

Tall Bear walked away, mounting his horse in one swift movement, using no saddle. A travois was tied to his horse, which he would use to take away Dark Owl's body, if it was allowed. He did not look back at the white woman, who was thin and plain. He'd seen the pain of loss in her eyes, and he could not help being glad that some of these whites had suffered the death of loved ones. Still, he was glad to know that little boy was alive. He led his horse at a slow walk toward the gallows, where the thirty-eight bodies were being cut down for burial.

"That'll teach 'em," one civilian grumbled.

"Best Christmas present I ever got," another declared. "I wouldn't mind celebrating Christmas this way every year."

"Do you think he's following us? Trying to find us?" Faith sat down beside Johnny on the train. She'd never ridden a train before, and already she was farther from home than she'd ever been in her life.

"Sure he is," Johnny answered, referring to Faith's father. "But how can he possibly know where we might go when we don't even know ourselves?" He laughed, putting an arm around her. "You're really free now, Faith. Relax and enjoy it! We're headed for a whole new life!"

Johnny still wore his Union cap, and one of the other passengers asked about the war, where he'd been, how it seemed to him it was going. Johnny proudly carried on about a few already-famous battles, stating he'd been there, and Faith admired his courage, little knowing Johnny had not been in any of the fighting he was bragging about.

"There's no doubt the Union will win this war," he told the inquirer with sureness. "If I hadn't been wounded, I'd still be out there fighting those rebs. Now me and the missus here are headed west to start a new life."

"Well, that's nice," the man answered, "but you're both mighty young. You'd best watch yourselves. I've always heard it can be pretty wild out there, hardly any laws, Indian attacks." He frowned. "Isn't it a little late in the year to be headed there?"

Johnny patted Faith's shoulder. "We'll find a place to winter. We'll be all right."

Faith wished she could be as sure as Johnny was about their future. She feared her father would catch them and drag her back to Pennsylvania to marry Henry Bartel, but she also feared the fact that Johnny had no definite destination or occupation in mind. Nor had they married yet. Johnny insisted they could not stop long enough to find a preacher, and besides that, they were still too close to home and might be reported. They had to wait until they reached Chicago before they wed. In the meantime they were to pass themselves off as husband and wife.

The trip to Pittsburgh had been miserable, hiding in the woods most of the way, fighting insects, sleeping on the ground. At least Johnny had not tried to have his way with her. She had insisted they wait until they were man and wife, and he had reluctantly agreed. He seemed such a gentleman most of the time, sitting up nights to keep watch, staying away when she bathed in a stream or pond. She was impressed with what he'd learned about survival in the wilds, and so far he had taken good care of her. But there was an underlying eagerness to his kisses that somehow worried her. She told herself it was just her own fear of the unknown that made her afraid, as well as being suddenly tossed into a whole new world with this young man about whom she still knew little. Besides that, she was concerned that Johnny was already running low on money, and every day he had a new idea about what he would do to make a living once they headed farther west.

His newest idea was to settle on free land under the Homestead Act. But then what? Johnny was no farmer, and she could not do all the work by herself. Besides that, being a farmer's wife was the last thing she wanted.

"Things will be a lot nicer for you now," Johnny told her. "No more sleeping on the ground and spending dark nights in the woods. Soon as we reach Chicago, we'll find us a preacher."

The train whistle blew, and Faith felt a jolt as the locomotive hissed and chugged and got under way.

Was she doing the right thing? She was so sure she could trust Johnny, but she could not forget his mother's warning that Johnny was not a man who knew what he wanted in life, and that she feared he was not going to settle anytime soon.

She forced back tears, not wanting Johnny to think she was unhappy with her decision. He was a grown, experienced man now. He wouldn't want her to behave like a silly little girl. She had made this decision, and she would stick to it. Fears and doubts aside, the fact remained that she dearly loved Johnny Sommers. Whatever lay ahead, it had to be better than wasting away in cornfields married to an old man who would make her feel like a prisoner.

She nestled into Johnny's shoulder. Everything would be all right. A whole new world full of exciting places and new people lay ahead for her.

"Gold," Johnny said softly.

"What?"

"That's where the real riches are out west. We'll find gold, Faith. All we have to do is find a good guide to take us up into Montana Territory. That's where the new discoveries are."

Faith sighed with renewed doubts. "I thought we were going to homestead."

He rubbed at her arm. "Heck, it takes too long to make any decent money that way. Too much hard work. We're gonna get rich quick on gold."

Again he had changed his mind.

Chapter Seven

Faith finished scrubbing another shirt, walked to where a clothesline was strung inside the back washroom of the boardinghouse where she and Johnny lived. Outside the snow blew into windswept drifts, the weather making it impossible to hang anything outside. Winter had come to Chicago, and also into her heart.

She draped the shirt over the line, then made her way back through the maze of clothes and took a moment to study her hands, her swollen red knuckles. Tears streamed quietly down her cheeks as she wrestled with guilt, disappointment, despair, anger. She would get old quickly if she had to do this much longer.

She and Johnny shared a room at this small, cheap boardinghouse outside Chicago, the only place left they could afford after Johnny had spent all his money, most of it at the poker tables in a tavern not far away. If she had not taken this laundress job for the boardinghouse, they would not even be able to stay there. Actually, between this job and taking in mending, as well as helping cook at a nearby restaurant, she had been able to save a little money.

She kept it hidden for fear Johnny would gamble it away. All he talked about was heading west "come spring," sure he would win big at poker and have plenty of money for traveling.

They would damn well go west and get out of this place, even if she had to earn all the money to do it herself! Maybe once she got Johnny away from that saloon and out someplace where he had little choice but to take responsibility for their marriage and their future, things would be better. Things *had* to get better.

She leaned down and dipped another shirt into the hot water, ignoring the pain in her knuckles as she scrubbed vigorously, more out of anger and frustration than to clean the shirt. From their very wedding night Johnny had begun to show his true colors. They had married as soon as they had reached Chicago, and the wedding night was far from what Faith had expected. An eager Johnny Sommers had given her little time to prepare herself for what she considered a sacred, special union. He had surprised her with his forcefulness, telling her not to worry. *It only hurts a little at first. You'll like it, sweetheart.* All the while he spoke he was practically tearing off her clothes, and because they were in a hotel with rooms on both sides of theirs, Faith had kept silent, not wanting to embarrass either of them.

She still had not quite gotten over that night, the realization that Johnny simply wanted to get inside her, with seemingly little respect for her feelings. He'd taken his pleasure in her several times over that night, with no gentleness whatsoever. She had been ready to forgive him for it, but for the first week he invaded her body every night and sometimes during the day, expecting her to just "lay back and enjoy it, honey." He made her feel like a prostitute.

At first they were able to take a room at a more pleasant rooming house, but Johnny soon found a saloon where gambling went on in a back room. He began going there nearly every night with big dreams of quick money, but he lost more often than he won, until they could no longer afford the nice room they had rented.

Now they were here, on the west side of town, in a depressing, unpainted excuse of a boardinghouse called

Fran's. It was run by Fran Babcock, a divorced woman who preferred to rent only to men. Faith had no doubts why. The woman had at least agreed to greatly reduced rent in exchange for help with chores, and it angered Faith that most of her hard work was only so they could keep their room and so Johnny would have money to gamble with. At least she had been able to save tips the men paid her for doing their laundry and mending, and the money she earned as a cook, but she had to work seven days a week in order to save what little she had.

Johnny had taken odd jobs, never kept one of them, always ended up back at the saloon as soon as he began to accumulate a little money. She was just as much in prison here as she had been back in Pennsylvania. She was a married woman, but she might as well not even have a husband. The only attention she got from Johnny was when he came home full of whiskey wanting to make love every night, if it could be called making love. She felt more like an object for him to use to relieve his drunken desires. She deeply resented the nights he would do that after she had worked herself to the bone all day just so they could survive. Didn't he understand she could not possibly be in the mood to have him pawing at her when she had worked so hard all day that everything ached?

There were times when she felt little pricklings of desire and enjoyment, when she wished Johnny would touch her lovingly first, caress her body, take his time. But Johnny was in too much of a hurry.

She could bear all of this only by convincing herself that "come spring" something wonderful would happen to change everything. Johnny was still young. He could change. He would take on a man's responsibilities soon enough once they were in dangerous, lawless country.

She sat down in a chair and stared at the washtub, the line full of clothes, wondering when this drudgery would end, wondering if her life would be this miserable forever. She could not imagine the shame of being a divorced woman, and she did love Johnny. She was not about to give up this easily. He was good at heart, of that she was sure. He just didn't know how to help himself. When she was through with the wash, she would go to the restaurant to help other women who worked there begin preparing a stew and baking bread for the night's supper. She would peel potatoes, knead bread, sweat over a hot stove, go back out into the shivering cold, and come back to the room to take down clothes. Then she would heat an iron over another hot stove and press the shirts, a tedious, tiring job. She would fall into bed at perhaps midnight, and probably sometime in the night Johnny would come home and make his demands. She would comply, only because she didn't want others in the house to hear them arguing, especially when the argument was about sex.

Again life had taken on a form of methodical sameness. She feared Johnny would decide to stay on in Chicago and never leave. She didn't like the city as much as she thought she would. It was noisy and dirty, and sometimes dangerous. She supposed that if a woman was quite rich, life was wonderful there, but it was not wonderful for the poor.

Fran came in from the kitchen then, wiping her hands on an apron. "There are two men here to see you, Faith. One of them says he's your father. They're waiting for you in the parlor."

Faith felt her chest tighten as she rose. "Oh, my! He can't see me like this! You didn't tell him what I'm doing, did you?"

Fran frowned, the many wrinkles around her eyes growing closer together. Her hair was black from too much dye, and her eyes were heavily painted. Fran was kind enough, but she had a hard look to her, the look of a woman well experienced in life. "What difference does it make, girl? There's no shame in hard work."

"I know that." Faith frantically pulled a couple of combs from her hair and retucked a few strands that had fallen from the bun she kept it in when she worked. "I just—you don't understand. I left without his permission, Fran, married Johnny without his permission, too. I thought we'd have a better life than this. I don't want my father thinking I made a bad choice."

Fran put her hands on her bony hips and grunted. "Hmmmph. You *did* make a bad choice, child. That boy *is* still a boy, not a man. There's no call for you to have to work so hard while he goes and gambles away the money, dreaming he'll win big and make his own money the easy way. You'd be better off getting rid of him and going back with your pa."

"Never!" Faith picked up a wet rag and rubbed it over her face, then went to the back door and opened it for a moment, letting some cold air rush over her to help her look fresh and revitalized. "I made certain vows before God to love Johnny, for better or for worse. Once we settle farther west, things will get better. I'll not break my wedding vows."

She breathed deeply for self-control, hardly able to believe her father had actually found her, or even bothered following her there. She turned to Fran. "Besides," she added, "anything is better than life back in Pennsylvania. Living back there was like being in prison, Mrs. Babcock. It killed my mother's spirit. I won't let the same happen to me."

She straightened proudly, taking another deep breath for courage, then headed through the kitchen. *You never should have written that letter, Faith Sommers!* she chided herself. She had thought the least she could do was tell her father she was safe and sound in Chicago for the winter. After all, he *was* her father. He must have some shred of love for her, enough to worry about her. He deserved to know she was all right, and now that she and Johnny were legally married, there was nothing he could do to stop them. Actually, she was surprised he had bothered to come all this way in winter to see her.

She braced herself for a chiding and walked into the parlor, realizing only then that it was Henry Bartel with her father. She had supposed it would be Benny. Seeing Henry only gave her more determination to stay put and stick it out with Johnny. She remained near the doorway. "Hello, Father. I was just in the kitchen helping Fran. You know how I enjoy cooking."

The man looked her over scornfully. "Is that all you have to say?"

"What else is there to say? I wasn't wanted back home,

so I left. You didn't understand my love for Johnny, so I married him anyway. We're wintering here, then heading farther west. You've seen me. You know I'm all right, so you can go back home and not worry about me."

"Just like that?"

"Yes. We're doing fine, and we'll do even better once we're farther west and settled."

"Settled! Johnny Sommers will never settle! Where is he now?"

Faith folded her arms, tucking her hands under each arm so her father would not see how red and swollen they were. "Working," she lied, feeling instantly guilty for it.

"Is he, now? And where might that be? I want a good talk with him."

Faith turned away, wanting to cry. "That isn't necessary. Please just go back to Pennsylvania. Why on earth did you come here, anyway? I told you in the letter I was all right, and you know I'm married now. Just go home, Father."

The man drew a deep breath, and even with her back to him Faith could feel his big, burly presence. Matthew Kelley had a way of filling a room and emanating authority. "I've come to see for myself that you are all right. Whether you believe it or not, I love you, Faith, and you *are* wanted back home. I've brought Henry along with me because he's still willing to marry you if you're ready to divorce yourself from Johnny Sommers. Surely by now you've seen he's only made of promises and dreams. He's not a man to depend on. Henry understands you're young and spirited. You'll get over that in time. We can arrange an annulment, and you can come home and live a proper life."

She faced both men. "Don't you understand I never want to go back there? I agree Johnny still needs to do some growing up, but he's—he's good to me. He loves me, and he has big dreams. I'm going to help him fulfill those dreams, just as he wants to help me fulfill mine. I've married him, Father, and I will not break the vows I made before God to love him till death." She glanced at Henry, shivering inwardly at the thought of being married to him. "I appreciate the fact that you are still offering to marry me, Mr. Bartel. But I am already married, and that won't change." She looked back at her father. "It's good to hear you say you love me, Father, and I love you. But I can't go back there. I can't deny my true self the way Mother always had to do. And you still have Benny. You always loved him best."

The man frowned. "He's my only son, girl. Favoring him doesn't mean I love you the less."

Faith blinked back tears, wondering if the man could ever understand how he'd hurt her all the times he'd punished her unnecessarily. "Father, I *can't* go back. I *never* want to go back. I can't live that way, and I won't make my children live that way. I'll be all right. I know how to work hard. I promise to write when we get settled out west."

Henry was shaking his head. "I am thinking perhaps she truly is too high-spirited for the likes of me," he said to Matthew. "I will walk back to the hotel and give you some time alone. I would like to take the train back to Pennsylvania tomorrow. I have matters to tend to, and children waiting for me."

After Henry took his leave, Matthew's eyes began to blaze in that way they looked whenever he was angry with Faith. "You will suffer for your wild heart, girl. You will learn there is no future with Johnny. You are headed into dangerous country, full of outlaws and wild miners and Indians, and you will find yourself *alone* against them! Mark my words." He walked closer, grasped her arms, and forced them apart. He held up her hands and studied them, then shoved them away and let go of her. "With all the hard work you did at home to help the family, your hands never looked like that! Tell me the truth, girl! Where is Johnny? Has he already left you?"

Faith moved away from him, forcing back more tears. "Johnny would never leave me. He lost his last job and he's looking for another job. . . . I'm doing laundry for Mrs. Babcock's customers. I'm doing it so we'll have even more money for when we go west. Johnny wants to look for gold. We'll need money to buy the kind of equipment he'll need, and for a wagon and oxen."

"Gold! Only fools go looking for it, and most do not find it!"

Faith closed her eyes and sighed. "No matter *what* happens, we will be fine." A tear slipped down her cheek and she quickly brushed it away. "I know you love me, Father, but to you love means that those you love must do everything you direct them to do, to live their lives the way *you* say they should live. I just want to be *me*, Father, and I can't do that back in Pennsylvania."

Matthew stiffened in indignation. He put his hat on his head, looked long and hard at her. "God be with you, Faith Kelley. You will most certainly need his grace."

She lifted her chin. "My name is Faith Sommers now."

"And I regret the day Johnny Sommers ever came into our lives. I pray *you* won't have the same regret someday. God bless you, Faith."

To Faith's surprise she saw tears in the man's eyes.

"I will miss you, Faith, just as I sorely miss your mother."

Faith nodded. "I miss her, too. I understood her better than you did, Father, because I am just like her."

"Oh, yes, how well I know that. And I suppose with that fiery spirit of yours, perhaps you *will* get by, in *spite* of Johnny Sommers." He leaned down and kissed her forehead. "I've done my duty as a father, made you an offer to come home and marry Henry. You have chosen against it, and I cannot be blamed for whatever life brings you. Good-bye, Faith."

Oh, how hard it was not to break down in front of him, but Faith was determined to appear strong, to make him believe she was happy. "Good-bye, Father." She stood rigid as the man left, waited for the door to close before she sat down in a chair and wept.

Faith took a nightgown from a bureau drawer, wishing she could first take a long, hot bath before getting ready for bed. But a bath cost extra money, unless she wanted to carry all the hot water herself to the tin tub in the bathing room at the end of the hall. She was far too tired for that.

She lay the gown out on the bed, and just then she heard the outer door of the boardinghouse open and close.

She heard Johnny's voice downstairs and wondered what he was doing home early. It was only eleven P.M. Lately he had been staying out most of the night and sleeping late in the mornings. She almost wished he hadn't come home so soon. She didn't want to talk, and she certainly did not want to make love.

She heard an unfamiliar voice; then Johnny came bounding up the stairs. After a tap at the door he entered, smiling.

"You're still up! Good," he greeted her, wearing his usual brash smile, as though neither of them had a care in the world. "I've got somebody I want you to meet. Come on."

"Johnny, it's after eleven o'clock! Can't it wait until morning?"

"Oh, it will only take a minute." He took her hand and pulled her to the door.

Downstairs in the parlor a tall, robust man with a grizzly beard stood in soiled buckskins. He removed a coonskin hat, showing a head that was mostly bald except for hair around the bottom edge that he had let grow long over his shoulders. It looked flat and oily. His eyes were a piercing, icy blue. The way those eyes moved over her when she came into the room, she might as well have been naked. She had to force herself not to avert her nose from the smell in the room, the smell of a man who did not understand the word "bath."

"Honey, this is Cletus Brown, and he's going to take us west, be our guide."

Faith shivered at the thought, hoping Johnny meant with a wagon train where many other people would be around.

"Clete, this is my wife, Faith," Johnny finished.

Faith nodded slightly to Clete.

"Evenin', Mrs. Sommers."

"I just won a bet with Clete," Johnny said, putting an arm around her. "Instead of money, I said if he lost, he'd have to guide us on farther west, up to the new gold discoveries in Montana. He's led lots of wagon trains, knows the west like the back of his hands, has even dealt with Indians and can speak some Sioux and Cheyenne. All we need to do is buy some equipment and we're on our way come spring. We've got enough saved for a wagon and all, don't we?"

We? Faith thought. *I have money saved, money you don't even know about.* "Whatever I can hang on to that you don't gamble away," she answered aloud, folding her arms authoritatively. She pulled away from him. "If you don't stop gambling, Johnny, we'll have nothing."

He shrugged. "I won good today. We'll be all right, and at least now we don't have to pay a guide."

Faith glanced at Cletus again, wondering if the man truly did not expect any pay. She suspected they had better keep their money well hidden on any journey they might take with Cletus Brown. "Well, Mr. Brown, we will certainly have to feed you, won't we? I don't exactly call that free guidance."

Clete smiled through yellowed teeth. "That's a fact, ma'am, but I'm a right good hunter. I'll shoot fresh meat most of the time. You can cook it. Johnny says you're a right fine cook, seein' as how you do the cookin' over at Flora's Diner. You ever cook wild-buffalo meat? Wild dear? Rabbit?"

"Deer and rabbit. Never buffalo."

"Well, it's not much different. You'll like the taste of it. Anyways, since I'll be killin' wild game for most of our meals, it won't cost you much to feed me."

Faith frowned with irritation. "You're really taking us all the way to Montana because of a bet on a card game?"

The man chuckled. "A man bets some foolish things sometimes." He looked her over again. "We'll all make do. I was fixin' to go to Montana anyway. If I can help a couple of young folks like you get there, all the better."

Faith looked at Johnny. "According to the papers the Indian situation in that area is very bad. Some forts have been abandoned."

"No fret about Indians," Cletus assured her. "I've been handlin' them since I was hardly out of my teens. You'll be all right. You might want to keep a hat over that pretty red hair, though. It might attract a few too many braves who've never seen red hair like that." He grinned at Johnny. "I gotta say, kid, you've got a right pretty woman there. You'll have to watch over her good if you're goin' to some of them mining towns. Women are mighty scarce in some of them places, and pretty ones like her . . ."

"I'll watch her good. You just remember to be around in a couple more months. We'll leave soon as it begins to warm."

Cletus replaced the hat onto his bald head. "I'll be ready and waitin'." He nodded to Faith. "Nice to meet you, ma'am."

Faith wished she could reply in kind but could not.

After Clete left, Johnny grasped Faith's arms and turned her to face him. "A free guide, Faith! We're practically all set. I'm sorry for all your hard work here, having to wait to realize our dream, but it'll come true soon enough, you'll see. We'll go to Montana and find gold, and you'll be a rich lady! No more scrubbing clothes for my Faith!"

Already she could see this would be one of those nights she dreaded. Whiskey was heavy on his breath, even though he'd come home much sooner than usual. "Johnny, if you don't stop the drinking and gambling, we'll never have enough money to go anywhere. Did you get that job you went looking for today?"

He waved her off. "That boot maker had already hired somebody else. Don't worry. I'll get something again. I'll work real hard the next couple of months, and we'll do okay."

"Johnny." She turned away dejectedly and smoothed a few strands of hair back from her face. "I'm beginning to see that you live in a dream world. You seem to know nothing about reality."

"Sure I do, sweetheart. I know I really love you and we're really going to Montana. We have a real destination now. That's all the reality we need."

She held up her hands. "I didn't plan on this! I didn't plan on being the one to earn the money so we could go! I didn't plan on you gambling away everything you had saved so that we'd be stuck here in Chicago!"

"Honey, honey, we're not stuck. You heard Clete. He's taking us to Montana in just a couple of months."

"I don't like Cletus Brown one whit, nor do I trust him. How can you put us at the mercy of a man like that? An experienced mountain man who consorts with Indians and smells like a skunk! You don't know anything about him, Johnny, or if he's even telling the truth about knowing what he's doing. I'm telling you I don't trust him, Johnny. I don't want to travel with that man! We'll find a wagon train."

"Heck, Faith, we don't need the headaches of a wagon train. If we go with Clete, we'll get there a lot faster. Wagon trains have breakdowns, and people have to wait. Sometimes somebody has a baby, or gets shot, or their horses or oxen give out. Sometimes they have outbreaks of cholera, measles, things like that. We're a lot safer going on our own. We'll make a lot better time and not have to get mixed up with other people's problems and diseases. Clete's okay. Hell, it's a good offer he's making us. Everything will work out, you'll see." He ran a hand through his hair in frustration. "Heck, Faith, I can't help it if it's hard to find work around here. And I'll be working plenty hard when we find us a claim and I start digging for gold. Before long you'll be living like a queen, I promise."

He pulled her close and kissed her, and Faith wanted to cry at the realization that she no longer felt the passion for him she'd once felt. The more she saw of the real Johnny, the less she desired him, in spite of his dashing looks and fetching smile. "Let's go to our room," he suggested.

She wrested herself from his embrace. "Johnny, don't you have any idea how tired I am? Every muscle aches in my neck and shoulders and arms from scrubbing clothes, and my fingers are burning raw! I'm working here like a slave while you sit in that tavern and play cards! This isn't what I expected when we ran away, Johnny. What if I should find out I'm carrying? How do you propose to provide for a baby? I certainly can't work this hard with a baby in my belly!"

The look in his eyes reminded her of a hurt little boy. "Heck, Faith, you should have known it wouldn't be all easy right off. I've worked, and I'm looking for work again. At least we're away from Pennsylvania. Isn't this better than being married to that old codger Henry Bartel? Isn't this more exciting than sitting in prayer meetings all day, or picking corn?"

Faith turned away. "I have to admit it is. Father came to see me today, Johnny. Henry was with him."

"What! Did they try to take you away? I won't let them—"

"No, Johnny. Father just wanted to know I was all right. I lied to him and said I was, and I said you were getting a new job." She faced him again. "He wanted me to annul the marriage and go back to Pennsylvania, but I'd never do that, Johnny. I made vows to you, and I intend to keep them. I just hope you intend to keep yours."

He put a finger to his lips. "Let's go up to our room first. We shouldn't be talking like this down in the parlor." He took her arm and led her upstairs, closing the door to their room. "Of course I intend to keep my vows, Faith," he told her then, rubbing at her arms. "How can you think I wouldn't?"

She sighed, studying his eyes, wanting so much to believe only the best about her Johnny. "You *will* look for more work tomorrow, and you *will* stop gambling, won't you? I've heard there is a lot of gambling up in those mining towns."

He pulled her close again. "I promise to look for work, and no more gambling." He kissed her neck. "If you want me to stay away from the gambling table the rest of tonight, let's go to bed, sweetheart."

She tried to fend him off. "Johnny, I'm a mess. I've been scrubbing clothes all day, and I'm tired. I ache all over, and I must look terrible."

"You're always pretty in my eyes," he responded. Without warning he picked her up and carried her to the bed. He moved on top of her and eagerly pulled off her clothes between kisses and promises. This was the last thing Faith wanted to do, and she knew it would take him even longer because he'd drunk too much whiskey again.

As he shoved himself inside her, she forced back the tears. She could not even think of her husband. All she could think of was how Cletus Brown had looked at her. She lay rigid while Johnny took several minutes to get his satisfaction. Finally he rolled off her, stretching and letting out a long sigh. "See? My gambling isn't a total waste. I got us a free guide all our own so we can get there that much sooner. I can't wait till the weather warms, Faith. Then it's off to Montana. Just the three of us."

Faith lay silent. *Just the three of us,* she thought with trepidation.

"Faith?"

"Yes, Johnny."

"I'm glad you didn't listen to your pa. Life wouldn't be any good without you."

She curled next to him. "What am I going to do with you, Johnny Sommers?"

"Just love me, girl. I'll make it worth your while, I promise."

Chapter Eight

May 1864 . . .

Tall Bear liked this new country where the Teton, Oglala, Hunkpapa and Brule Sioux lived. He decided this land farther west was surely a better place for the People. Most whites would not want to settle here. It was too high, too rugged. Here in this land even farther west than the Black Hills, majestic mountains rose like guardians of the land. It was beautiful here, and he had never felt so free.

A few of those with whom he had traveled had died on the rugged journey through winter winds and snows, but February had brought calmer, sunnier weather as they'd marched through the Dakotas and into territory they had learned from the Oglala was called Wyoming by the white man. Now they were encamped with the Oglala, some of Red Cloud's people, who were celebrating a winter of few soldiers to worry about. The white man's war and Indian raids had closed some of the white man's forts for the winter, and from what Tall Bear had seen and heard, he took great hope that here in Powder River country the

Sioux could continue dominion over the land. Red Cloud was a great leader, and new leaders were rising in prominence, men to take Red Cloud's place once he was too old to continue leading warriors, men like Sitting Bull, a Hunkpapa, and Crazy Horse, a very young Oglala warrior, who had already proved himself quite skilled with the lance and arrow, and with the white man's rifle.

The Sioux here were quite confident. Bellies were full, and Powder River country continued to be their domain. Being in a new place helped Tall Bear deal with his loneliness, and he had been welcomed as a member of the Crow Owner's Society. Soon it would be time to hunt buffalo. Many prayers were said over the pipe to Wakan Tanka that many buffalo would be found. Soldiers and miners were killing off the buffalo in great numbers, and now white men who hunted buffalo for their hides had also begun coming into Powder River country. The Sioux were determined to keep all such people out of their hunting grounds, and as long as they could keep soldiers driven out, they could rule the land.

He lived with an old Indian man called Fox Hunter and his wife, Kneeling Woman. He provided for them, as Fox Hunter could no longer do much hunting of his own because of his age. It was a good life, a last bit of freedom for the Sioux. Tall Bear was thinking about this as he worked on a war shield Kneeling Woman had made for him. He was tying scalps to it, the three scalps he had taken from the men who had killed Little Otter and his son, but he was interrupted when Kneeling Woman rattled the pieces of tin tied to the entrance flap to the tepee and ducked inside. She carried in some wood and stacked it nearby, then looked into an iron pot that hung over the fire, in which she had cooked a stew of turnips and buffalo meat.

"Traders are coming," the old woman told Tall Bear. "They say they come north from a place called Denver. They trade at Fort Laramie, then come into Sioux country to trade for buffalo robes and deer skins. I would like to go to them, perhaps trade for some colored ribbons." She looked over at her sleeping husband. "Will you go with me, Tall Bear? You speak their tongue."

He nodded. "I will go. But I do not like the thought of white traders coming here."

"The others say these are the kind of men who understand us, speak our tongue, respect our ways. They are not like the buffalo hunters and soldiers and miners. And they bring rifles."

Tall Bear set the shield aside. "How far away are they?"

"Not far. They will reach our village soon."

Already Tall Bear could hear yipping and shouting, the sound of Indian men welcoming strangers with a combination of friendliness and warning. "We had better go see them," he told Kneeling Woman. "Gather your robes. I will help you carry them."

The weather had finally warmed, and Tall Bear wore a buckskin shirt and leggings but did not need an extra robe. There was only a slight chill to the wind, made so by snow still packed on mountain peaks to the west and south of them, and patches of snow still on the ground in many places. Kneeling Woman tied a wolfskin cape around her shoulders and picked up three more wolfskins that lay at the side of the tepee, all thanks to Tall Bear's hunting. Tall Bear in turn took up two bearskins and carried them out.

"Save the buffalo hide and the other bearskin," he told Kneeling Woman. "We never know when another winter might bring a poor hunt and we will need the extra warmth."

They walked toward the pack train of approaching traders, who used mostly mules but also a couple of canvas-topped wagons—big, lumbering contraptions weighed down with all kinds of trade items. Dogs ducked around the wagon wheels, barking at the intruders.

"Sitting Bull says it is not good that we trade with the white man and begin to depend on him," Kneeling Woman said. "He says it will make us dependent on the white man, and maybe he is right. I need another cooking pot, and perhaps you have something to trade for tobacco and guns."

"I will see what they have first. The wild horses I caught last week are good, strong stock, and I need a good rifle."

Already the traders were opening the wagon gates and

displaying all sorts of trinkets, ribbons, beads, cooking utensils, blankets, and a hundred other items, including whiskey. The white man's firewater was one thing Tall Bear had tried to warn the Sioux to avoid. He always remembered his father's warnings that whiskey would someday be a tool the whites would use against the Indians to make them do foolish things, sign away their land, become so lazy they could no longer hunt. He had warned Tall Bear never to drink whiskey. Still, several other Indian men were already trading for the jugs of burning drink, feeling very cocky over the success they had had so far in keeping miners and soldiers out of their hunting grounds.

Kneeling Woman began dickering for an iron pot, offering two wolfskins. The man to whom she spoke looked the skins over. "They are very clean," Tall Bear told the trader, who looked familiar to him. His hair was white and his beard white mixed with red, but though he was obviously old, he was quite robust.

"Well, I reckon they're worth a cookin' pot," the man answered with a grin. He studied Tall Bear curiously. "You speak English."

Tall Bear nodded. "I learned it from my father, *mon père*. He was French."

"That so? Say, I knew a French trapper once, good friend of mine. We used to practically live with the Sioux over by Minnesota and them parts. His name was Alex Beaumont. You wouldn't know of him, would you?"

Tall Bear frowned, studied the man closer. "Jess? He had a good friend named Jess Willett."

The man's brown eyes lit up. "Gabriel?"

Tall Bear nodded. "My white name is Gabriel Beaumont. I have not used it for many years."

"Hot damn! Alex's kid! I knew I recognized them green eyes!" Jess reached out a hand to Tall Bear. "What the hell you doin' here with these Sioux, and you dressed just like 'em. What's happened to your pa, Gabe? I never run into him for years, and I always wondered what happened to him. I sure as hell liked that man. Honest he was. Honest as they come."

Tall Bear smiled, glad to see one of his father's old

friends. He shook the man's hand. "I am called Tall Bear now. I have lived among the Sioux for many summers, since I was ten. I am twenty-eight summers now." He lost his smile. "My father was killed by robbers on a riverboat when we were returning from St. Louis. My mother and I went to find her people, and I have lived among them ever since."

Jess frowned, saddened about Alex's death. "I'm sorry to hear about your pa, Gabe—I mean, Tall Bear, damn sorry." He brightened a little. "I sure do remember Yellow Beaver. She was a looker, all right. Is she still with you?" He yelled at the others with him to continue the trading and walked away from them with Tall Bear. "It must have been hard on her when your pa was killed. How did it happen?"

"Thieves on the riverboat. They stabbed him in the back and took his money." Gabe's eyes showed renewed sorrow and anger. "Yes, it was very hard on my mother, but she is also dead now. She was killed by soldiers at Blue Water Creek."

Jess shook his head. "I'll be damned. They're both gone." He looked Tall Bear over. "And you chose to stay livin' with the Sioux?"

Tall Bear stood a little straighter with pride. "I might have later left them, but I married a Sioux woman, and we had a little boy, but both of them were shot by buffalo hunters, for no reason."

Jess rubbed at his whiskers. "Lordy, lordy. I'm sorry you've lost so much, Tall Bear." He could see the look of a proud warrior about the young man as his green eyes turned to slits of hatred.

"I killed and scalped them . . . all three of them. Ever since then I have not wanted to go back to the white man's world. I have only wanted to fight them. Most of my mother's people have had to flee Minnesota, and now we are here with Red Cloud, where the Sioux still rule their land."

Jess sighed, rubbing at the back of his neck. "Sweet Jesus." He pushed his hat back a little, looking intently at him. "Tall Bear, you must know that it won't be long before whites will be here in Powder River country, too, in a lot bigger numbers. With gold up in Montana, settlers movin' into Nebraska and Kansas, gold discovered in the Rockies south of us, a big city startin' to grow there called Denver—they're all around, Tall Bear. It's a fact the Sioux and all other tribes is gonna have to face and accept. And you gotta remember you're half-white yourself. You ought to think about that."

"I think about it all the time, but I would not know where to go, what to do. I have no one now. These Sioux are my only friends."

Jess put a hand on his arm. "Well, son, you've got a friend in me, and that's a fact. You remember that. I'm usually around these parts someplace, around Laramie, or over to the Green River. Most anybody you ask at any of the forts around this territory knows me. If you ever feel the need to talk or give our side a try, you just come to me. Anything I can do for you is like doin' it for your pa."

"That is kind of you." He glanced over to watch Kneeling Woman. "Do you truly believe there is no hope of the Sioux keeping their hunting grounds?"

Jess sighed. "You've seen places like St. Louis. And right now the only reason the army can't quite hold its own out here is because of the war back east. You just wait till that war is over. There will be plenty of men to send out here to chase Indians, and plenty of people ruined by the war who will want to come west for free land and to start over. I can see the writin' on the wall, son. Your pa and me, we came from a different time, when the only white men out here came to trade and hunt, not to stay. We got along good with the Indians. These new ones that are comin' now, they're here to dig for gold until there's none left, and to claim the land for themselves, kill off the buffalo. Still, they ain't all bad, Tall Bear. You know that. Part of what's happenin' is just life, a change of times."

Tall Bear nodded. "I thank you for your honesty."

"And I wish you luck, Tall Bear. I'm sure glad to see you again, glad you're all right, and like I said, I'm right sorry about your pa. He was a good man."

Tall Bear nodded. "*Aye.* And how is it you are into the trading business?"

Jess glanced at the wagons. "Well, when it got so there wasn't no more demand for beaver, I started in guidin' wagon trains out here, then got into this tradin' business. I make enough to keep a horse, have plenty of whiskey and tobacco, and to afford to do some gamblin' now and then. That's all I care about."

Tall Bear grinned. "My father also never wanted much. You remind me of him." He put out his hand. "Whatever happens, I will always call you friend."

"Same here, Tall Bear." Jess shook his hand firmly.

They walked back to the trade wagons, and Tall Bear thought how good it felt to see someone from his father's past. To this day he missed Alexander Beaumont, the closeness they had shared. By now the Sioux were laughing and enjoying the trading, some getting a little drunk on whiskey they had bought. Tall Bear wished it could always be this way for white and Indian alike, but Jess was right. This could not last. The days of friendly trading with men like Jess Willett were nearly gone.

Faith thought how beautiful this country would be if she was truly settled here. How much nicer it would have been if they could have traveled by stagecoach. At times their path had crossed a stage route, and although it looked like a bouncing, dusty ride, at least those inside were seated and someone else was responsible for the coach and the horses. They could stop at way stations and eat and refresh themselves. They were with other people for conversation.

There was hardly any conversation now between her and Johnny. It was all between Johnny and Clete, who was filling Johnny's head with dreams of gold. Talk of settling under the Homestead Act had turned to talk of getting rich quick by digging for gold. Faith suspected there was a lot more to it than dipping a pan into a stream and coming up with golden nuggets, but that was how Clete made it sound.

The trip had been miserable, the heat and mosquitoes unbearable as they made their way through the Nebraska plains. Clete claimed it was best to travel as lightly as possible, which meant she had to walk most of the way rather than ride in the wagon. It didn't seem to bother Johnny much, but she had begun feeling sick the last two weeks, and she feared she was pregnant. Every step was an effort in physical stamina, and her fears were mounting, not just over when and if Johnny would truly settle, but where she would be when she had the baby. Would there be a doctor or anyone to help? How would that baby be provided for? She couldn't care for a newborn and also work, but if Johnny kept up his ways, she would be the one who would have to bring home money.

This was all Johnny's fault—the trip, the baby, her misery. If he had not squandered their money, they might have had enough, with what she had earned, to take a stage-coach part of the way rather than plod along with a wagon and four oxen. If Johnny had not insisted on mating practically every night, she might not be pregnant. The worst part about that was the realization that Clete knew what they were doing in the wagon at night. Often she could hear him and Johnny laughing about it over the campfire afterward. In the mornings Clete would look at her as though she were a whore, and his hungry eyes gave her the shivers.

They had been traveling for close to three months now, and Clete had made no move toward her, yet his presence made her uneasy. It was mostly the way he stared at her. Johnny trusted the man completely, admired his skills with gun and knife, which Clete had gladly demonstrated. Clete was "the most experienced man I've ever known," Johnny would say. He had at least proved he was not lying about getting along with the Indians. They had encountered a few Cheyenne in Nebraska, and although the Indians had frightened her to death with their war whoops and fancy riding around the wagon, as though to take their lives and perhaps take her captive, Clete seemed to calm the situation. He had spoken to them in their own tongue, and he had presented them with gifts of tobacco and cloth. They had brought supplies along for just such an encounter, and Clete had been right that they would need them.

Faith feared more Indian trouble. They were nearing the area where Clete said the Sioux had been making trouble for most travelers. Because of the Civil War, there were few soldiers out here for protection. The war, they had learned in a town called Julesberg, was still raging on. She would not have minded settling there, but Johnny insisted on going up to Montana, and now they were in rugged, mountainous country, peppered with a mixture of red-rock canyons and valleys green with grass and pine trees. They had encountered two rattlers, one bobcat, and a grizzly. Clete had "saved the day" on all counts, proving he was just as skilled as he'd promised, but each time he had looked at her as though to see if he had impressed her.

She was bone weary, and she felt more and more as though she was along only so Johnny would have someone to paw over at night and both of them would have someone to cook for them by day. Her disappointment in Johnny only added to her exhaustion, and now . . . now the baby. She had not told him yet.

Johnny didn't even seem to mind that while he and she walked most of the journey, Clete rode his big roan gelding, sitting with chest puffed out, wearing those soiled buckskins and sporting many weapons, putting on a show of the brave frontier scout. Faith couldn't help wondering how long he would have lasted if the Indians they had encountered had chosen to fight. And if Johnny was killed, how long would Cletus Brown fight for her honor? He would probably trade her for his life.

It was almost dusk, and Clete hollered for them to "hole up here." There was only a little grass nearby, but Clete claimed this was the best place to make camp. The oxen would have to forage as they could. Faith proceeded to stack some wood they had gathered earlier in the day when passing through an area of pine trees, and Johnny got a fire going, ordering her to heat some coffee and "cook us up some of that jackrabbit Clete skinned and cleaned for us yesterday."

Faith quietly obeyed. This was no place or time to argue. She would save that for when they finally reached civilization. There had been only hints of people and settlements here and there as they had passed by a couple of forts, even tagged along with a wagon train a time or two, until Clete told them of another "shortcut" that would save them time.

If only they had traveled with a wagon train, she would have other women to talk to, especially about babies. They would have companionship, more help in case of trouble. There might be a little music at night, the sound of children laughing, stories about settling that might help Johnny know for sure what he wanted to do. There might have been other men along who would have been a better influence on Johnny than Clete.

She heated some old coffee, used a spoon to dig the fresh rabbit meat out of a tub of thick lard used to preserve it, then placed a heavy black fry pan over the fire. It was the same tedious routine every night. She felt like an old hag, her skin dry, her hands looking too old for her age, her fingernails broken and dirty. It was slightly cooler here in Wyoming Territory, or at least that was where Clete said they were. But because of the heat she still wore no slips or even a camisole under her dress, and although she worried what this revealed to Clete's searching eyes, she was too hot and uncomfortable to really care.

The sun, which blazed hot and ornery by day, began to settle behind the mountains to the west, and both men ate voraciously. Faith had no appetite. She told herself this was still better than Pennsylvania. Once they reached wherever they were to land in Montana, she could clean up. Maybe they would have a little cabin somewhere. Clete could go his merry way and leave them alone. Clete said wherever there was a gold camp, there were usually little settlements, supply posts and such. They would have neighbors, a chance to make a normal life in a house without wheels. She would work if she had to, make money for herself just as she had back in Chicago. She had decided that if Johnny showed no hope of changing, she would divorce him. She would do whatever was necessary to live the life she'd always dreamed about even if she had to create it for herself and give up Johnny, who had so far broken every promise he had made to her.

The men finished eating, leaning against boulders that were scattered around the campfire. Johnny patted his belly, and Clete pulled his six-gun from a holster at his waist. He whirled the chamber, checking the bullets. "You might have to use your own gun a time or two to protect a gold claim," he told Johnny. "Sometimes men try to steal claims, but if they're caught, they're hanged for it."

Johnny lit a pipe, glancing at his own gun, which hung on a branch nearby. "You think we'll have much trouble getting through? They told us at the last fort that the Bozeman Trail is pretty much closed because of the Sioux."

Clete shrugged. "I've got a pretty good way with Indians. They won't mess with just three people, and we've got more tobacco and such to trade." He still held the gun, studying it almost lovingly. "Besides, I know another way to get up there. We'll head on west and go up through Yellowstone and the Tetons. It's a longer route, but way away from the Powder River country and the Bozeman. I got me some friends waitin' up there. They went on ahead of me to start diggin', but I told them I'd lost that bet with you and had to guide you myself. Said I'd be along behind 'em."

Johnny laughed. "That will teach you to bet something besides money."

Clete leaned forward, resting his elbows on his knees, still holding the six-gun in his hand. "Well, Johnny, some things is worth more than money to a man—like a pretty woman, you know?"

Faith could feel him looking at her, but she refused to meet his eyes.

"Heck, yes, I know," Johnny answered. "I got me a pretty one, and she feels right good in a man's bed."

He laughed, and Faith cast him a look of bitter anger. Her cheeks felt hot with embarrassment, and she was tempted to throw her coffee at him.

Clete chuckled. "I can tell by the noises you two make at night." He shook his head. "Mighty hard on a man, havin' to travel this far listenin' to that, no relief for himself."

Faith felt an eerie warning in the words, and all nerve

ends came alert. Pure instinct made her rise and walk toward the wagon. She wanted the men to think she was just climbing inside to get something—and she was . . . a small handgun she had bought in Chicago. She had never shown it to Johnny, because he would only laugh at her for not trusting Clete Brown. Now, in this one quick moment, she suspected she would need it, after all, and dread began to filter through her blood.

"I expect so," an innocent, trusting Johnny replied. "Sorry about that, Clete." He laughed, but suddenly the laughing stopped. Faith heard the click of a gun.

"Well, Johnny, I let you come this far and brought you up here on this out-of-the-way trail because out here we ain't likely to run into other travelers, and there's nobody around to hear a gunshot."

Faith scrambled to her trunk, dug inside for the pistol. She had never even had a chance to try using it, but the man she'd bought it from had loaded it for her. *All you have to do is cock the hammer here and pull the trigger. Might not actually kill a big animal, but it'll sure as hell stop it . . . or a man.* She prayed he was right. She found the gun.

"What the—"

Those were the last words Johnny Sommers spoke. Faith jumped when she heard the gunshot, knew instantly Clete Brown had just murdered her husband in cold blood.

Johnny! She ordered herself not to let panic or terror and grief get in the way. Clete himself had said that out in this country a man—or woman—had to be ruthless. Never more so than now.

"Come on out of that wagon, woman," Clete called to her. "Got somethin' to show you."

Faith knelt in a corner, waiting. Let Cletus Brown come to her. *She* had something to show *him*!

Chapter Nine

Terror so engulfed Faith she could feel nothing but the gun in her hand. She could not think about Johnny, or the fact that she was entirely alone and lost in Indian country. She concentrated only on the back of the wagon, watching, waiting, saying nothing.

"Come on, now, little lady," Clete taunted. "It's just you and me now. You're goin' to Montana with me as my woman, and if you try to tell folks what happened to Johnny, I'll make you suffer like you ain't never suffered. You was gettin' tired of him, anyway, I could tell. You let me have a little fun, and I'll take you to Montana like I promised and set you up real good. I know people there who can help you, make you a rich lady."

The voice was getting closer.

"Ain't that what you really want? To be rich? You're pretty, spirited, full of sass. Let me tell you, in a mining town you can make more money than any of them prospectors diggin' for gold. The real treasure is in the men themselves. You give them a pretty smile and let 'em have at you, and you'll be linin' your own purse with their gold."

He was almost at the back of the wagon now.

"Now, I know you ain't got no gun in there because Johnny's only handgun is still hangin' out here, and his rifle is propped outside the wagon. So why don't you make this easy on yourself? There's nobody to help you, nobody to hear you scream, and I don't want to hurt you if I don't have to. I been listenin' to Johnny go at you till my balls hurt. Now it's my turn, whether you like it or not. Take my advice and make it easy and let me take you to Montana, and you'll be a rich woman—and free to live however you want, wear fancy clothes, hire people to cook and clean for you."

There he was, his ugly bearded face peering at her from the back of the wagon. A lit lantern hung from above, so he could see her well enough . . . and she could see *him* well enough.

Clete grinned. "You look like a scared little rabbit. You don't have to be scared of me. I just got rid of somebody who'd be nothin' but a burden to you. You ought to be grateful. Come on, now. I'm givin' you a chance to do this the easy way." He started to climb into the wagon.

"Wait," she said.

He hesitated, looking surprised.

Faith scooted a little closer, keeping the hand holding the pistol behind her skirt. She had to get closer. The gun was small. Maybe at close range it would do more damage. She had to be sure to put him down, or he might shoot her, too.

"I . . . I want to bury Johnny first. It only seems proper."

He grinned again. "Oh, he'll keep for a little while. I promise to bury him right off, come mornin'."

To think that he could not only shoot Johnny with no warning whatsoever, then spend the night with the man's wife while his dead body lay stiffening made Faith want to vomit. It was all she needed to give her courage to do what she had to do.

"All right," she answered. "As long as you promise to

bury him first light. And keep his body close to the fire so the wolves won't get to him."

Clete nodded. "Sure enough."

She scooted a little closer, and Clete put his gun back into its holster and climbed a little higher. It was all done calmly, and Faith felt as though she were dreaming the whole thing. She reached out to him, held his eyes with her own gaze so he wouldn't even notice her raise her other hand.

She placed the pistol against his chest and pulled the trigger. The gun jerked slightly in her hand. At first Clete just stood there on the wagon step, staring at her, his eyes widening. Suddenly Faith feared the bullet had not done its job. She fired again.

Clete's mouth fell open as though he could not believe what was happening. He said nothing. He grabbed her wrist, terrifying her with his strength. Had the bullets done any harm at all? He was like a bear, hard to put down. Before he could push her hand away, she fired a third time. The sound reminded her of a firecracker.

Finally she felt his grip weakening. He began gasping for breath. She prayed one of the bullets had found his heart. Surely at least one of them had found a lung. He finally let go of her wrist, and she fired a fourth time. He clung to the wagon gate a moment longer. "You . . . bitch!" he muttered before finally letting go and landing on the ground with a thud. He began groaning and rolling on the ground.

Faith fought the panic that tried to grip her. Afraid he might still be able to grab her or shoot her if she climbed out the back, she went out through the front. She realized then that Johnny had never even unhitched the oxen yet. She knew how to drive them, had helped several times. She had to get away. Away from Clete Brown. She couldn't stay around there and watch him die slowly, nor could she bring herself to walk up and shoot him in the head and end it all, even though that was what he deserved.

She felt sick when she saw Johnny slumped over near the fire. "Johnny!" she groaned. She walked over to him and laid him out on the ground. "Oh, Johnny! Johnny!

Johnny!" The reality of the horror began to take hold. Johnny was dead. She had just shot a man four times, and he lay groaning and dying. She was alone in country full of wild things, including Indians, and she had no idea where she was, which way to go. Wolves howled in the distance. Johnny's body was already stiffening and had to be buried.

She tried to think. There was still a very tiny bit of light left, enough that she could at least drive the wagon a little farther on, get it away from Clete Brown. The trouble was, she had no way to pick up Johnny and put his body inside, and she couldn't leave it there for the wolves. She had to find a way to take it with her. She ran to the side of the wagon, where several feet of rope hung wrapped around a peg. She took it and went back to Johnny, tying it tightly around his ankles.

"Oh, God, Johnny, I'm sorry! I don't know what else to do," she said, wanting to scream. She could still hear Clete groaning. She hurriedly tied the other end of the rope to the side of the wagon, straining every muscle to pull Johnny's body close enough that as it dragged, it couldn't get caught under the back wheel. There was no other way to take him with her. As soon as she could see well enough, she would bury him. It seemed a shameful thing to do with the dead body of a man she had loved, but it would be worse just to leave him there. "Oh, Johnny, why didn't you listen to me?" A torrent of tears threatened, but she kept telling herself to be practical. She couldn't think too much about this yet. Not yet. Maybe it was all a nightmare, and she would wake up any minute.

She finished tying Johnny's body to the wagon, then peeked around the back again because she no longer heard Clete groaning. He lay very still now. Was he dead?

Just in case he was not, she walked carefully toward him, close enough to reach down for his gun. Quickly and gingerly she yanked it from its holster, realizing she might need it anyway. Her own little pistol would be no use against wolves or to shoot a man from a distance. She threw it into the back of the wagon. She retrieved Johnny's rifle and shoved it under the wagon seat. Then she tied Clete's horse to the back of the wagon. Now Clete would have no guns and no horse. His gear was still packed on the animal, so she would have ammunition for his six-gun, and his rifle was still with his gear. As soon as she could, she would practice shooting both six-guns and both rifles. She might have to defend herself. She might need to shoot straight in order to eat.

She walked back around to the front of the wagon and took the switch from under the seat. She snapped it over the heads of the oxen. "Come on, Brutus, Cleo. Get on there!"

The big animals reluctantly gave a tug and got under way.

How was she going to unhitch the poor animals? Could she handle the heavy yokes? She knew how it was done, had helped a few times, but Clete and Johnny had always taken care of the yokes. "Take one thing at a time, Faith Sommers," she told herself. "One thing at a time. Don't panic."

Tears began streaming down her face as she walked beside the oxen, determined to get at least a mile away from Clete before stopping for the rest of the night. She would build another fire to keep the wolves away from Johnny's body, and come morning she would bury him if she had to dig all day to make a hole big and deep enough. She fought against terror and hopelessness, and for the first time she truly missed Pennsylvania, even missed her father. Most of all she missed her mother, her precious mother.

More tears came until she shook with sobs, hardly able to see where she was walking. She refused to look back, afraid she'd see Clete coming after her, afraid to look at poor Johnny's body dragging along on the ground. She drove the oxen in the direction they had been traveling, not knowing what other way to go, aware only that they had been heading west, toward high purple mountains. How was she going to get over those mountains? And what about the baby she was carrying? How long could she go on alone like this?

She had no idea how far she had managed to go before darkness finally fell. By then she had cried so many tears, there were none left. She climbed inside the wagon. She turned up the wick of the still dimly lit lantern and hung it outside on the side of the wagon. With wood from the wood box and some dry sage, she lit a fire close enough to the wagon to keep wolves away from it and from Johnny. She still couldn't look at his face.

She would have to sleep near the fire, if she could sleep at all, so that she could wake up now and then to tend the fire. She dared not let it die down. She realized she should unhitch the oxen and untie Clete's horse, but she was afraid they would run away, stranding her. Come morning she would find a way to feed and water them. Right now she could not do another thing. She had to rest. She had to rest.

She prepared a bed for herself near the fire and lay down. Finally she allowed her gaze to move to Johnny's body, his face. It was only then she realized his eyes were still open, and she could see a small bloody hole at his right temple. "Oh, God, oh, God," she moaned. She turned away, sobs racking her small frame. "God help me," she wept. "Help me through tonight and tomorrow. Just that much. Help me through tonight and tomorrow." It was the first time, after all the prayer meetings she'd attended growing up, that she truly felt something, the first time she'd sincerely prayed . . . the first time she'd actually felt God's presence. She wept until she felt nothing again, and finally exhaustion took over, bringing on blessed sleep.

Morning dawned still and warm. Faith groaned from the pain in her arms as she awakened. At first she wondered why she should be so sore. Then the ugly reality came back to her. She rose to a sitting position with a gasp, realizing that she had let the fire nearly go out. She remembered that her arms ached from dragging Johnny's body to tie it next to the wagon. She glanced at his body then, stiff and grotesque now, beginning to bloat, his clothes torn from being dragged, his eyes still open.

"Johnny," she whispered, putting a hand to her stomach. "Poor Johnny." She had begun to hate him, but he didn't deserve to die like that. And once their new lives had begun, she might have loved him again.

There were no tears left in her. She didn't feel anything now except the pain in her arms. She would have to ignore that pain in order to dig a hole and bury Johnny. How she had managed to get through the night without wolves coming after her and Johnny and the animals, she wasn't sure. Maybe God was watching after her. One thing she did hope was that the wolves had turned all their attention to Cletus Brown for what he'd done to Johnny and had planned to do to her. She hoped the four bullets she'd put into him had finally ended his life, but she would not soon get over the fear that he would come after her. She would have to be very watchful.

There were only a few embers left of the fire, and she decided not to add any wood to them, since her supply was dwindling and she would need fires at night. On the other hand, maybe it was dangerous to light fires at night. Indians might see the flames and come investigating. She had no idea just what to do, where to go. This was the most rugged country she'd ever seen, both beautiful and menacing, dry and dusty in places, green and forested in others.

It took every effort just to get to her feet, and she wasn't sure how she was possibly going to dig a hole, considering how hard the ground was. She knew she was a mess with Johnny's blood on her already-dirty dress but she dared not even wash. Water was too scarce out here. She'd better save what she had for drinking and wait to wash until she found a stream.

She looked around, noticing that the land farther ahead rose into green hills. Maybe there was water there. And she saw pine trees, which meant dead wood for fires. She decided to head in that direction even before burying Johnny. It would be a good place for the animals to graze. She knew how to hobble them so they wouldn't run away. She was a little bit afraid of the big oxen, but she would have to overcome her fear.

She kicked out the fire, threw her blankets into the wagon. After relieving herself, she got the oxen under way again, surprised they would obey her at all. The poor things had been in yoke all day yesterday and last night with no relief. Maybe they sensed that there was good grass and possibly water ahead.

"Come on, you," she goaded, snapping the whip over their heads. "Let's go. I love you, Brutus, Cleo, Tilda, Bo. Right now you're my best friends."

The words brought a lump to her throat. She had no one now. No one. But she had chosen this path, and she would somehow survive.

For over two hours they plodded on until the ground became softer and greener. The grass and forest she had thought were only a few minutes away had turned out to be much farther. She chided herself for not realizing that. Nothing out in this big country was as close as it seemed. She guided the oxen farther onto the grass, and she dearly wanted to lie down in it herself and sleep again. She knew she should be hungry, yet she had no appetite at all. Somehow she kept herself going, untied and hobbled Clete's horse, removed its saddle and gear so it could graze comfortably. She would go through the gear later and keep what she would need.

She was astonished by her own stamina, and by how hardened she suddenly felt by what had happened. She'd shot a man, maybe killed him, and she didn't care. Why should she, after what he'd done? Ruthless. Yes, Clete Brown, one certainly had to be ruthless in a land like this, and she had a baby to think about.

From a bin on the side of the wagon she took out the leather straps for hobbling the oxen. It took all her strength to unhook the heavy yokes and lift the top half up and over the lead oxen, then let the full yoke fall to the ground. She unhitched the lead team from the second team, then unyoked the second team. The animals seemed grateful, quickly wandering out into the grass, where they began grazing. Then suddenly they moved a little faster, following Clete's horse, which, in spite of being hobbled, was walking clumsily toward a small dip farther ahead.

"Wait!" she called to the animals, but there was no stopping them. She hurriedly followed behind, coming to the rise and seeing there a stream of water where they were already drinking. She couldn't blame them, and she was glad she'd found a place where she could wash. But first she had to bury Johnny. She walked up to the oxen and quickly hobbled them while their attention was diverted by drinking, trusting that with grass and water right there, they would go no farther.

Mustering all her courage, she cut Johnny's body down, grimacing at how stiff it had become. Johnny, her sweet, spirited husband with the handsome smile. They had not even gotten the chance to say good-bye to each other. His intentions had been good and honorable. She had to believe that. At least he had married her, and he'd had plans to make them rich.

Carrying a shovel from the wagon, she looked for a soft spot in the grass to dig. Yes, this was better than the hard, rocky ground farther back. This was as pretty a place as any to bury him. When she reached civilization, if she wasn't killed first, she would write a letter to his parents and explain that their son was dead. She wasn't sure if she should tell them the awful truth. It would be too hard on them, and her own parent would worry, too.

She stuck the shovel into the ground and began the arduous task of digging a hole big enough for Johnny's body. A thousand thoughts rushed through her mind as she dug. She would never tell her father she'd killed a man, if indeed Cletus Brown was even dead. She couldn't think too seriously about it herself . . . not yet. It was just too much to bear. She dug and dug, sweat pouring down her face, soaking her dress. Finally she stopped to assess the size of the hole she had dug. She wanted to cry when she realized it was not nearly big enough.

"God help me," she whimpered. Her strength was running out. She needed to eat, to rest. She needed to think about the baby growing in her belly. She had never even told Johnny about it. Now the baby was all she would have of him, and she feared that the horror of what she'd been through, along with all this digging, might cause her to lose it.

She took several deep breaths, wiping at sweat with the sleeve of her dress. She began shoveling again, for another hour, two hours, the sun rising to almost straight overhead. Soon she would have to stop, find a shady spot to rest, force herself to eat something.

Finally she dropped the shovel. She drank from the water barrel, then took some bread from another bin, and a blanket from inside the wagon. She walked on weary legs to the stream, relieved to see the oxen and horse still grazed nearby. She spread out the blanket in the shade of a tall pine tree, where the fallen needles would make a soft bed. She splashed water from the stream over her face and hair, then let a light breeze cool her wet skin.

Her feet ached, her shoulders and arms screamed with pain. She forced down some bread, then lay down in the shade, relishing the chance to rest. For the moment she didn't care what time it was, didn't care that she was lost. She would do and think about one thing at a time, and today's task was to finish digging the hole so she could bury Johnny.

Soon she drifted into blessed sleep. When she awoke, the sun had drifted farther to the west. She realized then that she had not wound her mantel clock this morning. She had bought the clock back in Chicago, planning to set it on a fireplace mantel when Johnny built the cabin he had promised her. Now there would be no cabin.

She rubbed her eyes and sat up; then her blood ran cold. Just across the stream sat a man on a spotted horse with bear paws painted on its rump. He was Indian, and he was silently watching her.

Chapter Ten

Faith slowly got to her feet as the Indian guided his horse across the creek toward her. A gutted deer was tied over the horse's rump, its head hanging limp. Perhaps this man was only out to hunt, not to make war. She had seen Indians around Fort Laramie, knew some could be peaceful, but she could not even remember what tribe those were. Shoshone? Crow? Cheyenne? She couldn't think straight, her heart pounded so hard. She remembered other Cheyenne, with painted faces and a threatening countenance, who had frightened her to death when they had ridden in circles around their wagon when they'd come through Nebraska, yipping and whooping as though to make trouble. Clete had dickered with them, had managed to appease them with gifts of tobacco and a bottle of whiskey.

Now here she was not so far from country where the Sioux, according to Clete, had been making war, determined to keep whites out of their hunting grounds. She remembered reading about the horrible things the Sioux had done back in Minnesota two years ago. Now here was a man obviously a warrior, most likely Sioux. He was more naked than any Indian she'd seen. Besides a necklace that looked as if it were made of some kind of claws, he wore only moccasins and an apronlike piece of animal skin over his privates. She felt as though she should be ashamed to look at him, but she dared not take her eyes off him. With a sinking heart she realized she had left her guns back at the wagon.

Terror engulfed her. He had a powerful build, and he held a rifle in one hand. She noticed the curved handle of a big knife he wore at his waist, and white streaks were painted downward on his cheeks. His black hair hung nearly to his waist, across powerful shoulders. He had a proud look to him that seemed to say that this was a man who would do whatever he wanted with her. She'd heard Clete tell stories of what some Indians did to white women. He'd enjoyed terrifying her with his sickening tales.

The Indian rode his horse right up to her. She stood frozen in place, knowing it would do no good to run. Clete had once said Indians respect bravery. Yes. She would act brave, defiant. Maybe that would work. Or maybe if she did everything he wanted, she would at least stay alive. Ruthless. Yes, ruthless. She had to remember that word. In the last two days she had learned a hard, quick lesson about being ruthless out in this wild country.

The man looked around, curiosity in his eyes, eyes she only then noticed were green. Green! Maybe he wasn't all Indian. Maybe he was what Clete called a half-breed. She grabbed her blanket and stepped back, clasping it to her breast. "What do you want! Go away!" she shouted. "Go away!" She waved her arm, trying to make him understand.

He looked past her, his eyes again scanning the area. "Where is your man?" he asked.

He spoke English! She was relieved. At least she could converse with him, make him understand, learn what it was he wanted. "He . . . he's off hunting our supper," she lied. "He'll be back any minute, and he's got one of those big rifles they use to hunt buffalo." Clete had talked with buffalo hunters back at Fort Laramie. She'd seen those big guns, heard the damage they could do. "You—

you'd better get out of here. If he sees you when he gets back, he'll shoot you with that rifle. They make big holes. Big, big holes!"

If not for what he'd seen that kind of gun do to his own wife and son, Tall Bear would find humor in this woman's comment. He knew she was lying about her husband and his big gun, but he admired her courage. He'd hardly seen any white women since coming to Powder River country, and this was the prettiest one he'd ever seen, here or in Minnesota, in spite of her haggard look and bloody dress.

He was many miles south of the Powder, had come there with a hunting party following a herd of buffalo that was migrating south. There were women along for cleaning skins and curing meat, their village only a few miles to the north. After months of raiding with Red Cloud and his warriors, many white intruders had died, and the white man's road to the mining camps was all but closed. Now was a time for hunting rather than making war. Game was becoming scarcer, and finding enough food meant straying farther and farther from old hunting grounds. This was as far south as he and his hunting party had ever come, and it was pretty country. He had been on his way back to the village when he'd spotted this white woman sleeping alone near the creek. He had seen the grave she'd been digging, quietly ridden over to her wagon, and had seen the stiffened, bloated body of a white man lying near it.

"I know about the buffalo gun," he sneered. "And I know there is no husband and no gun here. Who is it you try to bury? Is *he* your husband?"

Dear God, he knows! she thought with failing courage. She stepped farther away. "What do you want? Please go away! I have nothing to trade. Just go away and leave me alone."

Tall Bear swung a leg over his horse's neck and slid off the animal, still holding the rifle in his hand. "I want nothing you have," he told her. "Do not be afraid of me."

Faith frowned in curiosity. This man not only spoke English, but there was a very slight accent to his words, one she could not quite pinpoint. "Why are you here if you don't want anything?"

He looked around warily again. "I saw the grave you dig. I saw the dead man. Do you need help?"

Should she trust him? Something in his green eyes told her she could. Why else would he ask if he could help? And she so dearly needed that help. She could only pray he wasn't lying. "I . . . yes." She put a hand to her belly. "I'm with child. And I've . . . I've been through something terrible. Now I have to dig a grave. I'm afraid such hard work will make me lose my baby."

His green eyes raked over her, and Faith was suddenly self-conscious of how she must look.

"How did that man die?" he asked. "His body is already many hours dead."

Faith put a hand to her aching head, tears wanting to come again. There seemed no sense lying to the man. "All right," she answered. "He is my husband." She stopped for a moment, an unexpected sob making her shoulders jerk. She threw back her head and breathed deeply to keep from breaking down. "We were . . . headed for Montana. Our guide was taking us around Powder River country because of"—she met his eyes again—"because of the Sioux making so much trouble up there. Are you Sioux?"

He nodded proudly. "Minniconjou."

"Aren't they the ones around—around Minnesota?"

He nodded again. "There was much trouble there. Many of us came here to live among our Oglala brothers because of that trouble."

She noticed scars on his chest, and long white scars on his forearms. "Were you a part of the awful massacres?"

He turned, shoving his rifle through leather straps tied around his horse's belly. Faith noticed that besides the deer slung over its back and the parfleche holding supplies that was also tied over the horse's rump, there was only a blanket on the horse's back, no saddle.

"I was there," he answered. "It is not important now." He faced her again, figuring she would be less afraid of him if he put his rifle away. "What happened to your husband? Where is your guide?"

"He's dead . . . I think."

Tall Bear frowned. "You *think*?"

She blinked back more tears. "I shot him. Four times. But the gun I used was very small, and he was a big man." She caught the scent of a strange odor and realized it must be Johnny's body. Poor Johnny! She had to get him buried. "I never trusted our guide. His name was Cletus Brown." And so she began to tell the Indian about what had happened in all its horror. When she finished, she met his eyes again. "Yes, I do need help. I have to get my husband buried. It makes me sick to have to leave his body like that." The tears came then. "I'm so weak and tired, and I'm afraid for my baby. Will you—will you finish digging the grave for me? I can cook something for you. That's about all I can do to repay you."

Tall Bear studied the woman before him, so beautiful but so sad. His heart went out to her. Last night must have been terrible for her, seeing her husband shot in cold blood, shooting a man herself. Cletus Brown must have been a man not so different from the buffalo hunters who had shot his wife and son. "I will dig the grave," he told her.

"Thank you," she sniffed. "What . . . what is your name?"

"I am called Tall Bear."

"I'm Faith. Faith Sommers."

Tall Bear took the reins of his horse and walked toward the grave site, and Faith followed. She lay the blanket over Johnny's body while Tall Bear started digging. Faith decided to keep busy or go crazy, so she made a fire from dry grass and kindling and set an iron pot full of water over it. She cut up some potatoes and threw them in, along with some dried peas and salt pork.

Occasionally she glanced at Tall Bear, sorry for his hard work, noticing sweat gleaming on his dark skin. It seemed strange to be looking at a man so nearly naked. Almost his entire buttocks was exposed, and she could not help noticing his powerful, muscled build, though not in the way a woman might admire a man she wanted, for she was too full of grief over Johnny for such thoughts. She only noticed because it would be impossible *not* to notice. There were not many men built like this one, and his mixed blood made her curious. He did not seem very willing to talk, so she said nothing, letting him concentrate on the digging so she could get the burial over with and put poor Johnny to rest.

She mixed flour, water, and yeast with a little salt and made biscuits, heating them in a Dutch oven over the fire, removing them as soon as they were raised and baked so they wouldn't burn. She left them in the pan to keep warm.

Finally Tall Bear climbed out of the hole he'd been digging, planting the shovel in a pile of dirt.

"I will bury him now," he announced. "You will want to speak over his grave. Are you Christian?"

Faith was surprised at the remark, which made her think of her parents, the prayer meetings. "Yes. My family are Quakers. Have you heard of Quakers?"

He scowled. "Some have come to the reservations to tell us everything we do is wrong. They understand nothing of Indian beliefs." She handed him a towel to wipe sweat from his face. Some of the white paint there smeared when he did so. "I worship Wakan Tanka, the Great Spirit," he continued, "but I believe He is the same as the Christian God. My father was French. He was what is called Catholic."

"I don't know much about Catholics," Faith responded. "But I guess they worship the same God as other Christians." For the first time Faith noticed a hint of a smile at the corners of his mouth.

"He is the same."

Faith felt suddenly embarrassed, not even sure why, except that this supposed heathen seemed to know more about the Christian religion than she did. "Well, to answer your original question," she told him, "yes, I do want to speak over Johnny's grave. After you put him in the grave, perhaps you'd like to go wash in the creek. You must be very hot and tired. I'll speak over my husband then, and we'll throw a little dirt in. Then you should eat something. I'll help you finish filling in the grave after that." She glanced at the blanket-covered body. "I . . . I hope you don't mind if I don't help you with the body. I don't think I could stand to touch it now."

Tall Bear did not relish touching it himself. Touching a dead body could bring bad luck. "I will tie rope around his wrists and drag the body. It is the only way I can get it into the grave."

Faith shivered. "All right." She turned away, breaking into sobs as she waited. She could hear the dragging sound, the thud of Johnny's body landing in the hole. The tears came harder then, and she stayed near the fire. Then she felt a hand on her shoulder, and she started, turning to find Tall Bear right behind her. Clete had said something once about Indians being the "quietest, sneakiest bastards ever born." Now she understood what he meant, but they were surely not all the devils he'd made them out to be. This one had worked hard digging a grave for her husband out of the kindness of his heart. He could so easily have ridden away and left her there alone . . . or done something worse.

His face was unpainted now, and she thought what a handsome man he was with those green eyes surrounded by dark brows and lashes and dark skin. But there was also that intimidating look about him, his size, his strength, his long hair. She reminded herself that this was a warrior, a man who had been a part of the Minnesota raids. "I'll get my Bible," she said, moving away from him.

She wished her father were there. One thing Matthew Kelley knew how to do well was pray and find just the right Bible passages for special occasions. Now that she had been away from him for several months, she was beginning to appreciate his good points, yet in spite of what she'd been through, she knew in her heart she would not go back to Pennsylvania. Not now. Not after all this. Clete Brown had tried to destroy her and Johnny's dreams, but he damn well was not going to succeed! Nor would she let this wild land or Indians or anything else defeat her. For Johnny's sake she would go on from here . . . somehow . . . and she would make a decent life for herself.

She went to get her Bible from her trunk. When she returned, Tall Bear stopped shoveling dirt into the grave. She thought she caught a glimpse of true pity in his eyes, and she was surprised that Indians had such feelings. Perhaps it was only the white in him. Then again, Indians *were* human beings, at least in appearance. Maybe she could learn more about them from this man. After all, if she was going to stay out there, she would need to know something more about them.

He was certainly a mystery, a look of wild savage about him, yet he'd helped her bury her husband and had enough respect for her religion to tell her to get her Bible. He actually knew about Bibles. He had a look of intelligence about him she had not expected to find in an Indian, and again she decided that was because he was half-white.

She realized then she was occupying her mind with wonder about this half-breed because she did not want to face the reality of the moment. Johnny Sommers, her handsome, brash, adventurous husband, whose head had been full of wonderful dreams, was dead and now he was buried. She fought a sudden urge to scream with the pain of it. She remembered wanting to do that when she had heard that first gunshot, when she knew Clete had killed her husband. But she had remained calm, calculating, waiting patiently for Clete to come to her so she could shoot him. She was discovering things about herself, discovering a strength she'd had no idea she possessed, a rather cunning aspect to her nature, an ability to shut off feelings when necessary. Maybe it was this wild country that did that to a person, or maybe it was simply an instinct for survival.

She glanced at Tall Bear again, realizing suddenly how Indians, at times, could seem so cruel and murderous, how they could be a people who seemed to have no feelings. Survival! They wanted the same thing.

She opened the Bible, remembering there was a passage from First Corinthians about death and resurrection. She thumbed through, fighting tears, silently praying that God would help her find the right passage. She scanned through the passages. . . .

"For the trumpet shall sound," she read, "and the dead shall be raised incorruptible, and we shall be changed. . . . O death, where is thy sting? O grave, where is thy victory? The sting of death is sin, and the strength of sin is the law. But thanks be to God, which giveth us the victory through our Lord Jesus Christ."

Her eyes filled with too many tears for her to see well enough to read any other passages, but she knew the twenty-third Psalm by heart, and she began reciting it. "The Lord is my shepherd; I shall not want. . . ." The lump in her throat was painful, and she stopped to swallow, shivering in a quick moment of unstoppable tears, then taking a deep breath to go on. She managed the next couple of sentences, then struggled through "Yea, though I walk through the valley of the shadow of death, I will fear no evil. . . ." Clete Brown. He had been the evil lurking in the shadow of death. "For thou art with me."

She broke down again, sobbing through the rest of the passage, the words coming out in a kind of squeak between tears. Yes, God was with her. She realized only then that she had learned that much from all the prayer meetings she'd been forced to attend. Perhaps shooting Clete Brown wasn't such a terrible sin. Maybe God had put that little gun in her hand. And God had surely sent this mysterious half-breed to help her bury Johnny.

"Surely goodness and mercy . . . shall follow me all the days . . . of my life . . . and I will dwell in the house of the Lord . . . forever."

She knelt beside the grave, sobbing uncontrollably for several minutes, until finally she felt strong hands on her shoulders. She thought how she should be afraid. She didn't know this man at all, and he was a Sioux warrior, in spite of his white blood. He was big and strong enough to do what he wanted with her, break her neck when he was finished. Yet she felt no fear.

"Come away now," he told her. "You must rest. I will finish filling in the grave."

"Johnny, my poor Johnny," she wept. "He didn't . . . deserve this. He . . . he had his faults . . . and sometimes . . . I hated him for . . . being so irresponsible . . . for breaking his promises . . . but I loved him so. . . ."

"Come. Lie down in the wagon."

She felt herself being led away from the grave, felt

strong hands at her waist as he lifted her into the back of the wagon. She crumpled into a pile of blankets and cried herself to sleep.

Birds sang and sunlight filtered through the back of the wagon when Faith awoke. She sat up, aching all over but feeling more rested. It took a moment to realize that the direction of the sun meant it was morning. Morning! She'd slept the rest of the evening and all night after burying Johnny.

Tall Bear . . . where was he? He had probably gone his own way, and now she was alone and lost again. An urgent need to relieve herself forced her to climb out of the wagon, and to her surprise Tall Bear was lying on a blanket near the fire. She remembered then, hearing wolves howl through the night, being too tired even to open her eyes to see if they were near, knowing somehow that this Indian man was out there protecting her.

His eyes opened when he realized she was up. He quickly sat up and nodded to her.

"Good morning," she said. "Thank you for staying here."

He got to his feet. "I ate some of the stew last night. It is still warm on the fire. You must eat this morning."

"I will." She walked toward a clump of rocks. "Please stay there." Could she trust him? It was silly to wonder about that now. He'd had plenty of chances during the night to take advantage of her weakened state, but he had not. She walked behind the rocks to take care of personal things, and when she returned, he was himself coming from behind a thick cluster of yucca bushes.

She glanced at Johnny's grave, noticed it was neatly covered now, the dirt mounded evenly, rocks piled on top of it. She looked back at Tall Bear. "Thank you. I feel as though I should pay you somehow."

He stretched his arms. "No need. I found a small barrel of salt and poured some into the carcass of the deer I killed to help preserve the meat. That is payment enough. I must leave today, take the meat to my village so the women can begin smoking and curing it before it spoils."

Faith was surprised at the realization that she did not want him to leave. What would she do then? And the mention of a village—women . . . "Do you have a wife there? She must be worried about you."

A strange look of bitterness came into his eyes. "I have no wife. She was killed, in much the same way your husband was killed. She was shot by buffalo hunters. As was my little son."

Her heart went out to him. "That's terrible! I'm so sorry!"

He put more wood on the fire. "It was in Minnesota." He met her eyes then. "Now perhaps you understand why I took part in the raids."

She slowly nodded, understanding even better the human side of this warrior, the reasons why he and his people did the things they did.

"You must wash," he told her. "In the stream. You will feel better. I will stay here and keep the fire going. When you are through, I will go and wash also. Then you must eat and gather your things. I will show you the way to a place where the white man's coaches stop for fresh horses and food and rest for the passengers. I rode past it only two days away from here. Perhaps there you can find help."

Faith felt great relief at the words. He would not leave her alone and lost, after all. "Thank you. I don't know what to do, what to say. I might have died out here if not for you. I have no idea where I am, where to go. I am deeply grateful for your help, but I don't understand why you're doing this."

He shrugged. "You are a woman alone who has done me no harm. Why should I not help you?"

She frowned. "Because you surely hate seeing white people come here."

"It does not matter so much here. It is in the north, in Sioux hunting grounds, that we do not want whites to come. I know some whites are good. My own father was a good man, as were some of his friends. I do not hate all whites, just those like the men who killed my wife and son. Go and wash now. I will wait here."

The words were spoken as more of a command than a

request, and Faith obeyed, trusting him not to try to take advantage of her while she was bathing. She climbed back into the wagon, dug out some clean clothes, and walked to the stream to wash, noticing that the oxen and horse were still in sight. She was glad of that.

A stagecoach station. That must be what Tall Bear was talking about, where he was taking her. He would show her the way, and then he would ride out of her life. How strange. She felt oddly disappointed that she would probably never see him again after that, but, then, she had much bigger things to worry about . . . like what she would do once she reached that stage station . . . where she would go from there . . . how she would survive and be able to take care of her baby.

Her baby. She was a woman alone in a strange land and carrying a baby.

Chapter Eleven

Faith guided the oxen through a wide valley and up a rise, following Tall Bear on his spotted horse. For all she knew, he could be taking her to his own camp to sell her to some other brave for some horses, but she did not believe that. How astounding that she was being led to safety by an Indian warrior, the very thing she had feared most in this land.

They traveled from early afternoon until dark, through open, grassy places studded with boulders and smaller rocks, through buttes and mesas, and higher mountains ever to the north, south and west. Tall Bear pointed out a small herd of buffalo. He waited while she stared at the great beasts as they ambled through a ravine below them.

She thought what a wild land this was, wild in beauty, wild in movement, in weather, in dangerous animals . . . and dangerous men. She had an unreasoning fear that Clete, as good as he was at tracking, might still try to follow her and exact his revenge. She looked back often, glad that Tall Bear was with her. He had spoken little since they'd left, mostly just to explain something she was seeing, telling her the Indian names for certain mountain peaks, pointing out various weeds that could be used for medicinal purposes.

"We will camp here tonight," he told her upon reaching a clear, grassy area at the base of a red rock mesa. "Tomorrow I will point the way, and you will find the white man's settlement on your own."

"Settlement? I thought it was just a stage station."

"If that is what you call it." He dismounted. "It is where the coaches carrying men west to forts and towns stop for fresh horses. I call it a settlement because it is a place where white people gather, and where white men stay to feed those who travel and to take care of the horses that pull the coaches."

Faith realized now that the slight accent she had detected was French, since he had told her his father was a French trapper. That was all the information he had offered, and she wondered about his childhood, what had happened to his father, why he'd chosen to live among the Indians instead of whites.

He ordered her to sit down while he unhitched the oxen, something she'd had to show him how to do, since Indians never used such contraptions, but he had easily understood, and she was grateful for his strength and help. "Indian men usually never do this," he said later, carrying an armful of deadwood he'd collected from a nearby stand of trees. "The women carry all the wood, make the fires, do the cooking, make the tepees, clothing, moccasins. They clean the animals, scrape and tan the hides, cure the meat."

Faith sat on a fallen log, watching him curiously as he piled the wood nearby. "That's not so different from what white women do. But, then, white men work hard at farming and such. The women help with that, too. Do your people farm?"

"Some do, on the reservations. None like it. It is better to hunt, find wild plants, kill the deer and the buffalo. But the whites are killing off the game. That is why we try to keep them out of what is left of our hunting grounds."

"Have *you* made war against whites? Since you left Minnesota, I mean?"

He finished arranging wood for a fire, building it in a tepeelike fashion over a pile of dry weeds. "I have," he answered without looking at her. "Light the fire. I will cut some meat from my deer and share it with you."

Faith did as he asked, glancing over to see him deftly slice off some meat with his big hunting knife. She wondered if he had used that knife to scalp some poor white man or woman. How strange that he was now helping her. He could so easily live like a white man, if he chose. He stabbed the meat onto a sturdy green branch he had cut earlier when they'd stopped to rest for a few minutes. She had wondered then what the stick was for but had not asked. He walked over and held the stick over the fire, saying nothing. Finally he met her gaze, and Faith felt embarrassed. He clearly knew she'd been staring at him.

"I have never known anyone like you," she admitted. "You . . . where I come from, for a man to wear almost nothing at all is considered very sinful."

"Sinful? What is sinful?"

"Bad. Wrong."

He shrugged and shook his head. "It is not wrong to stay cool when it is so hot. You should take off more of your own clothes."

Her eyes widened with indignation. "I'll do no such thing!"

There came only the second smile since he'd found her. Faith was astonished at how handsome he was when he smiled. She had never thought of an Indian man as someone who could be handsome.

"White women seem determined to be as uncomfortable as possible. I remember ones in St. Louis—"

"St. Louis! You've been to St. Louis? *I've* never even been there."

He turned the meat. "I used to go there with my father when he took beaver- and wolf- and deerskins to sell. We went by riverboat."

"Riverboat! *I've* never been on a riverboat! You're supposed to be an Indian, someone who knows nothing about whites, yet you've ridden a riverboat to St. Louis!"

He turned the meat again, and fat dripped into the

flames, making a hissing sound. "I was very young, perhaps ten. My father was killed on one of the trips. White men stabbed him for his money. That is when my mother and I went to Minnesota to find her family. Since then I have lived among the Sioux. My mother was called Yellow Beaver. She remarried when we came back to the Sioux, and she had a baby girl. They were all killed by soldiers."

Faith gasped. "I'm sorry." His father was killed by white men, his mother by soldiers, his wife and son by buffalo hunters. "I still don't understand why you're helping me, just because I'm alone. You should want to let me die. Surely you hate most whites."

He took a moment to reply. "There are good people and bad people no matter what their race. You are good. And you are carrying. The life within you is innocent. If I end your life, I also end your son's or daughter's. It is not fair."

Faith put a hand to her stomach. Did that mean he would have killed her or let her die if she had not been pregnant? "Do you have education?"

"Only what my father taught me. I read a little, but he did not have much education himself. He could read French better than English."

"What is your white name?"

He scowled. "White women ask too many questions. I liked it better when you were too tired to speak."

Faith straightened in indignation. "I was only trying to make some conversation."

"You should rest."

"I only think about Johnny when I rest. I'd rather not think about any of that. It hurts too much."

He nodded. "I know the hurt. It takes many years to go away." He met her eyes again. "Now I will ask you a question. How old are you?"

"Why?"

He rolled his eyes. "You answer a question with a question."

She sighed in frustration. "As far as I know, it's July. That means next month I will be eighteen. How old are you?"

He shrugged. "I know only by a stick I carry. My

mother told me to cut a notch in it each summer. I was ten summers when she told me that. Now there are eighteen notches on the stick." He grinned again. "See? I know how to count the white man's way."

She rested her elbows on her knees. "So you're twenty-eight." She wanted to ask about the scars on his arms and chest, but she was afraid to. Maybe they were from some secret sacred ritual, or maybe from fighting soldiers . . . or white settlers.

He turned the meat once more. "You are very young and with child. What will you do when you reach help?"

"I don't know," she sighed. "I guess I will decide when I get there."

"You will not go back to where you came from?"

She shook her head. "No. I wasn't happy there. Somehow I will make a new life for myself here."

He handed her the stick to hold for a while. "This is not a good place for a young white woman with a child and no husband."

"I'll survive."

Tall Bear admired her courage. "I think perhaps you will. You are a strong woman. You are also very beautiful. It will be easy for you to find a husband."

The words surprised her. He thought she was beautiful? And she was such a mess! She figured the part about her being strong meant more to such a man than being beautiful. "Thank you, but I don't feel strong *or* beautiful."

Again he smiled that rare smile. "I have never seen such red hair, except on a man who once hunted with my white father. He was from a place called Ireland, and he had many red marks on his face."

"Freckles," Faith told him.

He nodded. "I had forgotten what they are called."

Faith poured herself some coffee. "You say your father was French. Do you remember much of the language?"

He shrugged. "Enough to speak it a little and probably understand it if someone spoke it to me. I am not sure anymore."

"What was your father like?"

He stared at the flames. "Again you ask many questions."

"I'm sorry."

He sighed. "My father was a good man. His name was Alexander Beaumont, and we were very close."

Faith smiled slyly. "So I know part of your English name, or French, I guess I should say. It's Beaumont."

Tall Bear scowled, surprised at how easy she was to talk to, how easily she managed to get him to answer her infernal questions. "I must tie my deer carcass high in a tree near the fire. Wolves will come after it again tonight."

He rose and took something from his gear, and Faith realized it was clothes. She watched him pull on deerskin leggings and shirt, his body reminding her of a muscled animal. She felt relieved that he had put something on, had wanted to ask him to wear more clothes but was afraid it would be some kind of insult. She could not quite get over feeling guilty looking at his near-naked body.

He walked over to where he had left the deer lying over a log. Rope was already tied around the deer's hind legs, and he used it to drag the carcass to a pine tree. He threw the rope over a branch and pulled, hoisting the gutted deer until it hung high in the air.

"Did wolves come after it last night?" Faith asked. "I slept so hard, I didn't even realize."

"I was up most of the night keeping them away. I had to lay the deer on top of your wagon."

Faith was astounded she had slept through all that, and it gave her shivers to realize he'd been climbing around the wagon while she'd slept inside. He could just as easily have climbed inside. *But he didn't,* she told herself. She decided to ask no more about his father. It seemed to hurt him to talk about the man. He was suddenly quiet again, walked off to unload his gear and tend to the animals. He brought them all closer to the fire, tying them to various trees, and she noticed he now carried a six-gun, worn with an ammunition belt around his hips.

"There are many more wolves here than where we were last night," he told her. "It will be another sleepless night for me."

"I'm sorry," Faith answered.

"It is not your fault. It is because of the deer I have with me. I am very much accustomed to staying up at night to protect a kill. We will eat, and you must get your rest."

Faith thought it humorous the way some of his statements were like orders. *Yes, sir,* she felt like replying. She carried the meat to the wagon and put it in two tin plates, handing him one. She set them on the wagon gate, climbed inside, and took out knives and forks, but when she turned back around, he had already taken his piece of meat and was holding it in his hand and eating hungrily. She put his knife and fork back in the wagon, sat down on the gate, plate in lap, and ate using knife and fork.

Tall Bear finished quickly, drinking from the water barrel then and making up his bed beside the fire. He laid a rifle beside it and lay down, saying nothing more. Faith dipped some water into a wash pan and washed the plates and her utensils, feeling bad that Tall Bear would have to lie half-awake all night. Already she could hear the howling of wolves. She drank some water and added some wood to the fire, then climbed into the wagon. She did not bother putting on a nightgown, afraid she might have to jump out of the wagon to help Tall Bear chase off wolves.

She lay down, realizing how wrinkled she would be come morning, how terrible she would look. But out here she supposed it didn't much matter what a woman looked like.

Her eyes closed, and finally she drifted off. She was not sure how long she had slept before she was awakened by growling and snarling. Tall Bear! Was he all right? She sat up and looked out the back of the wagon to see him walking around the fire with a burning stick, waving it around and making growling sounds, trying to scare off wolves. She could see their yellow eyes, and Clete's frightened horse as well as Tall Bear's were whinnying and tugging at their ropes.

"I'll help you!" she told Tall Bear. She climbed out and pulled a burning branch from the fire.

"Do not go out of the light of the fire. If we keep them at bay long enough, they will give up."

Faith did as he was doing, darting back and forth, yelling at the wolves to get away. She screamed and turned when she heard a gunshot then. Tall Bear stood there with a smoking handgun, and a wolf lay sprawled not far from him. She began waving the stick again, but the yellow eyes had disappeared.

"The gunshot frightened them away for the moment," Tall Bear told her. He took the big hunting knife from his waist and leaned over the wolf. "Thank you, Spirit Wolf, for offering yourself to save us."

Faith frowned at the words. What did he mean? He deftly slit open the wolf's belly then, and she grimaced when he reached inside and cut out the wolf's innards. Her eyes widened when he began spreading bloody wolf guts in a ring around the campsite. "What are you doing?"

"The smell of their own dead will keep the others away," he told her.

She watched silently for a few minutes. He came over to the water barrel and asked her to pour water over his hands to wash them. She dipped a small bucket into the barrel and set it on the wagon gate. "Here. Just dip your hands in here and wash them." She studied him as he did so, thinking again what a handsome, virile, skilled man he was. "Why did you thank the wolf after you killed it?" she asked, handing him a towel.

He faced her, standing close. "All creatures have soul and spirit. We are all the same. Whenever we kill an animal for food or clothing, it is like killing one of our own kind. We thank it for offering itself to sustain us. This wolf offered itself to save us from the others."

She should think that was a silly thought, but she could see the sincerity in his eyes, and the way he said it made her believe it must really be so. "I never would have thought of it that way. He was going to attack you."

He shrugged. "Maybe. But he was only pretending, so that I would shoot him. Now the others will leave us alone."

"Are you sure? I can stay up and sit by the fire with you if you like."

Their eyes held, each wondering for a fleeting moment

what it would be like to stay together always. Tall Bear had never been attracted to a white woman before, but this one . . . he liked her courage. She was not a weeping, shrinking flower like so many others. She did not look at him as though he were dirt. He liked the way she had climbed out of the wagon and helped him scare off the wolves. "It is not necessary," he told her. "You must rest."

He walked back to his gear and took a piece of rawhide from it, coming over to tie it around the wolf's hind legs. He hung the animal low in a nearby tree, then returned to his blanket. Faith climbed back into the wagon, thinking what a strange turn her life had taken, lost and alone in the wilds of Wyoming, pregnant, widowed, fighting off wolves with a half-breed Indian she hardly knew, yet with whom she felt safe. She never would have dreamed back in Pennsylvania she would ever be in such a predicament.

Morning came on bright and warm. After sharing biscuits and coffee with Tall Bear, Faith climbed back into the wagon to change clothes and brush her hair. She twisted her thick tresses into a bun at the nape of her neck, then took a mirror from her trunk, frowning at the look of her sunken cheeks and the circles under her eyes. The skin of her hands was rough, partly from all the scrubbing she'd done all winter in Chicago, combined with exposure to the western sun and dust. She dug out a jar of cream she had purchased in Chicago and rubbed some on her face and hands. "I'll be an old woman by the time I'm twenty," she muttered.

She hoped the slat bonnet she wore every day was protecting her face. She tied it on, and having changed into a clean blue calico dress, she supposed she looked as good as she was going to look for meeting whomever she would meet at the stage station. Since she had to drive the oxen herself again, and Tall Bear had said it would be evening before she arrived, she supposed she would just be a dirty, haggard mess again by the time she got there, and what little primping she did now would be useless.

She lifted the canvas and climbed out of the wagon to see that Tall Bear had already cleaned up the campsite.

Clete's horse was tied to the back of her wagon. Faith wondered how much money she might be able to make if she sold the oxen and wagon and horse. Perhaps it would be enough to get her all the way to California by stage-coach. She could find work there, she was sure.

She watched Tall Bear finish hitching the oxen, thinking how easily he could live like a white man. He had already tied the deer and wolf to his horse, and she was glad he still wore his buckskin clothing. His hair hung loose, and there was a beaded ornament tied into one side of it. He still wore the claw necklace, and she realized she had never seen him take it off. She suspected it was special to him for some reason.

She tried to envision him in battle, raiding white settlements . . . killing . . . It was difficult to imagine, since he had been so good to her. Her heart felt heavy at the thought of having to say good-bye to him. She would always wonder what happened to him, if he was all right.

He turned, caught her watching him, and smiled. "To-day you will be with people of your own kind. I will always remember you, Faith Sommers."

Why did she feel like crying? "And I will remember you, Tall Bear. What . . . what is your white name?"

He walked to his horse. "It does not matter. I no longer use it."

"Well, I know your last name was Beaumont. Don't you ever think about living like a white man? You are just as much white as Indian, you know."

"I do not need to be reminded of that." He mounted his horse in one sleek movement. "White men have brought me too much sorrow. Come. It is time to go, or you will not reach this place by nightfall, and I must get back to my village. I will go with you only a little way, and then, if you follow where I say, you will find the station. It is on a trail that is easy to follow, a white man's road. You should come to no harm, but it would be wise to keep your rifle handy. Do you know how to use it?"

"I'll manage. Johnny showed me how to use it." Her chest hurt at the thought of Johnny.

"We must go." Tall Bear headed his horse out of the

stand of trees, and Faith followed, almost hating to leave the place. She realized she felt safer with this Indian man than she would once he left her on the "white man's" trail. She switched the faithful oxen into motion, and for the next three hours there was no talking, only walking, the sun growing hotter. They finally came upon a very obvious trail, two rutted lines of hard ground with a little grass growing between. Apparently many wagons and coaches had used the road. Tall Bear turned his horse west onto the road, then rode back to her, pointing. "That is the way you must go. Do not stop for long, and you should arrive before the sun sets. Perhaps while you are walking, you should carry that six-shooter gun you took from the white man who killed your husband, just in case other white men come along who have no respect for your honor."

She blushed at the words, realizing what he meant. "All right. I'll carry the six-gun."

Their gaze held their thoughts unspoken. Finally he nodded to her. "May your God be with you, Faith Sommers."

She felt a lump rising in her throat. "And yours with you, Tall Bear."

Tall Bear realized he did not want to leave her, but he had no choice. She was a white woman, and he was not ready to be a white man. "You will do well. I know this in my heart."

He turned and rode off before Faith could reply. She stood there watching him until he was out of sight. He never looked back.

"Never look back," she told herself. That was how life would have to be for a while. She must never look back if she wanted the strength to go forward. She decided she should begin keeping a diary, and her first entry would be about the man called Tall Bear.

Part Two

Chapter Twelve

At last Faith spotted several log buildings in the distance. It was nearly dusk, and she'd been afraid she would have to spend the night alone.

What big country this was! She had stopped on the crest of a rise at least a mile from the depot ahead, in a wide-open area surrounded by majestic mountains. These rolling foothills had only a few pine trees here and there, and boulders smattered the land as though God had taken a handful and thrown them down.

The little depot looked peaceful. Smoke curled from a chimney, and horses grazed inside a wooden fence. She goaded the oxen forward. As she moved up and down rock-strewn hills, the station sometimes disappeared from sight only to appear again moments later. The distance was farther than it appeared, and after forty-five minutes she finally came close enough to see a broken-down stagecoach sitting beside a shed.

She figured she had only about a quarter of a mile to go when she heard a noise behind her, a clattering, thundering sound, a man whistling and shouting. She turned to see what she knew must be an approaching stagecoach, even though she could barely see it for the roll of dust the coach and horses churned up. She was amazed at how fast it reached her, charging down the hillside over which she had just traveled.

The coach clattered past, its yellow wheels spinning. She saw a couple of faces inside, admired the charging horses and the colorful red coach with yellow-and-black lettering, HOLLADAY OVERLAND EXPRESS. She could not help wondering who was inside, where they were going, how they had enough money to be able to afford to travel that way. Back in Kansas she had checked on traveling west by stage, just out of curiosity, and she had been astonished to discover it would cost $320, a virtual fortune to get to Salt Lake City!

She coughed on the dust the coach stirred as it charged toward the station, and she got her own oxen under way again, her spirits reviving. People! It would be good to see people. She hurried the oxen as fast as it was possible for the big lumbering animals to go, and within fifteen minutes she made her own way to the small log station house.

A weathered-looking old man was unhitching the team of horses from the stagecoach, another man helping him. The doors to the coach were open, and as Faith led her wagon past the coach, she could see black leather seats inside. She wondered what it would be like to travel in such style.

She could hear voices now, the two drivers talking, other voices inside the station. When she'd been alone and lost after Johnny had been killed, she had wondered if she would ever hear such things again. She thought how strange this land was, so desolate and lonely, yet someone like Tall Bear had found her in all that emptiness, and here was a stage depot, in the middle of a land so big and threatening, it seemed no human would want to come there. Yet here they were. Where there was a will, man would find a way.

She had no idea what she was going to do now, had tried not even to think about it . . . or about Johnny. Yet how could she *not* think about him, buried out there somewhere in that lonely grave? She was on her own now. She had to survive any way she could find. But first she had to rest, perhaps find a chance to bathe. "Hello," she called out to the older man, who was leading two of the horses to a corral.

"Evenin', missy." He frowned, looking around. "You alone?"

"Yes, sir. Lost my husband about three days back."

"Well, I'll be." He scratched at a shadow of a gray beard, and Faith thought he was awfully small and wiry to be driving such a big team of horses; but for his size and age he was apparently strong and lively. "All by yourself?" he asked again.

"All by myself, but I've been through a lot and I need a few days' rest. Is it possible to stay here?"

"Sure! The woman inside that runs the station—her name's Hilda Banks—she'd be glad to put you up, glad for the company. These here stops get mighty lonesome between runs. Go on inside, and me and Cal here will unhitch your team for ya and put 'em up."

"I would be very grateful."

"Well, a man will do just about anything for a pretty little lady like you." The old man cackled. "Name's Buck. Buck Jones. This here is Cal, my shotgun." He nodded toward the younger man, who led the other two horses. Faith guessed him to be in his thirties. He was a rough-looking character of medium build, wearing dusty clothes and a floppy leather hat.

"Shotgun?" she asked.

"He keeps watch for outlaws and Indians, shoots anything that don't look like it ought to be in our path, if you know what I mean."

Cal nodded to her, then smiled, showing a tooth missing at one side of his mouth. "Somebody's gotta guard the passengers," he told Faith.

"I see. Well, I thank you both for your help." She put the switch in its holder. "I'll get some things from my wagon while you unhitch my team. Will the wagon be safe out here—my belongings, I mean?"

Buck shrugged while Cal took all four horses into the corral. "Who knows? These depots can be dangerous.

Never know when Indians are gonna skulk around at night and steal from you, or when outlaws might attack. Both are always after horses, but sometimes Indians like to steal other things—food, clothes, any supplies you're carryin'. Right now the Cheyenne seem to be concentratin' their attacks farther south, and the Sioux farther north, so maybe there won't be no trouble. It's just a chance you take."

Faith thought about Tall Bear. Where was he now? Would he go back to making war soon? Maybe he would be killed and she would never know it. "I'll take the chance. It's just so good to see people and have a place to stay, especially knowing I'll have another woman to talk to." She climbed into the wagon and stuffed a carpetbag with overnight necessities, assuming she would be able to sleep inside the depot rather than out here in the wagon. If Indians sometimes "skulked around" at night, as Buck had put it, she didn't care to be caught alone in the wagon. She climbed out and walked to the log building. Clucking chickens scampered about as she brushed past them. She pounded dust from her dress, wondering how dirty her face was. She looked up at a sign over the door. HOLLADAY OVERLAND MAIL & EXPRESS CO. it read.

Inside were three men and a woman sitting at a table drinking coffee, and an old woman standing at an iron cookstove stirring something. All of them looked at her, and she felt suddenly self-conscious. The woman at the table was beautiful, with white-blond hair and painted lips. Faith could not help wondering if she was one of those "dance-hall girls" Clete had told Johnny about several times, women at mining camps who wore fancy low-cut dresses and danced with the men for money. Sometimes they did more than dance. This woman wore a green linen dress beautifully cut to fit her perfectly, the ruffled bodice embarrassingly low, which she supposed the men didn't mind at all.

The man sitting next to her wore a fancy dark suit, a top hat on the table next to his plate. He was middle-aged, handsome, his hair graying. The other two men sat across the table from the fancy man and woman, one wearing a suit, the other dressed more plainly, cotton pants and shirt and a leather vest. The old woman at the stove wore a simple calico dress, her gray hair wound into a bun at the nape of her neck. Her face showed a thousand wrinkles, even more when she smiled, her aging brown eyes glittering with kindness.

"Well, who have we here? You folks didn't tell me there was another passenger."

The fancy lady looked Faith over. "This pretty little thing wasn't on the coach, Hilda. Where'd you come from, honey?"

Faith set her carpetbag on the floor. "I . . . my name is Faith Sommers. My husband and I were on our way to Montana when—" Should she tell them? Was there something wrong with what she'd done to Clete? How did people look at things like that out here? Surely she wouldn't be accused of anything. It was self-defense. Still, maybe somebody here knew Clete. "My husband got sick and died. Consumption, I think."

"You're *alone* out here?" the fancy lady asked.

"Yes. I . . . an Indian man came along and helped me bury my husband."

"An *Indian*!" Old Hilda shook her head. "I ain't never heard of no Indian helpin' a white woman. There's only one thing Indians do to white women. You all right, girl?"

Faith blushed. "Yes, ma'am." She explained about Tall Bear being half-white and speaking English, how kind he had been to her.

"That's the strangest story I ever heard," Hilda said. "My goodness, what you've been through! Sit down, child. I'll feed you some stew and you can sleep right in here. There's cots in the back room not awfully comfortable, but better than sleepin' outside. Oh, you poor thing. All alone out here. What's your name again, child?"

"Faith Sommers. I'm from Pennsylvania." Faith removed her slat bonnet and smoothed back some stray hairs. "That's where I met Johnny. We were going to come out here and homestead, but Johnny wanted to go look for gold first."

"Ain't many who will truly get rich looking for gold,

honey," the fancy lady told her. She patted the chair next to her. "Sit down, Mrs. Sommers. My name is Bret Flowers, and this fine man next to me here is my, uh, friend, Ben Carson."

"How do you do?" Faith replied as the other two men chuckled. She glanced at them, realizing with more certainty what Bret Flowers must be by the way the men were watching her.

"Joe Dugan," the man in the suit introduced himself.

"Matt Howley," the second man spoke up.

Faith nodded. "Please excuse my appearance. The last three days have been very hard, and I had to conserve my water, so I couldn't do much washing."

"Oh, don't worry about that," the old lady told her. She set a bowl of stew in front of her. "I'm Hilda Banks. Just call me Hilda. And I know what it's like to lose a husband. I lost mine to outlaws only a few weeks ago. I've been runnin' this station alone ever since, so I know how you're feelin', child."

"Oh, I'm sorry, ma'am, for your loss." Outlaws! Hilda's husband had been killed by outlaws. Who better to understand what had really happened to Johnny than this old woman? She needed to talk to someone about it. Maybe later, after these passengers left, she could tell Hilda.

The old woman set a basket of biscuits on the table and began dishing up more stew. "What are you going to do now that your husband's gone, child?" Hilda asked Faith.

"I don't know yet. This country is new to me. I'm not sure where to go, what to do with myself."

"Well, Ben and I are on our way to the mining camps in Idaho," Bret told her. "You can come with us if you want. I know one way you could get rich real quick, but then you might not be cut out for that. With your looks, honey, you could make a million."

The other two men chuckled again, but Hilda scowled as she set a plate in front of Bret. "I'll have none of that talk in here, Miss Flowers. She appears like a proper little lady to me."

Bret patted Faith's shoulder. "Oh, I don't mean no of-

fense. Just offering to help, that's all. If there's some other
way we can help, you just let us know. Ben here, he's a
gambler. Does real good, and he's real personable. We
could both ask around for you, help you find work or
something if you wanted to tag along with us. We ain't bad
people, honey. We just do what we do and we enjoy it, but
we don't mind helping out good folks."

Faith looked into the woman's gray eyes, and she saw
nothing but sincerity. She had never considered that
women like Bret might have feelings or a good heart—had
never thought to find herself sitting next to a prostitute and
talking to her. But there was something she already liked
about Bret, her honesty about what she was, the wild spirit
of the woman. She didn't believe what Bret did was right,
but she admired the woman's brash courage and the total
freedom about her personality. "Thank you, Miss Flowers,
but I think I'll just stay here a couple of days to rest up and
then maybe go down to Salt Lake City."

Bret laughed. "Honey, you don't want to go down
among those Mormons. You'll end up some preacher
man's fifth or sixth wife and never be heard from again. As
long as you're out here, honey, there's lots of ways to make
it on your own without having to do what I do for a living.
Might as well make the most of it and be an independent
woman."

"Miss Flowers, have some understanding for the poor
girl," Hilda scolded. "She's young and new out here, and
she's just lost a husband. She can't be thinkin' about bein'
independent and such things. Give her time to think and
rest."

"Oh, I'm sorry, honey," Bret said. "You eat up. You
look like you need it. Maybe later you can tell us more
about that Indian man who helped you. I've never heard of
a half-breed warrior who speaks English. What a combination! Was he good-lookin'?"

"Miss Flowers!" Hilda chastised. "Eat your stew and
leave the girl alone!"

Bret chuckled and began eating. As the men talked,
Faith listened intently, wanting, needing to know all she
could about this land and the people who roamed it. Al-

ready she was meeting a kind of people she would never have known back in Pennsylvania. A prostitute sat next to her. Beside her sat a man talking about gambling, about good poker hands, dice games. She learned Joe Dugan was a banker, on his way to Salt Lake City from Omaha to see about lending money to Mormons involved in a building project. The other man was a rancher from Colorado, headed for California to see about buying a special breed of horses called palominos, supposedly a beautiful breed that could prove to be quite valuable. He was considering bringing some back with him for breeding.

Faith relished the stew, the first good food she'd had in a long time, perhaps tasting better because she didn't have to cook it herself. Her emotions ran the gamut from sorrow to excitement and fear. She had not told any of these people she was carrying a baby in her belly. That would have a great effect on the decisions she would make. She had to think about the baby. Still, what an exciting place this was—prostitutes, gamblers, miners, stagecoach drivers and guards, an old woman who ran a stagecoach station out in the middle of nowhere, scouts, bankers, ranchers, Indians, outlaws. She had wanted adventure, and she had found it. It seemed to her that living in a remote station like this could be exciting. Just think of all the different kinds of people who must come through on their way to their own destinies. She only wished she knew what her own destiny would be.

Sleep. Blessed sleep. The passengers had stayed the night while Buck and Cal tended a mare that had fallen sick in its stall. They finally had to shoot the horse, then hitch it to a team and drag it off to bury it, which had taken the rest of the day and into dark, with Joe Dugan, Ben Carson, and the rancher all helping. The women slept in the back room, the men on bedrolls outside, Ben inside the stagecoach.

This morning Hilda had cooked a hearty breakfast of ham and eggs, promising Faith that once everyone left, she would get out a tin tub and let her take a real bath. Now she sat in that tub, glorying in the luxury of hot water, the luxury of just being truly clean again. Once the stage was gone, it was just she and Hilda. Faith enjoyed the peace, enjoyed talking to an understanding woman. She dressed and combed her wet hair, leaving it straight to dry. It didn't matter that it wasn't properly done up for the moment, with only Hilda there. She went into the outer room then, sitting down in a rocking chair. "I'm so grateful, Hilda. Thank you so much for the hot water."

"No trouble, child. I'm enjoying the company. Gets mighty lonesome out here between runs."

"How often does a stage come through?"

"I never know. Sometimes one three days in a row, then nothing for a week. Depends on a lot of things—outlaws, Indians, weather, breakdowns—a lot of things." The old woman walked over to sit across from her, handing her a cup of coffee. "Now, how about telling me the whole truth about your husband?"

Faith frowned, reddening a little. "What do you mean?"

"Honey, anyone can see by your eyes there's somethin' terrible wrong. I don't think your Johnny died of consumption. Is it that Indian man who killed him maybe? Maybe he violated you?"

"Oh, no! Tall Bear was very good to me. Honestly he was! He came along after . . . after Johnny was shot." She hung her head, retelling the story through tears. "I was afraid to tell anyone I shot Clete Brown."

"Nothin' wrong with that. It was self-defense, and he'd just murdered your husband." Hilda reached out and patted her knee. "You poor thing. Maybe you should just go home, back to Pennsylvania."

Faith shook her head. "I come from a family of Quakers, and my mother is dead. She was the only one back there I could talk to, the only one who understood me. My father is a good man, but very strict, and he was going to force me into marriage to a much older man I could never have loved. He never understood how much I loved Johnny." She wiped at her eyes. "But Johnny broke a lot of promises, and now he's dead. I don't know what I'll do, but I can't go all the way back to Pennsylvania. I have no way of getting back there, and not enough money left. And if I did make it back, I'd probably never find a way to leave again, and I can't live that way. I just can't!" She met Hilda's gaze. "Hilda, I'm carrying a baby. What am I going to do?"

"A baby!" The old woman clucked, shaking her head. "My, my." She leaned back in her chair, staring at a fireplace that was cold for the moment, since the cookstove created all the heat that was needed on chilly mountain mornings. It was only in winter that both the cookstove and fireplace were needed for warmth. "Well, it's for sure you can't go all the way back to Pennsylvania with no money and a baby growin' inside you. And since you don't know nobody farther west, and since it's dang dangerous country out there, I'd say you might as well stay right here with me." She leaned forward again, resting her elbows on her knees. "It's a fact I'm gettin' old, and I could use the help cookin' and all. Your board and food would be free, and we'd have each other for company. I borned four kids of my own, and I've helped bring other women's babies into the world, so I reckon I can help birth yours when the time comes."

Faith put a hand to her stomach, afraid of having a baby way out here with no doctor. Back in Pennsylvania she'd known women who had died in childbirth, and her own mother had lost babies. Still, she had little choice but to stay there for now. Someone like Hilda surely knew how to help. "Where are your children now?" she asked.

The old woman shook her head. "Well, three died before they got growed up."

"Oh, I'm sorry, Hilda."

"Well, you learn that death is just a fact of life, child. Anyway, the one that lived, my son, he went off lookin' for gold in California and never come back—don't know if he's dead or alive." Painful sadness was obvious in her eyes. "Me and my husband, we come here to work for Ben Holladay's Overland Express 'cause he pays good and we needed the money after losin' a supply business in Denver to fire. Then Pete, that's my husband, he was shot by outlaws who was after the spare horses."

Faith ached at the thought of all that the woman had

lost. "Does that happen often? Outlaws coming here to rob you?"

"Outlaws, Indians. Sometimes I scatter them off with my shotgun. No, it don't happen real often. I reckon the rewards is worth the risk, except it wasn't worth my husband's life." She blinked back tears and took a deep breath. "Well, that left me here alone, and I didn't have no place else to go, so I just stayed on. I know how to tend horses. I figured there wasn't nothin' I could do for that sick one that died yesterday. I'm glad Buck was here to help. Anyways, I can do lots of things. I can even hitch a team to a coach. I cook for travelers and give them a place to sleep. Ben Holladay, he pays for the accommodations. Nothin' fancy, but it's a roof over your head and a warm place to be come winter. You got weapons?"

"Yes, I have two rifles and two six-guns and a small pistol."

"Good. That'll do. We always keep shutters and doors closed and bolted at night. There ain't generally so much trouble. And if you want adventure and excitement, it comes through here every time a stage arrives. You never know who will be on it, and you meet all kinds of interestin' people. Maybe you'll meet a man come through here someday who you'll end up marryin'."

Faith smiled sadly and shook her head. "I don't know, and I don't really care right now. And if you really don't mind, then I guess I *will* stay, Hilda. I can cook, gather eggs, help with the horses. I always worked hard back in Pennsylvania. I don't need anything fancy. I just want my freedom."

Hilda laughed, her many wrinkles made more prominent again. "Well, that's one thing you get when you come west, girl. There's plenty of freedom out here, and hardly anybody to judge what you do or who cares. It's a real different life, and it's sure a place for the young, not the old. Maybe someday you'll end up runnin' this station yourself."

Faith leaned back and rocked slowly. "I never thought of that. Everything is so new to me, I can't think beyond the next ten minutes. I told myself all I can do is take one day at a time and not worry about tomorrow right now."

"Well, I'd say that's good advice. So you stay right here with me, and if you're to do somethin' else, the chance will come along when it's proper."

"Yes, I suppose it will. Thank you so much, Hilda, for offering to let me stay."

The woman waved her off as she rose from her chair. "Honey, you're doin' me a favor, bringin' me company, helpin' me with my work. It's sure no bother to me. Fact is, you can go out right now and gather me some eggs. If I've figured it right, there will be another stage come through here today. I don't know what's gonna happen when the railroad comes through, but for now the Overland is busy as ever."

"Railroad?"

"Oh, yes. The Union Pacific people was here not so long ago, sayin' when they build that there transcontinental railroad, it will come right through here. Do you think they'll really manage such a thing? I can't see how they'll get through the Sierras and the Rockies—but, then, man has a way of doin' what he sets out to do. I don't expect it will be anytime soon, but can you imagine a railroad stretchin' all the way across this country and through the mountains to California?"

Faith rose, shaking her head. "No, I can't imagine it."

"Well, it's not our worry for now. You go gather them eggs, and I'll heat some water for washin' dishes."

Faith walked out into the cool morning air. She liked Hilda. She was a wise old woman who was easy to talk to, and she had stamina. It felt good to be relatively safe for now, good to have something to call home, even though part of the time it was a place that had to be shared with strangers. This was beautiful country. She didn't even mind the danger. Helping Hilda with the place would help keep her mind off Johnny's grave back there . . . somewhere. She could probably never find it again if she tried.

She looked around the depot, log buildings with sagging roofs, chickens strutting about, her wagon sitting beside the main building. Life here certainly would be a far cry from the rich, glamorous life Johnny had promised her, but she certainly would not lack for excitement. Out here a woman alone had to grab whatever opportunities came along, and for now this stage station was her only opportunity for survival.

Chapter Thirteen

Faith was surprised and frightened by the pain, and right now she hated Johnny Sommers for causing it. Now he wasn't even here to see her suffering, to see his child about to be born. Hilda had tried to explain what to expect, but no explanations could prepare her for this reality. Deep, wrenching cramps clawed at her insides, and although she knew it was useless, she tried to keep the baby from coming, afraid of even worse pain as it was born. Hilda kept telling her not to fight it, but her voice sounded so far away. She wanted her mother, missed her terribly at this moment.

She was terrified that she would die here, two thousand miles from home, with no help, no one but Hilda to stand over her grave. And if her baby lived and she died, who would take care of it? Hilda was too old to be taking on a child. Maybe Matthew Kelley would come for his grandchild.

She had written her father, and Johnny's parents, made up a lie about how Johnny had died. Maybe this pain was God's punishment for lying to them and for killing Clete

Brown. She had told Johnny's parents that she and Johnny had traveled with a wagon train, and that Johnny had been caught under the oxen while pulling them across a river and had drowned. She'd written that she had gone on with the wagon train but had decided to stay with an old woman at a stagecoach station until her baby was born.

It seemed plausible. She had recently written a second letter to her father, explaining that she planned to stay at the stage station, that she enjoyed the work and this was a way to take care of herself. At least that part was true. Sommers Station was home now. That was what Hilda had decided to name the depot, thinking it needed a name more personal than just the Overland Express. Faith was proud of the name. She had something all her own now, freedom, independence, a respectable means to make money. She could do this and still care for her baby, though right now that baby was being mighty stubborn in arriving.

"It's coming!" Hilda said. Faith could not help another scream, even as she heard the thunder of horses outside. Perhaps Hilda had meant a stage was coming. "I'll be right back, child," Hilda told Faith, disappearing through the curtained doorway to the outer room.

Faith hated the thought of being in the back room screaming in childbirth while passengers came inside to clean up and eat. She wasn't even sure how long she had lain here, but she knew the next stage today was due around five o'clock P.M. She'd gone into labor around three A.M. Fourteen hours! Had she really been going through this that long?

Finally she heard voices again. "Oh, sometimes the first one is a real bugger. A woman's young body has to get loosened up and learn to give a little. They get easier after the first, don't you agree, Hilda?" That voice, a woman's, sounded familiar to Faith. "Course, I never had any of my own, but I've seen plenty of girls in my profession end up pregnant, and I've helped deliver plenty of them myself. It was one of them that told me the second one's easier than the first. She went and gave away two babies. Me, I'm more careful. I don't think it's right giving some poor kid the title of bastard."

The voice was close now. *Plenty of girls in my profession.* Someone pushed aside the curtains that divided the two-room depot, and the woman came prancing in wearing a beautiful fur coat and hat, a fur muff still caught on one hand.

"Bret!" Faith said. "What are you doing here?" Another pain came then, and she grasped the iron bed rails. Bret and Hilda both checked to see if the baby was showing yet, and Faith felt ashamed.

Somewhere amid her pain she heard Bret saying she and Ben Carson had decided there was too much Indian trouble farther north. Indian trouble. Was Tall Bear part of it? She had never forgotten him, never stopped wondering where he might be now, if he was all right.

It had been a hard winter with few supplies, Bret was saying, and she was tired of the danger and hardship. "We're headin' back south, maybe to Central City. It's not far from Denver, and there's still prostitutes and plenty of gambling there," Bret said. "And it's a lot safer. Lo and behold, we come through here and find out you're not only still here but you're having your baby, honey. I figured I could help. We'll stay over and take whatever stage comes along in the next couple of days. Ben doesn't mind."

The pain subsided again for a moment, and Faith watched Bret remove her fur coat and hat, complaining about the bitter winters in the mountains. They certainly were that. One snowstorm in February had barricaded the door to the stage depot so that Hilda had had to climb out a window to make her way to the horse shed. Another horse had died this winter, but six had survived. The only good thing about the weather was that it had kept away outlaws and Indians. There had not even been a stage run through there in all of January and February, and very few this month. But it was now almost the end of March, and a sudden warming last week had melted much of the snow in the foothills, although there was still plenty higher up in the mountains.

"I can't believe a stage got through them Rockies," Hilda told Bret.

"Oh, the whole trip has been a nightmare," Bret answered, leaning over and putting a cool rag to Faith's forehead. "We holed up in some of the most ungodly places. I'll tell you, I never want to go through anything like that again. I was sure we'd meet our Maker before we ever got this far—but, then, Ben Holladay hires some of the most experienced, rugged men he can find, and he gets his coaches through anything. Fact is, during one of the times we had to hold up because of weather, one of them drivers and me went off alone and had a right good time."

She cackled in her unique way of laughing that at the moment hurt Faith's ears. She wondered how old Bret was. Her face was so painted, it was hard to tell if it hid her age, or made her look older.

"When did you get that heating stove in here?" Bret asked Hilda. "I don't remember it."

"Mr. Holladay had it sent out on the last supply wagon that come in last November," Hilda answered. "One of the drivers set it up for me. I'm awful glad now. Even though we didn't have passengers who needed the room over the winter, it sure helped keep the whole place warmer, and now I can keep Faith here, warm, while she's in so much pain."

"Warm? For heaven's sake, Hilda, it must be a hundred degrees in here!" Bret complained, applying the cool rag to her own forehead. "Holladay's men must have cut you plenty of wood."

"Well, me and Faith, we cut some extra ourselves. You ought to see this girl work. Why, she's adapted to this life just fine—knows how to hitch teams, cleans out the coaches, cuts wood, does wash, and she's a damn good cook. Did you see the sign out front?"

"I sure did! Sommers Station." Bret cackled again. "You must be damn proud, Faith! And in a few minutes you'll be having a little baby to take care of. I have a feeling you can do that and still run a stage station. Looks like you're taking over for Hilda just fine."

At the moment none of it mattered to Faith, and it irritated her that neither of them seemed to realize how much pain she was in. Still, she supposed they were just trying to make her feel better. The pains became deeper, more gripping, and Hilda's and Bret's voices seemed far away. From then on all she heard was "Push!" "Breathe!" "Don't push!" "Push!" "It's coming!" "You're doin' good, girl. It's halfway out!" "Push!" "It's out!" "It's a boy!" "Cut the cord!" "Wrap him up!"

She heard a squeal, then the hardy cry of a baby. A boy! A son for Johnny Sommers . . . a son who would never know his father.

Bret massaged her stomach, saying something about forcing out the afterbirth. Hilda washed her and changed her gown. The baby kept crying. Bret helped Faith roll to her side, packing pillows behind her for support. She washed her breast and then brought the baby close. "You've got a kid to feed, honey."

Faith studied the tiny bit of life lying next to her, wrapped in blankets now, his face and fists beet-red from crying. She managed to pull him close, and he planted his tiny mouth over her nipple. The crying immediately ceased. *How strange,* Faith thought, *that after just being born a baby knows immediately he wants to eat, and he knows how to take his food. How very strange.*

She had come to this land to find freedom and adventure, to be a rich married lady. She had certainly found freedom and adventure, but no riches, and she was a widow with a new baby now. "I'll make a good life for you, little Johnny," she said softly. What else could she call him but little Johnny? Johnny for her husband, and Matthew for her father. She would have to put a new entry in her diary. Johnny Matthew Sommers, born March 30, 1865.

They had to be stopped, and Red Cloud and his warriors would stop them. This summer Tall Bear would not hunt. He would only make war. Forts had been burned, way stations along the Bozeman Trail had been burned, but that was not enough. Last fall Colorado Volunteers had massacred a village of peaceful southern Cheyenne, a tribe the Sioux considered brothers. They were Black Kettle's people and had made no trouble, but the Volunteers had murdered and mutilated women and children, even slaughtering women huddled in a ravine with their babies.

Survivors had fled north to tell of the terrible killings, and both the Cheyenne and Sioux were more determined than ever to save at least what was left of their land in the Black Hills and in Powder River country. More prospectors had tried to come, some shooting Indians down as though they were game to be hunted. More buffalo and other game were being killed. Trees were being cut down. Trash was left on beautiful Grandmother Earth, water polluted. More soldiers were sent west this summer, and Indian scouts had told them it was because the white man's war in the east was finally over.

Let them come! They would make them want to go back home! Tall Bear rode on many raids, attacking soldiers, forts, wagon trains of supplies and those bringing more people. Sometimes he and the warriors with whom he rode ventured almost as far south as Fort Laramie, not so far from where he had found the white woman alone last summer. He had not forgotten her, her hair as red as canyon rocks, her eyes as blue as deep waters, her skin fair but slightly burned by the sun. She was a small thing, but strong, not just physically, but on the inside. He had admired that woman, was surprised he'd been unable to forget her. He sometimes dreamed of being a white man, just to be able to see her again.

She was probably gone now, perhaps moved on to more civilized places like the city that was called Denver, or maybe all the way to Oregon or California. That was where most whites ended up. There were cities out there, big cities with many white-man attractions, as St. Louis had been. She would have no reason to stay in this country.

He would never see her again. But he could not stop wondering what she was doing now, if she'd had her baby, if she had taken another husband. Surely it would be easy for her to find a man, pretty as she was. She had been the first white woman he'd ever thought about this way, the first one he'd ever imagined in his bed. He could even remember her name. Faith Sommers.

Something about their run-in with each other had left

him with feelings of premonition, and a sense of something left undone. He strongly believed in fate, and he could not get over the feeling that there had been a reason for their meeting. Still, it made no sense. They lived in two different worlds, and now he had no idea where she had gone. It seemed foolish to keep thinking of her, and joining forces with Red Cloud on the warpath had helped him keep her off his mind . . . except deep in the night.

"Many wagons!"

Tall Bear jumped up from the fire he had made, as other warriors prepared for yet another raid. Charging Bear, one of the most bloodthirsty of their war party, was riding in a circle around their camp, rallying them to another battle. "On the white man's trail! Many wagons come, big ones with supplies for the miners! Soldiers are with them! It will be a good kill! If we can stop them, more white men at the end of the trail will give up and go home!"

Tall Bear gathered his weapons and ran into the tall grass where his horse, still bridled, was grazing. He quickly tied on his war shield and threw a blanket onto the horse's back. This Appaloosa was a fine war horse, swift, obedient. It was important the weight on his back be as light as possible. That was how the Sioux and their war ponies often outmaneuvered the bluecoat soldiers, whose horses were weighed down with heavy saddles, camping gear, men wearing heavy boots, too much clothing.

He wore only a breechcloth himself, nothing more. He had painted himself that morning for war, daily preparing himself for more attacks if they should arise. One side of his face was painted black for death, the other side had red stripes running from just under his eye to the bottom of his cheek, put there with paint on the tips of his fingers. They represented flowing blood. More red stripes ran down his chest. His hair was tied into a tail away from his face so that it could not blow into his eyes and affect his aim, and just yesterday he had painted arrows on his horse's rump, repainted the bear claws on the steed's shoulders and neck.

Always prepared! That was how it had to be when making war. He leaped onto the horse's back in one swift movement, clasping his rifle in his right hand. He wore a small tomahawk and his big hunting knife in a leather belt around his waist, and low moccasins.

He let out a piercing war whoop as he rode to join other warriors already circling the camp, the few women along to tend to them cheering them on as each man charged to the sacred war pole and touched it as he rode out, sod flying from under the hooves of swift ponies, dust filling the air. He touched the pole with his rifle and clamped his legs tightly around his horse's girth, heart pounding, blood flowing hot.

What choice did they have but to do this? It was too late to turn back the whites in Minnesota, but here . . . here there was hope. He and thirty-seven other warriors yipped and hollered as they thundered out of camp, up and down over rolling hills, until about twenty minutes later they came into sight of the trail. There would be no warning, no talking. Surprise was their best weapon. Tall Bear could already see the wagons begin to circle, saw little flashes and puffs of smoke that told him those driving the wagons were already shooting at them.

In moments he and the others were circling the wagons. He raised his own rifle as they rode, aiming, firing, proud of his marksmanship while on the back of a horse. He watched a man fall, rode past a wounded Indian at the same time. One of the war party had stayed behind to light little sacks of buffalo chips that were tied to the ends of arrows, and he had fired them into the tops of some of the wagons. Already three of the eight or so wagons were on fire. He could see the frightened faces of the white men who had taken refuge behind the big freight wagons. He shot another trader, all of them intent on keeping more supplies from getting to miners' camps. He took aim again, prepared to fire . . . then hesitated. Jess! It was Jess Willett, his father's old friend. He couldn't shoot Jess!

In that one quick moment, he would realize later, his life changed. He felt a stinging blow at his right shoulder, and his rifle flew out of his hand. He fell from his horse, knew he'd been shot, remembered being torn again by confusion. He'd been out to kill white men, yet there had been one he could not hate or kill. His white side had again come to life to haunt him, like the time he'd shot that little white boy back in Minnesota, something he would never forget.

His body hit the ground, and he felt a smashing blow to his head, thinking some white man must have hit him with something. Then he felt someone dragging him, heard Jess's voice. "Leave him be! You ain't gonna kill this one!" He heard more war whoops, more shooting, then the voices of white men cursing. He heard Jess's voice, closer now. "I ain't lettin' you die, boy. I owe it to your pa."

A white man was helping him, saving his life. Yet only seconds before he'd been out to kill every white man on this pack train. That was the last thing he remembered for hours.

Tall Bear awoke to unfamiliar surroundings. He opened his eyes to see a lantern hanging inside a small enclosure. After studying the white canvas over his head he realized he was inside a wagon, much like the wagon that white woman, Faith, had driven. Was he back at her camp? He blinked, confused, until a familiar face leaned over to look down at him.

"Finally awake, huh?"

He studied Jess's gray-and-red beard, the concerned look in his eyes. He tried to sit up then, but pain ripped through his right shoulder.

"You just lay still there, Gabe. You lost a lot of blood, but the bullet went clean through. I poured whiskey into the wound and wrapped it up."

It felt strange to be called Gabe. "I need water," he said.

The old man obliged, tipping a canteen to Tall Bear's lips. "Here you go."

After drinking the water Tall Bear studied Jess's eyes. "You should not . . . have helped me."

Jess corked the canteen. "You're Alex Beaumont's boy. He'd have wanted me to help you. I gotta tell you, though, I've had a time keepin' the rest of the men here from comin' in here and puttin' a bullet in your head. Only thing holdin' them back is you're half-white and your pa was my good friend."

Tall Bear closed his eyes, trying to think straight. "What happened to my horse? Where are my friends?"

"We finally managed to chase them off, but they done enough damage that we've turned back. I reckon they'll leave us alone if they see us goin' the other way. You and your friends won this round, boy. We can't survive yet another attack, and most of the supplies is burned up, still sittin' back there where we left 'em. Our extra mules is run off, so we figured we'd best head back, see if we can get a soldier escort before we head this way again. I don't know what happened to your horse. Your warrior friends have probably taken him off with them for safekeeping."

Tall Bear sighed. "You will take me to the soldiers? Have me arrested?"

Jess chuckled. "I didn't save you for that, boy. I wouldn't do that to Alex's son." He set the canteen aside. "Nope. I ain't aimin' for you to be arrested. I done told the others that anybody who tries to kill you before we get back to Fort Laramie is gonna feel my own bullet in his gut. I'll take you to the fort, and you can do whatever you want after that. I've got friends there among the soldiers in charge, men who listen to what I tell them about how to handle Indians. If I tell them not to arrest you, they'll leave you alone. You'll be healed some by then, and you'll be free to leave. I'll have done my part helpin' Alex's son."

Tall Bear looked around the wagon again, seeing pots and pans hanging everywhere, all sorts of other supplies. "You should leave me off here."

"You need more rest first. You took quite a blow to the head when you fell from your horse. I saw your head hit a big rock."

The wagon jolted as someone whistled and swore at the mules who pulled it. Tall Bear realized then that it was bright daylight. It must be morning. The attack must have happened yesterday, and he'd lain unconscious since then. "I do not want to go to a fort full of bluecoats."

"Well, you ain't got much choice, unless you want to try to run off on foot once you're well. I expect you have that right, but I want you to think about somethin' while you're layin' here healin', boy. I want you to think about why you're layin' here at all. It's because you hesitated when you took aim at me. You couldn't shoot me because I was your pa's friend, your *white* pa's friend. You holdin' off shootin' me is what caused you to get shot yourself by one of my other men. There's a part of you that belongs to our world, Gabe, and you've gotta face that fact. I want you to think about that, think about what your pa would think of you ridin' with war parties, killin' men not so different from himself."

Tall Bear rubbed at his eyes with his left hand, unable to move his stiff right arm. "He would understand."

"I expect he would, but he would also tell you there ain't no future in these raids, not in the long run. He'd tell you that whites is gonna keep comin' and comin' out here until it's impossible to stop them, just like all over back east, and like in Minnesota. He'd tell you you ought to think about your white blood, how you could use what you know about both worlds to help both sides."

"I do not understand," Tall Bear said, frowning.

"You understand the white world and Indian alike. If you truly want to help the Sioux, you should do what you can to make them understand that all this killin' ain't gonna do no good except to get more of themselves killed when more and more soldiers come to hunt them down, kill their women and children. The best way to survive is to give this up. I know it ain't gonna happen anytime soon, but men like you can help it along, Gabe. You can be a scout for the army, give the soldiers in charge advice about how to handle certain situations, and at the same time be a mediator with the Sioux."

"I will not help soldiers hunt Indians," Tall Bear replied flatly.

"Even if it means helping those Indians? Even if it means there could be peace, and the Sioux could still keep a lot of their hunting grounds? I can tell you right now that the government back in Washington is already talkin' about a new treaty. Their generosity is gonna depend on how soon Red Cloud and his warriors decide to stop the killin' and sit down and talk. You can help that happen, and it will save a lot of lives. I just want you to think about it, Gabe. I suspect you feel you don't fully belong in either the white world or the Indian. This way you can be a part of both and be doin' somethin' good, like your pa would want."

It all seemed too much to think about right then, as waves of blackness hit Tall Bear while Jess talked. "I must think a long time about this. It probably will not matter. Either one of your men will kill me, or the soldiers will hang me when we reach the fort."

Jess touched his arm. "I'm in charge of this wagon train, and these men know I'll kill anybody who tries to bring you harm. When we reach the fort, I'll talk to the commanding officer. I've got a strong feelin' that if you're willin' to act as a scout once we reach the fort, he'll go along with that. You think about it."

Jess climbed forward toward the driver's seat. "I'll take over for a while, Jake."

"That bastard half-breed awake yet?"

"He ain't no bastard, and yes, he's awake."

The wagon stopped for a moment. Tall Bear figured the one called Jake must be climbing down. He heard Jess whistle and shout then, and the wagon started rolling again.

Laramie! He was going to Fort Laramie, a den of bluecoats! He hated to admit it, but some of what Jess had told him made sense. He'd always been torn between both worlds. Maybe living between both was the answer. He had much to think about, but at least it would help keep his mind off that pretty little white woman he'd never see again.

Chapter Fourteen

Faith took aim through the hole in the shutters designed for the barrel of a rifle. She fired, and an Indian fell from his horse. *Pure, heaven-sent luck,* she thought, although she had been practicing her aim all summer. She had more than just the depot and its horses to defend. Now she had a five-month-old baby to protect, even more reason not to think about the fact that she had probably just killed another man.

One could not think about things like that in these situations. Hilda was at the other window, and when she fired her rifle, another Indian's horse took a spill. "Got ya, ya bugger! That'll teach ya. Ya try to take our horses, we kill yours!"

The horse's rider staggered away from the animal, then turned to face the depot, raising his arms as though in brave defiance and letting out a war cry. Hilda fired again, and a bloody hole appeared in the man's chest. He fell, silent.

Faith kept firing randomly, hitting nothing, just wanting to show the raiders she and Hilda were not about to give up easily, trying to scare them off and hoping luck would be in her favor. She noticed the one warrior she had hit still lay motionless, and she hoped God would understand and forgive her for killing him, just as she hoped she'd be forgiven for killing Clete Brown.

Most of the summer had gone by with no Indian problem, until the small raiding party outside had come riding down on the station, screaming their warcries, trying to get to the horses. Hilda had been outside when they'd approached from a distant hillside, and she had yelled for Faith to come help her get the six horses into the shed. Arrows had thudded into the doors of the shed just as they had closed them, and both women had run into the depot, bolted the doors, and closed the shutters, taking up rifles to defend themselves. Thank God the back of the depot was butted against a hillside and had no windows. They didn't have to worry about defending that side of the building, too.

This was Faith's first experience with such an attack, and her heart pounded with terror. She reminded herself she had her baby to think about. She could not let her fear overcome the necessity of the moment, which was to remain calm and keep her aim steady. She fired again, both women trying to keep the raiders from getting into the horse shed. The warrior at whom she fired fell from his horse, but he got back up and remounted, blood on his arm.

The raiders began circling the depot then, their faces frightfully painted. Both women fired and reloaded and fired again as fast as they could. Another Indian fell, but Faith wasn't sure if it was from her bullet or Hilda's. Thank God there was only a handful of raiders. They could only pray the braves would give up and rejoin whatever camp they'd come from . . . and pray they would not return with a hundred more warriors.

"This must be on account of that Indian fight last year down in Colorado," Hilda said, shouting over the gunfire. "Buck told us to expect plenty of trouble this summer."

Little Johnny lay on a blanket on the floor, crying from all the noise. Faith ached to go and comfort him, but there was nothing she could do. Briefly she thought how amazing it was that she was in a little stage station in a remote area of the Rockies shooting at Indians, and with a five-month-old baby to defend. What a far cry from the Faith Kelley who had run away with Johnny Sommers two years ago, her heart full of dreams.

When she stopped to reload, she was sure she heard more gunfire farther off.

"The stage is comin', I think!" Hilda shouted. "By golly, they've got a soldier escort! We're gonna be all right, Faith honey!"

Great relief flooded through Faith's veins when she looked through the gun hole to see the stage charging down a distant hill, several men riding with it. Two warriors reappeared, and Faith took aim.

"Let them go!" Hilda warned. "They've come to pick up their dead. Let them do it, or they'll just come back later and make more trouble."

Faith held off, watching the warriors quickly pick up the bodies of their friends and sling them over their horses. They rode away, bullets whizzing past them from the direction of the approaching stage. Moments later several soldiers rode past the station, still firing at the fleeing Indians, while the stagecoach and its team thundered and clattered to the depot, raising so much dust when the driver finally halted the vehicle that for a moment Faith could see nothing.

"Everybody all right in there?" the driver called out. It was Buck Jones, whom Faith had come to know well. She respected him for his skill and rugged independence. He was a gnarly, skinny, but strong man, probably in his forties, she guessed. He always looked as if he needed a bath and a shave, and he was rather rough in manner. But he was a good man, blunt-spoken, and full of wild stories about his experiences as a stage driver and former scout for wagon trains.

"We're fine, Buck," Hilda called back, setting her rifle aside and opening the shutters.

Faith picked up Johnny and patted his bottom to soothe his crying, while Hilda opened the door to shout more at

Buck. "You didn't get here none too soon. That's the first time any of them horse thieves have been around here this summer. Maybe it will be the last."

"At least they didn't get the horses," Buck answered.

Faith breathed a sigh of relief. She had survived her first Indian attack. There had been no trouble with outlaws this year, probably, according to Hilda, because of so much Indian trouble elsewhere. The territories of Wyoming and Montana and Idaho were not the safest places to be right now, not even for outlaws, yet Faith could not bring herself to leave the depot. Sommers Station had become home, and Hilda was not just a good friend. She was like a mother to her, and she couldn't bring herself to leave the woman there alone. Besides, where else would she go? She'd found something she could call her own, a new form of freedom and excitement, a place that tested her courage and stamina. Arriving passengers were always surprised to find two women in charge of a remote stage depot, and Faith had become used to the questions and comments, especially from men who just could not believe women could do such things.

"We can do anything, can't we, Johnny?" she said softly, kissing the baby's cheek while outside men were talking and shouting, some of the soldiers giving out war whoops of their own for having chased off the "sons of bitches." There was even some laughter. When Hilda returned, Faith, still shaken, turned to her. "Are you all right?"

"I reckon so. How about you?"

"I'm fine."

Hilda set her rifle aside and wiped sweat from her brow. Then she walked up to Faith and put her arms around her and the baby. "You'll get used to it, dearie. This Indian thing will get straightened around as more folks come west. They say they've started buildin' that railroad, and now that the war is over back east, you just watch how fast things grow out here. You'll do okay, honey. We've just proved we can handle anything, ain't we?"

Faith smiled through tears of relief. "I guess. I'm not so sure what would have happened if the stage and those soldiers hadn't come along. We'd better go and greet our passengers."

"I expect so." Hilda patted her cheek and turned to step back outside. Johnny's tears subsided, and Faith laid him in a wooden playpen a traveler had made for her two months ago.

She quickly checked herself in a mirror and wiped a smudge of gunpowder from her cheek and nose. Out here there would never be a need for fancy clothes and rouged cheeks. She had only the clothes she'd come out with, other than a couple of dartless, waistless dresses she had made for herself to cover her pregnancy. She had made a few clothes for Johnny and had ordered more material by mail from Omaha.

She licked her fingers and smoothed back a few wisps of auburn hair, tucking them under the braids wound around her head, then brushed at her gray dress and walked out behind Hilda, to greet the newly arrived passengers.

She had met people from all walks of life, people of every description and occupation; but she had also known great loneliness, bitter grief, and fulfilling love and joy. Her life was filled with hard work and anticipation, always waiting for the next stage, wondering who would be on it. She was learning how to make repairs to coaches, how to hitch and unhitch teams, mend fences, and care for horses. She cooked for the drivers and passengers, even sometimes nursed one who was injured or sick.

She looked around at the ring of mountains, north, west, south, majestic bastions of the West. She thought about her freedom there, how proud she was of what she had learned and how she could fend for herself, and she realized she could not leave this place now, in spite of the dangers. Maybe someday it would fold up and die, as her father had suggested, in his letters, would happen. By then Hilda would be gone, and she would be older, even better able to take care of herself. If she had to leave here, so be it. She would go someplace like Denver or maybe all the way to California and continue to make a life for herself, but she hoped she would never have to go.

Bricked streets, comfortable homes, schools, churches,

handy dry-goods stores, theaters, railroads . . . she would not enjoy such things for now, but maybe . . . maybe some day when the railroad came, Sommers Station would become a real town. Maybe then people would not just pass through, but rather stay and build businesses to serve the railroad and its passengers.

That dream was only a glimmer right now, but already she had been thinking of ways to make it reality, for she simply could not think about living anyplace else. She could not give up this wonderful taste of independence, and for that much she *could* thank Johnny . . . and a mysterious half-breed called Tall Bear.

"Welcome to Sommers Station," she told the new arrivals, putting on a smile for them.

A cold late-October wind hit Tall Bear's face with stinging sleet as he sat on a rise overlooking a small Indian camp. So far his scouting for the army had not been such a bad job. It had led to a few peace talks. But he still felt uneasy about finding these camps for captains and lieutenants who had little understanding of the Sioux, or any other Indian, for that matter. These new recruits were fresh from a victory back east and feeling cocky.

We've taken care of the Southern rebels. Now its time to take care of the Indians and get on with the growth of this country, one lieutenant had commented a few days ago. That was the same lieutenant, Nathan Balen, who had sent him out this morning to find the camp of a handful of Indians who'd been seen by a local farmer. The farmer had immediately panicked, considering the destruction the Cheyenne had been visiting on settlers all through Kansas, and Colorado and Nebraska. He had come running out to flag down Lieutenant Balen as he and his troops moved toward Fort Laramie, telling him he'd "better get after those renegades and give them what for!" The farmer had been very excited, obviously terrified, and Tall Bear had been ordered to find the tracks of the wandering band of Indians and trace them to their camp.

Tall Bear had no doubt the camp he was watching now was simply a band of Cheyenne trying to find small game for food. It was true the Cheyenne had been on the rampage ever since the Chivington massacre the year before in Colorado. He could see the reasons for terror and hatred on both sides, and that was what tore at his heart.

Maybe Jess had been right to advise him to take this job. Maybe he had no choice but to live between both worlds. For now, this was the best way to do that. He pulled his hat farther down his forehead to try to keep some of the rain out of his face. The Indians below could not see him. He could just leave and not tell Lieutenant Balen he'd found them. Still, peace could begin with these few Indians. If Balen, with Tall Bear's help in interpreting, could convince these Cheyenne to go back to their reservation farther south, maybe more would comply and lives would be saved.

That was supposed to be the army's purpose, although Tall Bear was not so sure all army leaders meant only peace. Some, he had no doubt, had come out there to make a name for themselves, and he suspected Balen, a rather arrogant man, was one of them. There were some officers he respected, and some he did not. He did not respect Balen. He had scouted for the man only two weeks now, had not seen him in action, but there was just something about his dark eyes, the scathing way he sometimes looked at Tall Bear, that made Tall Bear distrust the man.

He turned his horse and headed back to the army camp eight miles south. He'd taken this job. Now he had to perform it to the best of his abilities. His father would want that. He would report what he'd found and hope some good would come of it. He hunkered down into his slicker and made his way over undulating hills to Balen's camp, miserably wet and cold by the time he reached it two hours later. By then sleet had turned to snow in an early freak storm. Tall Bear had no doubt the weather would change again and warm a little before true winter set in. This was just Grandfather Sky's way of warning the little people who walked the earth that the long days of cold were coming.

It was not even noon yet when Tall Bear reported to Balen, a short, wiry man who had to look up at him. "I have found the Cheyenne camp, sir. I can go speak to their leader first, tell them it is best if they go back to the reservation. We could give them soldier escort so that whites would not be afraid and shoot at them and make more trouble."

Balen frowned, stroking a thin mustache, and Tall Bear thought how everything about the man was thin, his dull-brown hair, his bony cheeks, his sharp nose. "I believe I am the one giving the orders here, Tall Bear. A soldier escort all the way down to southern Kansas is out of the question. We will round up the scoundrels and take them to Fort Laramie, where some, no doubt, will be imprisoned or even hanged for killing those settlers we found a few miles back."

"You do not know that it was these Indians. Let me talk to them first, and I will know."

Balen snickered. "You really think they would tell the truth?"

Tall Bear bristled. "Neither the Cheyenne nor the Sioux lie about anything."

"Mmmm-hmmmm. So if they admit they killed those settlers, then you, too, would tell me the truth about that. You wouldn't cover for them, right?"

Tall Bear's hands moved into fists. "There is no use in having me scout for you if you are not going to believe what I say."

Balen studied Tall Bear's eyes, never able to quite trust a savage, not after seeing what some of them were capable of doing. He had even less trust for a half-breed. "I suppose that's true." He sighed, sitting down on a barrel behind a crude table inside his tent. "Do you think they're a war party?"

"No. There are women cleaning skins and smoking meat. The horses are not painted for war, and the men were sitting around campfires. I think it is a hunting party of southern Cheyenne who have strayed too far. If they were warriors, there would not be so many women along."

"Well, maybe they're just trying to fool us. We will ride in before nightfall and take them."

What a fool the man was, Tall Bear thought. "I ask

again that you let me go first and talk to them. There is no need to risk loss of life."

Balen—too young, Tall Bear thought, to be an officer making such decisions—picked up a pipe and tamped out old ashes. "They don't seem too concerned about taking white lives without warning or reason," he answered. "Tit for tat, Tall Bear. Just remember that your job is to find them, my job is to decide what to do with them." He shoved the pipe into a pocket. "Prepare to ride back out with us." He rose, pulled on a heavy woolen army coat, and donned a wool cap. "We'll leave in just a few minutes."

Tall Bear shook his head after Balen left. He ducked back outside, watching with disgust as Balen shouted orders above the wind to the men to arm themselves for possible battle.

Tall Bear could hardly believe what he was seeing and hearing. Tall Bear realized now that Lieutenant Balen was hot for a fight and saw this as an opportunity to score a "victory" for his career. He was fresh from another war, a war that was over now, which meant he had to find a new way to show his supposed courage and skill.

Tall Bear bent his head into the wind and snow and walked to a field where he kept a second horse, another Appaloosa, this one with black tail and feet and mane. The gray one he had ridden that day was worn out from the long ride. He would leave the first one there to graze and rest. He led the fresh horse to where he had tied his first mount, pleased with the beauty and swiftness of both horses. He could control them with just a touch of his feet and legs, while his hands were free to hold a rifle. Always before he'd used them that way in making war against the Crow, or against white settlers. Now he would be riding against the Cheyenne, close allies of the Sioux. It seemed he would never truly belong anywhere.

He took a fresh, dry blanket from inside the tent he'd pitched for himself and threw it over the back of the fresh mount, then changed his other gear over and leaped onto the Appaloosa's back, glad he'd chosen to wear his warmer, knee-high winter moccasins that morning. The fur was turned inward to act as a cozy lining. He suspected they were much warmer than the hard leather boots the soldiers wore.

He watched silently as men scurried everywhere, most of them behaving as though they were going after five hundred armed warriors. It would almost be comical if it weren't so sad. Quickly the troops were ready, thirty of them. Tall Bear guessed there had been perhaps fifteen to twenty Indian men in the camp he'd seen, another twenty or so women and children.

Balen sat straight and cocky on a large white gelding. The man liked to ride a white horse because it made him stand out from the others. Tall Bear rode up beside him. "I remind you, Lieutenant, that I do not believe that is a war party camped ahead. There is no need for so many men or to get them ready for a fight."

"Where Indians are concerned, we have to be always ready for a fight, Tall Bear. You certainly should know that. In fact, I'm not so sure I should trust you. I don't believe it's right having Indians scout against Indians. You'd better not be leading us into some kind of trap. That scout Jess Willett, up at Laramie, swears by you, but I think he's a fool to trust you. I didn't want you assigned to my mission, but now that I've got you, I guess I have to rely on what you tell me."

"Then you should listen when I tell you to approach the camp peacefully."

"Red Cloud and his Sioux have closed practically every fort along the Bozeman, Tall Bear. And the southern Cheyenne have been raiding and murdering all through this territory because of Sand Creek! I don't need to hear talk about peace. I'm not going to let this bunch slip through my hands and go on to kill more innocent settlers—not when I'm up for a promotion. Lead the way, Tall Bear, and remember: if you betray these soldiers, you'll hang!"

Tall Bear's horse turned in a circle, seeming to sense his master's anger. He headed north, and a column of men fell into place behind him and followed. Tall Bear wished Jess were there to help him reason with Balen. Jess was one of those white men who would know how to handle the situation.

For two hours they rode over rolling hills through an ever-stiffening wind, the sound of horses' hooves muffled by the fresh snowfall. They crested the hill that overlooked the Indian camp, and Tall Bear drew his horse to a halt. Below them smoke curled lazily from a few tepees, women wrapped in blankets hung meat over smoky fires, a few children ran and played in the snow.

"Do you see?" he told Balen. "They are not a war party. I will ride down and ask them to give up their arms peacefully. We can at least escort them to Laramie and make arrangements there to send them back south."

"Why do I have to keep reminding you that I make the decisions, Tall Bear—not you?" Balen spoke through a woolen scarf he had tied around his nose and mouth because of the cold. To Tall Bear's surprise and anger the man pulled out his sword. At about that same time one of the women below spotted the soldiers and gave out a cry of warning. Warriors emerged from tepees, many without their outer fur coats and other warm clothing, and Tall Bear knew they were warning the women to take the children and run for cover.

The next few minutes were moments of horror for Tall Bear. Balen ordered his men to charge. Thirty soldiers thundered down on the small camp, some with swords drawn. Two fell from their horses when a few of the warriors, though completely unprepared, managed to get to their weapons and take rifle shots at them. But soon the soldiers were shooting back in full force. Women and children fell. Tall Bear saw one soldier run a sword through a small boy, and he thought of Running Fox.

Where was his place in all of this, he wondered. He remained behind, refusing to take part in the senseless slaughter. If Lieutenant Balen could do this once, he could do it again. The man did not deserve to live. Tall Bear's hatred for such men welled into uncontrollable rage, and he pulled his rifle from its boot.

He raised the weapon and aimed.

"Tit for tat, Lieutenant," he muttered. Amid all the gunfire below, his own gunshot would not be noticed. But before he squeezed the trigger, Balen slumped in his saddle. Someone else's bullet had put him down.

With great satisfaction Tall Bear watched Balen fall from his horse. He turned his own horse, feeling no pity, wishing only that he could have been the one to pull the trigger. He headed back to base camp, where he would gather his things and his second mount and leave. He was through scouting for the army.

Chapter Fifteen

Faith saw someone approaching the station on horseback as she trudged through snow past her knees. It was April, and as often happened in those parts, a freak snowstorm had blown in off the mountains. She took comfort in the thought that this time of year snow didn't usually stay on the ground for long. And even with snow this deep it was possible for a stage to get through. Little Johnny, a year old already, was still sleeping soundly. Faith liked the quiet mornings, used them for prayer and to get chores done, which this morning meant raking out horse stalls.

She walked into the shed, shooing out eight sturdy horses. She'd been there almost two years already—had managed through two long, hard winters—and still she loved it. The year was 1866, the Civil War was over. There was more talk now of a transcontinental railroad, which would bring new settlers, people displaced because of the war. Her dream of building Sommers Station into a town was beginning to take on real possibilities.

She saw that the approaching figure was a heavyset man in buckskins. The rising sun was making the snow so bright that Faith had trouble seeing the man clearly. He was probably a scout or mountain man or drifting prospector come to see if he could get a little food and perhaps sleep the night in the shed. There had been plenty of men like that come through, and all had been respectful and paid their way. Still, she was always wary of strangers and never trusted anyone completely. Doors and windows were closed and bolted at night, and she and Hilda always kept rifles loaded, although they were hung in brackets high on a wall so Johnny could not touch them.

The horses trotted briskly into a fenced corral, and she realized she would have to spread some feed in the troughs for them. She took up a rake and raked out a stall. Later maybe she would have time to play with Johnny in the snow—it would be fun watching him try to stand up in it. She smiled at the thought, ignoring the muffled sound of the horse and rider's arrival. She expected they'd go into the station first, so she paid no heed and raked out a second stall, stopping only when she heard the door creak open.

She turned. To her horror the face she was looking into was that of Cletus Brown. Both of them stood frozen in place, Clete apparently as surprised to see her as she was to see him. She gripped the rake tightly, as his expression changed to anger, to hatred.

"You!" Clete snarled. "It's you!"

Faith could hardly breathe, could hardly find her voice. "What—what are you doing here! How did you get here?"

"You mean what am I doing alive, don't you?"

She stared at him in panic, remembering that her rifle was inside the depot. "What *are* you doing alive?"

"Your little popgun wasn't powerful enough for a man like me, you little wench," he snarled. "Oh, it put me down for a while, and I damn well suffered. Indians found and helped me. And all the while I was recoverin', I was thinkin' on how I'd get you for what you did! But by the time I was up and about, your tracks were gone. I figured you'd died tryin' to get help, or maybe you was well on your way with some wagon train to California. Either way, I never thought I'd see you again."

He looked around, his eyes glittering with something Faith could not quite read. Glee? Anticipation? Revenge? Oh, most surely revenge! She had put four bullets into his chest and left him for dead, and he damn well had deserved it. She told herself to stay calm, think clearly.

"How'd you end up at this place?" Clete noticed the rake in her hand and the pile of hay and manure at her feet. "Rakin' out horse stalls! You some station manager's wife now? Is there a man around here? A driver, maybe?"

Faith took hold of the rake in both hands. "None of your business. You get moving, Clete Brown, you *murderer*. If there was any law out here, you'd hang for what you did to Johnny!"

His scowl turned to a grin, and he rested his hand on a six-gun he wore on his hip. "Well, ain't this a miracle, and a lucky day for me," he said through yellowed teeth. "I can tell by the look on your face there ain't no man around. And you owe me, little lady. You owe me a horse, a six-gun, and a rifle . . . and a whole lot more."

Faith's skin crawled at the thought of what he meant. "After what you did to Johnny? I owe you a bullet in the *gut*, with a lot bigger gun than the last one I used!" She felt so helpless standing there with only the rake. He looked bigger and meaner than ever, his heavy beard unkempt, his eyes still full of lust and lies, his smell the same. She remembered it all as though she'd just left him for dead yesterday. "Where have you been all this time?" She took a defensive pose, moving away from the stall, holding out the rake in warning. "It's been almost two years!"

"Been all over, little girl, like always. Been huntin' buffalo, scoutin' for the railroad, did a little gold diggin'. I come through here on my way back to the railroad camps way out east to work for them some more. The railroad pays good. They're comin' through here, you know, next couple of years or so." He looked her over as though she stood there naked, even though she wore a heavy woolen dress and a wool sweater. "What the hell are you doin' here at a stage depot? This place ain't more than two or three days from where we parted."

"From where you murdered Johnny. You get out now,

Clete Brown, or I'll see you dead for sure this time! I'm here because this is my home now. I've got a little boy and I'm happy here, and I won't let you spoil it!"

He pulled out his handgun and cocked it. "You left me for dead, you little bitch. I was about to climb in your wagon an' get my due. Night after night I had to lay awake listenin' to Johnny Sommers hump his woman, me achin' to be doin' the same. I finally decided it was my turn, and I never got my due. Now here you are, like God himself led me here to you, and I aim to get what I got comin' for you puttin' them bullets in me and makin' me suffer like that! Put that rake down, you redheaded whore, and take what you've got comin', else that little boy you have will be growin' up without his daddy *and* his mama!"

He held the gun straight out, pointed at her.

"Drop the rake," he repeated. "We've got some talkin' to do, like you promisin' you won't tell the law who killed Johnny."

She slowly set the rake aside. "It wouldn't matter. There *is* no law out here—yet. And I've already told *plenty* of people who killed Johnny," she lied. She had told no one except Hilda and Tall Bear because she wanted to protect little Johnny from the truth. It was better he grew up thinking his father had drowned. "I have nothing to promise you. Just be glad you're alive and get out of here, Clete Brown. Be glad no one has seen fit to put a noose around your neck! You'd best ride far and wide from here. Go to California or Texas, someplace where you won't risk being found out."

He frowned, questions in his eyes. "How'd you get here on your own?"

"It doesn't matter now. Leave, and I won't tell anyone I saw you. The next stage will arrive within a couple of hours. I won't tell anyone on it that you've been here and you're alive. Be glad for that much and leave."

He shook his head. "And make it easy for you after you treated me like dirt, woman! You flauntin' yourself around, makin' me crazy with the want of you! Now here you are, ripe and ready and noplace to turn!"

He headed toward her, and all Faith could think about was Johnny. If she screamed for Hilda—

"Get them clothes off, little lady. I aim to see what it was that made Johnny pant after you every night." He held his gun in one hand, rubbed at his privates with the other. "Get 'em off!" he repeated. "Once this is over, I'll leave and you'll never hear from me again. I'll git, just like you want me to do, and you and your brat will be safe."

Faith scrambled to think. What choice did she have? Maybe if she let him get close to her, she could find a way to grab something and hit him with it. She pulled off her woolen sweater, began unbuttoning the front of her plain brown dress. Perhaps if she got his full attention, she could lure him into doing something stupid, but she did not have to go far before they both heard the click of a gun hammer being cocked.

"Drop that gun, mister!" Hilda ordered from the doorway.

To Faith's horror Clete whirled and fired. Hilda! Sweet Hilda! In an instant Faith grabbed a pitchfork just as Clete turned back around. She ducked when he fired again, then jabbed at him as hard as she could, sticking him in the left thigh. He cried out from the pain, aimed at her again. She rolled out of the way, heard another gunshot, thinking at first it was Clete shooting at her. But then Clete himself slumped to the floor, a bloody hole in his lower left back. The pitchfork was still stuck in his leg.

Faith turned to see Hilda in a sitting position, the rifle in her hand, a tiny bit of smoke coming from the barrel. She ran to the woman's side, taking away the rifle she still gripped. "Hilda! Dear Hilda, let me help you back to the station."

The old woman grasped her arms. "No, child. It ain't gonna make no difference." She managed a smile, but she was growing deathly white. "I saw him ride over here . . . wasn't sure if you was . . . safe. I come out to see . . . heard the things he said. He's the one . . . ain't he? The one . . . who killed Johnny."

"Yes, Hilda. He's the man who killed Johnny."

"Then I'm glad . . . I shot him." The woman's eyes

teared. "Take good care . . . of Johnny . . . and Sommers Sta—"

She did not finish the statement. Faith's heart tightened with sorrow as the old woman's eyes closed and she slumped away from her. "Hilda!" She shook her, but to no avail. She leaned close, felt no breath, felt for a pulse, but there was none. She looked over at Clete. He was not moving. With great effort she got up from Hilda's side and walked over to kick the man onto his back. His eyes were still open. Grimacing from having to touch him, she felt for a pulse and was glad to realize he also was dead.

At last! She no longer had to worry and wonder about him, but the cost of finally being rid of the haunting horror of Clete Brown was sweet Hilda's life. Grief welled up in her soul, and she felt as though she were losing a mother all over again. She staggered past Hilda's body and outside, her motherly instincts making her want to go to Johnny and make sure he was all right. She fled to the station and went inside to find her baby boy still sleeping on a cot.

She knelt beside it, never feeling more alone than she did at that moment, even after Johnny had been killed. Hilda was gone. They had become so close through two long, lonely winters. Now she was entirely alone . . . except for Johnny. Yes, she had Johnny. She could almost hear Hilda's voice, telling her she must go on now, telling her not to give up. The woman had been letting her run the place practically all by herself for months now.

She struggled to think straight. She would close the shed door and tell Buck what had happened when the stage arrived. They would not tell the passengers. Buck could send the stage on with the shotgun as the driver. He could stay behind and help her bury Clete and Hilda, which meant she would have to tell him the truth about what had happened to Johnny. She had never told Buck, but he was the kind of man who would understand.

More death. When would it end? When would civilization come to the wilds of Wyoming? She walked on weak legs to the door, out onto the porch, numb to the cold air. Maybe she should take Johnny and leave, go to Cheyenne or Denver. Maybe she should give it all up, after all, even though Hilda would have told her not to. She fought an urge to scream and sob, but she didn't want to frighten little Johnny. No. She had to be strong. She had survived so much already.

She walked off the porch, looked up at the sign. SOMMERS STATION. Hilda would say she could by-God run this place alone, and she'd do it. She'd do it. She glanced over at the shed.

"I love you, Hilda," she said, a painful lump rising in her throat. She felt responsible for the woman's death. If not for what had happened with Clete and Johnny . . . if she'd made sure Clete Brown was dead in the first place, he never could have come along and caused this terrible disaster.

She went back inside, deciding to get her wits together, stay in control for Johnny's sake. How was she going to explain to him where Hilda was, why she wasn't there anymore? She'd been like a grandmother to him.

"That's what we'll put on her marker," she whispered to Johnny, touching his hair. "Grandma."

Part Three

Chapter Sixteen

March 1867 . . .

The stagecoach rumbled into the depot, snow and mud splattering in every direction as horses and wheels splashed through thawing ground and standing water from snowmelt. Faith ordered two-year-old Johnny to stay on the porch of the station and out of the way. He sat down obediently, the buttons of his little woolen coat nearly popping because it was already too small for his growing frame. He was a good boy, charmingly handsome, as his father had been. He had Johnny's thick, sandy hair, his impish brown eyes, his fetching smile, which showed dimples in his chubby cheeks. Faith loved him more than her own life, and he was all she'd had to keep her company over the past winter, her first winter alone.

She so often longed for a woman's company and missed Hilda achingly. Few women traveled the stage route because of the dangers. Usually the only women who did venture into this country were ones like Bret Flowers. She smiled at the thought that she actually missed Bret sometimes. She was most certainly a "soiled dove," as she'd heard some men call such women, but there was a lot about Bret to like. She wondered how she was doing down in Colorado.

To think of Bret reminded her that she hadn't been with a man herself for almost three years, ever since Johnny's death. He had left her not particularly wanting a man in her life, or in her bed, though sometimes she would feel a deep ache for such things. And there was little Johnny to think about. He would be needing a father more and more as he got older. The trouble was, out there she saw men only in passing, and none stayed long enough to get to know well. She supposed that those who did come through didn't even see her as pretty or feminine anymore. She lived like a man, worked like a man, dressed plainly, never used color on her face, never wore her hair in a fancy do. Her hands were callused, her fingernails always worn down to stubs.

Besides all that, she'd done things no decent, properly bred woman would do. She'd tried twice to kill Clete Brown, left him for dead once. She'd killed Indians and once an outlaw, and she wouldn't hesitate to kill again if it meant protecting the station and Johnny. Some folks might consider it even worse that she had kept the dead men's belongings to sell. She now owned two horses, two six-guns, a pistol, and three rifles—much of that once the property of Clete Brown. She also possessed all his gear, two saddles, bridles, blankets, and even had kept the money she had found on him.

Wrong or not, all of those things could come in handy when she needed the money for Johnny, and when the day came to build Sommers Station into something bigger.

Finding a man would have to wait. For now she cared only about this wonderful freedom, this beautiful, wild land, her baby boy, and Sommers Station. When passengers asked about Hilda, she told them only that she had died of old age. Buck knew the truth. He had helped her bury Hilda behind the depot next to the woman's husband, but he had buried Clete Brown far off in a stand of trees, leaving the grave unmarked. No one would ever know it was even there now, and that was fine with Faith. The man did not deserve any recognition. She wished she knew the address of Hilda's son in California for she had no way of telling him the woman was dead. The man had never even written to his mother. It saddened her that he apparently didn't care about his mother's welfare.

Her sweet Johnny would never be such a negligent son. She watched him now, standing up and clapping his hands excitedly as passengers climbed down from the coach and gingerly made their way through the mud to the depot. One of them grumbled about the mud and cold, wondering aloud how people survived in "these desolate places." They all sported expensive-looking overcoats, obviously some kind of businessmen. Faith greeted each of them with a friendly smile, and each in turn seemed surprised to find a young woman and small boy there.

"Welcome to Sommers Station," she told them. "There is food inside, gentlemen. If you give me a few minutes, I'll serve you myself."

"And who are you, little lady?" one of them asked, removing a felt hat. Faith guessed he was only five or six years older than she. His dark-brown eyes were outlined with thick lashes, and a thin mustache accented his full lips. His hair was neatly cut, and Faith could not help taking special notice of him.

"I'm Faith Sommers, and I run this station."

His eyebrows shot up in surprise. *"Alone?"*

"I can hitch teams and cut wood and shoot a rifle good as any man, mister," she answered. "I've fought Indians many times, ridden out and rounded up horses they stole, and a gang of outlaws tried to steal our supplies once. I shot one in the rear and one in the head. They took the dead one and rode off and never came back. Does that answer your question as to whether or not I can run this place?"

The man nodded respectfully, but there was a rather cocky look in his eyes. "Yes, ma'am. I didn't mean to imply that you couldn't handle it."

"Yes, you did, but I'm used to it." She pointed at a water pump to the left of the depot while the others also stared at her. "You can wash over there if you've a mind. Our facilities aren't fancy, but the food is good. I'm not a bad cook, if I must say so myself."

"Thank you, ma'am," he answered, his eyes moving over her appreciatively. For the first time in years Faith felt self-conscious about her appearance. She supposed the man was wondering if she was really even a woman. "Actually, if you're the one in charge," he said, "you're the one we need to talk to inside."

"Fine. Go ahead and wash. I'll help the driver switch teams. If you don't mind, you could watch my boy for me. He's not bashful."

"Certainly!" The young one looked down at Johnny with a smile, then looked questioningly at Faith. "Where is the boy's father, if I may ask?"

"His father drowned on our trip west. I got as far as this station and decided to stay. The old woman who used to run the station died last year."

He shook his head in wonder. "My, oh my. Such a brave woman you are." He looked at the others. "Well, gentlemen, the lady says we should wash first, so I suppose we'd better." He herded them over to the pump, and a couple of them looked back at her as though she were something unusual and fascinating.

"I'll be damned," Faith heard one of them comment.

She shook her head and told Johnny to go inside with the men when they returned. She walked to the coach to help the driver unhitch the team. "Any problems, Buck?"

"No, ma'am. Course, you know me. I been doin' this for five years now, since afore you come here, so there ain't much I ain't seen. Took three bullets in me over the years and survived every one of them."

Faith grinned. Buck liked to brag about all the dangerous adventures he'd survived.

"The Indian situation seems to be calmin' down some," he added, smacking a horse on the rump and heading it toward the corral. "Now that the government is talkin' treaty with the Sioux, and Red Cloud has pretty much got his way, he's layin' low for a while. Trouble is, there's a couple of new troublemakers keepin' the fires stirred. Some leader called Sitting Bull and a young one called Crazy Horse. I don't expect that we're out of the woods yet, but, then, they stick pretty much to the Powder and the Black Hills. With the railroad comin' through next year, I think they'll stay away from this neck of the woods."

Faith walked with him, leading two other horses. "It's really coming, then?"

He nodded. "Track is laid almost clean through Nebraska already, headin' this way. Them men in there, they're railroad people, wantin' to talk about what will happen here once the stage line don't run no more. Watch out for the young one. He's a fancy-talkin' son of a bitch, seems like one of them spoiled rich boys, if you know what I mean. I hear he's buyin' up land for the railroad and investin' in plenty of it himself. I don't trust them kind. His name is Tod Harding."

Somehow the possibility of a railroad had remained unreal to Faith, even though surveyors had already been through there, about a mile to the south of the depot. She'd ridden out to see their stakes, and it worried her what could happen to Sommers Station once the stage line was no longer needed.

"What will you do, Buck, if they stop running the stage line?"

"Oh, I don't know. I'm gettin' old, you know. It's probably about time for me to quit anyway. I reckon I'll go to some minin' town and do some gamblin', find me some kind of work. I've got no family, so it don't matter much what I do."

Faith suddenly felt like crying. "I'd miss you, Buck. Maybe you could stay on here. With the railroad coming, this place will grow. I intend to see to it. There would be work right here for you."

He grinned and nodded. "Well, now, I'll keep an eye on things here, and I just might stay at that."

"I'd like that, Buck."

He sniffed, scratching at a scruffy beard, thinking what a brave little thing Faith Sommers was. He'd never known a woman so pretty who was willing to live the way she was living. Some thought her eccentric. He just figured she was a woman who knew what she wanted and wasn't afraid to go after it. "Well, I guess I'd like that, too." He turned and began walking again, taking the bridle of one of her horses. "You go on inside. I'll finish with the teams."

"Thanks, Buck."

Faith turned to the depot, eyeing the fancy red Concord coach, not looking so fancy now with mud splattered all over its yellow wheels. She was proud of running this place, proud of all she'd learned about horses and hitching, coaches and how to handle patrons of the Wells Fargo line. That's what it was now. Ben Holladay, who Hilda had told her was once one of the richest men around, and who had a monopoly on most transportation all over the West, had overspent and had been caught "stealing from Peter to pay Paul," as Hilda had put it. According to newspapers they received weekly from Denver the year before, the man had apparently broken some kind of federal laws and had paid huge fines and lost just about everything. He had sold the Holladay Overland Mail & Express Company to Wells Fargo & Company last year.

Now the railroad. She was not going to let Sommers Station die. She would soon begin inquiring through ads she planned to mail to newspapers in Denver and Omaha, asking people who might want to take advantage of the railroad and start new businesses or settle on railroad land to come there to Sommers Station. Growth would mean a need for carpenters, blacksmiths, store owners, bankers, and such. Once she managed to get a few more people there, growth would take place naturally, one thing requiring another, until the town would mushroom. More passengers meant that more food would be needed, which in turn meant something bigger in the way of a restaurant, maybe a rooming house for those staying the night.

Her mind was swimming with possibilities. How wonderful it would be if there were others there year-round—company, friends, other women! Whatever those men inside had to say to her, they were not going to talk her out of staying right there at Sommers Station. They were not going to take any of this from her. Let the railroad come. She would be ready for it.

She lifted the skirt of her rather ragged wool dress to avoid mud as she headed to the depot, again suddenly self-conscious of her appearance. She walked to the pump and washed her hands before going inside to see the men seated at the long table always set out for passengers. Johnny, who had not a bashful bone in his body, was sitting on one of the younger men's lap. Faith thought how he was so like his father, brash and outgoing, afraid of nothing.

She removed her stretched-out, badly worn woolen sweater and hung it on a hook. "I'll get you some stew, gentlemen." She could feel all of them watching her, sensed their curiosity. One by one she set bowls of buffalo stew in front of each of them, then put out a loaf of fresh bread and a bowl of fresh-churned butter.

"Do you do all this yourself?" asked the one Buck had called Tod Harding. "Make the butter? Do the cooking? Take care of the kid? Keep this place tidy?"

"Take care of the horses," Faith went on for him. "Clean out stalls, carry water, chop wood, whatever it takes. This is a far cry from the fancy hotels you men are obviously accustomed to, but it's warm and dry and part of your fare."

The others were already eating. "Very good stew, Mrs. Sommers," one of the older gentlemen told her.

"Thank you." Faith poured coffee into tin cups, then sat down at one end of the table. Johnny climbed onto her lap. "Buck says you men are all from the railroad," she said.

"Yes, ma'am," Tod Harding replied. He introduced himself, then added proudly, "My father is Nicholas Harding, owns a freighting wagon line down on the Santa Fe Trail. Now he's invested in the Union Pacific. He also owns several supply stores across the country. I'm here to investigate new places where he might open more stores as the railroad comes through. The rest of these men"—he nodded to a very distinguished-looking gentleman with white hair, then went on around the table—"Robert Belding, Marcus LeBlanc, Edward Hogan, Hank Beecher, and Larry King—they're all with the Union Pacific, here to check out other possibilities for railroad land. This place is on land that's part of the government land grant for the railroad—land that will one day be very valuable once the tracks come through. We feel that since there is already a stage depot here, and considering the distance between Salt Lake City and Cheyenne, it's a good place to use as a train depot also. It will be especially useful for trains coming east out of the desert, a good watering post, as well as a gathering point for cattle being shipped east from ranches directly north of here."

Faith brightened. "I am glad to hear that, Mr. Harding. I have already been planning ways to keep Sommers Station alive."

Harding grinned, a smile that Faith couldn't help noticing was movingly handsome. Again she was ashamed of her appearance. Women in places where these men came from surely were much more refined and fancy.

"Well, that's good news, and we can help you," Harding answered. "The railroad will grant you use of the land, but eventually you will have to pay for it. If you have some kind of business going here, or new ideas, you should begin setting aside some money. For all you know, Sommers Station will be quite a little settlement someday."

Faith straightened proudly. "That is my very intention, and I already have a growing nest egg for just that. I earn money from passengers who pay me to do mending, washing, earn tips for my cooking." She had told no one, not even Buck, that she kept money hidden in a secret place in the wall, and she would not tell these men, either. "I remind you that this land still runs with outlaws, so anything I tell you cannot go beyond these walls. You seem to be respectable businessmen, so I think I can trust your discretion."

"Of course," Belding told her.

Harding shook his head. "You surely are a wonder," he told her.

"I am just a woman trying to survive out here, Mr. Harding, and who has a son to support. I have already been thinking of placing newspaper ads for people to come to Sommers Station and take advantage of the coming railroad and the revenue it can bring."

Hank Beecher chuckled. "You're a smart woman, Mrs.

Sommers. I've never met a woman who was so independent at such a young age. You surely can't be more than eighteen or nineteen."

"I am almost twenty-one."

"Well, you are certainly an unusual woman," Mr. Le-Blanc told her. "We were told a young woman ran this place, but we didn't believe it. Tell me, don't you miss civilization? Don't you want to—well, you know—go to dances? Meet young men?"

Faith reddened a little. "I am much too busy to think about dances and courting, sir. If God means for me to marry again, He will send the right man at the right time. But that man will have to understand that I plan to continue building Sommers Station and will not sit home at a hearth knitting sweaters."

They all laughed at the remark, and Faith felt her pride and confidence growing.

"Well, of course, the cities that will truly grow with the railroad are Cheyenne and Salt Lake City," Tod told her. "My father is already building stores there, in readiness for new business. The West is going to mushroom now that the war is over, and the railroad will only make the growth that much faster. I'm sure Sommers Station will do well, and I intend to be back in a year or two to get something started here myself. I will see that tracks are laid from the main line to this point. I hope you're still here when I come back to open my own business."

"Oh, I will be, Mr. Harding. I promise you that."

His eyes glittered as though he was very pleased. "Good."

"Now, Tod, remember—the young lady said she had no time for men and courting," Belding reminded him.

Faith reddened more, but she noticed Tod Harding did not seem at all embarrassed. His brashness reminded her of Johnny, which attracted her, even as it set off the warning bells. She did not intend to fall in love with any man who might manhandle her the way Johnny had, and this man seemed like the kind of person who liked to control all those around him. Since he came from a wealthy family, he probably also expected women to sit home embroidering or attending social clubs and gossiping about each other. Men like that didn't marry women like Faith Sommers.

Why she even entertained such a ridiculous thought, she wasn't sure. She told herself that the aching loneliness she'd been ignoring for three years was getting the better of her, and she warned herself not to let that loneliness cause her to make foolish decisions.

"I have apple pie," she told them, rising. She set Johnny on his feet, and he toddled off to sit down on the floor and play with a small wooden horse. All the men voiced their desire for pie. Faith began heating water for washing dishes, then carved and served pie when everyone was through with their stew.

The men told her wondrous stories about how the railroad was being built, and she tried to imagine men drilling and dynamiting their way through the mountains, making tunnels big enough for locomotives. It had been a long time since she'd seen a train, but she certainly remembered how big the engines were. Before long they would be chugging and thundering their way past Sommers Station.

She listened intently to more railroad talk, investments that had been made, talk of millions of dollars. She noticed that Tod Harding seemed to enjoy impressing her by mentioning how much his father had invested. She reminded herself that being married to a man with money could end up being a life close to slavery, a life as confined as when she'd lived among the Quakers.

Buck came in and announced that the team was changed and he was ready to go. The men cascaded Faith with compliments about her cooking, and Faith wrapped a piece of pie for Buck in a cotton napkin.

"You should eat first, Buck."

"No, ma'am. We're runnin' a little late, and I want to make the next station before nightfall. You should know there's word of a new gang of outlaws runnin' these parts. They already robbed a stage carryin' an army payroll. One of 'em is a big Indian who they say is a half-breed and mean as hell. You keep an eye out."

"I will, Buck."

As everyone grabbed coats and hats and went out, Tod

Harding lingered behind. "Aren't you afraid when you hear talk about a gang of outlaws in these parts?" he asked Faith.

"I try not to think about it too much, Mr. Harding. God has protected me and provided for me so far. I have no reason to think He won't keep doing it. I grew up with Quakers, and prayer keeps me going. I'll admit I hated the prayer meetings when I was young, but I do have a strong faith."

His eyes moved over her curiously again. "I can see that. You're quite a woman, Mrs. Sommers." He buttoned his overcoat.

"Thank you, Mr. Harding. I'll take that as a compliment."

He put on his hat. "I must say you're too lovely to be buried here, though. You should go to a city—"

"I like it right here, Mr. Harding."

"Ready to roll!" Buck shouted.

Harding put out his right hand before pulling on a glove. "Nice to meet you, Mrs. Sommers. You remember what we said about growth. This is one location we think could benefit from the railroad. Others will close. Take advantage of what you have here, or others will run you out of business."

"I'll remember that, Mr. Harding."

He looked her over once more, a hint of arrogance in his eyes that made her a little uneasy.

"You'd better get on the stage," she reminded him.

"Oh! Yes. Good-bye, Mrs. Sommers."

"Good-bye, Mr. Harding." She watched him run to the coach and climb inside. Buck whistled and shouted and slapped the reins, getting the team under way. As the coach splattered past the station, she waved to Harding, who was watching through a window. He waved in return. Faith suspected there would be a good deal of conversation between him and the others about the strange woman who ran Sommers Station.

Suddenly all was quiet again. There was not even any wind today, only a still cold. She thought of Buck's comment about outlaws and a half-breed Indian. She thought of Tall Bear and wondered what had become of him. Buck's warning had left her feeling more uneasy than she'd wanted to admit. She rubbed the backs of her arms and went inside, closing and bolting the door, deciding she had better make sure all three of her rifles were loaded and ready—just in case.

Chapter Seventeen

April brought a sudden weather change for the better, and Faith awoke to a sunny morning and the singing of birds. She wrapped a shawl around her shoulders and stepped out onto the porch, unconcerned that she wore only a flannel gown. There was no one to see her in it. She breathed deeply of sweet morning air, took in the sight of wildflowers blooming amid green grass over many square miles of rolling hills. It was a sight to behold, the entire view ringed by distant mountains that were still covered with snow.

It was moments like this that she was most glad she'd stayed there, these moments of quiet beauty. She and little Johnny had survived another rugged winter. Just last month she had celebrated the boy's third birthday with a cake and a rollicking snowball fight in a wet March snowfall that soon melted into a warm spring.

Three years! That meant she had been here nearly four years now. She walked back inside and built up a fire in the cookstove to heat some water to wash. By then Johnny was sitting up on his cot rubbing his eyes. "Potty, mommy," he told her.

Faith smiled, thinking how sweet a child was when he was still warm and sleepy. She walked over and gave him a hug, then pulled some shoes on his feet and put a jacket on him. She kept her shawl on and carried Johnny outside to the privy, glad he no longer needed diapers. The boy liked calling himself a "big boy," often walked around saying so and pointing at himself whenever other people were around.

They each took care of personal needs, and when Faith left the privy, Johnny was standing in dewy grass pointing across the wide expanse of rolling hills.

"Buck," he said.

Faith studied where he pointed to see what looked like several riders coming. She frowned, watching them a moment before a hint of alarm began to filter through every nerve end. They were riding fast, and it was early morning. Indians liked to attack in early morning. And why else would riders be coming so fast this hour of the morning if not to try to surprise her and catch her off guard? Until she was sure who was coming, she had better be prepared.

She grabbed Johnny and ran back to the station, glad the horses were still in the shed. She had intended to let them out to graze before coming back inside, but that would make it easier for someone to steal them. She rushed inside and closed the door, bolting it with a heavy board that latched all the way across the doorway. She closed and locked the shutters, opening one outside window first so that she could point a rifle through the hole in the shutter made for that purpose. She'd warded off other Indians and outlaws, she told herself, so she would just have to do it again, if the men coming meant harm.

She hurriedly threw off her gown and pulled on a dress, not bothering with a camisole. There was no time. The important thing was not to be caught wearing only a night-gown. A woman had to be careful around strange men, whether Indian or white. At least Indians usually wanted only horses. Out in these parts a woman could be in more danger from lonely, lawless white men than from Indians. That's what Hilda had often warned her about.

She frantically fumbled with the buttons of the dress, managing to hook most of them. By then she could hear the sound of thundering hooves that sent vibrations through the ground so that she could almost feel their approach under her feet. Her rifles were always kept ready and loaded. She took down all three, stacking two next to her at one of the windows. She kept ammunition inside a little stand under the window. Keeping one rifle in hand, she hurried to a cupboard where she kept one of Clete Brown's six-guns on a top shelf, along with the holster that came with it, in which several bullets still rested. She carried the six-gun to the window and ordered Johnny to hide under his cot.

The boy just stared at her, looking ready to cry. "No," he answered, which was what he said to just about everything lately. Various passengers had teased her about the "terrible twos," and she could see that the theory that a two-year-old was difficult was certainly right; but now he was three and still being stubborn.

"Do as I say, Johnny," she told him. "We're playing a game. You have to hide as long as you can from whoever is coming."

He grinned then, happy with her explanation. With a squeal he ran to the cot, got down on fat knees, and crawled under it.

Faith shoved the rifle barrel through a hole and watched . . . and waited. She told herself to stay calm. The horses came closer, but she heard no shouting and war whoops. They couldn't be Indians. They always did plenty of shouting and yipping when they were on the attack, and by the heavy, thunderous sound of the horses, she guessed they were bigger than Indian ponies, probably shod.

White men. There was only one reason white men would come riding in so fast this hour of the morning. It was possible they were being chased by Indians, but that was not likely, since she'd heard no war cries. Besides, Indians seldom began causing problems this early in the season. Trouble usually arose only during summer buffalo hunts. The men outside were most likely outlaws, intent on overwhelming the station with a surprise attack.

She prayed Johnny would stay under the cot. "Mommy is going to practice shooting her rifle, Johnny, so don't be afraid. Remember, stay under that cot so nobody can find you."

The boy laughed again. Faith concentrated on the horses and their riders that charged in front of the station. She could hear more horses behind the cabin and was glad there were no windows or doors there.

"Get the horses!" someone shouted.

Faith saw two men head for the shed. She took careful aim and squeezed off a shot. One of the men cried out and fell from his horse.

"What the hell—" someone yelled.

A spray of bullets hit the front of the depot, one of them splintering the top edge of a shutter. Faith closed her eyes and ducked her head to keep pieces of wood from flying into her face. Anger began to replace fear then, and she looked through the hole and took aim again, reminding herself she had little Johnny to defend. She fired again.

"Ahhhh! Goddammit!" another man yelled, grasping his side. "Who the hell is in there?"

"It's just supposed to be some old woman!" another shouted.

Faith tried to count. To her best figuring there were seven of them, but she'd apparently killed one and badly wounded another. One more had probably made it to the shed by now. That left four shooting at her, and they were taking cover now. One led the wounded man and his horse behind a broken-down stagecoach; another dismounted and ducked behind a watering trough. One ran behind an area where several rain barrels sat abreast of each other, and the fourth man . . . where was the fourth man? She'd tried to keep track of each one, but the fourth one was gone now.

Everything had happened so fast, she was not even sure what any of them looked like. She did see that they were all well armed and wore long canvas dusters, their hats pulled down near their eyes so that it was difficult to see their faces. One had looked like an Indian, from what she could remember. He rode a spotted Appaloosa and wore buckskins, his long hair hanging wildly about his shoulders. She had caught only a brief glimpse of him, and she remembered Buck's warning about a half-breed who rode with outlaws.

More bullets ripped into the depot.

"Mommy!" Johnny whined, beginning to sound alarmed.

"It's all right, Johnny. Remember to stay there and hide. Don't let anybody find you." She kept her eyes on movements outside as she spoke, finding it difficult to keep from trembling so hard, she couldn't shoot straight. What kind of men were these to attack a stage depot that had only an old woman to defend it, or so they thought?

The shooting stopped for a moment, and outside the chickens continued to squawk and flutter about, distraught from all the noise. A couple of chickens lay dead from stray bullets.

"Come on out, lady, and you won't get hurt," someone yelled. "All we want is the horses and any food and supplies you've got inside. Then we're gonna wait for the next stage. It's got an army payroll on it. We ain't here to hurt you. We just want the payroll."

Fury gripped Faith's soul, as well as a deep alarm. How could she trust men like this not to violate her in the worst way? She would be defenseless against them. She was not about to let strange men touch her, nor let a terrified Johnny watch men hurt his mother. They might not hesitate to kill Johnny, for that matter. Her reply to their offer was to shoot at the man who raised his head above the barrels. He screamed, grabbing his face.

Good! Another one down. That left only two out front to shoot at her. She figured her practice shooting was paying off better than she thought, or she was just plain lucky to have hit three of them. Maybe God was doing the aiming. She decided to say nothing to them yet. She did not want them to hear a young woman's voice.

"Harv's dead! Let's take the horses and get the hell out of here! We don't need nothin' else!"

The shouted words came from near the shed.

"We ain't leavin' till the old woman gives up and lets us inside!" someone else yelled. "I ain't turnin' my back on the crazy bitch, and I ain't givin' in to no old lady who's got off a couple lucky shots."

"Lucky! She killed Harv, and it looks like maybe Mick! Pete's wounded bad. I don't call that luck!"

There was another moment of silence. "Come on out, old woman!" came the warning again. It was from the same man who had originally told her to give up. He was one of the two behind the stagecoach, and Faith suspected he fancied himself the leader of the bunch of them. "Don't make us have to come and get you!"

She still did not reply. She fired three warning shots of her own, her bullets spitting into the dirt under the stagecoach. She could see feet and legs, saw them jump out of the way. "There, you bastards!" she growled under her breath.

"There must be a man in there," the one in the shed yelled. "Ain't no woman can shoot like that."

"She's comin' out or we'll burn her out," the apparent leader answered. "You hear that, lady? You can't hold out forever. We'll burn you out, starve you out, whatever we have to do!"

Another moment of silence.

"How'd she know we was comin'?" one of the two behind the coach finally said. "We struck early. We should have surprised her."

"What difference does it make? She's in there and we're out here, and the stage will be coming around noon."

"We shoulda just attacked the stage like we planned."

"It's got soldier escort. If we attacked from the open like this, we'd all have been killed," the one who seemed to be the leader answered. "Surprising them from inside the station would have been the best plan of attack."

"Well, *this* plan ain't worked so far!" the second man grumbled. "I say we take the horses and light out of here before the stage and them soldiers get here."

"We've got time," the first man answered. "Maybe Indian has a plan."

Indian. So there *was* an Indian. Where was he? Faith kept her rifle aimed steadily at the coach, making sure she saw four legs. From her vantage point she could see the shed. If the man who had made it there came out, he would also be in her line of fire. Her only hope was to keep all of them at bay until the stagecoach and soldiers arrived.

Could she hold out for at least four more hours? That's how long it would take before the coach arrived, and it was seldom on time. In spite of the cool morning, sweat began to trickle down her forehead, and she could feel perspiration dampening the rest of her body. She closed her eyes for a moment, her neck aching from keeping a steady aim through the shutters. She wished she could see better to the side, worried where the Indian had gone. He couldn't get in anywhere behind her, so she wasn't too worried about that, but she remembered how quiet and sneaky Tall Bear could be, remembered hearing Hilda and Buck talk about how an Indian could, as Buck put it, "sneak up behind you even if he was wearin' boots an' spurs and walkin' on broken glass."

In the next moment she learned how true that was. She heard one of the men behind the coach laugh. Why was he laughing? Suddenly a powerful force grabbed the barrel of her rifle that protruded through the shutters, shoving it backward with such violence that the barrel of the rifle rammed against her chest. She fell backward, momentarily breathless. Before she could recover, the shutters were smashed open with the butt end of the attacker's own rifle, and the intruder charged inside.

Faith screamed, reaching for her rifle, but the man kicked it out of the way. She headed for Johnny's cot, crouched in front of it, telling a now crying and frightened Johnny to be still, but to no avail.

"Indian's got her!" she heard someone shout from outside.

Faith looked up at the one called Indian. Almost instantly her terror was replaced by utter astonishment. "Tall Bear!"

He stood there with painted face, pointing his rifle at her. There was a startled look in his eyes.

"Tall Bear, it's me—Faith Sommers. Do you remember me?"

"I remember." He looked past her then at the curtained-off room. "You are alone here?"

"Yes. Except for my little boy." By then Johnny had crawled out from under the cot and clung, sniffling, to her skirt.

Tall Bear looked down at him, memories coming back of another little boy—two little boys—his son, and the white boy he'd shot.

"Please make them go away, Tall Bear. I don't want my son to be hurt. And you know what they'll do to me if they find me alone in here."

His gaze moved over her in a way that made her shiver. She'd been so sure she could trust him when he'd helped her bury Johnny and led her there. Now she was not so sure. Something had happened to change him.

"What's happenin' in there, Indian?" one of the men shouted.

Tall Bear turned, going to the window. He put his back against the wall. "You must all leave!"

"What the hell do you mean by that?"

"I mean what I said," Tall Bear answered. "It is not the old woman. It is someone I know. Go back to our camp. I will meet you there."

"Without the horses?"

Tall Bear looked at Faith, and she shook her head. "Don't let them take the horses. Please! I couldn't go on here without them. I've defended this place alone for nearly two years now."

Tall Bear frowned, trying to remember when he'd seen her last. Two years? Three? He hardly kept track of days and seasons anymore. "They will not give up without the horses."

Faith slowly rose, setting Johnny on the bed and telling him to stay there and be very quiet. "I won't let them have them. I've killed other men for trying to take them. I'll kill them, too!" She ducked past the window and grabbed another rifle, holding his eyes squarely. "Are you going to help me?"

"They are my friends."

"*Friends?* I don't call men like that friends. They'll shoot you in a minute if they think you've turned on them."

He slowly nodded. "I have no doubt of that."

"Between the two of us we can—"

"What's goin' on in there?" someone outside shouted. "What is it, Indian? Can't be a woman. No woman can shoot like that."

Tall Bear glanced at Faith. "This one can," he said quietly. Faith was sure she detected a hint of a grin on his lips. "You take the other window. It is still protected by shutters. I will take this window."

Faith nodded, moving to the shuttered window.

"I am telling all of you to leave," he yelled. "It *is* a woman, and I do not want her hurt."

"Tell her all we want is to come in and wait for the stage."

Faith heard someone cry out as though in pain.

"Take Pete and get out of here," Tall Bear yelled. "He needs a doctor!"

Faith jumped when she heard a gunshot. "Not anymore he don't!" someone yelled. She looked at Tall Bear, horror in her eyes. Someone had killed the wounded man!

"Sonsofbitches!" Tall Bear swore. He crouched at the window and took careful aim. He fired, and the other man behind the stagecoach cried out and fell. Faith could see well enough under the coach to realize he was holding his leg. He was the only one left behind the coach now. One man was still at the shed, one behind the watering trough. She had shot the man who had hidden behind the barrels, as well as the second man who had gone to the shed. The one Tall Bear had wounded was cussing up a storm, calling the Indian every name he could think of, telling him he'd die someday for his betrayal.

Suddenly the one in the shed burst outside, running eight horses with him and staying on the other side of the animals so that it was impossible for Faith to shoot at him without hitting one of the horses.

"Come on! Come on!" The man who wasn't wounded made a dash to join the man behind the coach, and Faith could see they were mounting the horse they had managed to hide.

"I'll get you, you goddamn savage!" screamed the one who'd been shot in the leg.

It was difficult to get a shot at them, since the coach hid them as they rode off at a hard gallop. By the time they came into view, they had caught up with the first man who'd gone off with the horses, now out of rifle range.

"They got my horses," Faith said dejectedly.

"Not yet." Tall Bear jumped out the window.

Faith ran to it, calling out to him, "Tall Bear, wait!" Already he was out of sight, but in the next moment he came charging past her on his Appaloosa, long hair flying in the wind. In minutes he was gone. Had he gone to get the horses for her, or would he simply join the others again, or maybe kill them and keep the horses for himself?

She turned away to see Johnny on the cot sucking his thumb, tears on his chubby face. She touched his hair, leaned down to kiss his cheek. "Everything is all right, Johnny. Everything will be all right."

Would it, really? How easily she could have been raped and killed, little Johnny killed or left alone there to starve to death. If Tall Bear had been as ruthless as he was capable of being . . . if it hadn't been for the miracle that he knew her . . . if he had been anyone else—she and Johnny would be at the mercy of those men right now.

Her eyes teared as she straightened. "What kind of fool am I?" she thought. She'd been so sure she could make it there—had come so close. But it could be another two years before the railroad came through—two more years of all this loneliness and danger.

She told Johnny to stay on the cot. Then she took the board off the door and cautiously opened it. With her rifle she walked out onto the porch, slowly stepping down and walking toward the stagecoach, warily peeking around it to see a man lying there with blood staining his clothes at his side, a bullet hole in his forehead. She realized he was the one she had wounded and his "friend" had killed. She glanced over at the shed, where another man lay dead, the one she'd shot. She walked around the dead body near the coach and looked over at the barrels, where a third man lay dead, also killed by her. Three had got away . . . one of them wounded in the leg by Tall Bear.

It suddenly seemed too quiet. She began to tremble, realizing how close she had come to losing her life today. If not for Tall Bear . . . How strange that he had saved her life again, and yet to think he'd been among those who had attacked the station. Why? What had caused him to ride with such men? She let the tears come then, needing the release. After a few minutes she composed herself, not wanting to appear a helpless, fainting woman to the soldiers and Buck when they arrived. Poor Buck would have more bodies to bury now, but at least the outlaws' plan to attack the stage when it arrived had been foiled. She would warn them to be extra cautious heading into Idaho—but there were no fresh horses now for the stage, except for the four horses left behind by the outlaws. They weren't trained for harness, though, and were probably not big enough, anyway; besides that, they had already been ridden hard that morning.

Practicality again began to take hold of her thoughts. She had four more saddles now that she could sell for money to add to her savings. Two of the outlaws' horses still had rifles attached to their gear. She would go through their saddlebags and see what else she could find. Hardly able to believe what she was doing, she bent down and began rummaging through the pockets of the dead men, finding two wallets with paper money, a few coins, an expensive-looking chain watch, most likely stolen.

She felt guilt over what she was doing, but in this land the only rule was survival. "Forgive me, Lord, but I have no choice," she prayed. "And they have no more use for these things."

She took the items inside, hid the smaller things inside the wall.

"Mommy," Johnny sniffled forlornly. She set everything aside and walked over to pick him up, holding him close, unsure what to do next, who would show up first—Buck and the stagecoach . . . the remaining angry outlaws . . . or Tall Bear.

Chapter Eighteen

Faith washed Johnny's face and hands. His little body shivered in lingering sobs, and her heart ached at the sight. Perhaps her stubborn determination to stay there was taking too much of a toll on her little boy. Could she put him through at least two more years of this? She didn't mind so much risking her own life, but the thought of losing her precious baby, the guilt she would feel if something happened to him—that was different.

She stroked his hair again, put her arms around him from behind and kissed his cheek. "It's all right, Johnny," she assured him for the hundredth time. He was so sweet and receptive to people. To see him also frightened by cruel men tore at her heart. She patted his cheek and went to a cupboard, taking out some bread and slicing off a piece for him. She put a little butter on it and set it in front of him. "Mommy will cook you an egg." She realized then that she had not milked the cow that morning at the usual time. "You sit right there, and Mommy will go get some milk and gather some eggs. Promise Mommy you will stay right there in your chair."

The boy stuck a chubby finger into the buttered bread and swirled it around in the butter, nodding as he did so.

"And eat your bread, Johnny. Don't play with it." She smiled as the boy stuck his finger into his mouth to suck off the butter. She put all the guns up out of reach, not wanting Johnny to go near them while she went outside. She kept one rifle with her, taking it outside, not even bothering to put on a shawl first. She was too upset to notice the lingering coolness of the morning, although it was obvious the day was going to warm to a very pleasant temperature.

It was so quiet now. She had to stay busy or go crazy with the waiting. She decided she should move the dead bodies somewhere out of sight of the passengers who would soon arrive.

First she had to get some milk and eggs for Johnny and make him some breakfast. She headed for the smaller shed where the cow, called Betty, was kept, relieved to find the animal unhurt and munching away on hay, apparently unaffected by all the gunfire earlier. She set a bucket under the cow's udder, talking softly to her as she massaged the udder gently before beginning the milking, thinking how this was at least one thing she had learned back in Pennsylvania that was useful here. She had bought the cow from passing homesteaders who were headed back east and were worried the journey would be too much for the then-pregnant Betty. To Faith's disappointment the calf had died shortly after it was born, but she continued to milk Betty to keep the cow producing.

She filled half a bucket, then left the shed door open so Betty could wander at will. She went into the henhouse behind the cow shed and gathered what eggs she could find, scolding the hens for being stingy this morning. Still, it was not their fault. They were simply too nervous over all the shooting that had taken place only a couple of hours ago.

She picked up the skirt of her dress and placed the eggs in it, holding it up with one hand and picking up the bucket of milk with the other. The entire morning seemed so unreal now. She had killed two men that morning, and according to the mantel clock inside, which she could hear chiming, it was only nine o'clock. Now she was milking a cow and gathering eggs, preparing breakfast as though the morning were like any other. She worried sometimes that her heart was becoming too hard, that she had no emotions left except for her little boy.

She looked around, studying the horizons in every direction. There was still no sign of Tall Bear. Would the others manage to kill him? She didn't know whether to hope that he returned, or that she would never see him again.

She took the milk and eggs inside. She realized then that her dress was buttoned crookedly. What a sight she must be, her hair all askew from not having even combed and braided it yet that morning, her dress on crooked, no camisole or slips underneath.

She used the skirt of her dress to grab hold of one of the iron lids on top of the cookstove, lifting it to add yet another piece of wood to the fire beneath it. She replaced the lid and set a black fry pan on top, quickly cooking Johnny some scrambled eggs, then set them in front of him with a cup of milk. "Try to use the spoon, Johnny, not your fingers."

He was grinning now, apparently beginning to feel better about things.

While Johnny was eating, Faith took care of the bodies outside. She set her rifle against the broken-down stagecoach and took a deep breath before allowing herself to look again at the dead man who still lay there. She knew she couldn't drag the body very far, as he was quite hefty, so she decided to pull him over to the barrels, where another of the outlaws lay dead, the one she had shot in the face. She would try not to look at him too closely.

She turned around, positioning herself between the dead man's legs and picking up his booted feet, clamping one foot under each arm and pulling with all her might, feeling like a plow horse as she dragged the body behind her until she managed to get it to the barrels. She dropped the legs, not allowing herself to look at the other man. She dragged some of the water barrels around the bodies then, positioning them in a circle so that it would be difficult for someone riding in to realize there was anything inside the circle. Just

to be safe, she tipped a couple of barrels over the tops of
the bodies and added a couple more to the circle so that it
simply looked like a pile of barrels there and nothing more.

She hurried over to the horse shed then, dragging the
third dead body inside and out of sight. By then she felt
nauseated from having to touch the dead bodies, which
brought back memories of having to drag poor Johnny so
far before he could be buried.

She took a deep breath, holding her stomach for a moment, then went back out to gather the four horses left
behind. She led them into the shed, where they would be
out of sight, putting each into a stall but leaving them
saddled. She had to get back to Johnny. The horses would
have to be unsaddled and brushed down later. She went
out and closed the shed door, hoping the dead body left
inside wouldn't make the horses too restless. Hurrying to
the water pump, Faith washed her hands vigorously,
splashed her face with cold water, then went back to the
stagecoach to retrieve her rifle, looking around again. Still
no sign of Tall Bear. What if the others had killed him?
Would they come back for her? That was her biggest fear.

She set the rifle against a porch post and walked over to
a stack of lumber kept near the station for whatever purpose it might be needed. She picked up two wide boards
and carried them inside the station, taking a hammer and a
can of nails from a cupboard and placing the boards over
the window where Tall Bear had broken out the shutters.
He'd seemed like a wild bear when he'd come crashing
through, and it gave her a chill to think how strong he was,
what he could do to her if he chose. Yet he'd been so kind
when he'd helped her with Johnny. She'd seen so much
good in him.

She hammered the boards in place so that the window
was covered, then realized the whole front of the depot was
pocked with bullet holes. Of course, there had already been
many such holes there; perhaps no one would realize these
were new.

She brought in her rifle and closed the door, replacing
the thick wooden bar across it. Johnny was sitting on the
floor playing with blocks, and she noticed he'd eaten most

of his food. She smiled at how good he was most of the time.

Hurriedly removing her dress, Faith tied on her camisole, then pulled on two slips. She put on a different dress, choosing a blue calico that seemed almost to match the blue of her eyes. Then she brushed and braided her hair, wrapping it neatly around her head.

After she set aside the mirror, Faith cleaned up the little mess Johnny had left. She could not eat herself, still too upset from the morning events. Dead bodies lay outside, and the outlaws might still return. She shivered. It would be so easy to fall to pieces, which was why she kept trying to think of things to do to stay busy.

It was after ten now. The stagecoach would not arrive for a good two hours, perhaps longer. Until then she would have to worry and wonder, stay alert, listen for any sign of a horse or horses returning. She walked to the one window that still had shutters, deciding she would stack her guns there to wait.

The next hour seemed more like ten. Johnny quietly played, and she kept watch through an open shutter on the one good window. Finally she heard the faraway sound of pounding hooves. She picked up her rifle, all senses alert. The sound grew louder when a herd of horses suddenly appeared on the crest of a hill east of the station. She recognized one black one, realized then that they were the Wells Fargo horses one of the outlaws had herded out of there. A man on an Appaloosa with long black hair was whistling at them, guiding them to the station.

Tall Bear! Somehow he had gotten the horses back and was returning them. She was filled with both joy and apprehension. He drove the horses into a fenced corral and closed the gate, then rode up to the station. Faith opened the shutters fully and watched him through the window. She held her rifle ready. "Where are the rest of them?" she asked, thinking he looked pale in spite of his dark skin.

"Two are dead," he answered. He gripped his side, and it was only then she realized he'd been hurt. "One—got away—but he is one who is a coward without many men—to back him up. He will not come back."

"You're hurt!"

His breathing seemed labored. "I am shot."

Faith set the rifle aside. "Come in. Let me help you."

He shook his head. "Soldiers are—on their way with the stage. They will—arrest me."

"Not if they don't know you're here. I'll put you in the back room and hide your horse. The stage never stays long, and since they're carrying a payroll, they'll be in a hurry."

Sweat began to show on his face. "How do I know— you will not tell them about me?"

"You mean, can you trust me?" Their gaze held, and Faith could see he understood the irony of the situation. "The question is, can *I* trust *you?*" she added.

"I suppose—neither of us—has a choice," he answered. "If I do not—come in soon—I will fall off this horse and you will—have to leave me where I fall."

Faith moved to the door and opened it. She stepped outside, looking around again, then went to his horse. "Come on."

Tall Bear grimaced as he slid off his horse. He put an arm around Faith's shoulders, thinking what a small thing she was, but what big spirit and bravery she had. He was highly impressed by how she had defended the station all alone. He managed to make it up the step to the porch and went inside with her. When Johnny saw him, his lips puckered, and fear came back into his brown eyes.

"It's all right, Johnny," Faith assured him. "This is Tall Bear, and he's hurt. Mommy is going to help him."

Tall Bear felt an ache inside to think the little boy was afraid of him, and he was again haunted by the memory of shooting the little white boy. He staggered into the back room and fell onto a cot. Faith felt awkward and unsure as he lay there breathing heavily, blood staining the side of his buckskin shirt.

"I'd better have a look," she told him. "You should remove that weapons belt."

He unbuckled the belt that held many bullets and a six-gun, as well as the big hunting knife he always carried. Faith set the belt aside. When she pushed up his shirt, she could see the ugly hole in his side, and her chest went tight.

"I . . . I've never removed a bullet before. Do you think it's still in there? Maybe it went clean through."

He managed a sarcastic grin in spite of his pain. "Believe me . . . it is still in there." He grimaced again. "I need . . . water."

Faith hurried out to dip a ladle into a bucket of drinking water. She carried it in to him and helped him drink. He gulped it down readily.

"I think Buck can take out bullets," she told him. "He's the stage driver."

"He must not know . . . I am here."

"He can be trusted. He'll do whatever I ask. He's a good friend."

His green eyes moved over her, and he noticed she was dressed differently from earlier that morning. He'd liked the way her red hair had looked then, hanging long and loose, thick and beautiful, messy—like a woman just waking up in the morning. "There will be soldiers with him. He would . . . have to explain. He must keep driving."

"One of the soldiers can drive to the next depot. Buck can think of an excuse."

"No. . . . It is best he keeps going."

"I need him to help me bury the dead bodies out there. I hid them the best I could, but the weather is warming. I can't just let them lie there. They'll—" She felt sick again, remembering Johnny. "They'll start to reek. I have to think of the passengers. I don't want to alarm them."

He closed his eyes, breathing deeply. "Do what you . . . must do." He fell silent, and for a moment Faith thought he had died. She felt for a pulse, saw his chest rise and fall. She thought how strange it was that he had been one of those who had attacked the station, yet had risked his life to get back those horses, going after men who were supposedly his friends. He'd killed two of them. This man could be both wild and ruthless, yet kind and caring. She had never known anyone quite like him.

Johnny toddled into the room then, and she shooed him out. She then packed gauze against Tall Bear's wound to soak up the blood. He was too heavy for her to reach under him to wrap the wound, and it struck her how big he was. He took up the whole cot, his feet hanging over the end when she picked them up and placed them onto the bed. She left him fully dressed, hoping Buck would come in time to take out the bullet and save his life.

She remembered his horse then. She picked up Johnny and carried him outside with her, taking the reins of Tall Bear's Appaloosa and leading the animal into the cow shed. She left it there and closed the door, her mind racing with uncertainty. Was she crazy not to tell the soldiers Tall Bear was there? He'd probably be arrested and hanged. Much as he might deserve it, she could not bring herself to be responsible for such an end for him. She owed him, for saving her not once, but twice.

She headed back to the house, but before she went inside, she heard the familiar sound of thundering horses, the clanking and squeaking of soldiers' gear, the rattle of the stagecoach. She looked down the roadway to see it coming, just before it disappeared behind a hill. It reappeared on the crest of another, disappeared again. The stage was arriving much earlier than she had expected. Perhaps this was God's way of saving Tall Bear.

She hurried back inside to check on Tall Bear, who still lay silent. She set Johnny down and picked up Tall Bear's gun belt, putting it in a top dresser drawer so that Johnny couldn't touch it. She leaned close to Tall Bear then.

"You must keep quiet," she spoke softly, not even sure he heard her. "There are soldiers coming."

She hurried back into the outer room, closing the curtains and telling Johnny to stay near her. She put up her own rifle, then hurriedly picked up the splintered wood from the broken shutters and stacked it near the cookstove as kindling, hoping no one would ask why one window was boarded up. If they did, she would tell them one of the shutters had broken off and she'd put up the boards for safety, since she couldn't latch the shutters.

When the stagecoach reached the front of the building, she saw only two passengers inside, both men. Six soldiers accompanied the coach, and Faith invited them to tie their horses in front and come inside for apple pie, afraid that if they wandered around outside too much, they would spy the two bodies under the barrels, or find the one in the horse shed. She had decided not to tell them about the attack. They might want to stay and help bury the men, and she needed them to leave quickly so Buck could tend to Tall Bear.

The men gladly agreed to pie. Faith made sure they were all quickly served, sensing their desire to hurry on their way. After all, there was a lot of money being hauled on the stage, and they hoped to get it to its destination with no trouble. If only they knew that Faith Sommers was the reason they would encounter no outlaw attack.

In his usual winning way Johnny was soon on the knee of one of the soldiers and also eating pie. Faith served coffee, then hurried outside and called for Buck, who had partially unhitched the team.

"We're in a big hurry, ma'am," he told her. "Got a payroll on board."

"I already know that."

He frowned. "How?"

"Buck, I need you to stay."

"What!"

"Don't bother switching teams. The horses in the corral have already been run hard this morning."

"What!" he repeated, surprise and irritation in his eyes.

Faith put a finger to her lips. "Please. I can't explain right now. All I can tell you is there are three dead bodies hidden around here that need to be buried, and there is a man inside in the back room with a bullet in his side. I need someone who knows how to take out a bullet, and I need help burying the dead ones. I don't want the passengers or the soldiers to know, especially about the man in the back room."

Buck scratched his head. "What the heck is goin' on?"

"Please trust me, Buck. I'll tell you all of it after they leave. Have your shotgun or one of the soldiers go on to the next station and switch teams there. Tell the shotgun you're in such a hurry, you feel it would take too much time to switch teams. I'll tell the soldiers a rider came through here this morning and told me he'd seen a gang of men up ahead who looked questionable and that they had better hightail it for the next station and be on the lookout. I can tell them you're staying on here because I'm afraid of being attacked. Please do this for me, Buck."

He sighed, slowly nodding. "You all right? You look a mite shook up."

She smiled but felt like crying. "I'm all right." She touched his arm. "Thank you, Buck."

He nodded. "I'll go tell Gordy. He went to use the privy."

"I'll tell the soldiers. I expect they'll be ready to leave pretty quick once they hear. Tell Gordy to come get a swallow of coffee."

"Yes, ma'am." Buck turned, then hesitated. "How about Johnny? He okay?"

"Yes. He's inside right now sitting on a soldier's lap."

He chuckled and shook his head, walking off to find Gordy. What the hell had happened there that morning? Three dead bodies? The horses already run hard? A wounded man lying in the back room? It seemed there was never a dull moment where Faith Sommers was concerned.

Faith watched him, grateful for his kindness and friendship. She just hoped Tall Bear would not come round and cry out with pain, giving himself away. Maybe if he stopped his outlaw ways from now on and was no longer mentioned as a part of future raids and killings, the army would stop looking for him. Maybe they didn't even know the name of the "Indian" who had ridden with a gang of outlaws. Surely it wasn't too late for Tall Bear to change his ways. There was too much good in him to be wasted this way.

She went inside and told the others the stage would be leaving again momentarily. They had better use the privy and refill their canteens at the pump right away. They thanked her for the pie, complimented her baking, and a few asked her the usual questions about what a woman was doing out there running a stage station all alone. At the moment Faith had to ask herself the same question. With great relief she finally got them all out the door, telling them Buck would stay on until the next stage because she'd heard there might be outlaws prowling about. That got them moving even faster, sure they had to be alert now for a possible attack on the stage because of the payroll.

Faith closed the door, and Johnny toddled over to his cot and lay down with a stuffed cow Faith had made for him. Faith walked into the back room and watched Tall Bear. He opened his eyes and looked at her questioningly.

"The soldiers are gone. Buck stayed behind. He'll take out that bullet."

He closed his eyes again. "I am sorry . . . for your trouble."

She walked closer. "You helped me once, and again today. It's my turn to do something for you."

He looked at her once more, and it seemed just opening his eyes was an effort. "You are an unusual woman . . . Faith Sommers. I never . . . forgot you."

She felt a strange tug at her heart. "And you are an unusual man, Tall Bear. I never forgot you either." She knelt beside him. "Tell me. In case you . . . if you shouldn't make it through this . . . what is your white name? I never knew it. I could put both names on your marker."

Tall Bear ached at the memories of his early boyhood with his father. "My white name . . . is Gabriel. Gabriel . . . Beaumont."

"Gabriel!" She smiled. "That's the name of an angel."

He managed a faint smile. "I am . . . no angel."

"Oh, I certainly agree. But maybe the name will bring you luck."

He kept his eyes closed. "Just use Gabe. That is what everyone called me . . . many years ago. It is what my . . . father called me."

"All right. Gabe Beaumont." She studied his handsome face, closed her eyes, and prayed he would not die, yet wondered why she cared.

Chapter Nineteen

Faith and Buck managed to get enough whiskey down Tall Bear's throat to help dull the pain. Buck gave him a piece of rawhide to bite on, grumbling that he never thought he'd see the day he'd gladly pour whiskey down an Indian's gullet.

"Ain't nothin' more dangerous than a drunk Indian," he mumbled, using more whiskey to pour into the wound. "And I ain't so sure I want to save his life. You sure he's worth it?"

Faith sat down on the other side of the cot, watching Tall Bear's glazed eyes, thinking how here again was something she never would have experienced back in Pennsylvania. "He's worth it. I assure you, Buck, he's no danger to me. I owe him, and I appreciate your doing this for me."

"Well, he did help you a time back with your husband and all. I suppose you do owe him, but he could just as soon have killed you earlier today if he'd fired too quick once he got in here."

"He went after the horses and got himself hurt doing it, and he killed two more of those men. That's all we need to know. You've got to keep this quiet, Buck. I don't want soldiers coming after him."

Buck shook his head, removing the chimney of an oil lamp and holding Tall Bear's own hunting knife over the flame. "Whatever you say. I've always respected your opinions and wants, ma'am."

Faith smiled. "I wish you would call me Faith, Buck. It's all right."

"Well, maybe I can do that. I ain't never been much for callin' respectable women by their first names."

"Oh? And do you know a lot of women who are *not* respectable?"

He chuckled. "A few." He sighed and leaned over Tall Bear. "You'd best let go of his hand, else he might squeeze yours so hard, he breaks it."

Faith stood up, taking Tall Bear's hand and placing it on the round iron railing at the head of the cot. "Try gripping this with both hands," she told him. "It might help."

Tall Bear had said nothing since she'd come back inside the depot with Buck. He seemed dazed, and Faith figured it was from loss of blood. He gripped the railing as she'd suggested, and she was glad he seemed to understand. She was equally glad Johnny had fallen asleep on his cot, worn out from the frightening events of the day. She just hoped Tall Bear didn't cry out so loudly that he woke the boy up. She wouldn't want him to see Buck cutting into someone.

Tall Bear watched her, feeling as though he were floating in a different world. For almost four years he had thought about this woman off and on, wondered where she had gone. He had never expected to find her still here at the stage depot, let alone running the place by herself. He had never known such a brave white woman, didn't think they were even capable of the things this woman had done. She was as beautiful as ever, a hardy kind of beauty that spoke of strength and determination. She reminded him of some Indian women he'd known, reminded him of his own mother. White people like Faith Sommers made him understand that such settlers were there to stay, too stubborn and too brave to turn back.

Strangely, her presence gave him more courage to face

the awful pain of what Buck was about to do to him. He liked Buck, although he had not even spoken to the man yet. Buck was another tough one, the kind of white man who would fight an Indian to the death but still be respected by that Indian. Tall Bear knew that such men, too, were the reason no Indian tribe was going to stop whites from settling in this land.

He stiffened then when he felt the knife dig into him, grateful for the whiskey but wishing for oblivion. He'd heard Faith mention something called laudanum, but she did not have any, and she had only a couple bottles of whiskey, for "medicinal purposes," she'd said. She considered whiskey an evil drink when taken for pleasure, something Tall Bear himself had always believed; yet he had fallen into those evil ways himself a few months ago, turning to a life of lawlessness because he didn't know what else to do with himself.

Buck dug deeper, and Tall Bear bit hard on the rawhide, gripping the railing. He growled with the pain but did not cry out, for that would be cowardly. He drew on past experiences, the Sun Dance sacrifice, the times when he had cut his own flesh in mourning. He was not unfamiliar with pain, and he supposed he'd get through this pain, too. Somehow he felt that if he kept his eyes on Faith Sommers's beautiful blue eyes, so full of kindness, he would survive this. He noticed that her dress matched those eyes, and now she looked different from when he'd first attacked the station.

That hair. He remembered again how it had looked this morning, messy, hanging in wild waves and tangles, her dress buttoned crooked. He'd liked what he saw. He would be glad when this was over and they could talk. He was sorry for what had happened this morning, sorry for frightening her little boy.

His vision began to blur. Somewhere in the distance he heard Buck say something about finding the bullet. "Soon as I get this out, I'll bury the men," he was saying. He vaguely remembered hearing soldiers in the outer room earlier, hearing Faith tell them they had better get going, as she'd heard there were outlaws somewhere waiting for them. So the woman had protected him. She could just as easily have turned him over to the soldiers. Apparently Buck Hanner was also protecting him. He did not doubt that was for Faith, not because Buck had any liking for an Indian.

He kept his eyes on her. She was the kind of woman men would do anything to please. She apparently had a talent for taking charge of things, and just enough feminine charm to make a man do things he would never otherwise do—like ride after his own comrades, shoot them down, and take the horses back. She hadn't even asked—it had just been that look in her eyes at losing the horses.

He noticed she never took her eyes from his as he strained against the pain. Finally things went completely black, but he could hear her voice.

"Do you think we can stop the bleeding?"

"Help me wrap it tight. That's all we can do," Buck answered, "and hope it don't get infected."

Tall Bear felt hands, smelled the scent of a woman. Whatever they were doing, the pain had subsided a great deal. Apparently Buck had removed the bullet. Now all he had to do was heal quickly enough to get the hell out of there before soldiers found out about him. Faith Sommers couldn't hide him forever.

Tall Bear slowly opened his eyes, not sure what time of day it was. He looked around the room, trying to get his bearings, taking a moment to remember what had happened, where he was. He heard voices in the outer room then, familiar voices. After a moment he realized it was the man called Buck and the woman he'd almost killed this morning . . . if indeed this was still the same day.

"You sure I can leave you alone here?" Buck was asking Faith.

"I'm sure. Besides, right now he's weak and wounded, and I have my rifle. I'll be careful, Buck."

"Well, it don't seem right leavin' you here with a savage lyin' in the other room there, one who run with outlaws, besides."

Tall Bear heard someone shout from outside for Buck to

hurry up so they could go. He heard a horse whinny. He looked around for his own weapons, but someone had removed them all. He tried to rise, managing to get to a sitting position but feeling dizzy.

Buck argued more with Faith, then told her to be "damn careful." Tall Bear heard a door close, heard a whistle and someone shout "Giddap there!" Then there was the sound of several horses, squeaking harness, the clatter of a wagon or coach. He was just wondering how he was going to get himself outside to relieve himself when Faith came into the room, a rifle in hand. She looked surprised to see him up and awake. "You shouldn't be moving around. You'll cause that wound to start bleeding again."

He reached out and grabbed the edge of a chest of drawers to pull himself up. "I have something personal to take care of."

Faith thought how he seemed to fill the little back room when he stood up. Was she crazy to send Buck off with the eastbound stage and be left there alone with this "savage," as Buck had called him? It would be three or four more days before another stage came through. She pointed the rifle barrel toward a curtained-off area in the corner of the room. "There's a chamber pot behind those curtains. Use that. Just be sure to put the lid back on. You're too weak to try to walk all the way out to the privy."

"I don't want to make work for you."

She felt like laughing. "I already went through hell yesterday because of you, Tall Bear, and you scared the wits out of my little boy. Compared to all of that, creating a little work for me is nothing. Do what you have to do and don't worry about it. I'll go fix you some broth. You should eat something. And I'll bring you a cup of water."

He glanced at the now-open curtains to the doorway that led into the main room. "Are you alone now?"

"I'm alone, but you already know I can shoot straight. Remember that."

This time it was Tall Bear who felt like smiling, but he was in too much pain. "I will remember." He put a hand to his side. "This happened yesterday?"

"Yes. You slept all through the day and night."

He looked down at his bandages. "Your friend Buck must know what he is doing. I do not see much bleeding." He met her eyes. "You must know I would not harm you. I got back your horses for you. Doesn't that prove anything?"

Faith lowered the rifle. "We'll talk about it later." She left the room, her mind racing with indecision. Tall Bear was in no shape to leave yet. She would be alone with the man that day, probably that night, maybe more than a night. He was apparently capable of living two different lives—a man who could be kind and gentle, but also ruthless. How did she know when he might change from one to the other?

Maybe it had been wrong of her to tell Buck not to mention Tall Bear to the driver who had come through that morning. Buck had told him about the outlaws but had said he was the one who had shot them, that they had attacked the station the night before. He had explained that he had stayed there the night with Faith because she had seen suspicious-looking men who had come around earlier in the day, and she'd wanted him to stay. Buck had insisted that the man should not know Faith had killed two of the men and wounded another. She was grateful but a little amused by his efforts to protect her femininity, and she loved Buck for not mentioning Tall Bear.

Now at least the bodies were buried, and Tall Bear had a little time to recuperate. No one would know he had taken part in the raid, and maybe if he quit riding with outlaws now, he would not have to worry about being caught and hanged as a horse thief and, she didn't doubt, murderer.

As she stirred the chicken soup she was making for Tall Bear, she heard a movement and turned to see him standing at the curtained doorway, still wearing only his buckskin leggings. She and Buck had removed his shirt and moccasins. His middle was wrapped with gauze, and he still wore the bear-claw necklace he'd had on when he'd arrived. She remembered he'd worn it the first time she'd met him, and she wondered if he ever took it off.

"I told you you shouldn't be up."

He grimaced as he grabbed chairs and furniture, making

his way to the front door. "I will go outside to the proper place."

Faith scowled. "Don't be so damn proud. It's too dangerous for you to be walking around yet."

"I have suffered worse than this." He opened the door, glancing at Johnny, who sat on his cot holding a stuffed cow and staring at him with big brown eyes. He forced a smile for him, then looked back at Faith. "Tell him he does not have to be afraid of me. I am glad he was not hurt. I did not know there was a child in here."

Faith glowered at him. "No. You thought there was only a helpless old woman in here! Is there a difference? A human life is a human life."

"We were only going to ride in and surprise her, keep her out of the way while we waited for the stagecoach. We did not intend to harm her."

Faith's laughter rang of sarcasm. "Hilda would have given you just as much of a fight as I did. She was good with a rifle, fought Indians and outlaws on her own before I ever showed up. She—" Faith realized suddenly, as she felt again the pangs of guilt for being partly responsible for poor Hilda's death, that Tall Bear should be told about Clete Brown's coming back. "She was killed last fall. I'll explain later. And you owe *me* an explanation for why you were running with worthless white rabble like those who attacked this place. Right now you had better go take care of things and get back into bed. And don't you pass out somewhere out there. I could never drag someone your size back inside, and if someone came along, they'd see you, and there would be nothing I could do about it. I used every effort I had to convince Buck not to tell anyone about you, and I've not mentioned you to anyone else, so don't go ruining all my good efforts."

He looked her over, thinking how she could behave in an almost manly fashion, speaking with conviction and authority, her hands showing hard work, her face plain, leather lace-up work boots on her feet rather than the more feminine shoes he'd seen other white women wear. The outlaws he'd run with often hung out with white whores who did business with them at their various hiding places throughout Utah and Wyoming, and he'd bedded a couple of them himself. He found most of them grossly unattractive and was repulsed by their lewd lifestyle, but a couple of them had been pleasantly pretty and soft-spoken . . . and they had reminded him of Faith Sommers. He realized now that that was part of the reason he'd satisfied his curiosity about bedding a white woman, and at the moment he couldn't help wondering how this one looked naked. She was as pretty as he'd remembered—chapped hands, work boots, and all.

"I will not be long," he told her. "And my years with the Sioux taught me to rise above pain and weakness. I will not fall."

After he left, Faith shivered at the way he'd looked at her, so appraisingly. What irritated her most was that she had not minded. She walked over to Johnny and picked him up. "Everything is all right, Johnny. That man staying here is a good man. He likes you. He is called Tall Bear. Can you say 'Tall Bear'?"

The boy seemed much more relaxed than yesterday. "Tah Bay," he repeated.

"That's very good, Johnny." She kissed his cheek and set him at his own little table. "You sit real still here, and Mommy will get you something to eat." She dipped some of the soup into a bowl and brought it over to spoon-feed the boy, not trusting him yet to eat something like soup without spilling it everywhere.

She began feeding him, waiting, surprised Tall Bear could really walk all the way out back, worried he'd never make it. She remembered some of Buck's talk about Indians. *Them bucks is a tough bunch,* he'd said once during one of his tall tales about his experiences out here. *I've seen 'em get shot off a horse and get right back on and keep comin' after you. Some of them go through some kind of ritual where they starve themselves for four or five days and then somebody puts skewers under the skin of their chest and they're tied to a pole and hang from them until the flesh tears away.* Faith had scolded him for telling her such a lurid tale, and she could hardly believe it was true, but after Tall Bear had passed out yesterday and they'd taken off his shirt, Buck had pointed to the strange scars above his breasts she'd seen the first time she'd met him. *What'd I tell you?* he'd said.

Faith shivered at the thought. There certainly was a lot about Tall Bear she did not understand. Maybe he would explain some of it to her, why Indian men would do such a thing. Was it a test of strength? Of endurance?

When he returned, he looked pale and drawn. She got up from feeding Johnny and went to him. "You'd better get back on that cot. I'll bring you some water and broth."

He made no argument, but he refused to let her help him. He made his way into the back room and lay back down. Faith brought him soup and a cup of water.

"Will you eat something?"

When he looked at her again with that gleam of interest in his eyes, Faith wished she could read his thoughts. Was he laughing at her appearance? Did he think her pretty? Silly looking? Was she already starting to look old? Ever since Tod Harding had visited, she'd been studying herself in the mirror, trying to decide how she might look to others. She chastised herself for caring.

She set the food on a small table and pulled a chair next to the bed, then grabbed some extra pillows from the three other cots kept for guests and helped Tall Bear sit up so she could stack the pillows behind him. She sat down, dipped a spoon into the soup, and held it out.

"I will feed myself," he scowled.

"Don't be so stubborn. You've done enough just walking outside. To feed yourself, you'd have to sit up on the edge of the bed, and that might put too much pressure on the wound. You're lucky you haven't already opened something back up. The bloodstain on that gauze isn't any bigger than it was when you left, so be glad the bleeding has stopped again. Lie still and let me feed you, at least this one time. Maybe by tomorrow morning you can do it yourself."

Tall Bear had to admit it smelled good, and food could help him heal. He opened his mouth when she held the spoon next to it, and he swallowed the broth. "It is good," he told her.

"Thank you."

She fed him silently, their gazes often meeting, their eyes full of questions. Finally he reached over and picked up the bowl, tipping it and drinking out the rest of the broth. He sucked a couple small pieces of chicken into his mouth and handed back the bowl. "I will rest now. I will leave by tomorrow morning so that you can be at peace."

Faith took the bowl from him. "Not without telling me a little more about why on earth you were riding with men like that, I hope."

He drank some water and rested his head against the pillows. "Because I belong nowhere, not with my Indian people, and not with the whites."

"I don't understand."

He looked at her sullenly. "I am not surprised."

"Tall Bear, I *want* to understand. Please help me."

He studied her for several silent seconds, then sighed in resignation. In spite of the weakness of his voice his words rang with bitter hatred. "I told you my father was killed by white men. My mother took me back to her people, and I grew up among them . . . and then soldiers killed my mother and her new husband and their little girl. Later white buffalo hunters killed my wife and boy."

"None of that explains how you ended up with those men."

"For a long time I wanted only to kill whites. I rode with the raiders in Minnesota. I killed many white men, but one day I had the chance to kill a white woman." He hesitated, and it was obvious the next words were difficult. "I could not do it."

Faith felt a flood of relief, not even sure why it mattered.

"Not killing the woman made me feel weak, but I knew my father would have thought it was wrong." He took a deep breath. "The woman ran into the house, and I went in after her because I thought there was another white man inside. Her husband already lay dead on the front steps, shot by one of those who rode with me. But I knew that someone in there had a gun. When I got inside . . . I saw a movement . . . and I turned and shot at it." He was quiet again for a moment. "It was a young boy."

"Dear God," Faith whispered. "Did you . . . kill him?"

"No, but it is bad enough that I did shoot him and he suffered. I took him and the woman to a fort where the boy could get help. I rode off . . . so the soldiers would not catch me, and I later learned the boy lived. After coming farther west I . . . made war with Red Cloud. That is when I nearly killed an old man . . . who was once a friend to my white father. I knew then I did not fully belong with the Sioux. My father's friend convinced me . . . that I could help the Sioux by scouting for the army, act as an interpreter, help convince the Sioux and Cheyenne to go to the reservations and avoid more fighting. But then an army officer betrayed me, caused me to betray unwillingly some peaceful Cheyenne. I led soldiers to their camp, and then the soldiers attacked and murdered them, even though . . . they were making no trouble."

It was obvious to Faith that the pain of what had happened still ran deep. He paused, clearly hurting and growing weaker again.

"Tall Bear, if you can't go on—"

"I must explain." He grimaced as he shifted in the bed. "Again my heart was torn as to where I truly belonged. I wanted to kill the officer in charge, but he was shot during the fighting. I decided I belonged nowhere, and I just left . . . my people, the army, all of it. I wandered . . . and then I came to a place called Brown's Hole. I could see the white men there were bad, but it mattered little to me. For the first time . . . I tried white man's whiskey . . . and it made me feel good. One of them started mocking me because I am Indian, and we ended up in a fight. I beat him badly . . . then stabbed him to death. The others seemed to respect me for my fighting skill, said I should join them in raiding banks in small towns, stagecoaches that carry payroll . . . places like this, where we can get free supplies for the price of a bullet. I decided perhaps that kind of life was all I was good for . . . so I joined them. I have not been with them long, only long enough to learn to like whiskey and to shoot a handgun from the hip . . . to play the white man's card game called poker and to lie with—"

He paused and Faith reddened, astonished that she felt a pang of jealousy! She felt angry when a faint smile moved across his mouth. "With bad women. I did not like them so much. I prefer Indian women." He closed his eyes again. "Now I have betrayed both my own people and white men. . . ." His gaze rested on her again. "And I almost betrayed you. Again I could have hurt a small boy . . . and that hurts my heart. You must believe me when I tell you I would not have allowed the old woman to be hurt if she were the one who had been here."

She thought about all he'd told her, trying to imagine what it must be like to live between two worlds as he did. "All right. And if you want the truth, I feel responsible for that old woman's death myself. The white man who killed my husband did live. He came through here one day, found me. He tried to kill me, and he would have if Hilda hadn't found us and stopped him. He turned and shot her, but Hilda got off a shot herself and she killed him. She died shortly after. I've killed both Indians and white men myself, Tall Bear, things I never thought I'd be capable of doing, but we do what we have to do to survive. In a way that's what you've been doing. I've left my family back in Pennsylvania, vowing never to go back, so I suppose I understand better than you think about feeling as though you belong nowhere. The main reason I'm here is because I have no place else to go, but also because I am determined to survive, and running this place has given me a way to do that. Wells Fargo provides all the supplies. It gets very lonely sometimes, but when the railroad comes through, I think this place is going to grow. I just hope I can hold on that long."

A smirk moved across his lips. "You are a fool to stay here. Think about your son. And you are still young. You should have a man for yourself, a father for your son."

This last remark irritated her, but she had to admit there had been several times already when she'd needed Buck to help her. She hated being dependent on anyone, was determined to reach the point where she could do anything a man could do. Still, he was right. She had to think about Johnny and the danger to him. Yesterday had made that more apparent. The idea came to her then, but she hesitated, thinking he would laugh, would assume she truly had lost her mind. It was a ridiculous request.

"I know my son needs a father," she replied, "but I have no desire for—" She reddened. What was she saying! And to this wild Indian! "I don't care to be controlled by a man," she finished. "I like my independence here, and Johnny sees plenty of men, some fancy and important, others just good, honest, hard-boned men like Buck. If I can get a school in here someday, maybe build a little town, he'll have the education he needs. If life ever comes to that, maybe then I'll have time to think about marrying again, but right now it's the last thing I want."

She got up from the chair and picked up the bowl, leaving the cup, which still had water in it. She turned to the doorway, still not sure about her idea.

"I did not mean to offend you," he told her.

Faith looked back at him. "You didn't. In fact, you gave me an idea, something that could solve your own problem of not belonging anywhere."

"Oh?" Again he grimaced as he adjusted his position. "And how can I do that?"

Did she dare ask? It was a crazy idea. It was living this lonely life, that's what it was. Too long away from civilization had made her a crazy woman . . . or perhaps just a desperate woman. "You could . . . you could stay here—work for me."

He frowned in utter astonishment. "What do you mean?"

She set the bowl on top of a chest of drawers, the idea beginning to make sense. "You could stay here, guard the place for me, help with the horses, stacking wood, all the things that are so difficult for me now that Hilda is gone and I have a little boy to watch. You're obviously good with a gun, and outlaws are becoming more of a problem than Indians. The best part is that you can handle either one. You know how to talk to Indians. I'm sure that the authorities for Wells Fargo would let me hire anyone I want. I've been here long enough that they should trust my judgment."

He appeared upset, yet she knew he was thinking over the idea. "No," he answered. "It would not be good for me to stay."

"You could dress more like a white man. No one would know you're really Tall Bear, the Indian who rode with outlaws. I doubt they even know what that Indian was called. I heard him referred to only as 'the Indian.'" She drew a deep breath for courage. "The pay wouldn't be much, but you'd be out in wild country, which you love. You could take care of the horses and have free room and board, free meals, except that you'd have to go out and kill our meat once in a while. Since you say you have no place else to go, why not stay on right here? You can sleep in the cow shed. It's small but not such a bad place. Think about it."

He looked away, and she had not been able to read his expression before he did so. She left the room, figuring she'd given him food for thought, but certainly not out of any wisdom on her part.

She cleaned up the depot, washed Johnny's face and hands, and walked outside to enjoy the silence . . . and to think. What choice did she have if she loved Johnny? She either needed someone to help her here, or she would have to leave, and leaving would break her heart. Besides that, where would she go?

She let Johnny run and play, watched him carefully, played ball with him for a little while. When she went back inside, she looked in on Tall Bear to see what he would have to say, but he appeared to be sleeping. Later, after she put Johnny to bed, she peeked into the back room again. Tall Bear still slept.

She took down one of her rifles and kept a lantern dimly lit in the outer room. She sat down and read an old Bible of Hilda's until she was sleepy. She got up and checked on him once more. His breathing was steady, and when she reached out hesitantly to touch his forehead, his skin was cool.

She walked back to the main room and lay down on her

bed, pulling a blanket over herself. She left the rifle standing against the wall at the head of the bed within reaching distance. The tension of the day quickly caught up with her, and although she meant to take time thinking about the daring offer she had made to Tall Bear, her thoughts quickly drifted into sleep.

She had no idea how long she had slept before she heard it, the sound of a horse galloping away. She gasped and sat straight up. It was morning already—how had that happened? She was sure she'd gone to sleep only an hour or so ago. And what was that horse she'd heard?

She jumped up to check on Tall Bear. Her heart fell when she saw he was not on the cot. Surely he hadn't—

"Damn him!" she muttered. She grabbed her rifle and went out onto the porch. Everything was still. She hurried to the cow shed, where she had left Tall Bear's horse. It was gone. *"Why?"* she cried, surprised at her own disappointment. He had left without a word, not even bothered to say no, he couldn't stay and work for her. The least he could have done was give himself some time to heal, let her make him breakfast.

The realization of how alone she was after the trauma of the outlaw attack hit her hard, and although it seemed silly, Tall Bear's leaving made her cry. She *needed* to cry. She stood there weeping, feeling like a fool, feeling lost and abandoned.

She wiped her eyes. "Damn you! Damn you! Damn you!" she repeated. "I don't want to be alone anymore." What angered her more than his leaving was her own true reasons why she'd wanted him to stay. He was the most unusual man she had ever met, the first man since Johnny to whom she had felt an attraction. It made no sense.

She walked wearily back to the depot. She would have to be ever alert from now on. Maybe Tall Bear himself would return with Indians or more outlaws. Who could tell what he was thinking?

She felt bone tired, her nerves shattered, her heart hurting from disappointment. There had been so much more she had wanted to talk about. When she had first thought to have Tall Bear work for her, she had felt instantly safe at the thought of his being in charge of her and Johnny's safety. How strange that she should think that, after the events of yesterday morning. Still, she could understand his actions—a little. He was a very confused man.

And now she was a very confused woman.

Chapter Twenty

Faith counted her money from the sale of horses, saddles, and other supplies "inherited" from outlaws who had tried to ruin her. Some had been sold to drifters coming through, most to a supply salesman headed for Salt Lake City.

Four hundred dollars! She squeezed the money in her hands, sure she should feel guilty for how she had attained her little fortune, but unable to feel anything but victorious. She had earned even more money through her pay from Wells Fargo, and she had a total of seven hundred dollars in cash, some greenbacks, most in gold and silver coins.

She had intended to use the money to add a rooming house on to the station, maybe even find a way to build a real house for herself once Sommers Station became a full-fledged town; but now she still had to decide if she should even continue her life there. She was alone again, and she still had not received a reply to any of her ads. She had to face the fact that Sommers Station could become nothing but a brief moment in history once Wells Fargo's stage line went out of business. In spite of Tod Harding's promise that the station would become a major railroad depot, she had not heard from the man, and now with Tall Bear gone, she was for the first time truly losing hope for her dream.

She climbed up on a chair and returned the money to its new hiding place above a beam in the low ceiling. Mice had invaded the former hiding place in the wall, and she worried they would eat the greenbacks. She contemplated where she should go if she had to leave there. How much longer did she have the right to risk poor Johnny's future, perhaps his very life, by staying there?

The rest of April had brought a return of rainy, dreary, miserably cold weather, unusually wet for those parts, and the depressing weather only enhanced the depression in her own heart. She hated feeling that way, hated being afraid, being so uncertain about the future, her own abilities.

She climbed down from the chair, a new worry burdening her heart. Johnny was sick. So far she'd been able to treat him with hot tea and soup, but she didn't know what else to do for him. It seemed to be only a cold, and he was a healthy boy otherwise. She had taken for granted the likelihood that he would have the sniffles for a few days, and that would be the end of it, but his breathing seemed dangerously labored and was not getting any better.

She was already washed and dressed and had heated more water for tea for the child, but he seemed to be sleeping more soundly now. Still, she felt a strange alarm. She glanced at the mantel clock, listening to its soft tick. Nine-thirty. Johnny had never slept that late in the morning before. She walked over and bent closer to listen to his rattled breathing. That was when she noticed that his face was nearly crimson.

"Oh, God," she whispered. She reached out and touched his cheek. It was burning hot. "Johnny," she whimpered. What was happening to her baby? Maybe he wasn't sleeping at all—maybe he was dying. "Johnny," she said louder.

She wrapped his blanket fully around him and picked him up, sitting down in a rocker with him. He opened his eyes, eyes that were normally big and bright. Now they were only slits, the whites of his eyes bloodshot. He began coughing, a deep, rumbling cough that put terror in her heart.

She kissed his cheek, hot to her lips. "We'll sweat out the fever and you'll be all right, baby," she told him softly, struggling not to reveal her fear over how sick he was. She held him close. He was frighteningly listless. She remembered tales she'd heard among the women back in Pennsylvania when she was younger, about what prolonged fever did to a child. *It can damage the brain,* they'd said. She remembered a little girl among the Quakers who had died of "the fever." Lung congestion was also dangerous. Even adults sometimes died of fever and lung congestion.

"Oh, dear God," she whispered. "Not my baby. Not my Johnny. Please don't take him from me. He's all I've got." She rocked the boy, holding him close to her bosom. "I know I've done some bad things, God, but I didn't have any choice. I never wanted to kill anybody, and I didn't steal their horses and things, not really. I only sold them because they were left here. What else was I to do? I had to protect myself and my baby."

God wouldn't punish her this way, would he? Maybe he was angry for all those years ago when she wouldn't sit still and concentrate during prayer meetings. Maybe he was punishing her for killing men, for leaving Pennsylvania. Who could say? She'd done so many wrong things.

"God, please don't do this to me! I'll have nothing left to live for without my Johnny!" She'd had so much hope and courage until lately, had never doubted her decisions. There would not be another stage come through for at least four days. There was no one to turn to, no one to advise her on what to do for her baby.

She longed for her mother, missed her, needed her. Her mother would know what to do about this. Perhaps if she tried to force the sweat out of Johnny, she could rid his body of the poison that ravaged it. She wrapped his blanket even closer, her mind racing with indecision. She struggled to remember remedies she'd heard from Hilda and from her mother about what to do for such ailments, but in her panicked state she could think of nothing but to hold her baby close and try to comfort him, to make him sweat even more and hold him in a sitting position so he could breathe better.

The boy's body jerked, and he began coughing again, nearly choking on the phlegm. She reached into a pocket of her dress and pulled out a handkerchief, bending the boy over and patting his back as he coughed more, hardly able to stop now. He coughed up more phlegm, and she wiped it away with the handkerchief. Her heart ached at his obvious misery. It seemed every breath he took might be his last, and the fact that he said nothing and seemed so lifeless filled her heart with black dread that he was already very near death.

"Oh, God, oh, God," she whimpered. "Please, please help me. Show me what to do to save my baby. Don't let him suffer this way." She realized then how helpless Johnny would be if the tables were turned and she were the one who was sick. She could even die out here, and Johnny could freeze to death, starve to death, with no one to care for him. Yes, she had to leave this place. Once she got Johnny well, she would leave. If he died, she would shoot herself and be buried right there with him.

Finally the coughing subsided, but when she returned the child to the crook of her arm, he looked dazed. He didn't cry, he didn't talk. He only looked at her, pitifully helpless, seemingly asking his mother to please do something for him. But there was nothing she could do.

"I love you, Johnny. Mommy loves you. You'll be okay." She kissed his hot cheek again, aching for his misery, wishing she would see the normal brightness in his eyes, his boyish winning smile, the dimples in his cheeks. Maybe she would never see those things again.

She put her head back and rocked, humming a soft tune for him, secretly, desperately praying, struggling to keep from screaming and weeping. Her humming turned to mutterings to God, again begging his help. She rocked and prayed, rocked and prayed, stunned by this sudden terrible sickness. She was so lost in her dilemma and sorrow that she did not even notice the first knock at the door. When whoever was outside pounded a little harder, it startled her out of her near stupor, and she gasped with alarm. Who in

the world could it be? No stage was due, and she had not
heard anyone ride in. She got up from the rocker.

Maybe whoever it was could help her with Johnny!
She'd been praying for God to show her what to do.
Maybe this was her answer. She carefully laid Johnny back
down on his cot, then took down the rifle from over the
door. She went to one of the windows first. Buck had fixed
the broken shutters for her, and now she kept the shutters
of both windows closed and barred. She peeked through
the gun hole at a foggy, rainy morning. She saw a horse
tied outside the porch, an Appaloosa. Another Appaloosa
was tied behind it, used for a packhorse. The horses looked
familiar.

"Tall Bear," she whispered. He had come back! She
moved to the door. "Tall Bear, is that you out there?"

"It is," came the reply.

She lifted away the bar across the door and stepped
back. "Come in," she called to him.

The door opened, and Tall Bear walked inside to see
Faith holding a rifle on him. He closed the door, standing
there quietly, not surprised she still didn't trust him.

Faith stared at him in surprise. He'd been gone over
three weeks. Now he stood before her washed and shaved,
and he had cut his hair to shoulder length. He was wearing
dark cotton pants, leather boots, a white man's yellow
slicker, and a leather hat. Through the open front of the
slicker she could see he wore a six-gun belted to his hip,
and she saw a dark shirt and a short wool jacket. He was
dressed as a white man.

"Tall Bear, where have you been? Why are you—"

"I have decided I will stay and work for you," he interrupted. How could he tell her the truth—that she had
haunted his dreams? How could he tell her the reason he
left the first time was because he was afraid of his own
feelings for this feisty, independent woman—a woman
who would never be interested in a half-breed who had
raided and killed not only with the Sioux, but with white
outlaws. Still, he had not been able to stay away, and the
fact remained that he needed honest work.

Faith stepped back, lowering her rifle.

"I thought you would still want me here to help. If you want me to go, I will go."

Faith shook her head. "It isn't that. I—" She glanced over at Johnny. "It's just that I can't talk about this right now. I can't make any decisions." She moved her gaze back to Tall Bear. "Actually, you couldn't have come at a better time. I'm scared, Tall Bear. My son is very sick. I'm afraid—" The words caught in her throat, and she felt so helpless. "I'm afraid he's dying." She choked in a sudden sob and covered her mouth, letting the tears flow. In the next moment she felt a hand on her shoulder, and she was resting her head against his chest and crying. Never had she been so aware that she needed to be held, needed someone else's strength. In Tall Bear's arms she felt the first real comfort she had known other than when her own mother had embraced her.

"I don't know what to do, Tall Bear. He has a terrible fever and cough, and he's so listless. He looks at me as though he doesn't even know me."

She felt him removing the rifle from her hand, and she did not object. "Come," he told her. "We will see what we can do for him."

He led her over to the cot and leaned over Johnny, removing the blanket from around him and feeling his hot skin. "You are right," he told her. "This is bad. You must cool him down right away or he will die."

Faith wiped at tears. "I—I thought I should keep him wrapped tight, make him sweat it out."

He shook his head. "No. You must remove his clothing and immerse him in cool water. You must bring the fever down, or it will affect his brain. While you do that, I must leave. I will bring something back with me that will help. While I am gone, put a pan of water on the cookstove and heat it."

"No, don't leave me here alone! You won't come back."

"I promise that I will. I already came back once, didn't I?" He grasped her arms, forcing her to meet his gaze.

Faith saw truth there in his exotic green eyes.

"It is an old Indian remedy. You must trust me. I have caused you enough hurt. I would not lie to you about this.

Get your son into cool water right away, then wrap him again as soon as he is out so that he does not shiver with chill. Heat the pan of water. I will be back soon." He grabbed his hat and slicker again, leaving the jacket behind as he left without further explanation. Faith ran to the window and opened the shutters to watch him riding away. He had left behind his packhorse, which seemed to guarantee his return. She felt sorry for him, riding off into the cold rain, but if it was for something that would help Johnny, then so be it.

She quickly set a wash pan on the stove, then poured already-heated water from the kettle into the pan, building up the fire under the burner to keep the water in both vessels hot. Next she took down a washtub that hung on a wall and set it beside Johnny's cot. She poured two buckets of water into it, praying that Tall Bear was right about how to bring down the fever. It just didn't seem safe to put Johnny's little fevered body into cool water. She would never have thought to do such a thing, afraid it would kill him, but if this was something the Sioux had always done, perhaps there was some use to it. After all, they were a people who had to survive out here with no white man's help, no doctors, no fancy potions and creams. She remembered Buck saying once that the Indians had their own kind of medicine and seemed to do "right good" at treating their own sicknesses.

What other choice did she have? To leave things as they were would surely mean Johnny's death. She unwrapped him, and he made only a little whimpering sound as she undressed him. It was as though he did not have the energy to cry. Perhaps he had a sore throat on top of the fever and congestion. Perhaps he simply could not get enough air to cry. His little head rolled back and his arms hung limp when she picked him up, but his body jerked when she set him in the cool water. He made another whimpering sound.

"I'm sorry, Johnny, but Mommy is only trying to do what's best for you." She cupped water in her hand and began pouring it over his forehead to cool his skull, face, and neck. After a few minutes he seemed to come more alert. He kicked and splashed water, then began the awful coughing again, so fierce, she was sure he would choke to death on phlegm or die simply from the inability to draw enough air into his congested lungs. "Please hurry, Tall Bear," she prayed, still terrified for her little boy.

Finally the coughing subsided, but he seemed completely worn out just from the effort. She scooped more water over his face and head, leaned him forward, and poured some over the back of his neck and over his back. His skin finally seemed cooler, and she decided she had better take him out and wrap him before he became too chilled. She swaddled him in a blanket and carried him to the rocker to sit down and wait for Tall Bear, wondering if she was a total fool to trust him this way. She rocked Johnny, listening for the return of a horse.

After about twenty minutes she finally heard him returning. He came through the door, his big frame seeming to fill the room. He held what looked like pieces of bark in his hands, and he set them on the table, then removed his wet slicker and his hat, hanging both things on the wall. Faith noticed that without the extra coats he still seemed intimidating in size, and he still wore the six-gun.

"I have brought the bark of red cedar," he told her. "I will boil it in the water. As soon as it releases its oils, I will take Johnny over to the boiling water and put a blanket over us. You will have to watch the blanket to be sure it does not get near open flame. I need to make a kind of tent over us so that your son breathes the steam from the bark. It will help clear his lungs. My people have used this for many generations to chase away the lung sickness."

Faith clung to Johnny. "Does it always work?"

He walked over and broke the bark into little pieces, placing them into the wash pan, which was already steaming. "Most of the time."

"*Most* of the time?"

He poured more water from the kettle into the pan. "Nothing in this life is sure. I know only that this usually helps. The rest is in God's hands."

She thought it strange he should say that, as though he believed in her God. The room was silent for the next few minutes. Faith continued to rock Johnny, and Tall Bear poked at the bark, stirring it a little. He leaned down, sniffed it, and after several minutes told her to bring the boy to him, along with an extra blanket. Faith decided she had no choice but to trust him.

She carried the baby to Tall Bear, their gazes holding as she handed him over. "He's all I have," she reminded him.

"I know the feeling of loving a son," he answered, taking the boy into his arms, "and how it feels to lose one to death."

She saw the pain in his eyes. "I'm sorry. I'm thinking only of myself and my own son."

"That is as it should be. Put the extra blanket over my head. Once the water in the pan is boiling hard, I will take him over and sit on the cot with him. You can carry the pan and set it on the floor, and we will continue to sit over the steam, using the blanket to hold it in."

Faith tossed the blanket over their heads, and Tall Bear leaned over the pan. Faith checked all around carefully to be sure the blanket did not touch any open drafts on the front of the stove, and she made sure to keep lifting the hem so it did not rest too long on the hot wrought-iron stove. For several minutes Tall Bear held the boy over the water, and she thought how he must be getting hot and sweaty under there himself, and that his arms must be getting tired from holding Johnny, but he hardly moved. Finally Johnny began coughing again. He gagged, and she heard Tall Bear pounding on his back. He told her then to quickly bring the pan over to the cot, and he carried Johnny there, sitting down on the edge. He talked to the boy softly in the Sioux tongue, and Faith was amazed that the boy was not crying at being held by a stranger—such a big, intimidating man at that, a man he'd seen attack the station only a month ago. On top of that Tall Bear was talking to him in a strange language. Perhaps the boy was simply too dazed to understand what was happening to him.

She set the pan at the edge of the cot on the floor, thinking how good the steaming cedar smelled. Tall Bear hovered over it, he and Johnny covered with the blanket again. Johnny coughed more, but already his cough seemed even looser, so that he was able to bring up more phlegm, which she thought must be good.

"I'm sorry you have to sit under there like that," she told Tall Bear. "I can sit with him for a while if you want."

"I am fine," he told her. "I have sat in the sweat lodge many times for purification. It is much hotter than this. It is good for the lungs, and good for the soul."

Faith frowned, not sure what a sweat lodge was. It was something she would have to ask him about when this was over . . . if things ended happily. Nothing would matter to her if Johnny didn't make it. She would never forgive herself for staying where there was no doctor's help for her son.

Minutes seemed like hours, and finally a good hour did pass before she heard Johnny speak. "Ta Baew," he said. Her heart leaped with joy at the words.

"No," Tall Bear answered. "That is no longer my name, Johnny. I am Gabe. Can you say Gabe?"

"Gabe," the boy said after a moment. He actually giggled, but then he began coughing again.

"That is good, Johnny. Get all the poison out of your lungs. Don't be afraid of it."

Faith could hardly believe how gentle and patient the man was with Johnny, and it struck her how much he must have loved his own son, what an awful thing it must have been to see the child murdered. No wonder he had gone on raids against whites.

Tall Bear removed the blanket, his own face covered with sweat. To Faith's astonishment Johnny looked at her and grinned, a blessed sight indeed. "Johnny!" she said softly. "Come to Mommy."

Tall Bear handed him over. "He is still very sick. Rock him to sleep and keep him sitting up. I will reheat the water and do this again in an hour or two. We will keep it up all day and tonight. I think by morning he will feel much better."

Faith rose, clinging to her son. "I don't know what to say—how to thank you, Tall Bear."

He ran a hand through his hair. "There is no need for

thanks. I owed this much to you." He carried the water back to the stove, again adding a little more to the pan from the kettle. "He is not safely out of danger yet, so do not thank me too soon." He left the pan on the stove for the moment. "And call me Gabe from now on."

Faith frowned with curiosity. "All right," she answered. "Gabriel it is."

He smiled. "Just Gabe will do. Gabriel doesn't seem quite fitting."

She thought how she had prayed diligently for God to send help, and Gabriel was an angel's name. Gabriel Beaumont had shown up at her door and had probably just saved Johnny's life. "Gabriel is very fitting," she answered, "but if you prefer Gabe, then that is what I will call you."

Only a couple of hours ago she had felt so helpless, had lost all hope, was ready to give up and leave Sommers Station. Now here was this wild half-breed who amazingly had given her new hope, a new resolve to survive there, a deeper faith in her own God, who always seemed to be watching out for her.

"I will go put up my horses," he told her, putting on his slicker and hat.

"Fine. There is fresh hay in the horse shed, and some oats. You can put your things in the back room and sleep there."

He hesitated at the door. "One of the outbuildings will do."

"They aren't heated. You'll be as sick as Johnny if you sleep out there."

"It would not look right to your guests if they know I stay here and sleep in the same house." *How can I sleep so close to you without wanting to be in your bed?* he felt like adding. "I will survive until warmer weather, which is coming soon. In the meantime I will build a small place for myself out behind the horse shed so it is far enough away to be proper."

Proper? Faith thought. With all the things she'd done to survive there, the way she dressed now, her rough hands and sometimes-hardened heart, she wondered if it mattered if others thought her "proper." "Fine," she answered aloud, "if it makes you feel better."

It will just make things a lot easier, he thought. He went out without answering.

Faith rocked Johnny, who quickly fell asleep, this time seeming to be truly resting peacefully. She felt his cheek, and to her great relief it was cool. She felt like crying again out of sheer joy. She didn't know what to think of Gabriel Beaumont's return, other than that she was sure God had sent him. What would happen from here on was a mystery, but his presence would certainly bring relief to the loneliness and boredom of Sommers Station this time of year.

Chapter Twenty-one

Faith awoke to the welcome spring sound of birds singing. Her neck ached, and her eyes felt puffy. She still sat in the rocker, and Johnny still rested in the crook of her arm. She glanced at the softly ticking clock on the wall. Seven o'clock. She had slept only three hours. She had been awake all night, holding and rocking Johnny between the times Gabe had sat with the boy over the steaming water. Gabe had finally left the boy to her around four A.M.

She leaned down to listen to Johnny's breathing, and although he still sounded congested, his breathing was not as labored as it had been the day before, and she realized that during these last two or three hours he had not even coughed. She touched a chubby cheek to find it cool. She closed her eyes for a moment to say a short prayer. "Thank you, God. Thank you for bringing Tall Bear."

She rose, reminding herself Tall Bear wanted to be called Gabe now. She lay Johnny on his cot to let him continue sleeping, then built up the fire in the cookstove. Little shafts of sunlight shot through the cracks in the window shutters, and it didn't seem quite so chilly and damp that morning. Perhaps it would finally begin warming again, which would be a relief, since Gabe had insisted on sleeping in one of the sheds until he could build something for himself. And warmer weather would help Johnny.

She washed her face and hands, wondering if Gabe really meant to stay. It would be pleasant having someone around all the time again, although she dearly missed a woman's company—but just having anyone to talk to would be welcome. The trouble was, there were things about Gabe Beaumont that disturbed her in ways she had not been disturbed in years.

She set a kettle of day-old coffee on the stove, then walked into the back room to quickly change her wrinkled dress, wanting to start some breakfast before Gabe might wake up and come inside. She hoped he had not decided to leave again. She brushed out her hair and retwisted it neatly on top of her head, wondering what he really thought about her. There wasn't a lot left about her that was truly feminine, but as she studied herself in the mirror, she decided she still had a decently attractive face, and her mother had told her she had beautiful hair.

She looked closer in the mirror. No, she didn't have a lot of wrinkles yet. She opened a jar of cream and rubbed some into her skin, then into the skin on the backs of her hands, deciding she would never again have soft hands. So be it. She had her pride and independence, and now she had hope of staying at Sommers Station. If the work involved aged her, that was just the way it would have to be. She finished pinning her hair, chastising herself for caring how she might look to a half-breed Indian who had a knack for being here today and gone tomorrow.

She smoothed her dress and then checked on Johnny once more before going outside to take some bacon from the smokehouse. To her relief the sunrise brought a warmth that hadn't been in the air for nearly two weeks. She went back inside and set her favorite heavy black fry pan on the stove, laying some strips of bacon into it. She turned when someone tapped on the door. "Come in," she called.

Gabe stepped inside, wearing snug-fitting pants of black

cotton. Faith couldn't help noticing his slender hips, on which rested a wide leather gun belt that held his handgun. His pants belt showed beaded decorations, obviously something from his Indian world, as was the ever-present bear-claw necklace that peeked from the open neck of his red calico shirt. Although the shirt had slightly bloused sleeves, they could not hide the fact that they covered powerful arms and wide shoulders.

Faith felt a little ashamed to realize she had seen this man nearly naked and had never forgotten what a magnificent build he had. The thought almost startled her, for she realized she was appreciating his manliness, and he stirred feelings and needs she had not experienced since she'd first kissed Johnny Sommers. Then she had been so innocent, but now she knew the pleasure of lying with a man—or at least how pleasurable she suspected it could be when the man was gentle and understanding.

She thought how Gabe Beaumont was handsome in a different way from Johnny's brash good looks. Johnny could get what he wanted by smiling and fast-talking his way; but she suspected Gabe Beaumont got what he wanted by sheer force, or maybe just because of his size and the air of authority about him. This man was much stronger inside than Johnny had been, she sensed, and certainly much stronger physically. He was quiet, experienced, probably not even aware of his good looks.

"Good morning." She felt the color rising in her cheeks at her secret thoughts.

He nodded to her. "How is the boy?"

Gratitude swept through her. "He seems much better. There is no fever, and he's breathing better. I sat up with him after you left, like you told me to do. I laid him down only a few minutes ago. I'd like to let him sleep as long as he can."

Gabe nodded, thinking how pretty she was in spite of that plain, twisted hairdo, the simple gray dress she wore, no color on her face. This was a woman who would be easy to love. But she was white, and he suspected a man was the last thing on her mind. Faith Sommers was certainly a challenge for any man, but too much of a challenge for a half-breed. He would have to love her quietly. He would love her by staying there and helping her. He needed the work, needed someplace to call home. That place would be Sommers Station . . . unless it became too difficult to be near this woman and to ignore his desire to see her naked, feel her skin against his own.

"Sit down. I'll pour you some coffee. I'm afraid it's a day old and pretty strong."

"I like my coffee strong." He sat down at the table, and Faith poured coffee into a tin cup and set it in front of him. "I'm making some breakfast. I hope you like bacon."

He smiled softly. "There is not a man alive who does not like bacon."

Faith set the coffeepot back on the stove and turned the bacon, then poured herself a cup of coffee, facing him again. "I don't know how to thank you."

"I told you last night it is not necessary." He drank some of his own coffee. "Letting me stay here is thanks enough. I will clean out the horse shed and turn the horses out to pasture. You should stay inside today with your son."

"Fine. I will go out and milk the cow, though. She has to be milked every morning. Her calf died, but if I keep milking her, she'll keep producing."

Gabe leaned back. "I will leave that to you. I have never milked a cow."

Faith smiled. "I guess there are a few things I'll have to teach you."

"I suppose. But I learn fast."

She liked his deep voice, liked the way his full lips moved when he spoke, wondered how it would feel to be kissed by those lips. She turned away to finish cooking breakfast, frying some eggs in the bacon grease and putting three of them on a large dish along with a heap of bacon. She set the plate in front of him, then cut him some bread and poured more hot coffee into his cup. "One thing I've learned is how to cook. Sometimes I cook for several passengers. I actually enjoy it, in spite of the work. I'm hoping Sommers Station will grow when the railroad comes through, and I intend to open a rooming house then, maybe a restaurant. I'm so happy you're staying, Gabe. I was actually considering leaving before you came along, losing hope. But now I'm sure I can stick it out here until the railroad comes."

He ate voraciously as she spoke, mopping up the eggs with the bread. "Why did you stay so long?"

She shrugged. "I had no place else to go."

Gabe drank some coffee, thinking how alike they were in some ways. "Well, then, this place must have an attraction for people with no place else to go. It is the same for me."

Faith watched him devour the bacon. "I'm sorry you have no place to call home."

Gabe met her gaze, realizing she truly meant it. There was something about her that reminded him of Little Otter, even though Faith was not Indian. He swallowed the bacon and washed it down with more coffee. He set the cup down and sighed. "At one time I felt I belonged to another kind of world, my father's world. I traveled with him, hunted with him, lived easily in both the Indian and white world. But things were different then." He touched the bear-claw necklace. "My father gave me this. It is made of bear claws and was a gift to him from my Indian grandfather, Two Moccasins."

Faith tried to imagine what his life must have been like as a boy. "What was your father like?"

He stared at his coffee cup. "He was a big man, the kind your people call a mountain man. He was a good man, a friend to the Sioux. In the early days the Sioux did not mind such white men coming to their land. They came only to hunt and then they left again. They respected the Indian way, and many of them married Indian women. It is the kind of whites who come today who make the Indians raid and murder. They have no respect for the Indian way. They dirty the land and water, dig up Grandmother Earth, cut down the trees." He sighed. "I know now they cannot be stopped." He tipped back his chair. "I realize my father was also a man who lived in two worlds, even though he did not have mixed blood. He was a Frenchman, a fur trapper. He dressed like an Indian, lived like one most of the time." He buttered another piece of bread. "The only English I learned was from my father, but we usually spoke to each other in French."

Faith found this man utterly fascinating. What a wonderfully exciting life he had led, traveling to a city like St. Louis on a riverboat, living among Indians, scouting for soldiers, and, wrong as it was, riding with outlaws. "My life hasn't been quite so full of adventure as yours."

He rolled his eyes. "Most of it was not by choice. And I would not say you have not had an exciting life. Not many white women would choose to do what you have done."

She poured herself some coffee. "Not many white women are quite as crazy as I am."

Or as brave and beautiful, he felt like adding. "You are a strong woman."

She drank from her cup, then just stared at its contents. "I haven't felt very strong lately. Ever since . . ." She met his gaze. "Ever since you and those men attacked this place and I realized I couldn't hold off everyone who comes along, I've been very shaken, I'm ashamed to admit. Then that thing with Johnny last night." She looked back down at her coffee. "I felt so helpless." She glanced at his big hand. He was circling a finger around the rim of his cup. She thought how that hand could clamp around her throat and choke her to death in moments . . . but maybe it could also be gentle.

"There is no shame in being afraid. Your fear was for your son in both instances, not for yourself. It is a natural thing."

"Will you truly stay this time? If you don't, I'll have to leave, too. I can't keep risking Johnny this way, but I'm so sure that I can make something of Sommers Station once the railroad comes. I don't want to leave now, not when it's getting so close."

Gabe thought how the Sioux and Cheyenne hated the coming of the railroad, but he knew there was no stopping it. The Cheyenne had tried farther east in Nebraska, but they had failed. The iron horse was galloping ever closer to its destination, like an unstoppable monster. He looked into Faith's blue eyes. "I will stay. I owe you, for the attack that could have cost you your life . . . or Johnny's. I have lost everything that has meaning for me, so it makes little difference what I do now. By helping you I can at least make up for the wrong I have done you."

Faith had found herself half hoping he was staying because of personal feelings for her. "Why would you care? I'm white."

He rose, turning away. "You are not like other white women. I have told you that before." He slugged down what was left of his coffee. "I will go clean out the stalls. What else would you need done?"

"I'm not sure. You could fetch me some water, three or four buckets full. And you could bring in some wood. I want to heat the oven and bake several loaves ahead, get prepared for the next stage."

He frowned. "Indian men do not fetch wood. That is woman's work."

Faith looked at him in surprise. "What?"

"Indian men do not fetch wood."

She rose and put her hands on her hips. "Is that so?" She walked over and grabbed the cup from his hand. "I will remind you, Gabriel Beaumont, that you have decided to dress and behave as a white man. White men *do* fetch wood! They cut the trees and saw the logs and split them. They stack it and they bring it into the house. I've been doing that by myself for a long time, and if I'm going to hire help, that is one thing he is going to do for me."

He rubbed at his lips as though to try to wipe away the smile that showed itself there. He sighed deeply, his green eyes moving over her in a gaze that made Faith's blood tingle.

"There is another Indian custom you *will* like," he answered.

"I'm not so sure I'd like *any* of your Indian customs." She could not help noticing the way his dark hair fell softly around his handsome face. His eyes were set wide apart, outlined with dark lashes and eyebrows, set above high cheekbones. His lips were full, and when he smiled, his whole face became even more handsome, but he did not smile often. Right now he was grinning almost teasingly, and she didn't know whether to be angry or to smile in return.

"You will like this one." He leaned closer. "Indian men make a great show of being brave warriors. They hunt, raid, kill, scalp." He shook his head as though to pretend scorn. "They are wild and fierce, afraid of nothing . . . except their women. Inside the tepee it is the woman who gives the orders." He straightened. "Since you are a woman, and I am in your tepee, so to speak, I will do what you ask."

She could not help a grin of her own. "Good. We'll get along just fine, then." She walked back to the stove, uneasy about the feelings he stirred in her when standing close. "I will write to the powers that be at Wells Fargo and tell them I have hired someone to help me. I'll give them your white name. They'll never know the difference. I'll see if I can get their approval, and that way they will pay you. You don't have to stay here just for a place to sleep and eat. You deserve to be paid, and I can't pay you out of my own minimal wage."

"Good." He walked to the door, taking his hat from a peg and placing it on his head. "Will that man called Buck accept me?"

"Of course he will. He took the bullet out of you, didn't he?"

He rested his hand on the doorknob. "If soldiers come, use only my white name. Neither you nor Buck should ever tell them I rode with outlaws. They know only that an Indian rode with Chet Webster and his bunch. I killed Webster, and the one who got away is Ned O'Reilly. He's probably still running, if I know Ned. There is no one left to identify me, and all they ever called me was Indian. The army does not know the name Tall Bear as far as linking me with outlaws."

He turned and walked out, and Faith stared after him, shaking her head. Having Gabriel Beaumont there was going to be either a good thing, or the biggest mistake of her life. She walked over to Johnny's cot to check on him again. He still seemed to be sleeping comfortably, his breathing rhythmic, although still congested, his skin cool.

"It can't be a mistake," she said softly. Any man who would sit up half the night with a child not even his own had a lot of good in him. She went to the door and opened it a crack, peeking out toward the horse shed. She watched him turn out the horses, smacking some of them on the rump. He leaped up on one of his own Appaloosas in a single swift movement, rode it around, bareback, for a few minutes, not even using a bridle. He sat a horse as though he were a part of it, and that was the Indian in him. Yet here he was dressing like a white man. She liked this new Gabriel Beaumont. She breathed deeply, enjoying the sight of him, then turned away and closed the door. "Faith Sommers!" she scolded herself. She should not be looking at him as a man . . . a virile man . . . a skilled man . . . an utterly handsome man. He was a wild half-breed who knew nothing of the word "responsibility." He could disappear at any time, like a wisp of smoke. Gabe Beaumont was not the kind of man any woman should set her sights on. Sometimes she gave such thoughts to Tod Harding, but man for man, he couldn't hold a candle to—

There! She was doing it again. She must stop this! Gabe Beaumont was going to be underfoot twenty-four hours a day. She could not allow herself to be attracted to him. She glanced upward, wondering if God ever got tired of hearing her prayers. So far he had answered every one of them. Perhaps she'd better pray about this, ask God to help her overcome her sinful thoughts about Gabe Beaumont.

Faith hammered another nail, hoping her repair job would fix the leak in the wood-shingle roof of the depot. A heavy spring storm the night before had revealed the leak, and she was only guessing its source, based on where the water had dripped through. Gabe had offered to do the work, but she had insisted she could fix it herself. She'd made roof repairs before. *Besides,* she'd told Gabe, *what would you know about fixing roofs? Repairing a tepee skin might be more up your alley.* She'd sent him off with a wagon to start gathering rocks. She wanted to stockpile them to use later with cement to build a foundation for an addition to the depot, whatever might be called for when Sommers

Station became a real town. She had decided to think positive from now on. This place would grow, and she wanted to be ready.

She studied the repaired area, seeing nothing that looked as though it could leak. The western sun was mean on wood, quickly drying it out, curling it up, always creating problems. She was proud she had learned how to repair such things, proud she could survive out there as good as any man . . . well, almost as good. She looked far out in the foothills, where she could see Gabe performing the rather grueling work she'd given him, lifting rocks of all sizes and lugging them to the wagon.

"Lord knows there is an endless supply of rocks out here," she muttered.

Gabe had taken Johnny with him. Nearly a month had passed, and the boy was healthy and full of vinegar again. He had warmed to Gabe almost immediately, and now he followed the man everywhere. It was almost comical, and Gabe was ever patient. She suspected he didn't mind because Johnny helped heal the wound in his heart from losing his own little boy.

A pang of guilt stabbed at her for her rather cruel remark earlier that she could probably fix a roof better than he. After all, he was a man, and a man had his pride. He could probably have done it just as well as she, but lately she'd had this anger inside her, and it was her own fault. She was angry over her feelings for Gabe Beaumont, and she was taking that anger out on him, trying too hard to show him she didn't care, hurtful words coming out of her mouth almost without control. Here Gabe had saved Johnny's life, and already she could see the tremendous help he was going to be, and she was finding ways to insult him. For the first time in years she had a few chances to relax, more time to play with Johnny. It was good having him there, and he had not complained about a thing, and yet she had this anger to deal with. She felt truly safe and unafraid for the first time since settling there, and Gabe had been courteous, had kept to himself, never bothered her at night. He had—

Damn it! She knew deep inside that was the problem.

He had never bothered her at night. The only reason for her anger was because she was fighting her own emotions. She was alarmingly attracted to the man, and it was wrong. She was taking her own weaknesses out on Gabe, doing everything she could to make him hate her, to make sure he never got any ideas about her. And yet there were times when she caught him watching her, and the look in his handsome green eyes—

She angrily threw the hammer to the ground. If she kept treating him the way she had been, he would surely leave, and she realized how lonely she would be if that happened . . . how much she would miss him. She scooted down the roof, dragging along the bucket of nails. She started to put her foot on top of the only ladder she had, which was getting old and also becoming dried out. The moment she stepped on it, she heard a strange cracking sound and felt it giving way. Quickly she scrambled back onto the roof, and the ladder tilted sideways. She was afraid to try to use it again. The last thing she needed was to break a leg and be laid up.

"Damn!" she swore again. She glanced toward the spot where Gabe had been gathering rocks and noticed he was in the wagon and headed back toward the depot. It was almost lunchtime. She climbed back up and sat down on the roof to wait. She could see little Johnny sitting between Gabe's legs, pretending to be driving the team of horses. The boy already all but worshiped the man, and that made her own feelings even more difficult to deal with. Gabe was even already teaching Johnny how to ride.

"Indian boys begin riding this young," he had told her, "someone with them, of course. By the time they are four or five, they are riding just fine by themselves."

She could hardly believe that, but, then, she had to consider Gabe's own riding skills. Indians seemed to do everything at an earlier age, according to Gabe . . . including marrying.

The wagon came closer, and she thought how in this land one could watch something like that, thinking it would arrive any moment, but it would take much longer. She had watched the stagecoach this way, winding along the twisting road, disappearing behind a foothill, appearing again, a thundering, clattering, noisy vehicle, yet soundless when it was far out in the rolling hills. Sometimes it seemed more like a vision, silently winding its way on the horizon. Buck had said that the hills acted like a sound barrier, that a whole tribe of Indians could be behind one of those hills and one would never know it, never hear them. She could see how true that might be.

Finally they came close enough for her to hear Johnny's squeals and laughter. Gabe let him hold one rein, and the boy snapped it up and down, already wanting to be a "big man." Three years old. She had never dreamed he might understand these things yet, would never have considered putting him on a horse or letting him pretend to drive a wagon. These were things a boy needed a father for, and Gabe had a way with little boys. He treated Johnny like his own—

She closed her eyes, again fighting the thought of what a good father the man would make, telling herself not to let the pity she felt for Gabe, because he had lost his own son in such a gruesome way, run away with her. After a few more minutes the wagon pulled in front of the depot, and Gabe looked up at her.

"It's getting hot," he told her, climbing down and lifting Johnny from the wagon. "I'll gather more rocks tomorrow morning. I hope you don't mind my letting Johnny hold a rein and do a little driving of his own."

Faith laughed. "Well, if he wants to think he was really driving, I suppose there is nothing wrong with that. Lord knows he'll need to learn someday anyway."

"I'll take the wagon over to the spot where you said you wanted the rocks piled and begin unloading," Gabe told her. "Just give a call when lunch is ready."

For a fleeting moment Faith thought how they were almost living like man and wife . . . except for one thing. "There will be no lunch until I get down from this roof. The ladder cracked and I'm afraid to use it."

Gabe had already started to climb into the wagon. He turned, climbed back down, and walked over to where she sat on the edge of the roof. He checked the ladder, set it aside, and looked up at her, smiling. "That roof isn't all that high. Why didn't you just jump down?"

Faith scowled. "And break a leg? No, thank you. Besides, I'm kind of afraid of heights. It looks a lot farther down from up here than it does from down there."

He reached up, still grinning. "Come on. I'll catch you."

She studied the distance. His arms certainly were a lot closer than the ground, tall as he was, and she had no doubt he was strong enough to catch her. Still, that meant she'd be in those arms. "Just drag something over I can climb down on," she protested.

He shook his head. "This is a lot quicker. Just jump down and get it over with."

She sighed, handing down the bucket of nails first. She leaned forward over the edge then, and Gabe laughed and shook his head.

"Turn around. Feet first. Scoot down off the edge and let go. I'll catch you. Trust me."

Trust you? She turned around, scooting down so that her feet hung off the edge. She was not even aware that her dress had caught on a shingle and was pulled up as she scooted down, so that Gabe saw her slips and caught a glimpse of her ruffled bloomers.

Little did she know that Gabriel Beaumont had been fighting his own desires, telling himself this independent, bossy white woman was the last type of woman he should set his sights on. But there was no fighting the beauty beneath all that rough way about her, the real woman she tried to hide. He reached up. "Come on. You will not fall. I promise."

Faith let go, and in the next moment strong arms came around her waist from behind. She waited for him to set her feet on the ground, but instead he held her tight in a grip that told her she'd be helpless if he decided to do anything more. She grasped the hard rock of his forearms that were wrapped around her from behind. "You can put me down now."

"I am well aware of that."

Faith frowned. "Then why don't you?"

He lifted her a little higher, and in the next moment she

felt his lips at the side of her neck. He kissed and licked her there, sending a fiery tingle through her blood, but also shocking her.

"Gabe—"

His lips were at her cheek. Why was she turning her face toward him? "Gabe, don't—"

His lips were on her mouth, and her own lips parted. His kiss burned deep, and one strong hand moved to grasp her breast.

It had been so long! So long since she'd allowed any such feelings, since she had truly wanted a man. But not this man—it shouldn't be this man. Yet why did it feel so wonderful? Johnny had never made her feel like this. It was only the first few times they were together that she had wanted it as much as he, that she had truly enjoyed her womanliness, yet even then he had been quick and forceful. Gabe was also being forceful, wasn't he?

No, there was something different about this. It was as though he could read her needs, as though he'd waited for just the right moment. She sensed that if she truly wanted him to stop, he would. Johnny never stopped, never cared what her own wants and needs were. The trouble was, she *should* want Gabe to stop. This was not the kind of man she should desire. Maybe this was just a case of being too long without a man, too long lonely, too grateful for how he had saved Johnny's life, too relieved to have the help . . . and perhaps too overwhelmed by his virility, his looks, the mystery about the man, the fact that he should be totally forbidden.

He left her mouth and slowly set her on her feet. "I'm sorry," he told her.

She stood there close to him, on fire, confused, embarrassed, aching. "I . . . have to look after Johnny."

"He is tired from helping me, still needs his rest. Maybe if you put him down, he will fall asleep."

She nodded, refusing to look up at him. "Maybe." She knew what he meant. If Johnny could be put to sleep, they would be free to become lost in each other. He put a big hand to the side of her face.

"Gabe—"

"Do not fight it, Faith. It is time you were a woman again. And I love you."

The words shocked her. He had said them so easily. "You—you still hardly know me."

"I know enough. Out here there is not much a man needs to know, except that a woman is brave and strong and loves the land."

She finally looked up at him. "I . . . I don't aim to give up what I have here, nor my independence."

"Did I ask you to?"

"I don't know if we—"

He cut off her words with another kiss, this one deeper, hotter, more suggestive. He pressed her close, crushing her breasts against his powerful chest, and she felt a hardness against her thigh when her leg slipped between both his legs. She realized then she had an ache to feel a man inside her again. Once a woman knew that pleasure, it was difficult to go without it forever. She couldn't even tell him yet that she loved him, was afraid to feel that way again. Johnny had broken all his promises. Maybe this man would, too. Maybe he would ride off next morning and never come back. She wondered if she would ever get over that worry. Yet why didn't that possibility stop her?

She felt her arms moving around his neck, and neither seemed to care they were warm and sweaty from their morning's work. Nothing mattered but to feel this passion, to satisfy this terrible hunger. She returned his kiss wildly, wrapping her legs around his waist when he lifted her slightly. Their kisses grew hotter, almost frenetic. His tongue slaked in and out of her mouth suggestively, and he moved one hand under her dress, grasping her bottom. He moved his fingers between her buttocks and to that secret place only Johnny had ever touched and invaded. He pressed against it, creating a fiery need deep inside. She wanted him to touch her there, wanted to feel this man of men surging inside her.

He left her mouth and kissed at her neck when she threw her head back.

"Let me go put Johnny down," she told Gabe. She could feel him actually trembling. He slowly let go of her, saying nothing. He only nodded, backing away and going to the wagon. He climbed up almost as though in pain, and he drove off.

Faith turned to see Johnny sitting on the porch picking leaves off the viney plant that had started growing around the porch posts. She picked him up and carried him inside, her body almost hurting in a need to be satisfied by a man. She gave Johnny a little something to eat and laid him on the cot, telling him he should take a nap. She gave him his stuffed cow, and he turned on his side and closed his eyes. She was surprised at how quickly he had obeyed, for he had been fighting his naps lately.

Was this another sign from God? Did this mean what she and Gabe were about to do was right? How could it be? As far as she was concerned, nothing could be more wrong, yet she knew that would not stop her. She heard Gabe's footsteps on the porch then, turned when he opened the door and came inside. She looked at him, feeling flushed, afraid, on fire, weak.

"Don't just use me, Gabe."

He shook his head. "I would not do that—not with a woman like you." He turned and placed the board over the door to bar it so no one could come in who might happen to pass by. He walked over and picked her up in his arms, carrying her to her own bed in the corner.

Chapter Twenty-two

Never had Faith experienced anything like what was happening to her now. There had been so many times when she had wished Johnny would slow down, touch her in special ways first, show his love and adoration of her body. Everything she had wished Johnny would do when making love to her, Gabe Beaumont was doing now. He, too, was urgent in his desire for her, yet this was so different.

There was a mature manliness about him that told her he knew how to treat a woman, and there was a look in his green eyes, a sensation in his soft, deep kisses that told her he did not just want quick pleasure. He adored her, cared that he pleased her. He had a commanding way of bending her to his will, and yet she did not mind obeying that command. Part of her felt that this was wrong, but the woman in her had been too long without a man, to care what was right or wrong.

Her clothes came off almost magically, kisses and licks at her lips, her shoulders, her breasts, her swollen nipples. She gasped at the sensation of his soft lips pulling at her breasts. Johnny had never stopped to do this. He had usually grabbed at her almost painfully, but Gabe seemed to savor every taste and touch. His lips moved downward as did her dress and camisole, which he unlaced then and threw aside, kissing her belly, her hipbones. Farther down the clothes came, and he kissed at the hairs of that secret place only Johnny had seen and invaded.

But Johnny Sommers had never lovingly caressed her there. She felt her clothes pulled the rest of the way off her legs, including her long stockings, her drawers, her boots. She curled up as he removed his shirt, his six-gun . . . everything. Johnny had given her little chance even to look upon that secret part of him with which he so eagerly invaded her practically every night. Now she could not help studying Gabe Beaumont's body, from his powerful arms and shoulders to his broad chest, the scars above his breasts from that which was Indian about him, the scar at his side where she and Buck had saved his life not so long ago, the scars on his arms from mourning after the violent deaths of his wife and son. She had been horrified to think a man could mutilate himself like that, but she was trying to understand the Indian in him.

His torso was magnificent, his belly flat, his hips narrow, his thighs muscled, his most manly part reminding her of a proud stallion. She waited for him to climb on top of her and quickly have his way with her, but instead he lay down next to her, taking her into his arms and caressing her with kisses all over again, deep, hot kisses that made her forget all reason. His lips trailed to her breasts again, while he gently moved a hand to secret places, exploring, bringing out the sweet nectar of woman, making her ache to be invaded by Gabriel Beaumont.

Johnny had touched her there only roughly and eagerly, had never waited for her to build her own desire. She had thought that was the way it was supposed to be, but this . . . this was surely the best way. She felt wonderful sensations rising in her soul, heard herself whispering Gabe's name, asking him please to not stop touching her there. She felt her legs parting willingly, felt her hips rising in response to his touch, as though to invite him to come inside. She felt a pulsating climax deep inside then, a sensation that made her arch against his hand. He pressed his fingers tightly against that magic spot, and now she was the one kissing him wildly, begging him to enter her. She was the eager one, the one being too quick. Johnny had never made her feel this wanton, this bold, this wild. She rose against Gabe, needing to feel her breasts crushed against his bare chest. She kissed him almost violently, her fingers digging into his arms. She arched against him as he moved between her legs, and she cried out in ecstasy when suddenly he was inside her, his hot, hard shaft penetrating deep, almost hurting her with its size.

He moved in sweet, slow rhythm, teasing her with exotic circular motions. Finally his thrusts became more urgent, his rhythm faster. He rose on his knees and grasped her under the hips, pulling her to him. She groaned with the utmost pleasure, amazed that sex could be this wonderful. She felt his life flow into her, and she lay still as he lay down beside her. She could hardly believe then that she had allowed Gabe Beaumont to make love to her, yet still she hardly knew him. Had this lonely life brought her so totally into lawless behavior that now she was capable of lying with a near stranger like a harlot?

"What have we just done?" she asked.

A big hand moved across her breasts, and he turned on his side to kiss at her neck. "We have made love. By Indian custom you are now my wife."

She frowned, not at all sure she wanted to be anyone's wife. "Not by my customs," she answered. "We need a preacher."

"Then we will find one."

"I don't know if I want one. I don't want to be tied to a man again."

"I would not tie you in the way you are saying." He moved on top of her again, resting his arms on either side of her. "Your independence is what I love about you, Faith Sommers. I would not change that."

She reached up and touched his face, still on fire for him. "You could have just made me pregnant."

"I hope I have. I would like another son of my own. Would you not like a brother for Johnny?"

"Only if his father plans to stay around and live the life of a normal family man—by white man's standards."

He kissed her lips gently again. "I would not have done this if I did not plan to live your way."

She sighed, closing her eyes. "I can't imagine what you think of me."

"I just told you. I think of you as my wife. I think of you as the most beautiful white woman I have ever known, not just your sky-blue eyes and your hair red as clay, but inside. You are brave and strong, and you have remained that way through things that would have made other white women run back to where they came from. I do not just love you. I admire you."

He leaned down and gently kissed her breasts, her neck, reawakening all her womanliness. She was still warm from their first lovemaking, and deep inside she already wanted more. This time she did not need all the touches and kisses. She needed only to feel Gabe Beaumont surging inside of her again.

"How can you know so quickly this is what you want?" she asked.

He smiled softly. "Because I have thought of no one but you since the day I found you lost and alone four summers ago. For years I have not known where I belong. Now I know."

She traced her fingers over his lips. "You won't turn Indian on me, will you?"

The remark made him laugh heartily. "What is that supposed to mean?"

How she loved that smile! Handsome. So handsome. "Well, you know. You won't suddenly strip down and paint yourself and go riding off to fight soldiers or something, will you?"

He was still smiling, and he caressed her hair with one hand as he spoke. "I will *always* be Indian, because that is what half of me is. But I no longer choose to live among them. And I will always be white, because half of me is also white. I have chosen this because of you. If I were to lose you, perhaps then I would go back to my Indian ways, and even now I will sometimes go to a distant hill where I can be alone and I will pray with the pipe, for strength, for wisdom, for the ability to care for you as you should be cared for."

She pouted. "I don't need caring for. I can take care of myself. I just need someone to hold me once in a while, and I need a father for Johnny. He worships you already."

He raised his eyebrows mockingly. "You don't need caring for? What if it had been some other wild Indian who broke through your window the day we attacked you? How much longer could you have continued doing all the chores and still caring for Johnny? Who would have buried the dead bodies of those outlaws I ran with if Buck had not come along? Who would have got you down off that roof today? Who would have helped bury your husband? Who would have led you to this place and kept you from being lost and starving to death, or being eaten by wolves, if—"

"All right!" She rolled her eyes. "I admit I need a little caring for, but I would have found a way out of all those situations if I'd had to."

He shook his head. "I think I have chosen a very stubborn woman who will lose no freedom in marrying. It is I who will lose his freedom."

She felt his shaft growing hard again. "I will lose some freedom of my own, Gabe, because I'll never want to be without you. I—" It was so hard to say. The last time she had said it, it had cost her dearly and had become such a disappointment. "I love you, Gabe Beaumont."

"And I love you, Faith Sommers. Now tell me that you also love Tall Bear."

She studied the dark skin, his straight black hair, remembered how wild he could look . . . and behave. "I love you, Tall Bear."

He grinned slyly and nodded. "Then you truly love all of me."

She sighed deeply. "I will want to stay right here, you know. I still have a dream of building this place. And I want to keep calling it Sommers Station, even when we marry. It just seems to fit, and it was Faith Sommers who hung on to it to keep it alive."

"That is fine with me. And you can have all the freedom you want, as long as you are in my bed at night."

"It's the same for you, as long as you are in *my* bed every night."

He rubbed himself against her thigh. "I will be here."

She smiled. "I have to admit it will be nice having a man around."

Their gaze held as he slowly pushed himself inside her again. She drew in her breath, letting out a long sigh of sweet satisfaction. He began the rhythmic movement again, and she leaned up to kiss his chest. There was no more talking between them, only lovemaking . . . sweet, urgent, deeply gratifying. They were two people with wild hearts in a wild land, belonging nowhere but to each other.

Gabe unloaded another wagon full of stones, adding them to the pile for what they had decided would be their future home. A man and wife could not live a decent, private life inside a stage depot. Johnny was with him, and he stood throwing little stones into the pile, thinking he was helping. Gabe hesitated when he heard the clatter of an approaching stagecoach, for he also heard something he never liked hearing. His keen ears and his experience with soldiers over the years told him some were coming now. He could detect the unique sound of soldiers' gear.

There had been several stagecoaches come through in the four weeks he had been there, but never had any soldiers been there since his arrival. He could not help the apprehension and distrust that pulled at him as he slowly set down the last stone. He picked up Johnny and carried him to greet the stage. If he was going to stay there forever with Faith, he needed to face everyone who came through and get over his basic distrust of whites and soldiers.

He wore no gun today, just cotton pants and dusty boots, and a shirt that hung open because of the heat. He nodded to the driver, recognizing him as the man who had taken the bullet out of him. For some reason Buck had not been through there since Gabe had returned to stay. Buck looked at him in surprise as he drew the coach to a halt. He wrapped the reins around a post and climbed down.

"Tall Bear?"

Gabe glanced at the soldiers and shook his head. "Gabriel Beaumont," he answered, still feeling uneasy over the soldiers. One of them looked familiar, and he thought it best they did not know his Indian name. He hoped that in the noise of calling orders to halt, the scraping of hooves and squeak of saddles, none of them had heard Buck call him Tall Bear.

Johnny reached out. "Buck," he said, smiling sweetly.

"Howdy, little guy," Buck answered, pretending to shake his hand. He looked at Gabe again and saw the warning look in his eyes, the way Gabe glanced at the soldiers again. "Everything okay here?" he asked.

Gabe knew he was referring to Faith. "Everything is fine. Mrs. Sommers asked me to stay on and work here, and to help protect the place. I decided to take her up on her offer. When I arrived a month ago, I found Johnny lying near death with bad lungs and a high fever. I helped heal him and then I just decided to stay."

Buck nodded, glancing at Johnny again. "Is the little guy okay now?"

"He will be all right."

"Looks like he took a shine to you."

Gabe nodded.

Buck rubbed his lips thoughtfully, glancing at Faith as she came out of the depot to greet the soldiers and passengers. She was wearing a yellow-flowered dress, her hair done up in curls, lace-up shoes on her feet. He looked back at Gabe. "Did Faith take a shine to you, too?"

Gabe grinned. "It is a long story. In a way we have known each other a long time. We wish to be married."

"Married! Faith?"

Gabe set Johnny down and let him run to his mother. "She *is* a woman, you know, and her son needs a father."

"A half-breed outlaw?"

Gabe was glad the man had said the words quietly. "I did not think you the sort of man who would judge another by his blood or his past."

Buck removed his hat and ran a hand through graying

hair. "Well, I ain't—but considerin' how you first came here—"

"Buck! I've been worried about you," Faith called, running up to surprise the man with a hug. "It's been nearly a month since I've seen you. The other drivers said you had been kicked by a horse."

Buck looked a little embarrassed. "Hate to say it, but a mean ole mare did get the better of me—broke my damn arm. It's still wrapped tight, but I can use it now." He held up his left arm, and Faith could see the bandage wrapping under his folded-up shirtsleeve. "Looks like you've made some changes since I've been gone," he said, glancing at Gabe.

"Yes. Gabe has come back to stay, Buck. We're going to be married."

Buck shook his head. "So I hear. You sure have a way of keepin' a person on his toes. I ain't never met a more unpredictable woman."

Faith smiled. "I'm glad you're all right, Buck. And be nice to Gabe. He's a good man, and I love him." She glanced at the passengers. "We'll talk more later. I have to take care of these—" She hesitated. "My goodness! It's Tod Harding. It's been a year since he was here last."

She left them to greet the passengers, and Gabe watched a well-dressed, handsome man remove his hat and bow slightly to greet Faith. He felt a pang of jealousy at the way the man looked at her. "Who the hell is Tod Harding?" he asked Buck.

Buck jerked a harness off one of the horses and let it trot away. "Oh, he's just some rich fella involved with the railroad. He's after Faith to put her claim on this land—part of railroad right-of-way, somethin' like that. He figures to keep this place alive as a stop-off for trains once the railroad is done, says Faith can eventually build a town here. I expect she's told you she wants to do that."

"She has," Gabe replied, still watching Faith and Harding. They were walking toward the depot. "He's quite the fancy man, isn't he?"

"Oh, he likes to put on airs. I don't exactly trust him."

Buck faced him. "Let's get back to you, though. Last I knew, you was ridin' with outlaws."

"That is behind me." Faith was inside the depot now, and Gabe's gaze moved to the soldiers, studying the one who looked familiar. Finally he met Buck's eyes again. "I wish to be called only Gabe now. That is my white name. It was by mistake and confusion that I rode with those men. They are all gone now, and I have chosen to stay here."

Buck slowly nodded. "Livin' out here, I've seen and heard just about everything. I've seen total strangers marry on wagon trains west, a woman with kids who's been recent widowed and needs a man to look after her—that's usually the case. So I ain't surprised by this." He frowned, looking Gabe over. "Thing is, Faith ain't exactly the kind of woman who thinks she needs lookin' after. She must have strong feelin's for you to want to marry again."

Gabe grinned. "You are right. She does not like to think she needs taking care of." He leaned closer. "We will not tell her that is what we both have been doing."

Buck chuckled, folding his arms. "By God, I think maybe I like you, Tall—I mean, Gabe."

Gabe nodded. "And you are one of the few white men *I* like. I owe you my life. I never had the chance to thank you."

Buck waved him off. " 'Twern't nothin'. I've took out so many bullets, I ought to be given a doctor's diploma. Trouble is, I wouldn't even be able to read it."

They both laughed, and Gabe helped Buck finish unhitching the team, feeling uneasy at the way the familiar soldier kept staring at him.

Inside Faith tended to the passengers, one married couple traveling to Idaho, and two railroad men, one of them Harding. He seemed eager to explain that the railroad had already reached her area, stretching one mile south of the depot. Sommers Station would soon begin to grow. They expected to complete the railroad by next summer, at which time the Union Pacific would build the loop to Sommers Station.

Faith served coffee and fresh biscuits to the passengers, listening to Harding, excited about what it all could mean.

"I am planning to hire someone to build a house for me so that I can use the depot as a rooming house," she told him. "By the time tracks are laid to Sommers Station, I will be ready with a place for passengers to stay."

Harding watched her, thinking how pretty she looked, much more feminine than the last time he'd been there. Here was a forward-thinking, hardworking woman, with a body that made a man ache. It was obvious she didn't have much in the way of money and never had. Maybe if he helped her out, she would eventually be "grateful." Women seemed to gravitate toward men with money. Besides, his entire plan for Sommers Station included gradually making this woman almost fully dependent on him.

He had to be clever about this. Faith Sommers had the capabilities to build Sommers Station into a profitable little town. He needed her right now for that very purpose, since he was too busy to give the place full attention himself. Once Faith had made this real estate valuable, he would move in and take over—legally. But he could not let the very feisty, independent Faith Sommers realize his plan until it was too late for her to stop it.

It amused him to think how eager people like Faith were to settle on railroad land grants, thinking to get rich somehow at their ventures. They would work hard to bring value to otherwise unsettled land; then men like himself would take over, getting rich from the labor of others.

"I could float you a loan if you need it," he told Faith aloud.

"I'll get by, Mr. Harding." Faith poured him more coffee. "I have saved my money faithfully, and I have advertised for people to come here and settle. I'm sure I'll find a cooperative carpenter to help me out."

Harding put a hand on her arm. "Call me Tod, Mrs. Sommers. And may I say, you look quite beautiful today?"

"Quit the sweet talk," the man with Tod teased him. It was Robert Belding, who had accompanied Tod on their first visit. "We've got to be on our way, soon as the team is changed. You don't have time for spooning with pretty young women."

The woman passenger blushed, but her husband

laughed. Faith turned away with the coffeepot. "I prefer to call you Mr. Harding," she replied. She faced him. "And I feel I should tell you my name will soon be Mrs. Gabriel Beaumont, as soon as we can find a preacher coming this way."

Tod's face fell, and Faith thought she actually saw a little anger in his eyes. "*Mrs.?* When and how did you meet a man way out here in the middle of nowhere? I thought you ran this place alone!"

Damn! He had not planned on this, and he had been so sure Faith would accept a loan. His plan was going to be a little harder to execute than he'd thought. Now there would be a husband to contend with. He had thought to woo Faith himself, just enough to make her trust him completely. That should have been easy. He had never had trouble fancy-talking a woman, but Faith Sommers was no ordinary woman.

"Well, I couldn't quite handle everything alone," Faith was saying. "Especially if Sommers Station is to grow. A man came here looking for work, so I gave him the job, and . . . things just happened."

Tod rose. "That man I saw helping Buck when we first got out of the coach?"

Faith faced him calmly, already reading his thoughts. "Yes."

"He looks Indian!"

She shrugged. "He *is*—half-Indian, Mr. Harding. And he's a good man, skilled with a gun, which I certainly need, and strong for work."

Tod scowled, taking on a stance of authority. "Mrs. Sommers, I feel compelled to ask you—are you sure this isn't just a case of your being lonely? Wanting a father for your charming little boy?"

Faith put her hands on her hips, angry for the embarrassing remark in front of the others. "It is really none of your business, Mr. Harding. This station is being run just fine, and I still intend to build Sommers Station into a railroad depot and a full-fledged town. That should be all you're concerned about."

A look of challenge and arrogance came into the man's

eyes, renewing Faith's original suspicion that Harding was not a man to be fully trusted. "Yes, I suppose you're right," he answered.

Buck came inside then, announcing that the new team would be hitched within five minutes. "We'll leave in ten."

The dusty, sweaty female passenger groaned at the thought of boarding the coach again.

"I hope you haven't made a grave mistake, Mrs. Sommers," Harding told Faith. He tugged at the lapels of his fancy suit jacket and walked out with Robert Belding, who looked at Faith and shook his head before also leaving.

"I don't like that man," Faith addressed Buck.

Buck only grinned. "That makes two of us."

"Four of us," the other woman remarked. "He's been bragging about himself and the railroad since we left Omaha."

They all laughed, and the young couple left. Buck turned to Faith. "You real sure about marryin' Tall Bear?"

"I am," Faith answered boldly. "And don't call him Tall Bear. He doesn't want that name used here."

Buck shook his head. "I always said you was a strange, unpredictable woman. You've gone and proved it again."

Faith shrugged. "*You* like him, don't you, Buck?"

He nodded. "I didn't think I would, but I already do."

"Good. I am glad. Find us a preacher, will you, Buck? It's kind of . . . urgent . . . if you know what I mean."

Buck snickered, and Faith could feel her cheeks turning crimson. "I'll find one," he answered. "Have I failed you yet?"

Tears came into Faith's eyes. "No. You're a good man, Buck. I hope you'll continue to consider settling here. Things are going to start growing real soon."

He nodded. "I'll think on it."

They both walked outside, and Gabe was checking the harness on the team. Tod Harding was watching him, pacing. Finally Gabe straightened and faced the man. "Something I can do for you, mister?"

Gabe towered over Harding's much slighter frame. "I am told you intend to marry Mrs. Sommers."

Gabe frowned, looking the man over. "What business is that of yours?"

Harding folded his arms authoritatively. "I am Tod Harding of H and H Enterprises, not that you would know what that is. Suffice it to say my father and I own several companies in Chicago, Cheyenne, Omaha, and St. Louis, and we have invested heavily in the coming railroad. I've been here before, talked to Mrs. Sommers about helping this depot grow once the railroad comes through. I'm quite fond of the woman, have a great respect for her. I am only asking because I hope she will be well taken care of."

Gabe saw right through the man, feeling a twinge of jealousy at knowing a white man with power and money was interested in Faith. He also read the man's prejudice. "Faith Sommers is not the type of woman who considers herself as needing to be taken care of, Mr. Harding. She does a good job of that all by herself."

Harding studied Gabe's handsome face, furious inside. He had fully intended to come to Sommers Station soon to stay and build some businesses for his father, at which time he would have wooed Faith Sommers and got the pretty but lonely woman into his bed—while he stole away everything she had worked to build. This half-breed bastard could foil all his plans. "Yes, she does manage well alone," he answered Gabe. "I will be coming back here soon, Mr. . . . Beaumont, is it?"

Gabe nodded. "It is."

"I hope I do not find that Mrs. Sommers has been abused, or perhaps abandoned by her husband."

Gabe felt his anger rising. Here was the kind of white man he detested. "*I* hope you don't try sticking your nose into our personal business, Mr. Harding! That could be a bad move on your part." He watched Harding stiffen, saw the sudden fear in his eyes, even though he held his chin a little higher and pretended bravery.

"It is my opinion that no white woman should marry an Indian. No insult meant, Mr. Beaumont, but it's just a fact of life."

"Oh, I think you *definitely* meant an insult, Mr. Harding!" Gabe walked away from the man, afraid he would punch him if he stood near him any longer. He walked over to stand next to Faith while passengers boarded, Harding sitting next to a window so he could look at Faith. He turned away when Gabe moved an arm around her waist.

Buck climbed aboard and snapped the reins, and the soldiers fell in place alongside the coach. One held the reins to a riderless horse, and Gabe realized it belonged to the soldier who had made him uneasy, the one who had looked familiar. That one had not spoken to him, but now he rode inside the coach with Tod Harding. Why? A soldier and a white man with power could be a bad combination if both had something against him. He just was not sure what it could be. Perhaps the soldier knew about his outlaw ways. Maybe he was even wanted. He only knew something was not quite right, and he did not like this feeling of danger; but he decided not to mention it to Faith.

"What did Mr. Harding say to you?" Faith asked him.

Gabe scowled, looked down at her. "How well do you know the man?"

She shrugged. "This is only the second time he's come through here. All I know is that he is a pompous ass with money. He has offered to help build Sommers Station into a railroad depot, and for that I am grateful, but I suspect he's the kind who likes to think he owns people. I am not a person who can be owned. He offered me a loan, but I refused."

Gabe grinned, grabbing her close and lifting her feet off the ground. "That man has an interest in you, woman. Didn't you give some thought to what it might be like being married to a rich man like that?"

She grinned slyly. "Oh, a passing thought. But men like that don't marry rough-and-tumble women like me, and women like me could never be happy with that kind. We like our men just as rough, men who can handle themselves in a fix, men who are afraid of nothing." She moved her arms around his neck. "We like strong, rugged men who understand real life and know how to work hard and aren't afraid to sweat a little."

He laughed lightly, meeting her mouth in a hungry kiss.

"I can think of better ways to sweat than by working," he said after releasing the kiss.

"You'll just have to wait until Johnny goes down for his nap, Gabe Beaumont."

He set her on her feet. "We have to get a preacher here soon. Doesn't matter to me. As far as I am concerned, we are already married, but I know it matters to you."

"Buck said he'd find one and bring him soon as possible."

He nodded. "Good. Go ahead and clean up inside. I will brush down the horses that just came in."

Faith left him, chasing after Johnny, who decided to run from her then, daring her to catch him. Gabe watched after the disappearing stagecoach, still feeling uneasy about Tod Harding . . . and that soldier who had stared at him but said nothing. The two of them were in that coach together. Maybe it all meant nothing. Life was good now. He'd found a place to call home, a woman to love, even had a family. He had more purpose in life than he had ever had. Nothing was going to spoil that, or take Faith Sommers from him. He would make damn sure of it!

Chapter Twenty-three

Faith looked up from hoeing her garden to see two men approaching on horseback. Gabe came from the horse shed, Johnny toddling behind. Gabe wore deerskin leggings today, which he said were cooler in hot weather than white man's heavy cotton pants. He wore a leather vest but no shirt, and his dark skin glistened in the sun. There were still times when it struck Faith that this man had once ridden with the wildest of warriors. It was hard to imagine when he so gently made love to her in the night, but not so hard when she saw him this way, dressed in buckskins, a rifle in his hand.

He set the rifle aside when he realized one of the riders was Buck. Faith laid down her hoe and walked toward them, noticing the other rider wore a black suit, vest, and hat, a white shirt under the vest. He held a Bible in one hand.

"Found you a preacher, folks!" Buck called to them.

Faith's heart beat with joy. Buck dismounted and introduced "Preacher Louis Ames. Came across him conductin' services for railroad workers to the southwest of here."

The preacher shook hands with Gabe and Faith as they introduced themselves.

"Thank you for coming, Reverend Ames," Faith told him. She could see the doubt in his eyes as soon as he realized it was Gabe she was marrying. She suspected, though, that the man was growing accustomed to the unusual in this country, as the doubt turned quickly to gentle acceptance, no questions asked. "Always glad to unite two people ready to settle and bring growth to the West," he told them.

"And we're glad to find a preacher out here!" Faith answered. "It always surprises me the different sorts of people who come through this place."

"Well, more and more are choosing to stay, and I have come to travel to the various settlements and bring them the Word of God, conduct funerals and weddings and such."

"This is so sudden!" Faith exclaimed, suddenly self-conscious about her appearance. She wore a plain brown dress of coarse cotton, her mannish leather work shoes, and no slips. Her hair was twisted into a tight bun to keep it out of her face because of the heat, and her hands were callused and dirty from gardening. "I'm dressed for digging in the dirt, not for a wedding! I can't get married looking like this! All of you come inside and have coffee and biscuits while I go in the back room and clean up."

"You are always beautiful," Gabe told her.

"No woman looks like this when she marries, Gabe Beaumont!" She hurried inside, and the men chuckled, shaking their heads.

"Buck explained the situation," Ames told Gabe. "Mrs. Sommers's first husband drowned on their journey west, and she ended up staying here. He says you helped her out once during an outlaw attack."

Gabe glanced at Buck. "Yes, I guess you could say that." He picked up Johnny and introduced him to the preacher.

"I can see the boy already loves you," Ames said when Johnny hugged Gabe around the neck.

Gabe nodded. "I already think of him as my own."

Johnny wiggled to get down again, and Gabe set him

down and shooed him into the depot. "Well, Buck, as long as there is going to be a wedding today, and since it is already late afternoon, perhaps you and the preacher can stay the night in the depot," he said, turning to face the two men again. "Is that possible?"

Buck shrugged. "I reckon. I ain't makin' no runs this week, so I ain't in no hurry. If the preacher here can wait till tomorrow to go back down to that little settlement, we can stay."

"That will be fine," Ames told him, "but . . . well . . . won't the two of you want to be alone?"

Gabe grinned. "We *will* be. I'm hoping maybe the two of you can keep Johnny for us. You know what a good kid he is. He wouldn't be any trouble."

"Sure, I'll watch out for him. But where will you be?" Buck asked.

Gabe winked. "This is my wedding night. I think it would be nice to spend it out under the stars."

Buck grinned, and the preacher raised his eyebrows. "Whatever suits you," Buck told Gabe.

They went inside and waited, the preacher telling Gabe that government men were coming out that summer to talk treaty with Red Cloud. "Buck says you lived with the Sioux for a time."

"I did." Gabe hoisted Johnny to his knee. "I chose to end that life and live like a white man. Many things led to the decision, but I think I am where I belong now." His heart raced with excitement as they talked about a hundred other subjects. Soon Faith Sommers would be his wife. She would belong to him totally. It had been two weeks since that first glorious afternoon of making love with her, and every day and night they had shared bodies again. He already knew every inch of her body, and she knew every inch of his. It seemed silly that they needed a piece of paper to prove they were married, but if that was what his white woman wanted, that was fine with him. In Faith's eyes they had already been "living in sin" these two weeks, and enjoying every minute of it.

"I have some clean clothes with some of my other things in a shed outside," he told the preacher. "I think I'll go out and wash by the water pump and change myself. And I need to take a tent out of my gear. This is the time of year when the nights are just cool enough to sleep close, and early enough that there are still no insects. The way the weather has been, it should be pretty tonight."

"You ain't gonna be noticin' the stars," Buck teased him. "Only stars you'll see are the ones that'll be in Faith's eyes."

"You men stop that talk!" Faith called from the back room, raising her voice to be heard above their laughter. "I heard every word!" She stuck her head out from between the curtains, keeping the rest of the curtains closed. "And what's this about a tent and stars?"

Gabe headed for the door. "You and I are spending the night alone out in the foothills," he told her. "Buck and Preacher Ames will look after Johnny."

"Out in the foothills! Whatever—" She stopped to think, her face turning red again. How else could they be alone? They certainly couldn't ask the preacher to go sleep in the horse shed. She said no more as they all chuckled again, and she returned to changing her underclothes and pulling on slips. How delightfully exciting it would be to sleep out under the stars. That was how things were when she'd first met Gabe . . . Tall Bear . . . lost in the foothills, surrounded by wolves. She'd felt so safe with him there. She always felt safe with Gabe Beaumont by her side.

She brushed her hair vigorously, pulling back the sides with combs. Gabe liked it brushed out long, so that was how she would wear it for their wedding. She pulled on her best dress, a blue linen with a ruffled skirt. She had not worn it since leaving Pennsylvania—had no reason to. Now it was a little tight in the waist, for she'd had a baby since then, but it still fit.

What a surprising day this had turned out to be. Most of it had been like any other, and this afternoon she had helped Gabe haul wood from a site where he'd been cutting. She never dreamed this would be her wedding day. In spite of the dangers and hardship, life had been such an adventure here, every day unpredictable.

"June fifth, eighteen and sixty-eight," she muttered.

"Today I married Gabriel Beaumont, who is half–Sioux Indian. His Indian name is Tall Bear. . . ."

The next hour seemed a moment of unreality to Faith. She had never felt quite so pretty; the way Gabe looked at her told her he thought the same. He had picked her a bouquet of spring flowers, which she held while she told him she loved him, would honor him, keep herself only for him, till death they must part.

He looked wonderful! He wore a beaded, fringed shirt and leggings that were bleached almost white, and one feather was tied into the side of his hair. He had decided to be Tall Bear for her, and it was a good choice. This was the man she had first met when she was so alone and terrified after Johnny had been killed, and when he dressed this way, he looked so virile and handsome that she shivered. Even though they had already made love many times, this was different. This time he would truly be her husband.

She watched his exotic eyes as he repeated his own marriage vows. She would be someone's wife again, but this time her husband would not demand she give up her freedom to build and grow. He would not treat her as less than he. He would not grope at her in the night when she was so tired she could hardly move. He would respect her, love her for who she was, not just for something to have in his bed.

The ceremony ended, with Buck as a witness. The preacher gave them a paper to sign, and Buck signed it also. Johnny reached up for Gabe, saying "Daddy," and Faith told him yes, Gabe truly was his daddy now. It felt so good to be able to tell him that.

The men visited while Faith put some biscuits into a cloth sack and picked up a tin of tea leaves and a small water kettle. Gabe filled two canteens and told her that was all they needed. They would be gone only the night, and he had packed everything else they would need. Faith found herself saying good-bye to the preacher and Buck. She kissed and hugged Johnny, and in the next moment Gabe was hoisting her up on his Appaloosa as though she weighed nothing. He leaped up behind her and took up the reins of his packhorse, then rode off into the foothills as the sun was already beginning to sink behind the Rockies.

"The first chance I get, I will ride to Cheyenne and find you a wedding ring." Gabe stirred the coals of the campfire, and Faith lay on a blanket studying the stars.

"I'd like that. I know it seems silly to someone like you, but it's important to me."

He lay back down beside her. "It does not seem silly. When a Sioux man marries, he must bring his wife's father gifts, usually horses, tobacco, blankets, and such. I paid many horses for Little Otter."

Faith turned to face him, tracing the beading on his shirt. They had decided to take their time tonight. It had seemed enough at first just to lie there under the stars and talk and plan. "Do you love me as much as you loved her?"

He smiled sadly. "Of course I do. I just loved her different. She was Sioux, and highly respected among her tribe. I was much younger then, and I loved her blindly, as you loved your first husband. I think perhaps love changes as we grow a little older. It becomes even deeper, more fulfilling. That is the kind of love I feel for you. Still, except for your white skin and hair the color of a sunset, you are not so different from Little Otter. You have her quiet strength." He put a hand to the side of her face, then leaned closer to kiss her lightly.

Faith turned on her back to study the stars again. "You are *very* different from Johnny. When I look back on it, I realize he knew nothing about how to truly love someone. He had no respect for my feelings and needs as a woman. You make me feel very special, Gabe. It's been so long since anyone made me feel that way. I'm not sure I've *ever* felt this way." She faced him again. "You sure you don't mind staying right here to live?"

He toyed with her hair. "I am well aware of your dreams. I would not destroy them."

"I'll have to go to Cheyenne soon myself to lay claim to the area beyond the railroad land under the Homestead Act. We'll go together. Maybe I can get Buck to come back again and keep an eye on things so we can both go and leave Johnny here." She smiled at the idea, breathing deeply and watching the stars again. "Oh, Gabe, all these years I've stayed right here. I've never been to Cheyenne, never left this place, never even ridden on a stagecoach! It would be fun going with you to a real town, shopping for my own things instead of always having to order them sent to me. How far is it? How long would it take to ride there?"

"It is about sixty miles, a good three-day ride. We could get there quicker by stage, but it would be better to ride and take packhorses for supplies. Besides, it would be more peaceful. We would have much time alone together."

She snuggled closer. "I would like that. I don't think it would hurt for me to be away a week or so, just once. I've never left this place in all this time. It will be wonderful to see people again, some kind of civilization. And we have so much planning to do, Gabe. We need a house, and I want to turn the depot into a rooming house. You can hunt for our meat. I have some money saved, and—"

He cut off her words with a kiss, moving on top of her. "There is plenty of time for such planning," he told her, moving his lips to her neck. "This is our wedding night. From here on we will talk only about our love for each other, and we will show that love by sharing bodies."

Faith delighted in the fact that he seemed to have a way of making each time a little different, and she thought what a lovely idea he'd had in coming out here to lie under the stars, amid the soft night sounds, where they could be truly alone. "I love you, Tall Bear. Sometimes that's the only way I can think of you, as the Indian man who helped me four years ago."

He grinned, removing the combs from the sides of her hair and running his hands through its thick tresses. "And you are the woman who has haunted my night dreams ever since." He met her mouth again, deciding he would never get over his desire for her. She could be totally beautiful and feminine, yet she was not vain like some white women. She could work as hard as any man, shoot just as straight, and was just as brave. It was hard to believe she was really his wife, that she had so quickly and willingly agreed to marry him. But some things simply were meant to be, and as far as he was concerned, this was one of those things.

Faith was lost in her own surprise that she had so quickly decided she wanted to be a wife again. She was Faith Beaumont now . . . wife of Tall Bear. Her husband was a mysterious mixture of Indian and white, a man from worlds far removed from anything she had ever known. He was a man of great passion, and she did not mind some of that passion being spent on her now as he gently unbuttoned her dress, unlaced her camisole, and reached inside to caress her breasts almost worshipfully. He rose and pulled the dress down, off her shoulders and arms, and she lay there with her camisole still on but unlaced. Her feet were already bare, as she had taken off her shoes and stockings when she'd sat down on the blanket. He pulled her dress and slips the rest of the way off, leaving only her drawers and camisole. He leaned down, kissing her belly, slowly pulling down her drawers, licking little circles around her belly button, on down to the crevices at her thighs.

Indeed, this was no time for talking. Her drawers came off, and he kissed a pathway back up her legs to the red hairs that hid her lovenest. She shivered with a totally new ecstasy when his tongue moved to that magical spot he had touched only with his fingers until now. This was something totally new to her. Johnny had never done anything like this. He had never brought her so alive, made her feel quite so wanton and full of such urgent desires. He licked his way back down again, massaging and kissing her feet, her ankles, her legs, her knees, the insides of her thighs, making her want to open herself to him.

He gently tasted her again. She was astounded she could be so brazen with him, yet it felt so right. She stared up at the heavens, aching at his touch, quickly feeling the sweet, pulsating climax that made her cry out his name. Johnny had never brought her to this point, had never caressed her there, never caused this terrible need in her.

In the next moment his leggings were unlaced and he was surging inside her before he had even removed his clothes. He'd worn nothing under the leggings, wanting to be ready for this moment.

Gabe himself had not known such pure satisfaction since first taking Little Otter, but this was so much more satisfying, because he had been through so much since then, and this woman understood that. They shared more in common than one would think, both alone, both having suffered the loss of a spouse, both victims of this wild land, both free spirits. It felt so good to be inside her, to be able to please her. Her sweet juices still lingered on his lips as he devoured her mouth and claimed his new wife.

Faith arched against him, meeting his rhythmic thrusts, wanting every inch of him buried deep inside. This was her man. He had come to stay this time. He would not go away again. They had both found their place in this world where once they both had been lost. It felt good to be held, loved, caressed, respected, wanted. It felt good to be cared for and protected, much as she hated admitting she needed those things.

Gabe kept up the exotic mating for several minutes, wanting to please her totally. Finally he was unable to hold back his own near-agonizing pleasure, and his life spilled into her in pounding surges, leaving him spent and weak. He lay down beside her then, pulling her into his arms. "We will do this again. I want to take you many times tonight. We will be wild like the animals, free as the wind."

He sat up and untied and removed his precious bear-claw necklace, pulled off his buckskin shirt, leggings, and moccasins, then stretched out beside her, damp skin against damp skin. He pulled a blanket over them so she wouldn't get chilled. "It is strange," he told her, "how we are so close and yet in so many ways still strangers to one another. How can this feel so natural?"

She kissed his chest. "I don't know, except that it must be God's will. I never realized how much my parents taught me about faith until I came out here. Every time I've had a need, God has provided it. When Johnny was shot and I was out here alone, I prayed for God to send help, and then you appeared, and you came again when little

Johnny was sick. I think even then the Lord meant for us to be together."

He smiled softly. "Then this God of yours has great wisdom and great powers."

"He's the same God as your Wakan Tanka, I'm sure," she answered, snuggling against him. They lay there quietly before she spoke again. "Gabe, I've never let . . . I mean, no man has ever . . . done to me what you just did. I . . . I never felt like that."

"It pleased you?"

She felt herself blushing. "It pleased me greatly."

"There are many ways to enjoy each other."

The thought that he might have learned some of those things lying with whores when he rode with outlaws brought forth a fierce jealousy, and she reached around his neck, kissing him vigorously. "I want to know all the ways," she said, kissing at his neck then. "I want to please you as much as you please me."

He laughed lightly and sat up. "First we will wash. Then I will teach you more." He poured some water left heating over the fire into a bowl and added some cooler water to temper it. He made her lie still and washed her himself, the mere act of allowing him to do so bringing on more heated desire for Faith. She decided this was going to be the most glorious night of her life. Although she'd already been married once and had a baby, Gabe made her feel so special, almost as though this were her first time.

A wolf howled somewhere in the surrounding hills, but she was not afraid. Gabe Beaumont was as much a part of this wild land as those wolves, and God meant for this night to be one of wondrous love and ecstasy. The wolves would not bother them tonight.

Chapter Twenty-four

August 1868 . . .

Faith felt elated, little realizing until now just how far removed from civilization and social amenities she had been for much too long. Cheyenne was wild and dusty, but it bustled with excitement, a growing city with people from every walk of life crowding its boardwalks, horses, buggies, and wagons clattering up and down the streets. The ever-present Wyoming wind chased the dust everywhere, bringing with it the odor of horse dung and smells from cattle pens outside of town, but those were smells to which she had become accustomed long ago. She enjoyed the movement, the people, the many shops. The Union Pacific now reached Cheyenne, and it was obvious the town was experiencing a sudden burst of growth because of it. That meant that someday Sommers Station just might grow as big. Work on the railroad loop to be built into Sommers Station was already in progress.

Buck had already decided to quit Wells Fargo and had come to Sommers Station to stay—a grand population now of four! Because Buck could watch things, including little Johnny, Faith and Gabe had their chance to come to Cheyenne, and right now she felt like crying with joy as she sampled gold wedding bands. Gabe had promised her a ring, and now he was making good on that promise. The man who ran this jewelry store and clock shop didn't seem too pleased selling a wedding ring to an Indian man who had married a white woman, but his displeasure showed only in his eyes. He said nothing, only nervously showed both of them a variety of bands, extolling the wonderful value of each one.

Faith finally decided on a plain gold band that was not the cheapest, but certainly not the most expensive. "We have to be careful with our money, Gabe. We have so much building to do now, things to do to get ready for the railroad." Already crew leaders and more railroad executives had begun stopping at the depot for a good meal and to scope out the area. Her dream of a real town was becoming a reality, and much as she hated to admit it, Tod Harding was greatly responsible for that.

To her relief, during all these last few weeks that tracks had been laid through the area south of Sommers Station, the hellish settlement of prostitution and gambling that followed the railroad crews had stayed a mile southwest of construction, which kept it over two miles from Sommers Station. Buck had been there, and his description of the decadence that went on there gave Faith the chills. Soon the "dens of iniquity" would move even farther west as the railroad progressed several miles a day. Gabe had joked about going to see for himself what went on in what some railroaders called Hellsville, but Faith knew he would not really go. He had led such a life once, but only for a short, unhappy time. He was happy now; both of them were happier than at any time in their lives.

Gabe slipped the ring she had chosen onto her finger. "I want you to be happy with whatever you choose."

She studied his eyes lovingly. "I am happy with the *husband* I chose. The ring is only a symbol of my love for you."

They kissed lightly and Gabe paid for the ring, then

picked up Johnny, who had been standing at a grandfather clock, watching the pendulum swing back and forth. "Let's go, son. We have more shopping to do." He held the boy in one arm and put the other around Faith. They walked out and headed for the land office, only to be stopped by none other than Tod Harding, who had a man with him who wore a badge.

"Well, Mrs. Sommers!" Harding spoke up, putting on a smile Faith could tell he thought was charming.

"It is Mrs. Beaumont now, Mr. Harding."

His eyebrows shot up in surprise, and there was no mistaking the anger and jealousy in his eyes. "Oh? So you *did* find a preacher willing to marry a white woman to a half-breed."

Faith bristled, and she could feel Gabe's anger rising. "We found a preacher who believes in the Christian principle of loving all men the same, Mr. Harding. If you will excuse us now, I am going to the land office to put my claim on that railroad land you told me about, as well as even more land under the Homestead Act."

The man glanced at the jewelry store from which they had just emerged. "Buying a wedding ring, I presume?" He glanced at her hand, and the man with him stood with his legs apart in a threatening stance.

"My personal life is none of your business, Mr. Harding," Faith told him, irritated at the way he had of intruding when she still hardly knew him.

"I suppose not. I must say, though, that you are much too beautiful for such a plain gold band. You deserve much better."

"What the hell do you want, other than to try to insult me, Harding?" Gabe spoke up, handing Johnny to Faith.

Harding shrugged. "Just to say hello and let you both know I'll be staying in Cheyenne for a while, opening two new stores for my father, keeping an eye on the progress of the railroad."

"Good for you," Gabe answered with obvious sarcasm. He took Faith's arm to urge her off the boardwalk so they could walk around the two men, but the one wearing a badge grabbed Gabe's arm.

"I'm Sheriff Joe Keller," he told Gabe.

"Get your hand off me," Gabe warned him. He towered over the slender man.

"Gabe, keep your temper," Faith warned. She knew how he felt about this kind of white man, who looked at him with such derision.

Keller let go, but he took a deep breath and raised his chin as though to pretend he was not afraid. "Just thought I'd warn you most folks in this town are not too fond of anyone with Sioux blood. A lot of people around here have had some bad experiences, and they've got no tolerance for breeds who go around pretendin' they're civilized white men when in fact they're nothin' more than murderin' savages."

Gabe leaned closer. "Maybe I should accommodate your suspicions by slicing off your scalp, but I really couldn't do that in front of my wife and son, now, could I?"

"What is this?" Faith demanded, glaring at Harding. "You are deliberately trying to start trouble! Why? What has either one of us ever done to you?"

Harding put up his hands defensively. "My deepest apologies to both of you. I just happened to be walking with Sheriff Keller here when the two of you came out of the store." He looked at Keller chidingly. "Joe, you really ought to apologize for insulting Mr. Beaumont."

Keller looked at Harding angrily. "I don't make apologies to renegades." He looked back at Gabe. "And that's exactly what I think you are, Beaumont. My job is to keep the peace in this town, and men like you have a way of causin' trouble. I'm just warnin' you to mind your business and stay out of town as much as possible."

Gabe fought a need to hit the man. "I will mind my business, Sheriff. You just be sure to do the same."

The two men eyed each other a moment longer before Keller finally tipped his hat to Faith and walked around them.

"I truly am sorry for that man's behavior," Harding told them.

"And what about your own?" Faith asked.

"Oh, well, it was just the jealous man talking," he said, putting on a smile again. He'd hoped Faith had changed her mind about marrying, but now he supposed he would have to go through with his more recent idea—a way to get rid of Gabe Beaumont and leave Faith alone and vulnerable again.

"I must admit that I had an eye for you, ma'am. I have a great appreciation for your endurance and determination." He looked at Gabe. "You can't blame a man for admiring such a lovely and brave woman. I'm sure that is part of the reason you love her."

Gabe forced back an urge to land a fist in the man's face. "The reason a man marries shouldn't be another man's concern."

"Oh, I agree, but you have to understand that when I met Faith a year ago, I had every intention of getting to know her better as soon as the railroad reached Sommers Station. I never expected to come there a few weeks ago and find her ready to marry someone else. I ask your forgiveness for allowing my own envy make me insult you. I truly am sorry." He put out his hand. "Congratulations, Mr. Beaumont, on marrying the best woman this end of the Union Pacific." He flashed his most charming smile again.

Gabe did not shake his hand.

Harding's smile faded, and he dropped his hand. "By the way, Beaumont, whom did you scout for in the army?"

Gabe felt a new alarm. "How do you know I scouted for the army?"

"Oh, I have my sources."

Gabe thought about the soldier who had shown up at the station several weeks ago the same time Harding had—remembered the way the soldier had stared at him. "It makes no difference now," he told Harding. "That is long past and should be of no interest to you."

"Tall Bear, right? Were you called Tall Bear?"

Gabe did not reply. He took Faith's arm and led her past Harding, walking with such a determined pace that Faith practically tripped over her skirts to keep up. "Bastard!" Gabe mumbled.

"Gabe, there will always be men like Tod Harding to deal with. Once we're home, it won't matter. And we'll run Sommers Station however we want. There won't be men like Harding and Keller to answer to. I'm just sorry about their insults."

"You do not need to be apologizing. Never do it again. I know men like that very well, and they are *beneath* you!"

"And *you*!" Faith stopped walking and faced him. "I love you, Gabe. Let's go put our claim on that railroad land and then some. We'll get our supplies and go home." She grasped his hand. "Home. That's what we have now, together. Men like Tod Harding can't take that from us. You've got to get used to men like that if you're going to be Gabriel Beaumont and not Tall Bear."

Gabe took a deep breath to control his anger. "I would like to show both of them how a true warrior defends his honor!"

Faith shivered at the thought of just how wild and fierce her husband could be, and yet she felt only pride. "I know it's hard, Gabe. But the way you handled yourself just now—you've proved you're no savage who will kill at the drop of a hat. They tried to rile you, but you held your own. Please try to put it out of your mind."

Gabe glanced to where the men had been standing. Keller was gone, but Harding was leaning against a storefront watching them. "I do not trust that man. Why did he ask me about scouting for the army?"

"There is nothing he can do to us. We're legally married, and soon we'll lay legal claim to Sommers Station. Your days as an Indian are long behind you, and why would someone like Harding possibly care about your Indian side? He's just trying to upset you, to remind you you're part Indian and try to make you feel the lesser man for it."

"White men like him—those with money—have much power."

"Nothing is as powerful as our love for each other."

He met her eyes, his own bright with anger and determination. "I will not let anything or anyone take you from me."

She squeezed his hand. "If you believe in my love for you, you will know there *is* nothing and no one who could possibly come between us."

He sighed in resignation, taking Johnny back from her. "Your mother is not a woman to argue with, Johnny. You remember that."

He began walking again, and Faith followed beside him, feeling uneasy about Harding's insults and Keller's threats. They did not frighten her. They only angered her and made her more determined to realize her own dreams. Those dreams now included Gabe Beaumont, and they had damned well better understand that and not try to get in her way!

Johnny came running to Faith as she hung some clothes out to dry in the clear autumn air.

"Mommy! Mommy! Buck says Daddy's coming!"

Faith finished pinning a shirt to the line, then turned and picked up her son. "Well, let's go watch!" She could already hear the thundering hooves of the wild horses. Finding them and herding them to where he wanted them to go was as natural to a man like Gabe as breathing. He was shirtless because of the heat, and because he was a man who liked to feel the sun on his back. She could hear him yipping and shouting at the horses, the Indian in him coming alive when he rode free like that, the wind in his face.

He had decided that if Sommers Station was going to grow, he would be ready with his own means of income. He would catch and break wild horses, open a livery, sell and trade horses. Buck had suggested they could also sell saddles and bridle and all the other gear needed for horses.

Sommers Station was finally beginning to blossom. A blacksmith had answered one of Faith's ads, and two more men had replied and would be coming soon to see about settling there. Already a carpenter had joined them. His name was Henry Baker, a middle-aged man who had come west to homestead but who had lost his entire family to cholera on the way. They had been too poor to travel by train or stagecoach, had taken covered wagon. After his family's death Baker had wandered rather aimlessly, following the new railroad line until landing at Sommers Station, a heartbroken man with no idea what he was going to do with his life. Faith's offer that he stay and help build her town had given him something to do, and after building a one-room cabin for himself and Buck, he was now building a home for Faith and Gabe. He was working as fast as possible, since winter would soon settle in the mountains.

Things looked bright. They had heard that the Sioux had signed a treaty with the government that everyone hoped would mean peace and no more danger of Indian attack. They'd had only one encounter with Indians since Gabe had come to stay, when a band of Sioux had decided to camp near the station. Because Gabe was so much a part of them, he had been able to converse with them and keep the peace, convincing them not to try to take any of his or the stage line's horses when they finally headed to the new reservation farther northeast of the area.

Two weeks ago three men had ridden in bearing threatening looks and even more threatening weapons. Faith had had enough experience out there to know what they were after, but this time she had not had to barricade herself in the depot and try to shoot it out with them. One look at Gabe standing on the porch with a rifle in his hand had made them think twice. One had gone for his gun, and he now lay buried in the distance with Clete Brown and the other outlaws who had tried to make trouble at Sommers Station. The other two had left with no further argument, and Faith had no doubt that completion of the railroad and the growth of Sommers Station would end future Indian and outlaw troubles.

The railroad was still not finished, but already trains were coming as far west as the tracks allowed, some just bringing supplies to finish the building, others bringing more people to settle there. Already they often heard the echoing sound of a train whistle as locomotives headed for the end of the track. The sound of the whistles carried over the land as though to signal the coming of a new era, and it was like music to Faith's ears.

Soon many more people would come when the railroad was complete, men and women traveling beyond Cheyenne onward to California, with stops along the way, including Sommers Station. She and Gabe and Johnny had gone to watch some of the track crews once, and it was a sight to behold, crews working in rhythmic, determined steps—preparing the railroad bed, laying the ties and the iron rails, pounding in the spikes. It was amazing how fast they had come through; the tracks would meet by next spring, somewhere in Utah.

Faith's own next project was to add on to the depot and enlarge it into a rooming house. Maybe after that she would build a restaurant. Then she would be well prepared for the first travelers who came to Sommers Station by train. Her claim to railroad land was filed and valid now. Once the railroad was finished, she would be able to buy the land for $2.50 an acre, which meant she would own most of Sommers Station. She had claimed another one hundred adjoining acres under the Homestead Act, sure Sommers Station would grow beyond the railroad land. Those extra acres would be very valuable someday. She could sell them as town lots.

"Daddy," three-year-old Johnny said, pointing to the approaching herd, and to Gabe, who rode behind them, turning his Appaloosa first one way, then another, the animal obeying his every command as man and horse forced the wild herd to run toward a new corral Gabe and Buck had built for them.

Faith carried Johnny closer to watch Buck help force the horses into the corral. He shouted and whistled, waving his hat, chasing some strays back into the herd, while Gabe did the same from behind. It took several minutes to maneuver all sixteen horses through the gate, and Gabe let out a victorious war cry when the last horse was through and the gate closed. "Thanks, Buck!"

Henry waved his hat from the rooftop of the house he was building for them. "Beautiful horses, Gabe!" he yelled.

Gabe waved in reply, then rode over to Faith, jumped down from his horse, and gave her and Johnny a hug. "They are a good bunch," he said. "They all look healthy."

"I'm glad for you, Gabe."

"We still need a blacksmith. In the meantime I have to

study the hooves of each horse, make sure there are no deformities. For now I will brush down my own horse and be in soon for supper." He tousled Johnny's hair and gave him a kiss on the cheek, then met Faith's eyes. "Maybe Johnny will fall asleep early tonight?"

Faith felt a warmth move through her veins at the words. "He probably will. He did a lot of running today."

Gabe grinned the handsome grin Faith loved to see. She watched him walk off with his horse, thinking how she had not regretted one moment with Gabe Beaumont. Life was good now, and it was going to get better. The house would be finished soon—nothing fancy, a five-room frame home behind the depot so they would be close to the water pump. Fancy did not matter. It would be their first real home. Gabe had never lived that way, but he seemed eager for it. He was happy now, and she in turn never thought she could take so much pleasure in a man's arms. Now she was already carrying their first child together. She had not told Gabe yet. She was saving the news until she was absolutely sure.

She went inside and finished preparing supper, and soon Gabe came in, having already washed at the pump outside. "I think I will make that trip back to Cheyenne," he told her. "I need horseshoes, and last fall I spoke with the grown son of a blacksmith there who expressed an interest in coming here to start his own business. That one who wrote you has not shown up yet, and these new horses must be shod. We also need more supplies, and with the stage line running less often, we cannot always depend on getting what we need in time. By next spring the train will begin bringing supplies."

"I have a lot to do here," Faith told him. "Maybe you should go by yourself this time." She could not tell him yet the real reason—that she did not want to do anything that might lead to losing the precious life in her belly. Gabe had already lost so much in his lifetime, and now he had a chance for a new family. She did not want to spoil that.

"I had already planned on going alone. I want to surprise you with something when I come back, and I cannot do it if you go with me. With Henry and Buck here, I will not worry so much about you. The Sioux are at peace—for the time being, anyway—and because of those who camped here last winter, they know you are my woman and the horses out there belong to me. They will not make trouble."

Faith liked the way he called her his woman. Yes, he owned her, and she didn't mind at all. Not many men cared about their woman's dreams, but Gabe did, and he was doing all he could to help her realize that dream.

"What on earth can you surprise me with?" she asked.

"If I told you, then it would not be a surprise." Gabe felt excited at the thought of selling some of his horses in Cheyenne and bringing home some furniture for their new home. Faith had carried on about a grandfather clock she had seen at the jewelry store where they had bought her wedding ring, as well as a fancy table and chairs at another store. He also intended to buy her some of the prettiest material he could find to make herself a new dress, and more material for curtains for their new home.

Faith set a plate of venison stew in front of him. "When will you go?"

"In a couple of days. I will try not to take too long. I do not like the thought of being apart. We have not been apart since I first rode back here to work for you."

Faith sat Johnny at his own special little table with a bowl of stew in front of him. She had drained out most of the sauce and left only meat and potatoes and corn. She handed him a spoon and told him to try to eat like a big boy and not make a mess.

"Big like daddy," he said, taking the spoon.

"Yes, big like daddy," Faith repeated, smiling. Gabe chuckled, and she moved back to sit down near him with a plate of stew for herself. "He loves you so, Gabe."

His smile faded. "And I love him." He looked her over, and Faith dearly wanted to tell him about the baby, but she didn't want him to worry while he was gone. If he had a surprise for her when he returned, she would have an equal or better surprise for him.

"All this time I spent here alone, and now it will seem

strange and lonely without you, Gabe, even though it's only been six months."

He stabbed a piece of meat. "I won't be long. I just hope I do not run into that fancy railroad man again. I am not so sure I could hold my temper again if he insults me."

"He's probably gone by now, on to another city to build his father's wealth. He does so love to brag about that."

Gabe met her eyes. "He will probably come here next. I do not like the thought of his looking at you."

"Gabe Beaumont, the man knows we are married now. Besides, men like Harding marry only their own kind. Lord knows I don't belong in that world, nor would I want to. I have everything I want right here."

"Men like that do not give up easily."

"Gabe! Stop worrying where there is no need. Besides, I've seen him only twice. I hardly know him. It's not as though he was beating down my door. His real interest isn't me at all. It's Sommers Station and what kind of businesses he can have here. And I'll even own the land he builds them on, so he'll have no hold over us of any kind, which means he's harmless."

"Men like that are never harmless," Gabe grumbled. He decided not to go into it further and worry her. How could he explain the uneasy feeling he had about Tod Harding? He still could not get off his mind the way that one soldier had looked at him last spring, the fact that he'd suspected the soldier was talking to Harding when they'd left on the stage that day. He would not think so much about it if Harding had not asked him whom he'd scouted for in the army. The entire encounter had weighed on his mind ever since. Nothing more had happened, so perhaps he had nothing to worry about, after all. He finished his stew and bread, sat down with a pipe, and watched Faith clean up. He called Johnny to come over and sit on his lap, and he held the boy close as he watched Faith wash dishes. He hoped she was right that people like Tod Harding could not come between them. The Indian in him who hated men like Harding was rearing up to cause doubts and worries where there probably should be none, and he realized that part of him would never change.

They put Johnny to bed, and Gabe barricaded the door and shutters to the depot, then retired to the back room, where they had moved their bed so they would not be too close to Johnny. Gabe sat down on the bed and removed his boots, watching Faith brush her hair. "I've never seen hair like yours," he told her. "It reminds me of a sunset."

She smiled, setting the brush aside and unbuttoning her dress. "I'm surprised it isn't gray already, with what it's taken to live out here. And every day it seems I find a new line in my face."

He removed his shirt and walked up behind her, grasping her hair and enjoying the feel of it tumbled in his hands. "Your face is beautiful, and it will always be, even when it starts showing lines." He leaned closer, gazing into the new mirror she had bought on their trip to Cheyenne. He ran his hands over the sides of her neck and down the front of her, reaching inside her camisole, and Faith closed her eyes and grasped his strong wrists, breathing deeply with the pleasure of his touch. "You will hurry back from Cheyenne as fast as you can, won't you?"

"You know that I will." He leaned down and lifted her out of the chair in front of the mirror and carried her to their bed, a homemade pine bed with rope springs and a feather mattress. He laid her down and moved onto the bed, hovering over her. "You have never regretted marrying me?"

Faith frowned. "Why would you ask such a thing?"

He kissed her lightly. "I am not sure. Sometimes I am afraid I will lose you, the way I have lost everyone else in my life."

She reached up to smooth back some of the thick dark hair that had fallen across his face. "I will always be here, Gabe. But I have to tell you, *I* worry about losing *you*, to that wild heart inside you, the man who once rode with the Sioux and made war against people like me. Maybe someday you will miss that life and go back to it."

He shook his head, smiling lovingly. "Never. Not as long as I have you."

He met her mouth in another kiss that told her he meant every word of it, and both felt an urgent need to seal the

promises. They were still dressed, and Gabe pushed up the
skirt of her dress and her slips, then deftly helped her out of
her drawers. He unbuttoned his pants, and in the next
moment he was deep inside her, neither of them needing
preliminaries this time, not even undressing completely
first. It was important simply that they be together this
way, that he brand her again, and that she offer herself to
him in the promise of eternal love. He took her hard and
fast, burying himself deep, wanting her in an almost angry
possessiveness he could not explain.

It was over quickly, and he rose and helped her undress,
removed his own clothes, and took her again. Faith found
her breath coming in gasps as he moved in hard, wild
rhythm. She sensed his worry, knew this was something he
needed in more ways than just a man needing sex. He was
laying claim to her, reminding her she belonged to him. His
life surged into her once again, and finally he relaxed beside her.

"I am sorry," he told her. "I was not very gentle."

She curled next to him. "It's all right. But I wish you
would tell me what is wrong. Something is bothering you,
Gabe. Surely you aren't still thinking about Tod Harding
or considering he could have any affect on us."

He sighed deeply. "That is part of it, but it is not just
him. It is white men in general. If this place grows, there
will be many men come here who are like him—white men
with education and money—men who can offer more than
I will ever offer."

"Oh, Gabe," she sighed. "I can't believe you're saying
these things. You have already given me everything I have
ever wanted. I thought we agreed we belong together, that
we're actually very much alike in the loneliness we knew
when we met, the freedom we both love. We have so much
here, so much to build on and share." She kissed his chest.
"Get some sleep, Mr. Beaumont."

He grinned, pulling her close. "I always sleep well with
you next to me."

Faith closed her eyes and did not bother to get up and
turn down the oil lamp. It felt too good just lying there in

the safety of her husband's arms. It was a good feeling not being alone anymore, never being afraid.

Somewhere in the distance she heard another wail of a train whistle. It suddenly dawned on her how different it might be for a man like Gabe to live in a full-fledged town, such a contrast to anything he had ever known. Just as he feared losing her to that growth, she in turn feared losing Gabe to the Indian in his blood. Gabe Beaumont could live in and adjust to a white settlement just fine. But could Tall Bear?

Chapter Twenty-five

Gabe pocketed the money he had made selling five horses to the livery owner in Cheyenne, confident that one thing he had learned from the Sioux that could be used in the white man's world was how to judge good horse flesh. He had made seventy-five dollars each for three of the horses he'd sold, one hundred dollars each for the other two. Four hundred twenty-five dollars! He had plenty for supplies, plus that material he wanted to buy for Faith, and perhaps the grandfather clock and some furniture. Maybe he would buy some kind of toy for Johnny.

He took hold of his horse and ducked into the wind-storm that had arisen overnight. He bent his head against stinging sand and walked toward the supply store, holding on to his hat. He tied his horse near the supply store and stepped up onto the boardwalk, but before he reached the store, something slammed into his ribs from behind. He felt someone take his six-gun from his holster as he grunted and fell, and he grabbed at his attacker's hand, giving a vicious tug.

For a brief moment he caught a glimpse of Sheriff Joe

Keller. He landed a big fist on the man's jaw and sent him sprawling. Quickly he felt for his gun, hoping Keller had not already managed to take it away, but there was nothing in his holster. The sudden attack and black pain in his ribs, as well as the blinding sandstorm, kept him from gaining control of the fight before something hit him again, this time in the head. Everything went dark, and he could not move, yet he could hear voices.

"You're under arrest for murder, Beaumont."

"Let's take him around the back way," came another voice.

"The son of a bitch almost broke my jaw!" came the first voice. "I ought to kill him!"

"We've got to make this look more legal than that," came the second voice.

Gabe felt himself being helped to his feet, pain ripping through his head, dizziness and the howling wind keeping him confused. He staggered between the two men who held his arms, not sure how far they went before he fell against some steps. Then he sensed he was inside a building. His vision began to return as he was shoved to the floor, and someone removed his gun belt and rummaged through his pockets.

"Got a lot of money on him."

"Keep it. You've earned it," came the reply. "I'll get rid of his horse where nobody sees it. I'll have it shipped farther east to a buyer I know there."

Gabe heard a loud clank, the rattle of keys. Moments later there was only silence. He managed to pull himself to a seated position, opened his sand-filled eyes. It took a moment to focus before he realized where he was when he saw iron bars all around him.

Jail! Darkness came over him again, and he slumped to the floor.

Gabe slowly regained his senses, not sure how long he had been shut up alone in this cell. His head pounded, and his ribs ached so bad, he could hardly breathe. He scrambled to think straight, remembering someone had taken his gun and money. Keller? Poor Faith would probably never see any of his money. Maybe she wouldn't even be told where he was.

After what seemed hours he finally heard voices outside the heavy wooden door that separated the cells from the outer office. The door swung open, and Keller stepped in, two other men standing just outside the doorway. Gabe had never seen them before.

"You're going on a little trip with a couple of bounty hunters," he told Gabe. "They've been waiting here a few days, Beaumont. We thought you'd never show up. Didn't want to go arrest you in front of your white bitch of a wife and the little kid. Figured you'd be comin' back around here sooner or later. Now you can keep on goin'—south— to Indian Territory, where you'll be hanged."

Gabe felt instant fury beginning to rise in his soul. He slowly rose and grasped the iron bars of his cell. "What the hell are you talking about? Hanged for what?"

"For killing an army officer, Lieutenant Nathan Balen."

"Balen!" Gabe scrambled to think. "That was three years ago! How do you know I scouted for Balen?"

"Oh, us lawmen have our ways. Besides, when you kill a superior officer, sooner or later the army will have your hide for it."

"I did *not* kill Balen! I saw him shot down in an Indian fight. If I had killed him, why has no one come for me before now?"

"Well, maybe they just didn't know where to find you."

"Who says that I killed Lieutenant Balen?"

"Can't say. All I know is someone saw you do it. Says he reported it, but you ran off before you could be caught. The army couldn't find you, but not long ago a soldier recognized you when he saw you at Sommers Station. He reported it to me."

"To *you*? Why you and not his own commander? This stinks, Keller, and you know it! Harding is behind all of this, isn't he?"

Keller shrugged. "All I know is I'm supposed to arrest you."

"You know a hell of a lot more than that, you thief! You

stole my money! You know this is all a farce! The army should come for me, not bounty hunters!"

Keller grinned. "Life just ain't quite fair when you're a half-breed, is it?" He folded his arms. "Arrangements have been made to, uh, waive a hearing, you might say. I have all the proper papers here. There's no price on your head, but the two men waiting for you are being paid well to take you to Indian Territory. You can go peacefully, or painfully, whichever way you choose."

Rage ripped through Gabe's blood. "You cannot do this! I should be allowed to talk to whoever has accused me! I have a right to a trial!"

"You're half-Indian. Like I said, things just ain't fair for ones like you." Keller unlocked the cell door.

"This is Tod Harding's doing!" Gabe repeated. "*He* has arranged this, hasn't he?"

"I don't know what you're talking about," Keller answered. "Come on out of there. You're going out the back way."

"What about my wife? Someone must tell her! Return my horse, give my wife the money I earned for selling the other horses today, you bastard!"

Keller shook his head. "You shouldn't have called me a thief, Beaumont. Now I don't feel like doing you any favors. Now, let's go."

The two bounty hunters entered the room then, smelling of perspiration from the hot day and from clothes worn too long without being washed. Their beards and clothes and the looks on their faces reminded Gabe of the buffalo hunters who had killed Little Otter and Running Fox. Bounty hunters! Such men were the scum of the earth, as far as he was concerned. He had to get out of there!

He slammed the cell door against Keller, knocking him backward, then heard a gunshot before he could do anything more. Hot pain bit at the back of his right leg, and he crumpled in the doorway that led to the outer office. He looked up, and that was when he saw him—Tod Harding—standing in the outer office with a smirk on his face.

"Bastard!" Gabe roared.

Before he could rise, the bounty hunters began landing

feet into his face, his ribs, pummeling his entire body with
kicks. He was hardly aware of being dragged out the back
door and thrown into the back of a wagon, cuffed spread-
eagled to the wagon bed and covered with straw and blankets so no one would see him. No one bothered to wrap the
gunshot wound in his leg, put there, he surmised, by one of
the bounty hunters. He groaned as the wagon hit a bump
when it got under way.

Inside, Sheriff Keller was being helped to his feet by Tod
Harding. One whole side of Keller's lip was badly swollen,
and already his face was showing bruises. He wiped at a
bleeding nose with his shirtsleeve.

"Good job, Keller," Harding told him. "You'll be paid
well, as will those men when they return and let me know
he's been hanged."

"The son of a bitch packs a punch," Keller answered,
putting a hand to his already-sore jaw. "I hope you know
the trouble I could be in if people found out about this. I
need their votes, you know."

"And you'll get them. I backed you the first time. I'll
back you again, as long as you keep doing me favors. I'll
get you elected, and then I'll be on my way to new horizons—establishing another business in the new railroad
town of Sommers Station."

Keller shook his head. "Don't forget the Sommers
woman *married* this guy. She won't exactly be wanting to
think about anybody else, no matter how much you do for
her town."

Harding chuckled. "She will when she realizes her wild
Indian husband has run out on her. Men like that aren't
made for settling. I'll convince her of that eventually. I'll
get rid of his horse, and there will be no trace of Gabriel
Beaumont, also known as Tall Bear. The only thing Faith
Beaumont needs to know is the man came here, sold some
horses, and just kept on riding with the money. The pres-
sures of civilization must have got to him."

Keller sat down behind his desk, wincing with pain.
"You figuring on marrying her?"

A sneer moved over Harding's lips. "Knowing she's
been bedded by an Indian?" He shook his head. "My pri-

mary goal right now is to help her build that town of hers into something valuable. Then she'll find out she's going to have to pay a lot more than she thought for those railroad lots." He shook his head. "You know, I just don't get it. Why would a fine woman like that marry a half-breed? I was sure she'd wait to see what I had to offer."

Keller shrugged. "Some women like their men big and dark, and he's not exactly ugly."

Anger glittered in Harding's eyes. "If she'll lie with that breed, she'll lie with anybody . . . in time." He took a deep breath as though to brush away the thought. "But whether she does or not is beside the point. I had her all set up to suck her into my plans for building Sommers Station. She's so excited about it, she'll be a great help. She just doesn't know she'll slowly lose control and eventually be forced to leave. Gabe Beaumont is a smart and skilled man. He just might have gotten in the way. Now I don't have to worry about him, and being a woman deserted and badly hurt like that, Faith Beaumont will be like soft mud in my hands, to mold however I choose." He tipped his hat to Keller. "I'll be back with your money."

Keller nodded and watched him leave. "You pompous bastard," he muttered. He hated Tod Harding, but the man paid well for favors, and a sheriff's pay wasn't much. A man needed a little extra to get by.

"Daddy come." Johnny stood outside the screen door, his brown eyes full of hope. Faith's heart ached not just for herself, but for Johnny, who had become Gabe's shadow, and who had waited faithfully for his new father for days now. She hoped he was right that it was Gabe who was coming, but deep inside a hopeless feeling had engulfed her. She walked outside, taking Johnny's hand and waiting for the approaching rider. Henry Baker had also noticed and was walking toward her. Already Faith could see that the rider was Buck . . . coming back alone. When he came close enough to dismount, the look in his eyes only made her feel sicker inside.

"Where daddy?" Johnny asked.

Buck forced a smile for him. "Oh, he can't come yet,

son." He glanced at Faith with a look that said, "I'm sorry."

"Johnny, go play with the kittens in the barn," Faith told him. "But be careful with them. Don't hold them too tight."

"Okay, Mommy." The boy ran off, and Faith was grateful that a cat had strayed to the depot, probably from some settlement not far away, and had had kittens in the barn. It was a good diversion for Johnny. She faced Buck again. "What did you find out?"

Henry had come closer, a plain, quiet man who had continued to work on the house he was building for Faith and Gabe.

Buck sighed with disappointment. "I hate to say it, ma'am, but everything points to Gabe just ridin' off. Only thing I could find out was he sold them horses at the livery for good money, and nobody saw him after that. He didn't do no shoppin', wasn't seen in no taverns, nothin'. I checked with the sheriff, and he said seein' as how he didn't like no Indians in town, he'd have noticed him, but he says he never saw him. Only thing I can think is he sold them horses and then lit out."

Faith straightened more, trying to be strong. It was her biggest fear now realized, but she simply could not believe it would really happen. "Something is wrong, Buck. Something is terribly wrong. He wouldn't do this to me." She turned away, fighting tears. "He told me he wanted to surprise me with something. Maybe . . . maybe he had to go somewhere we don't know about."

"Well . . . maybe. But he did say he'd only be gone the seven or eight days it takes to get to Cheyenne and come back. I don't mean to try to make you feel bad, ma'am. I'm just tryin' to make you see what could be the truth. Gabe is half-Indian, and livin' the settled life, stayin' in one place, it might have just got to be too much. There's nothin' but talk around here about this place growin' to a town, and you're havin' that house built. He's been feelin' the pressure of providin' for a family the white man's way. So maybe—"

"He would have told me if he had problems with that," she interrupted.

"Maybe. Then again, maybe he just didn't know how to tell you. Maybe he just took the easy way. He don't strike me as a man always able to speak his true feelin's."

Faith turned and faced him, fire in her eyes. Henry Baker meekly looked away, saying nothing. "He loved me, Buck! He *married* me, the legal, white man's way! He wouldn't have done that if he didn't mean to live out our married life like a white man. And over there!" She pointed to the corral. "There are eleven horses left over there that he captured himself! Horses mean *everything* to an Indian! He wouldn't leave without taking them with him! A lot of his gear is still here. His other Appaloosa is still here. He wouldn't ride off and leave all that behind! Something has happened to him, Buck! You've got to find out what it is!"

Buck removed his hat and ran a hand through his hair. "Ma'am, I did everything I could, talked to just about everybody in town."

"Did you talk to Tod Harding?"

"No, ma'am. He was out of town on business. The man who runs his lumber business there claims he's been gone a couple of weeks, since before Gabe would have gone there."

A tear slipped down her cheek, and she quickly wiped it away. "Maybe he lied. Gabe didn't trust Harding *or* that sheriff! They tried to make trouble for us when we went there two months ago. Did you check inside the jail? Look in the cells?"

"Yes, ma'am. He wasn't there. Sheriff Keller had a pretty swolled-up jaw, but he said he got it breakin' up a bar fight a couple weeks ago. I checked the livery and all around town, but there was no sign of his horse anyplace either."

Faith grasped her stomach. Gabe's baby was growing inside her. She should have told him. Maybe if she had told him, he would have had more incentive to come back. *Stop it!* she chided herself. Gabe had not left her. He wouldn't do that! He loved her, and Johnny, too! He'd been so happy when he left, so eager to sell the horses and to surprise her with something. He wouldn't do this. He just wouldn't. Still, three weeks had gone by since he'd left.

"You've got to go back, Buck. Chances are Keller's swollen jaw is from a tangle with Gabe, but we'll never know. This time check all the outer settlements. Check along the railroad. Go to the end of the track. Ask everyone you can if they've seen Gabe. He's easy to describe. Not many men are built like him or look so Indian. People will know it if they've seen him." She wiped away another tear. "You rest tonight. I'll make you a nice meal. Then I want you to leave in the morning and try again. I would go myself, but I have Johnny to look after, and I'm"—oh, the pain of it—"I'm carrying Gabe's baby."

Buck closed his eyes and sighed. "I'm real sorry, ma'am, for what's happened," Henry said, pulling his hat a little farther down over his eyes. "I'll get back to work on your house. I'm sure your husband will come back, and the house will be all ready when he does."

Henry walked off, and Faith turned around, crying quietly. Buck patted her on the shoulder. "I'll go back and try again. I don't mean to make you cry, ma'am, but I've lived out in this land for many years. I've seen just about everything there is to see, and men like Gabe . . . Well, I think he's a good man, but that Indian spirit in him just might have took over."

"No," she protested again. "I won't believe that. He promised. He promised me this was what he wanted for the rest of his life."

Buck sighed and turned away. "I'll go tend my horse and come back later."

She nodded, her back still to him. "Thank you, Buck, for going to look for him."

"It ain't no bother. I liked the man a lot. Maybe you're right. Maybe somethin' happened we don't know about. If you want, I'll even go check at Robber's Roost, Brown's Park, some of the outlaw hangouts. Some of them men knew him. Maybe somebody there knows somethin'."

"Yes!" Faith turned, wiping at her eyes with her apron. "That's a good idea. Check the whole territory of Wyoming if you have to!"

Buck nodded, his heart aching for her. "I'll do that, ma'am. If he's to be found, I'll find him. Hell, I'll check at the forts, maybe ride to the Sioux reservations."

Faith brightened even more. "That's a wonderful idea! If . . . if he did leave because of his Indian blood, he would probably go there. And if you find him, Buck, tell him I'm going to have a baby. He'll come back if he knows that. Tell him . . . tell him I love him and want to be with him. Tell him I'd even leave Sommers Station and go live on the reservation if that is what it takes."

Buck ran a hand around the back of his neck. "I'll tell him, ma'am." He turned away, not sure if he should be worried about Gabe Beaumont or hate the man. If he discovered Gabe had simply run out on Faith, he'd be tempted to shoot him. One thing was sure, though. The woman sure as hell loved Gabe, and he ought to appreciate that. As much as she'd put into running Sommers Station, all her dreams about building a town here—yet she'd be willing to leave it all for Gabe Beaumont. That would be a great sacrifice for her, and right now he wasn't sure Gabe Beaumont was worth it.

Faith turned away and let the tears come, wanting to get them out before going to get Johnny for supper. Of all the things that had happened to her, all the things she had been through, nothing had hurt this much, and nothing had so sorely tested her faith in God and man.

Gabe Beaumont had suddenly disappeared from her life, and she was alone again. It was as though something or someone did not want her to be happy. She told herself she must hang on. She must keep the faith, and trust in Gabe's love.

"He'll be back," she told herself. "Unless he's—" No! He wasn't dead. Not Gabe. He was strong, and his love for her would bring him through whatever had gone wrong. She had to believe that, or she wouldn't want to go on living herself. She *had* to go on—for Johnny, for the new baby inside her. She would never stop believing that Gabe Beaumont would come back to her.

Part Four

Chapter Twenty-six

1870 . . .

Bret Flowers climbed down from the train platform, smiling at what she saw on the sign over the depot. SOMMERS STATION. The station was apparently becoming a bustling new town, and she could see several new structures, including a livery, a supply store, a little building that simply read HOTEL, and a rooming house with a sign overhead that read "BEAUMONT'S—ROOMS FOR RENT." The train station was also a new structure, and she was glad that it and the town were still named after Faith Sommers. She was anxious to see Faith again, and she called to Ben Carson to "Hurry up and get down here."

"You're always in a hurry, woman," Ben told her, disembarking with two of her bags. "I'll get your trunk and our other bags and find someone to cart them for us. Do you see a hotel around?"

"Well, there's a sign over there, for one, but that rooming house there—" She pointed. "That looks like the old stage depot, doesn't it? Looks like they've added on to it.

I'll bet Faith runs that place. Let's check that out first. There's a new house behind it. Maybe she lives there now." She smiled, waving her arm in a sweeping motion. "Look at this, Ben! Do you think Faith is still here? Is this all due to her?"

"It must be. The ad said to contact Faith Beaumont."

"Well, when we left her, her name was Faith Sommers. The girl must have married. I'm damn glad of that. She struggled on her own long enough."

"Let's find her and tell her our plan."

"You go ahead with the bags. I'm going to walk over to the rooming house." Bret strutted off, twirling her ruffled pink parasol that matched her ruffled pink dress. A few people gawked at her, but she was used to stares. She sauntered across the dusty street to the rooming house, stepping onto a new front porch, where potted plants sat on either side of the front door. Lace curtains hung at the oval glass in the door, and a wind chime tinkled when a gust of hot wind blew sand against Bret's face.

"Damn wind," she mumbled as she knocked. "It never stops blowing up here." Through the lace curtains she saw the shadow of a very large woman coming to the door, and when the door opened, a hefty, stern-faced woman looked her over with obvious disapproval of her dress.

"Yes?"

"I am looking for Faith Sommers. I believe her name is Faith Beaumont now. Does she still live around here?"

The woman looked her over again. "Faith lives in za house back of zis one," she replied with a strong German accent. "I am Maude Grummond. My husband makes and repairs boots and shoes. I run this place for Faith. You come here to start a business, too?"

Bret forced back an urge to laugh. "You might say that. I'm really not sure yet. Actually, I've known Faith a long time. I just want to see her, see how she is doing."

"Not so goot since zat no-goot husband of hers deserted her, but she's a strong lady. Folks in zis town admire her a lot. She is fair to us on renting our lots, does good with za rooming house here. She is the kind that just keeps on going, you know?"

Bret remembered well. "Yes. I could see that for the short time I knew her. Thank you." She turned. "Oh, and do you have a vacant room to rent?"

Maude frowned, still obviously doubtful of Bret's respectability. "Zere is one available—but only if Faith approves. I vill hold za room. Just come back after you talk to Faith."

"Sure. And if a man comes here looking for me with a wagon full of baggage, tell him to leave mine and go on over to the hotel and find a room for himself." She twirled the parasol and smiled. "Thank you." She left, full of wonder over the woman's comments. A no-good husband who had lit out on Faith? Why would any man not appreciate a woman like her enough to stay with her? Poor Faith! She'd been through so much. Now apparently some man had deserted her.

The sound of pounding hammers filled the air as she walked to the new house behind the rooming house. Sommers Station was definitely growing, and each gust of wind carried with it the smell of fresh lumber. Beyond town she could see a few small homes. The train at the depot belched out several short whistles, signaling it was preparing to depart again. All sights and sounds that spoke of a growing new town.

Faith's house was painted white with blue shutters and trim, and flowers bloomed around the porch. A little bit of scrubby grass served as a small lawn, already drying up for lack of rain. Apparently the flowers were kept watered, since they looked as though they were doing well. She went to the screened door and knocked, noticing that the inner door was open. A handsome little boy with big brown eyes and curly brown hair came running down the hallway, and he pushed open the screen door.

"Hi!" he said, putting on a charming, dimpled smile.

"Hello! Don't tell me! Are you Johnny?"

He nodded his head. "I'm five!"

"My, oh my! Let's see . . . it's 1870. Why, yes, you *are* five! I can't believe it's been that long since I saw you being born!"

"You saw me borned?"

"I sure did. Where's your mommy?"

"She's in the bedroom. She's feeding my little brother. His name is Alex."

A little brother! Her husband not only had run out on her, but he'd left her with a new baby! Poor Faith sure didn't have much luck with husbands. The first one drowned, and now this one left her.

"Who is it, Johnny?"

The boy ran back down the hall and into a room. "It's a pretty lady."

Bret stepped inside. "Faith? It's Bret Flowers."

"Bret! Oh, just a minute."

Bret waited, walking a little farther to gaze into a small but tidy parlor on her right. The room had a small fireplace, a couple of love seats, a rocker, and two fancy oil lamps. A small round table sat between the two facing love seats, and the lamps were on tables at one end of each seat. Lace curtains hung at the window, and a couple of Oriental rugs were scattered on the polished wood floor. She could see the end of the hallway and what looked like a kitchen, for she spotted a porcelain cookstove and a table and chairs. To her left was a room that looked like an office, with shelves of books and a desk that had papers scattered over it. Two more doors beyond these were most likely bedrooms, but she didn't want to appear too snoopy.

Faith emerged from one of those rooms, still buttoning the front of her dress. She left a few buttons undone at the top, and the look of joy in her eyes warmed Bret's heart. "Bret! Oh, it's so good to see you!" Faith literally ran to her with open arms, and Bret sensed her sadness in spite of the joy of the moment.

"My goodness! I didn't expect such a warm welcome!" She hugged Faith, patting her back. "Let me have a look at you, Faith Sommers. Or I guess it's Beaumont now, isn't it?" She pulled away. "You're more beautiful than I remembered. Maybe it's because you've turned into much more a woman than the half child I met when you had that baby. How the heck old are you now, anyway?"

"I'm twenty-four. Johnny is already five years old!"

"Yes, he told me. And what a handsome child he is. His father must have been a looker!"

Faith smiled sadly. "Johnny was very handsome."

Bret folded her parasol and set it aside. "Well, Ben and I, we saw your ad in the Denver papers asking people to come and settle in the growing railroad town of Sommers Station. We knew it had to be you who placed the ad—always wondered how you were doing. They're starting to get pretty uppity in Denver about people like us, so we thought, heck, let's go to Sommers Station and see about having our own business. We were just working for other people in Denver—running gambling tables and such. Say, where's Hilda?"

Sadness filled Faith's eyes. "Hilda . . . died . . . four years ago. Oh, there is so much to tell you, Bret." Bret never even knew the truth about how Johnny had died, and to explain about Hilda meant telling the truth about Johnny. So much had happened since then. "Do you have time?"

"I have all the time in the world. Ben and I came here to open a saloon, if you'll allow one in this new little town of yours."

Faith put a hand to a strand of hair that had fallen out of her plain bun. Ever since Gabe's disappearance she had not cared much how pretty she was. She'd never worn her hair down and loose again. The thought of what Bret did for a living, the colorful way she was dressed now, made Faith more aware of her own plain appearance. "Well, I . . . I suppose. Every town has a saloon—usually several! I just wouldn't want . . . well . . . I don't think it would be right to have . . ."

"Prostitution?" Bret waved her off. "Heck, I didn't plan on that. Just a legal establishment—beer and drinks, men can play cards, that sort of thing." She studied Faith's appearance. Yes, she was beautiful as ever, but there was a terrible sadness in her eyes, a tired look about her. And she was too thin. She took hold of her hand. "Now, my dear, first things first. We'll talk about the saloon later. I want to know about Hilda—and I especially want to know more about what the lady at the rooming house told me—something about a husband lighting out on you—and now Johnny says he's got a new baby brother. What in the world is going on?"

Faith closed her eyes against the endless pain. "I wish I knew, Bret. You're a worldly woman. Maybe you will have an idea what I should do."

"Well, I don't know about that, honey, but I'll try. Let's go into the parlor and talk about it."

Faith nodded. "You go sit down. I'll put Johnny down for his nap. Where is Ben?"

"Oh, he's taking care of baggage and such. He'll fend for himself for now."

"You have no idea how good it is to see you, Bret. You're one person I know I can talk to and you'd understand anything. One thing I want you to understand right now is that my husband did not 'light out' on me, as you put it. I will never believe that. I may never know what happened to him, but I'll never believe it was his own doing. Come into the bedroom and see the baby." She led Bret down the hall and into her own bedroom, where Johnny sat playing on the floor near the cot where his little brother slept. Faith ordered Johnny to go lie down, and the boy climbed onto his own homemade bed, sinking into the feather mattress.

Faith gently stroked her second son's straight black hair. "He's fourteen months old already. His name is Alexander, named after his grandfather Beaumont."

Bret studied the child's dark skin and hair. "Beaumont. That's French, I think. That boy looks more Mexican or Indian."

"His father was half Sioux Indian." Oh, how it hurt to talk about him! "Gabriel Beaumont, called Tall Bear by the Sioux. Gabe's father was a French trapper. It's such a long story, Bret." She met Bret's eyes. "I loved him more than I could ever love another man again. And I know that if he could, he would be here right now. I don't know if he's dead or alive, and I don't know what to tell Johnny or the new baby—if I'm a widow, a free woman, or still married. But it doesn't matter. I'll never be interested in another man."

Bret put her hands on her hips. "You're only twenty-four, and you have two sons to raise. You have to consider marrying again, Faith."

Faith shook her head. "I got along on my own just fine before Gabe came along. I didn't marry him to have someone to take care of me. I married him because I loved him and wanted to share my life with him. I won't love another man that way, although I know the boys need a man in their lives." She met Bret's eyes. "I'd wager with all the men you've known, you've never seen one as handsome as Gabe Beaumont. He's the one who saved my life after Johnny—" She closed her eyes and sighed. "Let's go into the parlor. I'll make some tea and explain it all to you. It's so nice to have you here. There are a lot of women in this town, but they're all new friends, and I've never felt able to really talk to any of them about intimate things. None of them understands how I feel about Gabe. They all think I'm crazy to still believe he didn't run out on me. They think I should get a legal divorce and start my life over."

"Well, you tell it all to me and maybe I can help. I have to say, it's nice to be so welcome. Most women won't walk on the same side of the street with me, if you know what I mean." Bret followed Faith into the kitchen, where Faith put on a kettle of water to heat. She began explaining, needing to get it all out, and for the next two hours, over several cups of tea and through an occasional venting of tears, Faith told Bret everything, from Johnny's death, how Hilda had died, how Gabe had come back into her life as an outlaw, then returned to work for her . . . that first night he'd come to her bed . . . their agreement to marry, how and when he had disappeared.

"Since then I've stayed here not so much to build my town, but to be here if and when Gabe comes back. I want him always to be able to find me."

"My, my, my," Bret said softly, shaking her head. "You've been through so much, Faith. I could never be as strong as you've been."

"What do you think? Do you believe Gabe just deliberately rode out of my life?"

Bret shook her head. "I don't know what to think. I've

seen all kinds of men, and Lord knows half of them aren't worth two cents. There's plenty who will desert their wives and families for another woman, gold, or just because they've got the wanders. The way you describe Gabe Beaumont—I just don't know what to tell you, Faith. A woman like you, a wonderful little boy, a new baby on the way—"

"He didn't know about the baby. I was going to wait and tell him when he got back from Cheyenne."

Bret ran a finger around the rim of her teacup, which bore lipstick stains. "Tell me more about this Tod Harding."

Faith walked to the back door, looking out toward the mountains. *Where are you, Gabe?* Oh, how she had ached for him every night for over a year now. "I don't know what to tell you except that I can't help believing he's played a part in Gabe's disappearance. I have no truly valid reason to believe it, but the way he looked at Gabe in town just two months before he disappeared . . . it was so threatening, so hateful. Harding is wealthy and obviously a man who does not like to be outdone by anyone. He apparently had an eye for me, and he seemed very surprised I had married. I have this deep, deep feeling it was more than that, though, yet I can't quite figure what it was. Whatever his motive, I can't believe anyone could be so vengeful and cruel as to arrange something like Gabe's disappearance and let a wife and mother worry and wonder what has happened to her children's father." She turned to Bret. "Maybe it's all my imagination, Bret. It does seem rather preposterous."

Bret thought how much she admired this young woman of such courage. "Maybe not so preposterous. As far as I'm concerned, no man in his right mind would run out on someone like you. I don't have an explanation for your husband's disappearance, either, but I'd like to meet this Tod Harding."

"You'll get the chance. He's written me a letter telling me he's coming to Sommers Station soon to open a lumber-supply business here, maybe even a hotel."

Bret folded her arms. "Good. He doesn't know how well we know each other, and I have a way of getting things out of a man. Maybe I'll get acquainted with him, get him to talk a little, if there's anything for him to tell." She pushed back her teacup. "Sooner or later every man in town will visit our saloon, including Tod Harding."

"I don't know, Bret." Faith sat down again. "Harding is a smart man. He's the kind who would know how to cover himself if he'd done anything illegal. He wouldn't be careless enough to say anything."

"Maybe not. We'll see. You don't know how clever *I* can be at worming information out of a man."

Faith smiled, shaking her head. "When I first met you, I was shocked, but I quickly learned to like you. You're brave in your own way, freer than even I could dream of."

Bret grunted in laughter. "Not so free, honey. I'm stuck with this reputation. No decent man would ever marry me now, and there are times when I'd like to change my life, marry, have a kid. Don't go envying me."

"What about Ben? Why don't you two marry?"

Bret laughed aloud then. "Ben? We're just good friends, always have been. Ben is the last man on earth I would marry. It would just spoil a good friendship." She leaned forward on her elbows. "So tell me about Sommers Station. Looks to me like it's really growing."

Faith smiled. Helping build this town was the only thing that had kept her from going crazy with worry these past many months. "It happened almost overnight. The UP built a branch close to the stage depot, and that was it. People started coming, just as Tod Harding said they would. I hate to admit he was right about anything, but he was right about that. Buck—the stage driver I told you went looking all over Wyoming for Gabe—he has stayed on to run a livery. He buys and sells saddles and bridle equipment, too. It was something he and Gabe were going to do together. You met Maude. She and her husband are from Germany—came here to homestead, but things got too hard and they were making no money. The man who does most of the building around here is Henry Baker, a man who was widowed on the way west. Others came in answer to my ads. Some are part of those who just travel the railroad looking for places to settle, start new businesses. When they first get here, they need a place to stay, so I enlarged the original depot and started the rooming house."

She rose and picked up the teacups, carrying them to the sink. Bret noticed that a water pump had been installed so water could be pumped by hand inside the house.

"One business leads to another," Faith continued, looking out the kitchen window. "I needed a carpenter. A carpenter needs lumber, tools, hardware. Wives come with husbands, and they need cloth for making clothes, food for cooking. People with such businesses come here and provide those things. Farmers outside of town bring the food, men who once were scouts and such are now hunters, bringing meat to town. That calls for a butcher, who also orders in beef from surrounding ranchers. Storing meat means needing someone to haul ice down from the mountains to cool the meat, which calls for a warehousing and freighting operation. More people means a church is needed, a school, and, yes, even a tavern. And so the town just keeps growing. We have a preacher, Louis Ames. He's the preacher who married me and Gabe. He was a circuit preacher. Now he's decided to stay here and build a church, holds services for now outside the little shack he lives in."

"Well, well, well. It's just like you dreamed it would be, isn't it? You wanted something all your own, to show yourself and your family you could make it. All those years of loneliness, the hardship, fighting outlaws and Indians—it all paid off."

Faith returned to the table. "Monetarily, I'm doing all right. I'm not making big money, mostly just making ends meet. I have a ways to go to be completely on my feet, but I know I can do it. I used the first money I made to pay for this house, to add on to the rooming house and build the railroad depot. I've found another woman who will help me open a restaurant next to the hotel. I laid claim to the railroad right-of-way land and several more acres north of it, and people who build on those lots pay me rent. I've held meetings, established a town tax on profits that we keep in a special fund for future growth. We'll use it to find a way to bring in water from the mountains, maybe brick the streets, plant some trees, figure out a more modern sewer system instead of people just putting up privies."

"My, oh my. Faith Beaumont, you've thought of everything. It's amazing!"

Faith smiled bashfully. "Would you believe I'm the mayor of this little place? A woman? I'll bet I'm the first woman mayor this country has ever had. I decided we needed to organize, maybe even hire a sheriff."

Bret laughed. "Just wait until Ben hears about this!"

Faith's smile faded, and her eyes teared. "I'd give it all up in a second, if it meant having Gabe back." She quickly wiped at her eyes. "Right now I have to stay here. I have two sons to support. If I could, I'd leave and search the whole country for Gabe, but I wouldn't even know where to begin. Buck tried everywhere, even went to the Sioux reservations. That's the main reason I suspect foul play, Bret. If he did feel he had to leave, he would have gone back to his people. Someone among them would have known where he was. He wouldn't just disappear completely. And a man like Gabe would be remembered by someone. He's big and dark and handsome, very unique."

Bret felt tears forming in her own eyes. "I'm so sorry, honey. I'd sure like to have known the man. Sounds like quite a catch to me. Hell, Lord knows you wouldn't have settled for just any John Doe. It would take quite a man for somebody like you to decide you wanted to be with him the rest of your life, especially after the lesson you learned on that first husband." She sighed. "What a life you've had. Hell, they could write a book about you."

Faith shook her head. "Hardly. This all started out with my being a foolish, headstrong girl who was determined to have her own way. I was a child married to a child, and running off cost both of us dearly. Everything else that happened was just—I don't know—fate, I guess. The result of knowing I had to survive somehow, for my son. Now there are two sons who need my care."

The baby started crying, and Faith rose. "I'd better tend to Alex. Johnny is probably awake, too."

"Sure. I'll go unpack and freshen up." Bret got up and

stretched. "Ben and I will find that builder—oh, by the way, I need you to put in a good word for me with Maude. I don't think she much approves of me. She said she had a room left, but she needed your okay to let me stay in it. I sent Ben on to the hotel. I don't think Maude would put up with us sleeping in the same room, although we've done it plenty of times."

Faith shook her head, wiping at more tears. "How on earth did you two end up together?"

"Oh, we go way back—both orphans in New York City. We just always got along, ran off to work on riverboats for a while. Ben, he got into playing cards, got pretty good at it—makes his living now just gambling, but that's being outlawed in a lot of places. We figured we'd come here and open a legitimate business together, just run a saloon, maybe hire a piano player. I sing some. I'll probably put on a couple of shows a night, and Ben can run the bar. We'll build our own rooms upstairs and live there eventually."

Faith walked up to the woman and hugged her again. "Well, I'm glad you're here."

"So am I, now that I know *you're* still here and you need somebody to talk to. Believe me, there isn't anything you can't tell me, honey. I'm only thirty-five, but I've lived enough I ought to be eighty. I guess it's time I got out of the business of prostitution. There aren't many men who'd pay much for a used-up woman like me."

"You're still quite pretty, Bret, and I think you know it."

The woman smiled, several lines creasing around her eyes. "Well, thanks, but I know when it's time to quit. It all started with—" Her smile faded. "Some man on the riverboat decided I must be there for more than just cooking for the crews. I put up a good fight, but he was stronger." She shrugged. "After that I didn't have much pride left, and it was like you—I had to survive. I picked the only way I knew how. It was wrong, but I was young and scared. After a while I just fell into the business like any other business a person might have. I knew I wasn't fit for any decent man after that, so I just kept at it, and me and Ben, we just traveled the country doing what we knew best. Would you believe Ben and I have never slept together?"

Faith could feel the woman's pain, sensed her loneliness. "Yes. I believe it."

Bret put on the face of someone who could brush off anything with little effort. "Good. I don't think anyone else would ever believe that." She walked out and down the hall to take up her parasol. Alex was still fussing, but Faith saw Bret to the door.

"Welcome to Sommers Station, Bret. You and Ben, you come back here for supper—six-thirty. Will you do that?"

Bret's mouth twitched slightly, and she was obviously fighting a need to cry. "Sure. That's real nice of you, Faith."

The woman turned and went out, and Maude was just then approaching the house. She stopped short when she realized Bret must have been visiting with Faith this whole time. "I vas just coming to see if I should keep holding a room," she called to Faith.

"Yes," Faith answered. "Miss Flowers will be renting one for a while until she can build a place for herself."

Maude shrugged. "All right." She turned away, shaking her head, and Faith and Bret both laughed.

"A dollar a night or five dollars a week," Faith said.

Bret nodded. "That's fine. I'll have Ben pay you five dollars for our first week when we come back at six-thirty."

"I'll be waiting. By the way, Buck Jones will be here, too."

"Good. I'd like to see him again." Their gaze held a moment longer, two women from two different worlds, who had a total understanding of each other. It seemed so ironic to Faith that the arrival of Bret Flowers was the first truly uplifting thing that had happened to her since Gabe's disappearance. She was someone from the past who had returned. Maybe it was a good sign. Maybe some day Gabe would also come in on a train, or ride in on a horse.

One thing and one thing only kept her believing he was out there somewhere and would come back to her, and that was this constant feeling of closeness to him. She could almost feel him standing beside her at times, lying next to her in the night. He'd told her once that the Indians believed in spiritual travel, that through concentration and sacrifice they could be one with the wolf, or the eagle, or the wind. They could take themselves anywhere they wanted to be, including with their loved ones. She'd felt Gabe with her, knew somehow deep inside that when she felt that way, Gabe Beaumont was thinking about her.

Chapter Twenty-seven

1871 . . .

Gabe closed his eyes, again drawing on what strength was left him, reminding himself of the Sun Dance sacrifice, the starvation he'd suffered, the thirst, the pain of the skewers in his breasts. His years with the Sioux had taught him stamina, courage. Most of all he had learned the importance of spiritual removal from the body.

He concentrated again on taking himself away from the horror and filth he lived in. From what he could determine, he had been thrown into a cell in the basement of the two-story brick building that served as a courthouse at what he had learned from other half-starved, disease-ridden prisoners was Fort Smith, Arkansas, Indian Territory. He no longer noticed when rats crawled over his body, and his nostrils had become accustomed to the smell. There were no windows, but when he closed his eyes, he could be on a mountain, see the sky, the eagle. He could smell the sweet scent of pine. He could see Faith's face, her beautiful hair. He could hear her voice, instead of the groans and coughing of his fellow prisoners. He could smell her lilac water, taste her lips. He could hear Johnny's laughter, see his sweet smile.

He saw real sunshine only once a week, when he was released for two hours to walk in circles around a court-yard for exercise, but even then his ankles were chained together, as well as his wrists. The first four months he'd been here he had not even enjoyed that much freedom, for he had been unable to walk at all. His wound had been left untended for two weeks, until finally one of the bounty hunters who had brought him here decided to take out the bullet in a horrifying, painful procedure with his hunting knife beside a campfire. It had been a sloppy job, and he hadn't been able to use his leg at all for weeks afterward. He literally had to learn all over again how to walk, with the help of some of the other prisoners. Now he exercised daily in the cell any way he could, wanting to keep his muscles as strong as possible under these conditions.

Someday he would get out of here . . . someday. He had to believe that. He must think only of sunshine, fresh air, Faith, Johnny, freedom. What must poor Faith think by now? He suspected Tod Harding would try to convince her that her husband had deserted her, and he would not blame Faith for believing it. Days, weeks, months had gone by . . . years. He had tried to keep track by making marks on the wall, but he wasn't sure he'd remembered to mark every day when he'd first got here, he was in so much pain. To the best of his knowledge he had been here almost three years. He had contemplated all kinds of ways to escape, but none of them would work. He asked every day to see the judge who presided over the territory, but the man had refused to see him. He was here without trial, without a chance to defend himself, without a proper, legal sentencing.

His only appearance before the judge had been when he'd first arrived, when he was too sick and weak from the wound and botched bullet removal even to speak up for himself; but he remembered that the judge had appeared to be drunk at his hearing, completely uncaring and unable even to conduct a legal trial. He had simply ordered him thrown in a cell and had refused since then to see him.

A lot of people had obviously been bribed to put him here, and the only way he kept from going crazy over his situation was using his ability to remove himself spiritually, to be with Faith and Johnny, to feel Faith lying next to him. He had contemplated ways of escape, but so far three other men had tried and had been shot. There was no way of digging out of this basement prison with its cement walls and floor, and just above was the courthouse and jailers. Whenever the prisoners were outside, their ankles and wrists were chained. After his wound had finally healed the best it would heal, his health would improve no further, his body kept weak from the lack of fresh air, from foul water and bad food, from occasional rat bites. And to run from prison would only make him a hunted man, still unable to go home to Faith. He had hoped to find a jailer willing to write Faith and tell her where he was, but so far none had obliged him.

He opened his eyes, stared at a damp wall, shifted his position on the hard cot he lay on. The men who had brought him here had told him they had papers saying he was to be hanged, but that had not happened. One of his jailers had said that because the crime did not happen in Indian Territory, the judge had decided he did not have the authority to hang him. Gabe suspected there was more reason than that. The man might be afraid of being found out by the federal government, which was the overseer for this territory. A hanging would create too much paperwork—paperwork that might lead to the discovery of the judge's dishonesty and drunkenness. It was easier to just throw him down here and forget about him, let his name and existence be forever forgotten.

His last shred of hope lay in the news from one of the more recent prisoners that the current judge might be replaced. There had been numerous murders in Indian Territory, and it was becoming a haven for outlaws. The government was seriously discussing what should be done to bring more law and order to this wild, unruly land. A new judge could mean Gabe's salvation . . . or his demise. If the man would review his case, he'd see he did not belong here—but then again, maybe he'd be hanged, after all.

He closed his eyes again. He had to stop thinking about the horror of the place. Every day it was becoming more difficult to keep up his hope, to find the spiritual power to remove himself from this hellhole and take to the mountains, to Faith. He could not think about the possibility of having to stay here the rest of his years, although under these conditions that would not be so long. He had to concentrate on Wakan Tanka, on his own inner strength. He had to pray that the love he and Faith shared was strong enough to overcome this separation, strong enough to hold them together in spirit, and that their prayers were powerful enough to bring a miracle.

"Faith," he whispered. "Hang on. I love you."

At that very moment Faith sat up in bed, sure she'd heard someone whisper her name. She shivered at how real it had seemed, but surely it had just been a dream. She rose and pulled on a robe, walking to a window to crank it open. She could hear a few noises from town, but this window looked out at the distant mountains. She shivered again at the feeling that someone had been in the room with her, standing over her bed and saying her name.

"Dear God, is it Gabe?" she said softly. "Please, please bring him back to me. Please let him be alive." The hope was growing dimmer. Nearly three years had passed. If his spirit had spoken to her, maybe it was because he was already dead, but she had never been able to believe that. For the first time since she'd left home, she wished she could participate in a Quaker prayer meeting. Sometimes the power of prayer from an entire group could bring miracles.

She closed her eyes and prayed again with all her heart and soul for news about Gabe, then just listened for a moment to the howling of wolves in the distant foothills. Wolves always reminded her of Gabe, wild and free, a part of this land. "Come back to me, Gabe. I'll wait here forever."

She closed the window and climbed back into bed, empty . . . so empty.

A crowd of surrounding settlers and local business owners gathered at the train depot to welcome the new schoolteacher. Faith had insisted the teacher be a woman, and the town vote had supported her. After all, their mayor was a woman, and out here in the West people liked to think they were more forward thinking than back east. Allowing women to have jobs normally held by men was simply another sign that in this land of opportunity new settlers experienced a totally new kind of freedom. According to newspapers from Cheyenne, Wyoming citizens even thought women should have the right to vote for President some day. For now, here in Sommers Station, women were allowed to vote on various town decisions, and hiring Miss Sandra Bellings was one of the decisions they had made.

The slender, middle-aged woman disembarked from the train, her sober face brightening when she saw her welcoming committee. She had been chosen from among several applicants who had answered ads Faith had placed in newspapers in Denver and Omaha, and Faith suspected that most had voted for her because they had decided a thirty-year-old woman who had never been married was most likely highly moral and would set a good example for the children. And without her own family, she would be able to commit all her time and attention to her students. A little log schoolhouse had already been built about a half mile north of town, close enough for the children of the townspeople, yet far enough out for outlying settlers to be able to bring their children in. Miss Bellings was from Omaha, and in her letter she had expressed her desire to see the beautiful West, her appreciation for the fact that women had more freedom here, and her wish to offer the children of Sommers Station the opportunity of an education.

As Faith approached the woman with a bouquet of flowers, she suspected Miss Sandra Bellings had an ulterior motive for coming there. Men far outnumbered women in the town, and many single women came west for the very purpose of finding a husband. She smiled inwardly at her suspicion. It was fine with her if the woman had come there to find a man, as long as she was a good teacher. It was already the fall of 1871, and Johnny was six years old. It was time for him to go to school. Alex was two and a half now, an active, wild little boy, with long black hair and his father's green eyes. Every time Faith looked at him she saw Gabe, and having him around kept the wound of her aching love for Gabe constantly open.

She handed the flowers to Miss Bellings. "Welcome to Sommers Station, Miss Bellings. I am Faith Sommers Beaumont."

"Oh! You're the woman who runs this town, so I understand."

Faith felt a little embarrassed. "I don't know about that. I sort of started this whole thing, but most decisions are voted on by everyone, including the women. I just oversee things, I guess, but I don't really run things."

"Well, I am honored to meet you, Mrs. Beaumont." The woman took the flowers, and others surrounded her, leading her toward a wagon that would take her to the little schoolhouse, where cake and coffee would be served as a welcoming party. A two-room frame house had been built next to the school as living quarters for the new teacher.

Faith felt proud and satisfied that Sommers Station was turning out to be everything she'd hoped it could be. They now had a church and a school. Bret and Ben had built their tavern, and they ran it quite professionally, with Bret's singing so lovely that sometimes even some of the women stood outside and listened. Ben was careful not to allow any one man so many drinks that he became drunk and violent, and the only gambling allowed was poker.

Some people thought Sommers Station should have a sheriff, but so far there hadn't been the kind of trouble that would warrant one. Still, Faith supposed that could happen, and perhaps they should be ready. It was just another thing that would have to be voted on, maybe next spring. She turned to go to Bret, who was watching Johnny and Alex. They would board their own buggy and head for the school. She walked toward them, but a man stepped down from one of the train platforms and put out his hand to stop her.

"Well, hello, Mrs. Beaumont."

Faith felt a flood of emotions move through her at the sight of him. It was Tod Harding. She had not seen him since their encounter in Cheyenne in sixty-eight. He had sent men to Sommers Station to build a grocery store and a feed-supply store, but he had never come himself. Faith had always wondered if it was because of a guilty conscience. Maybe she had been wrong all along about the man, and her suspicions were unfair. She would probably never know now.

"Hello, Mr. Harding. I am surprised to see you here." He still dressed in his dapper manner, wearing a short wool chesterfield overcoat, under which she could see a white-collared shirt and a silk tie. He removed a silk top hat and bowed to her.

"Well, I am *not* surprised to find *you* here. I must say you are more beautiful than I remembered. The years only seem to make you more lovely." He stepped back and looked her over. She wore a deep-blue velvet dress with a lighter-blue apron overskirt trimmed with a satin ruffle and satin bows. Her cloak was plush velvet, also dark blue, trimmed with gimp cord. It was fitted at her still-slender waist and had shawl sleeves. Her blue velvet empire bonnet covered her red hair, which was wound into a chignon, held in place by white beaded netting. "My, my, we are even dressed in the latest fashion. It is obvious you are doing very well here, Mrs. Beaumont. Look at you! What a far cry from the plain, work-worn woman I met when there was nothing here but a little stage depot!" He looked up the street. "Just look at this place! It's all you dreamed of, isn't it?"

"We're doing quite well, Mr. Harding. What on earth brings you here after all this time?"

"Oh, I have some wonderful plans, and I came to tell you about them myself. And I am doing some investigating for the railroad, seeing how things are coming along at the various depots along the way." He looked around again. "I can see I'll be able to report that Sommers Station is doing very well."

Bret approached them, holding Alex's and Johnny's hands. "Well, who is this, Faith?"

Faith realized she was staring, and she hoped Harding didn't misinterpret her intentions. She stared because she was trying to read his eyes, trying to gauge the man's honesty. She would never get over the feeling he'd had something to do with Gabe's disappearance. She finally tore her eyes from him to address Bret. "This is Tod Harding, Bret, the man I told you about, the one who built the grocery store and feed store and who originally told me about claiming railroad land."

"I see! So you're Tod Harding." Bret looked him over as though he were a piece of candy. "Pretty fancy."

Harding brightened, a worldly man who did not take long to realize the kind of woman Bret was. She dressed more demurely now, out of respect for Faith and Sommers Station, but women like Bret had a flair about them that could not be hidden. "Pretty fancy yourself, ma'am. And who might you be?"

Bret folded her arms, glad finally to meet this man Faith had always suspected had something to do with her husband's disappearance. "I'm Bret Flowers—came here with a friend to open a tavern." She turned and pointed. "Right up the street there—'Flowers and Wine.' Come see us sometime."

Tod looked her over appreciatively. "I'll do that." He glanced at Faith. "I take it you don't allow anything more than drinking and a little card playing in your fair little town."

"No, I don't, Mr. Harding."

He waved her off. "Oh, stop with the 'Mr. Harding' thing. Surely you can bring yourself to call me Tod. After all, I am partly responsible for helping you build this place, am I not?"

Faith didn't like the suggestion that she couldn't have built the town without him. She liked even less the hint that perhaps she owed him something. "I had plans long before you came along, Mr. Harding." She could tell by his eyes he was miffed that she insisted on not using his first name.

"And if not for me, you might not have known about the railroad land, don't forget."

Faith could see that his smile was forced. She sensed the crueler man behind the fancy clothes and charming smile. "I have to go, Mr. Harding. We are having a reception for our new schoolteacher. You are welcome to come with us."

He brightened a little again. "I would like that. After all, I want to get to know the others in this town. I intend to stay awhile. I never told you my personal reason for coming here. I am going to build a hotel—a very fine one, I might add. And if you would like to rent part of the lower level, you may open a restaurant there. Just a suggestion. You must be quite busy, what with two children and being the mayor of your own little town." He frowned. "I must ask, though, if you have ever heard from your husband. I was told by Sheriff Keller in Cheyenne that you had been searching for him a couple of years ago. He, uh, ran off on you, I believe?"

Faith picked up Alex and faced him squarely. "Believe what you want. Gabe did not run off on me. Something happened to him. I don't know what, and I may never know, but I will never believe he left me deliberately." She turned and exchanged a knowing look with Bret, and both women walked away, Bret leading Johnny beside her.

"I'll be damned," Harding mumbled to himself. "The woman still doesn't believe he deserted her." He'd had high hopes she believed exactly that, and that she would be so disgusted with Gabe Beaumont by now that she would be ready to throw herself at any other man just for spite and to go on with her life. The man had been gone three years! That meant she likely hadn't been bedded in all that time. Surely she was getting hungry to be a woman again. Between the loss of her husband, needing a father for her children . . . and his own plans for making her completely dependent on him . . . it shouldn't take terribly long to get her into his own bed. He'd never had a woman turn him down the way Faith had, certainly not one in her position, one who could benefit so greatly from his wealth and connections. *Give it up, Faith Beaumont. Your husband was hanged in Indian Territory. He's been dead for three years.* How he wished he could tell her without giving himself away.

So be it. If he could not get into her bed, there were plenty of other women for that purpose. His real purpose there was to claim the town of Sommers Station for himself, take title to all the property, and add it to his growing real-estate fortune.

The hammering continued and Sommers Station grew, even through the long, cold winter. The Harding Hotel became a reality—three stories, lace curtains at the windows, and a fine restaurant on the first floor. However, Faith refused to have anything to do with the hotel or the restaurant. She had told Tod Harding she did not want to be partially dependent on anyone else for her income. Opening a restaurant in the hotel would mean paying him rent, and it would appear they were in business together, which might not look proper.

She studied herself in the mirror now, proud she'd kept her shape after two babies. She wore a yellow-checked dress of light cotton, with short sleeves trimmed with the same white lace that adorned the slightly scooped neck. The yellow narrow-brimmed bonnet that she tied on matched the dress, the color making her hair look even redder. She wished Gabe were there. He'd never seen her quite so gussied up as this, and it felt good to be feminine again, to feel womanly, attending ladies' gatherings and spring dances.

That was where she was going this evening, to Sommers Station's first spring dance. Tod Harding had been after her all winter to allow him to court her. Over and over he had expressed his regrets over her "misfortune," lamenting that if she had been his wife, he could never have left "such a beautiful, strong, self-reliant woman." There were moments when he seemed totally sincere in feeling sorry for her predicament, but deep inside she still did not trust the man and never would. He had offered help from his own attorneys in declaring Gabe legally dead, or getting a documented divorce so that she was free to see other men.

Never! Faith thought. She would go to the dance alone. She might dance with a few men, ones like Ben and Buck perhaps, maybe even Tod Harding; but everyone in town would know she was dancing only to be sociable. They all knew that Faith Beaumont was still waiting for her husband to come home. She knew many whispered, and maybe even laughed, about it, thinking her a fool to believe that after nearly four years he would show up again, but she could not let go of her love for Gabe.

She just wished she knew if she was right in her feelings and suspicions about Harding. Bret had cleverly questioned him a few times when he'd visited the saloon, and the wily woman had told Faith she could read a man's eyes as clearly as most others read books. *He knows something,* she'd told Faith not long ago. *He hasn't come right out and said it, but he's hinted. A man full of liquor sometimes says things he'd never say when he's sober, and Harding hinted to me the other night that maybe Gabe had been arrested. Maybe he'd even been hanged.*

Hanged! Surely if that was so, she would have heard about it. She'd sent Buck back to Cheyenne, but there was a new sheriff there now, and he knew nothing about Gabe Beaumont. Buck checked in surrounding towns, and Faith had written several forts and larger cities, asking if there was any record of a Gabe Beaumont being arrested or hanged. None had any news about him.

Maybe it was time to face reality. She had two sons who needed a father, and she was not sure she could live out the rest of her life without a man to hold her, a man to love in return. After having a man like Gabe, a woman missed those things.

She turned away and walked out of her room to the porch, where Maude was sitting in a porch swing reading to Alex and Johnny. She watched her boys a moment, each a replica of his father, seven-year-old Johnny so outgoing and charming, a quick, bright smile, dancing brown eyes. He usually got his way about things because he knew how to use those eyes . . . just like his father. Alex, now three, was dark, and she'd let his hair grow to his shoulders because it just seemed right. His green eyes stabbed at her heart, for in those eyes she saw the only man who had truly made her feel like a whole woman. He was the daring one, with a wild, free spirit that made him adventurous, the kind of child who had to be watched constantly or he might get hurt. He was always playing around horses, had absolutely no fear of them whatsoever. She remembered how adeptly Gabe could ride a horse, how easily he worked with them, as though one in spirit with them.

"Are you sure you don't want to go to the picnic and dance?" Faith asked Maude. "We can take the children."

"Oh, no, dear. You know zis little one here," she answered. "He would be into everzing. You should not have to worry 'bout zem. Me, I get tiret at places where der are so many people. I like just to relax here. I watch za children for you. You be free to have fun—maybe dance vit some men, huh? You got to find you a man, Faith. You are too beautiful to go on alone. Za boys, zey need a papa. You think about zat Harding fella. He got money and he good-looking. Everbody knows he has an eye for you."

Faith smiled and shook her head. How could she explain to anyone else her suspicions about the charming, dapper Tod Harding, who was so sociable and who had contributed so much to the town? "Thanks for watching the boys," she answered. She walked out to the carriage to which she had already hitched a horse, and she climbed in, taking up the reins and heading the horse toward the other end of town, where a warehouse that Tod Harding had built would now be used for the spring dance. Women would bring food, and Faith had already taken over three pies earlier in the day. She could hear music as she drew closer, provided by a few men in town who were reasonably adept with fiddle and guitar. Bret had shipped over the piano from her saloon, and the old man who played for her would lend his talents to more music for the dance.

She pulled the carriage to a hitching post, and Buck came out to greet her. "I'll take care of your horse and carriage, ma'am," he told her. "I agreed to look after everybody's animals." He came around to help her down. "Say, now, ain't you the pertiest woman here!"

Faith blushed a little. "Thank you, Buck." She squeezed his hand. "What would I have done all these years without you?" She looked him over. He wore a suit, nothing fancy, just Buck's best attempt at dressing up. "And don't you look nice yourself!"

The man chuckled. "Can't wait to get out of these duds."

Faith laughed in return. "Well, you be sure to come inside and get all you want to eat. And I insist on a dance, Buck Jones." She leaned closer. "I'll bet Miss Bellings wouldn't mind a dance or two herself. She has an eye for you, Buck."

He waved her off, looking embarrassed. "Don't you be tryin' to get me together with that teacher. I got me a feelin' she's a single-minded woman who'd have a leash around my neck in no time."

"You like her and you know it."

He laughed, shaking his head. "Well, maybe I'll go over and say hello."

Faith heard a woman's voice then, someone singing a lovely tune with a voice that floated on the evening breeze. "Sounds like Bret is entertaining everyone," she told Buck.

"Yeah, she's been singin' off and on between square dances. You'd best get inside. Everybody is waitin' for Mayor Beaumont to arrive."

Faith sighed, thinking how perfect everything would be now if only she knew where Gabe was, if he was dead or alive. "Well, then, I suppose I had better get in there."

Buck grasped her arm. "Harding is waitin', too. He asked earlier about you. He's all spiffed up, expectin' some dances, I reckon."

Faith rolled her eyes. "Oh, I'm sure he is."

"I gotta tell ya, he's got somebody with him, somebody he's been introducin' around to everyone, spreadin' the word that it's time Sommers Station got itself a sheriff, built a jail, made sure we've got law and order here on account of we're growin' so fast."

Faith frowned. "Well, that's true. I've mentioned it at

town meetings. We had planned on bringing someone in for the job sometime this summer."

"I know that, but . . . well, ma'am, the man he's got with him is that Joe Keller, the one who was sheriff in Cheyenne for a while."

Faith felt a surge of apprehension and resentment. "Joe Keller!"

"Yes, ma'am. Apparently him and Harding know each other good. Harding is puttin' on a big show with him, getting people to agree he'd be the man for the job."

Faith looked toward the warehouse, feeling deep alarm. "I don't like Joe Keller, Buck. I don't trust him *or* Tod Harding. I never will."

"Well, Harding is workin' on the crowd good. He's already got people all fired up, and Keller, he's puttin' on a good show himself. Harding is sayin' as how he has to leave so often to tend his other businesses and go to company meetin's and such, on account of his pa died and he's taken over everything, he wants to be sure his businesses here in Sommers Station is safe and protected when he's gone. Now that he's opened that bank, he says it's more important than ever to have a sheriff to watch over things. He's got folks convinced it ought to be Keller, on account of he's got experience. Him bein' sheriff in Cheyenne for a while, that's got folks impressed."

Faith sighed with frustration. "And any argument I try to present would make me look silly. I have no proof those two had anything to do with Gabe's disappearance. To bring up such a thing would only make people think I was losing my mind." She met Buck's eyes. "I don't like this, Buck. Harding seems to be trying to take over this town, impressing people with his wealth, all his businesses, opening that bank. Now he's bringing his puppet sheriff to Sommers Station, and he's got people looking up to him more and more. I feel as if I'm losing control, and I think that's just what he wants. Maybe it's been his plan all along."

"Well, you just remember that everybody in town loves you and supports you. You stick to your guns and don't let Harding get the upper hand. If we have to accept Keller as our sheriff, so be it; but everything we do here has to be voted on, so if Keller don't do a good job and people don't like him, he can be voted out."

"Well! It's about time you got here!"

Their conversation was interrupted by Tod Harding himself, who approached Faith, Joe Keller walking behind him.

"My, my, look at you!" Harding said, his eyes raking her almost hungrily. "Such wasted beauty. It's time for you to dance and be happy and enjoy yourself, Faith Beaumont. And I want every dance!"

Faith did not even look at him. Her eyes were on Joe Keller, and all her distrust was awakened. He was not a big man, but he had two six-guns strapped on, and his pock-marked face had a hard look, his dark eyes seeming to drill right into her. He drew his fingers across a thin mustache and nodded to her, a smile beginning to show, but not a friendly one. Faith saw it more as a smile of victory, and she could not help thinking the victory was that he knew what had happened to Gabe Beaumont.

"What is Joe Keller doing here?" she asked, finally meeting Tod's eyes.

"Joe? Well, Mayor Beaumont, you know Sommers Station needs a sheriff. Keller's got experience, and I know him personally, so I can vouch that he would do an excellent job." He moved an arm around her waist in a familiar gesture Faith resented. "Don't be so resentful, Faith. That little incident back in Cheyenne—heavens, that was years ago. Joe is sorry about that, aren't you, Joe?"

Keller looked her over rather scathingly. "Sure," he answered.

You know! she thought. *You know what happened to my husband.* She pulled away from Harding, facing him. "He is not sorry for anything. I probably can't stop you from convincing people this is the best man for the job, but he had better be fair and honest and cooperative, or he can be voted out just as easily as he's voted in. You know how I feel about Joe Keller, yet you've brought him to Sommers Station. Don't expect any dances today, Mr. Harding."

She turned and headed for the warehouse, putting on a

smile for the first people who greeted her. Harding and Keller glanced at Buck, neither one of them caring for the way Buck looked back at them, a strange, knowing look in his eyes. "Tend the horses and mind your own business, old man," Harding told him. "And if you're such good friends with Faith Beaumont, why don't you try to reason with the woman? Sommers Station needs a sheriff, and Keller here will do a good job. As far as hope that that cheating half-breed she married is ever coming back to her, help her see that's never going to happen."

Buck folded his arms. "Oh? And how would you know that?"

Harding rolled his eyes. "It's just common sense. What's it been? Four years since he disappeared? Open your eyes *and* hers. She's much too good a woman to waste herself like she's doing."

Buck looked him over. Like Faith, he felt this man knew something, and so, too, did Joe Keller, he was sure. "If Faith Beaumont was my own daughter, I couldn't care more for her, Harding. You better never hurt her, else you'll answer to me."

Harding just snickered. "And you would in turn answer to Joe Keller." He turned and went after Faith.

Keller looked Buck over threateningly before also going to rejoin the good citizens of Sommers Station. *This place is going to be a piece of cake,* he thought. The people were innocent and eager, proud of their town, excited to have a new sheriff. Once Harding was through with them, Keller would easily be voted in, and then he would hire deputies—men he knew well, men who were good with the gun. In no time at all he would own this town, and Tod Harding would own Faith Beaumont.

Chapter Twenty-eight

Gabe faced Judge Isaac Parker squarely, hating the thought of how he must look—thin, unclean, his hair grown nearly to his waist. Prisoners were allowed one shave a week, and his had been four days ago. He wore the striped uniform of all other prisoners, allowed to change, too, only once a week.

The chance he had wanted was finally here, but it was doubtful he could take hope in the fact that a new judge had been appointed to rule Indian Territory. Already they were calling this man the "hanging judge." He did not hesitate to order hangings when they were recommended, and sometimes even when they weren't recommended. He had weaned out several prisoners who had still been incarcerated when he'd arrived, freeing some, hanging others. Gabe's turn had come to stand before the man, and because his original papers supposedly had recommended he be hanged, there was little doubt what the judge would decide—but Gabe would damn well have his say first. Judge Parker, a rather round man with a mustache and goatee and very discerning eyes, asked him to state his name.

"Gabriel Beaumont, Your Honor."

"You look Indian."

"I am half-Sioux. My Indian name is Tall Bear."

The judge nodded. He took a long, hard look at Gabe, pulling at his goatee. "I have to tell you, Mr. Beaumont, that I can find no papers on you."

A glimmer of hope beamed through Gabe's heart. "If I may have the privilege, sir, I believe I know why."

Parker's eyebrows shot up in curiosity. "You speak good English. I am catching a tiny hint of an accent. French?"

"Yes, sir. My father was French. He was a trapper in the Upper Missouri country."

The judge nodded. "So what is your explanation as to why I can find no papers on you? What were you accused of?"

"I was accused of a murder I did not commit and was sent here without trial, Your Honor. The man who claims he saw me kill the victim has never shown his face, never come forward publicly to accuse me. I was never even told his name."

"Then how did you end up here?" Parker asked with a frown.

Gabe explained how he'd been falsely arrested and sent to prison with no trial, explained about the beating and gunshot wound and never even being able to tell his wife what had happened. He mentioned no names. He had his own plans for the men who had put him there!

"I was brought here by two men who claimed they were bounty hunters, Your Honor, whose names I never was told, yet there was no bounty on me. The judge who was here then had me thrown in prison without a trial. The bounty hunters told me I was to be hanged, but I have instead spent the last—" He thought a moment. "Excuse me, sir, but what year is this?"

He heard a chuckle from someone in the room, and Parker pounded his gavel. "This is not a laughing matter! This man has been imprisoned without trial and with no legal papers to keep him here! It is a sad situation that he is not even sure how long he has been here!" The room quieted again, and Parker looked at Gabe. "It is August, eighteen and seventy-two, Mr. Beaumont."

Gabe closed his eyes. Four years! What must Faith be thinking by now? What had she told Johnny? Maybe by now she had given up on him and married someone else, thinking he was dead or never returning. "I was sent here in sixty-eight, sir," he answered.

Parker leaned back in his chair, pulling at his goatee again. "I am confused, Mr. Beaumont. Who sent you here? The army? The man who accused you? The sheriff of Cheyenne? Who paid the bounty hunters if there was no bounty on you?"

Gabe ran a hand through his hair. "I do not know who paid the bounty hunters." He knew damn well it was Tod Harding, but he was still determined not to reveal the man's name. "I only know there was a wealthy man in Cheyenne at the time who was good friends with the sheriff, and who—" He struggled against the rage he felt at the thought of Tod Harding touching Faith. "He was interested in my wife, sir."

"Your wife? She's white?"

"Yes, sir. Her name is Faith Beaumont. She lives at Sommers Station in Wyoming. I was never allowed to contact her after I was arrested. As I said, I believe she has no idea where I am. The sheriff took the money I had earned from selling my horses. I believe he kept the money, and that neither he nor the wealthy man told my wife what happened to me."

"What is this wealthy man's name?"

Gabe held his eyes squarely. "I would rather not say, sir. I do not want him contacted. I do not want him to know I am still alive. Besides, sir, this man would deny everything if he was questioned, as would the sheriff who was involved. They claimed to have sent papers along ordering my hanging. I believe the wealthy man forged those papers, and the judge who was here then might have been bribed by this man to take me and keep quiet about it. I do not mean this as an insult to judges, sir. However, others here know that Judge—"

"I am well aware of what the situation was here before I arrived," Judge Parker interrupted. "That was the reason I was appointed, to clean up this territory, which has become a haven for outlaws. I intend to change that. However, that is not your concern at the moment. And *my* concern is that you were brought here all the way from Wyoming. Your crime evidently did not take place in Indian Territory, which, as far as I am concerned, means you should not be jailed here. If there were papers ordering a hanging, I can find them nowhere, which leads me to believe you are right about the man who preceded me. He probably destroyed the papers because he knew it could be proved they were forged." He leaned forward. "Now, Mr. Beaumont, contrary to what you may have already heard about me, I am a fair man. I find it reprehensible that you were sent here without trial, that you were shot and beaten while a prisoner, and that you have lived in that stinking hole below this courthouse for four years with no proof of any crime. What I will do is contact the powers that be in the United States Army and ask if there is any record that a Gabriel Beaumont or a scout named Tall Bear is wanted by army officials for the murder of Officer Balen. If there is a record of such a crime, I will be sure you are afforded a fair trial before army officials and insist that your accuser be present to testify. You will be given a chance to speak for yourself. If there is no record of such a crime, I will release you—but only on one condition."

Gabe felt like giving out a wild cry of joy. "Yes, sir."

"I don't want you going back to Wyoming and murdering this wealthy man you think put you here. I may be exonerating you from the charge of murder, Mr. Beaumont. Don't embarrass me by going back home and *committing* a murder."

There was nothing Gabe wanted more than to sink a blade into Tod Harding and rip it from his balls to his chin. The judge's request was a difficult thing to promise, but it could mean being with Faith again!

"You have my word, sir." He might not kill Harding,

but he'd damn well find a way to make the man *wish* he were dead!

"Do you want me to contact your wife?"

Faith! Was she even still there? Of course she was. She wouldn't leave Sommers Station. He ached at the thought of seeing her again, touching her again. "Sir, I have no idea what her situation is right now. She already had a son by her first husband, who died. It is possible she believes I am dead and has remarried so her son will have a father. I would rather wait until you get your report from the army. If I am freed, I just want to go home. I will tell her the truth then. If I am to be hanged or kept in prison, then she must be told. For now I do not want to build her hopes or interrupt her life until we know."

Parker nodded. "All right. Whatever you wish." He pounded his gavel and ordered one of the jailers to take the prisoner back to his cell.

Gabe stopped in front of the bench, joyful hope welling up in his soul. "Thank you, sir. There are not many white men I honor and respect, but I will always hold great honor for you."

The judge pointed a finger at him. "Mind you, I still might have to hang you, Mr. Beaumont."

"Then you would only be doing what you must do. If I have a fair trial, then nothing more can be done. At least my wife will know what has happened to me."

The judge nodded, studying Gabe closely. "You have an honesty about you that I like, Mr. Beaumont. Just keep your promise to me about not killing the man who you believe sent you here."

Gabe nodded. *I did not say I would not torture him,* he thought. The Sioux had many methods of torture. He would have to weight them all and decide which was best for Mr. Tod Harding. But first he had to get out of there. He would pray to Wakan Tanka that Judge Isaac Parker would find that the army had no record of his being wanted for murdering Nathan Balen.

Faith led Tod Harding into her parlor, offering him some tea, which he refused. She thought he was behaving rather strangely—all business, rather than his usual flamboyant, charming self. He opened a briefcase, taking out some papers.

"Well, apparently you want to get right down to business," she said. "I have the money ready. Two dollars and fifty cents an acre for fifty acres comes to one hundred twenty-five dollars. I am glad the railroad is finally ready to square up with people who settled the right-of-way land. I suppose you have some deeds with you?"

"Yes, but I am afraid there are some changes, Faith." He spoke the words crisply, and Faith felt a hint of alarm. Harding had been gone for two months, having traveled back to Chicago on business, and returned to tell her it was time for those who had claimed railroad land to take care of paying for it. As a railroad official, it was his job to do some of the collecting.

"What kind of changes?" she asked warily. She was well aware of what a powerful political and financial entity the railroads had become. The newspaper out of Cheyenne had been carrying stories of corruption and political bribery. *We have our transcontinental railroad at last,* one article had read, *but what will be the real cost? And how many politicians in Washington, including the President himself, were bribed by the railroad to grant them far more land than was necessary for construction? How many railroad officials own the very construction and supply companies that were paid by the railroad companies for their services? Is it possible those bills were padded to line the pockets of those companies' owners? At the same time, our government has been subsidizing the railroad for their "expenses."*

"I am afraid the price has gone up," Harding told Faith. "The government gave the railroad permission to sell excess land given them in the land grants, with the intention of helping the Union Pacific and Central Pacific pay the debts incurred in building the railroad. Those debts were far higher than we had imagined, and we are asking more for the land. Thirty dollars an acre."

Faith felt a chill move through her, and anger began to move into every nerve end. "Thirty dollars! That's *rob-*

bery! I don't believe for one minute the railroad is that much in debt. You had all kinds of help from the government! I have papers right here from when I laid claim to the right-of-way land saying I would pay two dollars and fifty cents an acre once the railroad was completed."

"That was your promise, that's true. You signed your name to those papers. But we did not promise that the price would not change. We underestimated the cost, and now it is thirty dollars an acre. There is nothing I can do about it. It's the same for everyone."

Faith fought an urge to cry. "That's fifteen hundred dollars! You know I can't come up with that kind of money!"

Harding shrugged. "Just charge your tenants more for their lots. Or you can sell them to me. I'll buy them for three dollars an acre from you, and then I'll pay the railroad their asking price. You'll make some money, and I will own the land."

"And charge much more for renting the lots, I suppose," she answered. Harding met her eyes, and she saw a look of evil victory there. She felt her own power in Sommers Station slipping all the more. She was losing her little town, her dream. Sheriff Keller had hired deputies who were more like thugs than legitimate policemen. They hung around town in threatening stances, arresting people on flimsy charges and charging high fines. Last week Clancy Dee's hardware store had burned down. Luckily it was not close enough to other structures to cause them to catch fire too, but in a secret meeting at Faith's house a few townspeople questioned the cause of the fire. Clancy told them that Sheriff Keller had been harrassing him about a fine he had refused to pay for "public drunkenness." Clancy claimed he'd had only two beers at the Flowers and Wine and had tripped on something on the way home and fallen. He'd been arrested for being drunk in public, which he swore was not true. Now he suspected his store had been burned down as an example of what happened to people who didn't pay their fines. Besides that, Harding was building a hardware store of his own, much bigger than

Clancy's. Already Clancy was giving up and moving out of Sommers Station.

"Why are you doing this, Mr. Harding?"

Anger showed in Harding's eyes. "Are you ever going to call me by my first name?"

She threw her papers aside and rose, walking to a window. "Is that what this is all about? You're angry because I won't call you Tod? You're angry because I have never agreed to see you socially? Angry that I refused to dance with you at the spring dance?"

He leaned back in the love seat where he sat. "You think too highly of yourself, Faith. What is happening here is strictly business."

She folded her arms, thinking that if she had a gun, she could easily shoot him. "How many other small towns like this one have you already taken over through your deceit?" she asked, facing him again. "In how many other towns have you built your own businesses, knowing that eventually you would own the land, too? In how many other towns have you planted your own lawmen, men who threaten and harrass town citizens so that eventually you control everything? You've had this planned all along, haven't you? You thought that by now I would be like clay in your hands, perhaps sharing your bed, which would make all of this even easier!"

He shook his head. "You're letting your imagination run away with you."

"Am I? I don't think so, Mr. Harding. It's very obvious what you're doing. You knew from the beginning I'd never get this property for two-fifty an acre. Or would you have stuck to two-fifty an acre if I had been more . . . friendly? If I had not married someone else?"

He gathered some papers and put them back in his briefcase. "Believe what you want. I'm through trying to deal reasonably with you, tired of your damn dream that that half-breed husband of yours is coming back—tired of your idea this place belongs to you. You're losing Sommers Station, Mrs. Beaumont. That's life. As far as your dead husband—"

"Dead? How would you know he's dead, Mr. Harding?" Faith noticed a flash of guilt in his eyes before he had a chance to put on a show of innocence.

"I just supposed." He shrugged. "The man has been gone four years. If he isn't dead, then he sure as hell has no intentions of returning."

She stepped closer, facing him squarely. "And the reason I have never responded to your advances is because I believe *you* had something to do with Gabe's disappearance—you and Sheriff Keller! Besides that, Tod Harding, I don't believe you ever *were* interested in me! You were interested only in what I was trying to build here. You saw an opportunity to move in and take over Sommers Station. God knows how many other communities you've done this to. You duped me into agreeing to buy railroad property, waited until I had invested every dime into businesses of my own, built my town, attracted good, honest, hardworking people here, people who would also put every penny of *their* own into their dreams. Then you brought in your henchmen, leading us to believe it was important to have a sheriff here. You have slowly been taking over Sommers Station all along, and now you tell me the railroad property is going to cost me fifteen times as much as originally agreed! Now you can take hold of all that property and own Sommers Station."

She turned away so he could not see the tears beginning to form in her eyes. Why did she always cry when she was this angry?

"You can't own what doesn't exist, Mr. Harding. If you keep this up, everyone will leave, and you will own a *ghost* town! You deliberately burned out Clancy Dee, and now he's getting out, which I am sure you planned on, since you're building a hardware store of your own. Now you have no competition."

She silently prayed for courage, then turned and faced him again.

"Who is next? Buck's livery? Bret and Ben's tavern? Your ultimate goal, of course, is *me*! Well, I assure you I will be the *last* to go, and when I do, there will be nothing left here for you, and you will lose everything you have invested in Sommers Station!"

Tod closed his briefcase and stood up, clucking. "Such passion, Mrs. Beaumont. I don't know where you get your ideas, but your imagination is incredible."

"Is it? You planned this all along, and you knew that Gabe Beaumont just might have the skill and the guts to stop you from your little plan, so you got him out of the way before you came here to finish the plan."

He snickered. "I really believe living here all these years has made you crazy." He turned. "Think what you want. The railroad has given all homesteaders two months to come up with the money to buy the lots, or you can pay in installments. Which way do you want to handle this?"

Faith had never hated anyone, not even Clete Brown, as much as she hated Tod Harding right now. "I don't know yet. I obviously have no power to fight this, but the citizens of Sommers Station *can* fight the way you and your thugs are taking over this town. We will find a way, and *I* will find a way to hang on to what I have here!"

"Well, good luck to you," Tod smirked. "I am leaving for a couple of weeks on more railroad business. Have an answer for me when I get back."

He walked out without another word, and Faith walked to the door. Maude had taken the children so Faith could talk to Harding. She walked to the boardinghouse, and she looked up the street at the bustling town of Sommers Station—such a far, far cry from the lonely little stage station it once was. From there she could see Clancy's burned-out store, and it tore at her heart. Tod Harding and Joe Keller were slowly taking over, and once she sold her land to Harding, if that was what she had to do, she would lose control of everything, lose her primary source of income . . . lose her dream. This had been a happy, vital town, everyone eager to make their little settlement grow. Now, since Clancy's misfortune, everyone else's dreams were fading, too. She could feel it in the air. If she didn't find a way to stay in control here, Sommers Station would fade away into history.

Where would she go then? Back home? Pennsylvania had ceased being home years ago, and how could she face her father after all this time and tell him she had failed? To lose Sommers Station would also mean failing her sons, who depended on her. How would she take care of them?

She stepped around to the side of the boardinghouse where no one could see her, and she let the tears come. If only she knew what had happened to Gabe. Perhaps she could bear all of this if only she knew the truth about her husband. And if he were there, not even a man as powerful as Tod Harding could hurt her.

Chapter Twenty-nine

You are a free man, Mr. Beaumont. I have found no legitimate charges against you. In fact, Lieutenant Nathan Balen is not even dead. He is fine and healthy, a colonel now. He was shot in a battle with Sioux Indians, just as you claimed, but he recovered.

Gabe heard the words over and over in his mind. Free! Free to breathe fresh air! Free to return to the mountains! Free to be with Faith again! But he could not go to her like this. He was thin and weak, a shadow of the man he'd been when he'd left her. He had to regain his strength and stature. He had to do a lot of praying, rebuild his inner strength. He had to find a way to earn some money, buy decent clothes, a horse . . . a gun.

No man hated anyone more than he hated Joe Keller and Tod Harding! He'd made the judge a promise not to kill Harding, but he was not so sure he could keep that promise, and he had made no promises regarding Keller. Right now he had to think about how to contact Faith. He had to find shelter and food, some kind of help. And before he set eyes on Faith again, he had to know if she had given up on him and married someone else. He couldn't bear setting eyes on her again and not be able to have her for his own.

He'd be a sorry sight if she could see him now. He finished washing his face in a stream and returned to his campsite. He'd been turned out of prison with nothing but an ill-fitting set of clothes, a ragged coat, a couple of blankets, a small pack of food and one pan, one plate, one tin cup and one coffeepot, a pair of previously worn boots, and ten dollars. It wasn't much to start with, but anything was better than the hellhole he'd lived in over four years. By the time he'd left, Judge Parker was building a new jailhouse for those who remained.

He cleaned up camp and slung everything tied into a blanket on his back, then made his way up the road. Ahead of him he saw someone herding a few head of cattle. The man guiding them on horseback had long black hair that was tightly braided into two plaits Indian style, but he dressed like a white man. Gabe hurried to catch up, calling out "Hello!" as the man led the cattle to the stream. The rider turned to look, and Gabe could see he was obviously Indian. He had a stocky build, and even though he was on a horse, he looked short. His round face showed dark eyes that were wary but gave hint he was basically friendly. Among Gabriel's own people everyone took care of each other. Those with the most shared with those who had little, and he suspected it was that way with most tribes. At least he hoped so. Since he'd been told this area was mostly occupied by Cherokee, he guessed this man might be from that tribe.

"What can I do for you?" the rider asked, trotting his horse closer.

"I need work. I need a place to stay for a while."

The stranger looked him over. "You look sick."

Gabe smiled. "I am not sick, I promise you. I have just been released from the prison at Forth Smith, four days ago."

The man frowned. "That is a bad place."

"I committed no crime. I have papers to prove it. Can you show me where to go to find work?"

The man sighed, glancing at his cattle to check on them before turning back to Gabe. "What is your name?"

"Gabe. Gabe Beaumont. My father was a French trapper, my mother Sioux."

The stranger's eyes widened in surprise. "Sioux! What is a Sioux doing down here?"

Gabe removed his backpack and set it on the ground. "It is a long story. I wish nothing more than to go back to my homeland. I have a wife and child there. But I need to rebuild my strength first, and that will take time, food, money. I need a horse, more clothes. Can you help me?"

The man looked him over skeptically. "Perhaps. I have a ranch not far from here. You could work for me."

"I would be grateful. What tribe are you?"

"I am Cherokee." A look of great pride came into his eyes. "We have our own settlements here now, ranches, schools. My name is Charlie Jefferson, for government record. My real name is Runs with Horses. What is your Sioux name?"

"Tall Bear. I lived first in Minnesota for many years, then my people were chased west into the Dakotas."

Charlie nodded. "Someday there will be no land left for us."

Gabe felt a stab of pain in his heart, but he could not think about the future of the Sioux right now. He had to think about his own future . . . Faith. "I am good with horses. I can catch wild ones for you, break them. That is what I do best."

Charlie nodded. "Then that is what you will do for me. But you also must learn about cattle and do chores, cut wood, sling hay."

"I will do whatever you want. I just want to get started as soon as I can so that I can go home by spring. I will give you the winter."

Charlie looked toward a horse that drank and grazed among the cattle. "Can you ride bareback?"

Gabe grinned. "You ask a Sioux if he can ride bareback?"

Charlie chuckled. "I suppose that was a stupid question.

That is my spare horse. You can ride him back to my home. My family will welcome you."

Gabe picked up his backpack and eagerly walked over to the sturdy sorrel mare, slinging the supplies over his back again and easing up onto the horse. "She is a fine animal."

"I call her Fancy Dancer," Charlie replied with a grin. "She is good at dancing around the cattle and keeping them in line." He turned his horse and clucked his tongue at the cattle, shouting at them and getting them under way. "I will teach you about herding cattle. These are some strays I was taking back home. A lot of white men are coming here to settle now, on Indian lands the government has opened up to them. You see? Even in Indian Territory we lose our land. Anyway, we have to be careful to keep our cattle on our own land, or sometimes the white men steal them. Yet they call *us* thieves."

"You do not have to tell me about how white men behave. When we have more time, I will explain how I got here."

"White men?"

Gabe nodded. He rode beside Charlie, grateful for the man's help. "Do you know how to write?"

Charlie frowned. "Why?"

"I need to send a letter to my wife in Wyoming, let her know where I am and that I am all right. I am sure she was never told what happened to me. I want her to know why I can't come back right away, and I need to know if she even *wants* me to come back. I have been gone over four years. It is possible she thinks I am dead and she has perhaps married someone else."

Charlie left to chase a wandering cow back into the herd again, then returned to Gabe's side. "I have a son who is sixteen and well schooled. He can write a letter for you."

"Good." Gabe felt a flutter in his heart at the thought of contacting Faith. What if she wrote back and said she didn't want him to come home? What reason would he have left to live? Where would he go? "Thank you." He rode out after another wandering steer, managing to work it back to the herd. It felt good to be on horseback again, good to be free! Free! All he needed now was to know Faith was all right . . . and that she still wanted him.

There was one other thing he needed to do then. He had to find Tod Harding, let the man know he was still alive! It would feel good seeing the look of fear on the man's face!

Bret stoked the potbelly heating stove in the middle of the saloon. Here it was March, but no relief from the bitter winter had yet arrived. Still, the cold came just as much from the cool, dark depression that hung over the town as it did from the weather. Everyone knew Faith had been forced to sell her railroad lots to Tod Harding, which meant that now she had to pay rent to the man for her own boardinghouse and her home, which both sat on someone else's property. The man had raised everyone's rent, and a few more people had left town; harassment by Joe Keller and his men was added incentive to do so.

Still, many stayed out of loyalty to Faith and a determination to hang on to "their" town. Faith still owned considerable property beyond the railroad land, and she refused to give up and leave. The townspeople thought highly of Faith, and many couldn't bear to skip town, leaving her alone to fight Harding and his henchmen.

Bret told herself that somehow they would get through this. Faith had held several secret meetings, and the citizens of Sommers Station had discussed their options, including hiring a gunman to go up against Keller. The trouble was, that still left Harding owning half the town. How did they get rid of him?

Bret closed the stove door and opened the draft slightly, turning to watch a young man, barely more than a boy, who had drifted into town earlier in the day. He was playing cards, and he had been ordering whiskey all evening, apparently newly on his own and wanting to prove he could handle his alcohol. What bothered her more than a kid getting drunk was the fact that one of Joe Keller's deputies was standing inside watching him. Keller had begun the practice of placing deputies all over town, saying it was his way of ensuring the peace. As far as Bret was concerned, it was his way of making people feel threatened. In another secret meeting at Faith's house, Sam Kettering, who owned a farm-supply business, admitted that Keller had threatened him. If he did not begin making weekly payments to Keller for "protection," his business could end up burned to the ground like Clancy Dee's hardware store. Even Buck had been threatened, and both Bret and Faith were worried about him. He was a stubborn, brave man, not easily threatened or forced to back down.

Let the bastard come after me, he'd said at the meeting. *I'll be ready for him.*

Faith had argued with him to cooperate until she could decide what to do, how to get rid of Keller and his bunch. Everyone in town was afraid of them, yet most had spent their last dime investing in Sommers Station and could not just up and leave.

Bret didn't doubt it would be very long before Keller came to pay her a visit, asking for part of her profits. The deputy at the doorway now was Dave Kuzak, a big man, tall, hefty, a look in his dark eyes that made even Bret nervous. She'd been around long enough and dealt with enough men that there were few who could intimidate her—but this one did.

Damn them, she thought, feeling sorry for Faith, who had put so much work into building this community and now was losing it. Her thoughts were interrupted when the young stranger ordered yet another whiskey. Where he got his money for gambling and drinking, Bret didn't know or care. She only knew he didn't dare drink anymore, or Keller's thug would use drunkenness as an excuse to throw the kid in jail and "fine" him every last cent he had.

"You've had enough, young man. No more tonight." Bret picked up his whiskey glass, and he grabbed her wrist.

"Hey, pretty lady, you gotta get me some more."

"Sorry, honey. I don't want you to spend the night in jail."

"Wait!" He stood up as Bret turned away. "I asked for a drink. You gotta bring me one."

Bret set his glass on the bar, and a few people in the tavern stopped their talking and turned to watch. Bret approached the young man authoritatively. "I don't *gotta* do anything, honey. Now, why don't you just leave before you get in trouble? You're just a kid."

"A kid!" He grasped her arms. "I'm man enough to go upstairs with you. You got a room up there?"

Bret wrested herself from his grasp. "I just own and run this saloon, kid. No prostitution. Now, you can sit down and finish your card game, drink some sarsaparilla or something. But no more whiskey."

"Come on, honey." The young man had had just enough whiskey to give him romantic notions. "You can change the rules for a lovin' young man like me, can't you?" He stuck a finger into the cleavage of her full bosom, well displayed by her low-cut taffeta dress.

Bret pushed his hand away, but stopped at the sound of a clicking revolver.

"That's enough, boy!" The words were growled by Dave Kuzak. "You're comin' with me, and so are you, Bret Flowers."

Bret stepped away from the young man and faced Kuzak. "What the hell are you talking about? I haven't done anything."

The other men at the gambling table got up and backed away.

"The young man here is drunk, and you're soliciting for prostitution." He shook his head, a haughty grin on his face. "You know that's not allowed in Sommers Station. We just might have to run you out of town, Miss Flowers."

"You know damn well I was trying to turn the boy away!"

"That's not how I saw it."

"You're not taking Bret anyplace," Ben spoke up from behind the bar.

"Please don't get involved, Ben," Bret asked him.

"I've been looking out for you since we were kids. Keller's just using this as a way to start getting money from us, and it's not going to happen."

Kuzak waved his pistol at both Bret and the drunken young man. "I make the decisions here, and I say they're both going to jail."

Bret turned to Ben, her faithful friend, still so handsome

and dapper. Ben could charm just about anyone into anything, but none of that would work on Dave Kuzak, and even Ben knew it. He raised a sawed-off shotgun and aimed it at Kuzak. "I say Bret stays," he told Kuzak.

The room went silent, and Kuzak's face literally distorted with surprise and anger. "Put that thing away, Carson!"

"Ben, put the gun down," Bret pleaded. "I'll go over to the jail. I'm not worried about this."

Ben met her eyes. "You weren't soliciting that punk."

"Ben, what difference does it make? Everybody knows what I once was, and they don't care. I'll spend a night in jail, and that will be the end of it. It's not worth your getting hurt. What would I do without you?"

Ben glowered at Kuzak. "You'd better treat her decent."

Kuzak slowly raised his gun hand, aiming his pistol at Ben. "And you'd better know you're in trouble, pointing a gun at a deputy. Put it away, Carson."

"Ben, please! If you shoot him, the others will come. Keller will have you hanged!"

Ben knew Bret was right. He slowly laid the gun on the bar, but just before he let go of it, to Bret's shock and horror, Kuzak fired his pistol. Everything happened so fast that there was no time to think, no time to wonder how or why it had happened, except to know that Kuzak had apparently made up his mind he wanted blood that night. Ben crashed backward into a stack of glasses, a hole in his forehead. He slumped to the floor, glasses falling and crashing all around him. Amid the noise Bret screamed his name and ran toward him, and the drunken young man, whose name no one even knew yet, made a dash for the door.

Kuzak's gun fired again, and the boy went down with a bullet in his back. Everyone else inside the saloon backed away, appalled at what they had just seen. Kuzak whirled, waving his gun at all of them. "You all saw it!" he said, more of a command than a question. "Ben Carson threatened a law officer with a sawed-off shotgun! And this boy here was trying to escape arrest!" He turned and walked around behind the bar, where Bret was kneeling over Ben, crying his name, clinging to him, not even aware that as she knelt beside him, she had cut her knees on broken glass.

"Let's go, bitch!" Kuzak ordered. "You're still under arrest for whorin' with a kid."

Bret slowly rose. "Murderer!" she screamed at him. "This was murder! He'd already put down his gun!" Tears streamed down her face, making white lines through her rouge and powder.

Kuzak grabbed her arm. "Keller will decide what was right and wrong about this, and he'll decide what to do with *you*! Now, let's go!" He dragged her away from Ben forcefully, all the while Bret screaming Ben's name. She stared at the dead young stranger as Kuzak took her through the saloon door, only then aware that the boy had also been shot, and in the back! He wasn't even armed!

"Murderer!" she screamed again, unaware that blood was streaming down the front of her legs. "This town will find a way to get you for this! We'll bring in the army! We'll do whatever we have to do, you bastards!"

Kuzak dragged her out into a cold wind filled with stinging sleet, not even allowing her to put on a cloak first.

Faith held Alex's hand, and the little boy seemed to understand he had to stand still and not make any noise. Eight-year-old Johnny stood on his mother's other side, staring at the open grave, the mounds of fresh dirt around it dusted with fresh spring snow. The coffin inside was plain, and Ben had no family, yet the whole town had turned out for his burial.

People were angry. Sheriff Keller had declared that Dave Kuzak had every right to do what he did. People pooled their money to get Bret out of jail, and the new town doctor had treated the wounds on her knees. She stood on the other side of Johnny now, dressed in black, and under her long black skirt her knees were wrapped in gauze. She walked with a limp because of stitches, and the old smiling, devil-may-care Bret Flowers had disappeared behind a black veil. Because of the cold weather she'd worn the hat and veil beneath the black hood of a fur cloak. She had said nothing through the whole ordeal. Faith had arranged everything, even a funeral for the unnamed young man who'd been shot in the back. Most of the town had also gone to his funeral, simply as a show of solidarity against Keller and his men. The dead young man had no identification on him. His stone would read "Name Unknown."

Faith moved around behind Johnny and put an arm around Bret, who had not even cried since being released, but now she broke down as the minister read from the Bible. In spite of their reputation as nothing more than a roving gambler and a long-time prostitute, everyone felt sorry for Bret, and all were angry over what had happened. A few managed to get through a hymn, "Shall We Gather by the River," but Faith could not even sing the words without more tears of her own stopping her. Again she wished she could be present at one of the Quaker prayer meetings and ask all of the worshipers to pray for Bret, and for Sommers Station. Keller had to be stopped, but she wasn't sure how to do it. She had already sent a letter to the commanding officer at Laramie, but his reply was that the army was much too involved in continuing Indian problems to be concerned about a town's problems with its sheriff. He had suggested they simply vote him out and hire someone else.

If only the man understood how difficult that would be. Any move made against Keller and his bunch was considered a crime, and though the townspeople were angry, they were also all afraid—except for Buck. Faith had had to argue with the man not to go after Keller alone—an impossible task. They had to plan a strategy. They had to stay calm, play along with Keller a while longer. It was obvious Keller had ordered Kuzak to find a reason to kill Ben Carson. That left Bret more vulnerable. Now they could move in and try to take over her saloon.

The service ended, and several people came up to express their sympathy to Bret, who was surprised to see so many there—more surprised to be receiving so much attention and sincere concern. Maude took the children with her, and Faith stayed behind with Bret, who bent down, took some dirt into her fist, and gently dropped it onto the coffin.

" 'Bye, Ben," she said softly.

Faith was glad to hear her say anything at all. A stiff wind blew against them, billowing their skirts and making the hood of Faith's wool cloak blow off her head. She pulled it back around her hair and ears and took Bret's arm. "We've got to get in where it's warm, Bret."

The woman faced her, and even through the veil Faith could see the dark circles under her eyes. "He was my best friend," Bret said brokenly.

"I know."

"I loved him. Not like you love a man you want to sleep with." She closed her eyes. "Ben was . . . just different. I loved him like the father I never had. The brother I never had. The friend I never had."

Faith grasped her cold hands. "Bret, you have a whole town full of friends now. We'll get you through this. And the Bret I know won't let it break her. That's what they want, Bret. Don't let them do it. I'm fighting it myself, and I need your help, just like you need mine."

Bret nodded, shivering in a sob. "It isn't . . . just losing Ben. It's more than that, Faith." She sniffed, wiping at her eyes with a handkerchief. "I never thought . . . it could happen to me . . . of all people. Some would say it isn't possible for somebody like me."

Faith frowned. "What isn't possible, Bret?"

The woman hesitated, blowing her nose. "That I . . ." She cried again, blew her nose again. "He . . . raped me, Faith. That bastard Kuzak . . . raped me in jail."

Faith felt her blood running colder than the winter air. "My God!"

"It wasn't like . . . you know . . . like being with somebody because it was my job and I agreed to it. It was . . . different. Just different. Can you understand that?"

Faith pulled her into her arms. "I think I do, Bret."

"You've gotta . . . be careful, Faith. He said . . . he said they'd get you, too. I think they're just waiting . . . for Tod Harding to say it's okay."

Faith felt sick to her stomach. What could she do if they

came for her? She couldn't shoot it out with two little boys in the house. Things were different now from when she'd been alone there guarding the depot. How strange that she'd felt safer then, knowing outlaws and Indians were always lurking about—safer than she felt now in the middle of a settled town with a sheriff to keep the law. How convenient that Tod Harding hadn't even been there when all this took place. He was very clever at disappearing when trouble descended on the town. "Let's just go back to the house for now," she told Bret. "We have to get out of this cold wind and get some rest."

"I can't leave Ben out here in the cold."

"We have no choice, Bret. And you have to keep the saloon open, in Ben's memory. Don't give up." She was so close to giving up herself. She felt guilty for having invited all these fine people to Sommers Station only to bring them so much trouble and heartache. How many more would leave now because of this?

She managed to get Bret back to the house and inside, making her sit down in a rocker beside the heating stove in the parlor. She stoked it a little more, then turned when Maude came in to hand her an envelope. "That Dennison boy bring zis from za postal office," she told Faith. "You know how he likes to bring all people zer mail."

Faith took the envelope. "Thank you, Maude. Could you fix Bret some hot tea?"

Maude nodded, thinking how she had disapproved of Bret Flowers when she'd first come to town, but now she felt very sorry for her.

Faith looked at the envelope, noticing that the return address was from Fort Gibson in Indian Territory. "Who in the world would be writing to me from Indian Territory?" she muttered. She sat down across from Bret near the stove, still wearing her woolen cloak. She removed her gloves and carefully opened the envelope, which was slightly battered, looking as though it had been through many hands and maybe even a little mud in getting there. She unfolded the yellowed paper and began reading, and suddenly all despair left her. She barely got past the first paragraph before letting out a gasp and coming out of her chair to sink to her knees. "Dear God," she whimpered.

"Faith?" Bret removed her own hood, then her black hat and veil, concern for Faith momentarily overcoming her own sorrow. "Faith, what's wrong? Is it your father?"

Faith looked up at her, and to Bret's surprise the woman was smiling through her tears, her blue eyes showing only great joy. "It's Gabe!" she whispered, glancing toward the door before looking back at Bret again. "He's alive!"

Chapter Thirty

Bret got up and walked to the parlor doors. "Would you wait on that tea and leave us alone for a moment, Maude?" she called to the woman. "And keep an eye on the boys." She reached out and swung the parlor doors together. She hurried back to Faith, who still sat on the floor, holding the letter in her shaking hand.

"Are you serious? Gabe is alive?" She spoke the words softly, not sure anyone else should know yet.

Faith looked up at her, handing her the letter. "I only got past the first . . . couple of sentences," she answered with a shiver. "I . . . I can't finish it, Bret. I'm too shocked . . . too nervous." Her whole body jerked in a sob, and Bret took the letter from her, all her own senses suddenly alive and kicking. She didn't even know Gabe Beaumont, yet this news brought her great elation.

"Get up, honey. We have to be careful about this. Let me read the letter to you, and we'll decide what to do. If it's true Harding and his henchmen tried to get rid of Gabe, maybe *they* don't know he's alive. Don't be telling anyone yet. Maybe the letter is some kind of trick."

"Oh, Bret, it can't be! This has to be real!"

Bret helped Faith back into her chair, then pulled her own chair closer, leaning forward so Faith could hear her read the letter softly.

"It's dated November sixteen, 1872. That's four months ago! It must have gotten lost for a while." She studied the letter a moment before starting to read. "Dearest Faith. This letter might be a shock to you. I have no idea what you have been told about me, but let me start by saying I am alive, and I want to come home." Bret blinked back her own tears of joy for Faith. She took a deep breath and swallowed before continuing. "The son of a Cherokee family for whom I am working in Indian Territory is writing this letter for me. I asked a dispatcher at Fort Gibson to send it on its way, with a prayer that it will reach you. I could have wired you, but I was not sure it was safe. It might be possible that the wrong men would hear about the telegram. A letter is more personal. Faith, please believe me that you should not trust Tod Harding or that sheriff from Cheyenne, Joe Keller. They are the reason I have been missing all this time. It is too long a story to put into a letter, but you must believe me when I tell you I did not leave by choice. I have been in—"

Bret hesitated, horrified at what had happened to the man. "In prison all this time, but now I am free."

"Dear God," Faith moaned. "Prison! They must have somehow made up some charges against him. How could anyone do such a thing!"

"Hush," Bret told her. "Keep this to yourself." She patted Faith's arm and continued. "I will explain everything when I see you again, but first I need to know if you want me to come. Perhaps you thought I was dead or had abandoned you. Perhaps you have already married someone else. I would not want to spoil whatever happiness you have found, but I pray you have waited. I thought about you every night of the four years I was in prison, and I tried to be with you in spirit. I hope that you have never given up on me, as I would never give up on you. I was not well when I was released, and it will take time for me to gain weight and get my strength back. I wanted to be strong again before I came home. I will winter here and return in the spring, as I don't feel strong enough right now to travel so far in winter snows.

"Faith, I have never stopped loving you. Please reply in care of Fort Gibson, Indian Territory, and tell me if you want me to come home."

"How could he think I wouldn't want him to come!" Faith sobbed.

"Honey, he has no idea what you were told, what you thought. He didn't want to just show up on your doorstep and shock you to death. For all he knew, you'd greet him with a rifle out of pure anger. Besides that, he apparently suspects Tod Harding has moved in on this town, and he's right. Harding and Keller apparently sent him off illegally. He can't just come prancing into town in full view of Keller and his thugs. He's using his good sense, Faith, and we've got to decide what to do, what to tell him."

"What to tell him? I'll tell him to come home! Oh, Bret, he's alive! And I know if he were here, Keller wouldn't get away with half the things he's done! Gabe would stop him! Gabe would—"

"Faith, stop and think!" Bret set the letter aside and grasped her wrists. "I just told you he can't come riding into town in full sight, not with Keller and his men still here. We have to warn him. We have to decide the best way to handle this."

Faith nodded, wiping hastily at her eyes. "Oh, Bret, I *can't* think straight, not when I know this wonderful news! Gabe! My Gabe is alive, just as I always believed! God has answered my prayers. This could be the answer to so *many* things. And Gabe doesn't even know he has a son of his own. He has to be told! And—oh, Bret, maybe he thinks I don't want him to come. The letter took so long getting here. My God, four months! It's 1873. He's been gone close to five years! What if he isn't even at Fort Gibson anymore? Maybe he gave up on me."

She started to rise, but Bret kept hold of her arms. "Faith, he will be waiting. He knows winter weather might have held things up, and he told you he would be there till spring. If he never gave up on you after four years in prison, why would he give up on you now that he's free? He has to be told everything that's going on here now. The question is *how* to tell him and keep it secret; *what* to tell him, and how to get you and him back together. The other problem is time. Who knows how long it would take for your reply to reach him? You need to send him a wire, but you can't do it from here. We can't trust the telegrapher. He might tell Tod Harding about the message."

"Then I'll go to him myself!"

"No!"

Bret was up and pacing now, rubbing at her lips thoughtfully. Faith watched her in surprise. A moment ago she had been a broken woman. Now she had something to think about, something to give her hope. The fact that Gabe was alive could give the whole town hope. He was living proof of the corruption of Tod Harding and Joe Keller! He could go to a U.S. marshal, the army, anyone in authority and tell them his story. He had prison records to prove it. The trouble was, Tod Harding had power, and friends in high places. How did they know who could be believed?

One thing was sure. She'd been right all along about Tod Harding having something to do with Gabe's disappearance. Gabe was alive! She had to see him, had to go to him! "Why not, Bret? It's the only way."

Both women spoke in excited whispers, both still wiping at tears that were a mixture of joy over Gabe and sorrow over Ben.

"Don't you see?" Bret answered, coming closer to keep her voice low. "Everybody knows you would be the *last* one to leave Sommers Station. If you pack up and go now, they'll wonder, and Joe Keller and his bunch will suspect something, maybe even follow you. *I* have to go!"

"*You!*"

"Yes!" Bret's eyes lit up with excitement. "Keller and Harding will think they've defeated me. Harding will probably take over the saloon, but I don't care. I'll leave town a broken, defeated woman, or at least that's what they'll *think*. If I have to come back later with a message, I'll just say I decided all my friends were right here in Sommers

Station and I wanted to come back." Her smile faded. "Faith, I have to do this. I can leave town with no one suspecting a thing. I *need* to do this, you see? It will help keep me from thinking about poor Ben, what I've lost. It will give me a purpose for the next few weeks. I'll go to Denver and send a wire from there, tell Gabe to get on a train and meet me in Denver at a designated place. I'll explain the situation so he'll be aware before he gets here. Then he can decide what to do about it. Then I'll come back to Sommers Station, supposedly to visit you. I'll let you know then what Gabe is going to do."

Their eyes held in mutual understanding, two women from such different worlds, yet each understanding the other's sorrow and joy.

"It's a wonderful thing you're doing for me, Bret."

A cold hardness came into Bret's eyes. "Honey, you're just about the best woman friend I ever had, but I'm not doing this just for you. I'm doing it for Ben, and for Sommers Station. If Gabe Beaumont can find a way to show Keller and Harding for what they are and can get Keller out of this town, I'll feel like I've had a little part in doing something to avenge what happened to Ben."

Faith embraced her, and the two of them clung to each other. "I'm so sorry about Ben," Faith told her. "But it's like I said, Bret. You have a lot of friends in this town. You can always stay here, keep your saloon, whatever you want to do."

"I know . . . and thanks." Bret pulled away. "I'd better go pack. I've got some traveling to do. Say, you don't have any pictures of Gabe, do you?"

"No." Faith closed her eyes and smiled, clutching the letter in one hand. "But you don't need a picture. You'll know him when you see him—tall, dark, black hair, and the most exotic green eyes. He's the kind of man who makes women look twice, and—" She hesitated, studying Bret closely and smiling. "You just remember he was in prison for four years."

Bret smiled through tears. "And hasn't been with a woman in all that time, and probably not since. My, my." She gave Faith a wink. "This could be an interesting trip."

She sashayed to the parlor door and turned. "Don't you worry. You know I'd never dream of bedding my best friend's husband—but even more, I suspect your Gabe isn't the kind of man who'd settle for anyone but the woman he loves, Faith Beaumont. I'll probably have a hell of a time keeping him from charging up here to see you like a bull after a cow in heat."

"Bret!" Faith reddened. "Such talk!" She felt a rush of desire sweep through her at the thought of being held by Gabe again, touched by him, being a woman to him again. She prayed the letter was not just some kind of ruse. "Tell him I love him, Bret."

"You really think I need to?"

Faith smiled sadly. "He'll know. But tell him anyway. And tell him it did work, his thinking of me in the night. Tell him I felt him with me many times, and I never gave up believing he was alive and coming back to me."

Bret nodded. "I'll tell him." She rested her hand on the doorknob. "You know something? I'm feeling much better. I think I'll skip that tea and go back to the saloon and order a round of drinks for everyone, in Ben's memory. You just remember not to go around town looking too happy." She picked up her hat and plopped it on her head, pulling down the veil. She threw on her hooded cloak and pulled the hood up over her hat. "I'll do the same. We don't want anyone to suspect. And hide that letter some-place safe."

"I will. Thank you, Bret."

The woman smiled sadly. "Sure."

She turned and left, and Faith looked down at the letter, reading it again. "Oh, Gabe," she whispered. This was no ruse. No one but Gabe would know just the right thing to say. No one but Gabe would have known to tell her he'd be with her in spirit. She folded the letter and shoved it into the front of her dress, inside her camisole, next to her heart.

Gabe disembarked from the train, amazed at what a big city Denver was. With the pace at which the West was apparently growing, he surmised St. Louis must be many times bigger now than when he'd been there as a boy, and Cheyenne had probably also grown far beyond what he remembered, now that the railroad was completed.

Passengers and their greeters thronged the depot of the Denver & Rio Grande, and Gabe stood a little taller than most of them. He scanned the crowd for the woman called Bret Flowers. She'd said she had blond hair and would be wearing a green velvet cloak. His gaze locked on to a woman who fit that description. It was a cold, but calm day, and she had left the hood of her cape down so her hair would show.

Gabe walked closer, carrying a carpetbag. He thought she had a look about her that spoke of what one might call an "experienced" woman. How could such a woman be Faith's best friend? She turned and noticed him as he approached, and her eyes roved his body appreciatively. It was obvious she was buxom, even though most of her was covered by the velvet cape. Her face showed a little too much powder and rouge, and although it was obvious she was once very pretty, she was now showing some age and had the hard look about her of a woman who'd been around too much whiskey and smoke. He would have much preferred Faith standing there waiting for him, but he understood from this woman's telegrams that it was not safe for him to go directly to Sommers Station. He needed little explanation after learning that Joe Keller was sheriff there. He suspected he already understood the whole picture, and he worried what kind of hell poor Faith had been through.

"You are Miss Flowers?"

Bret could not help being stirred sexually by the sight of Gabe Beaumont. This one was all man, that was sure. There were hints of what he'd been through, still looking a little gaunt in the face, his eyes hinting of the horror he'd suffered. She nodded in reply to his question, drinking in his handsome masculinity. Every feature of his face was perfect—full lips, high cheekbones, deep-set eyes surrounded by dark lashes. Faith was right about those eyes being exotic. Their sea-green color was only accented by his dark skin. He wore a wide-brimmed felt hat, and his black hair was pulled back and tied at the nape of his neck.

"I sure am," she replied in answer to his question. "And there is no doubt in my mind who *you* are. I figured Faith had to be exaggerating about how handsome you are, but now I see her glowing praises were an understatement."

Gabe grinned. "I suppose I should thank you." He looked toward the baggage and cattle cars. "I have to get my gear and horses. The horses are a gift from a Cherokee friend I worked for. I intended to stay a little longer, since I am not full strength yet. But after hearing that Joe Keller is in Sommers Station, I knew I had to come right away. Wait here and I will get my things."

"Sure. I'll be in that buggy over there. We'll go to my room at the Brown Palace. I've rented an extra room for you—my treat. I'm glad to be able to do this for Faith."

Immediately his eyes showed a new softness. "How is she?" he asked. "She has not been harmed, has she?"

Bret smiled, glad to see the love in his eyes. "She's fine— physically. We'll talk about it when we get to the hotel. You go get your gear so we can get over there and out of this cold."

He nodded and she watched him walk away, wondering what he meant by "full strength." What she saw certainly looked strong enough. It was obvious that under the heavy winter canvas duster he wore was a man with a mighty fine build. She noticed he limped a little. Faith had never mentioned a limp. His hair was very long, hanging in a tail outside the back of his duster. She walked to the buggy she'd rented, climbing into the seat and asking the driver to wait. Several minutes later Gabe rode up beside the buggy on a sturdy black gelding. He led a packhorse behind him. Bret ordered the driver to take her back to her hotel, and Gabe followed. A young boy who worked for the Brown Palace greeted them when they arrived, and Gabe paid him to watch his horses and gear. He looked up at the five-story brick structure, still surprised by the size of Denver and its buildings.

"This looks pretty fancy," he told Bret, taking her hand and helping her down.

"It's the best hotel in town. I figured after what you've been through, you deserve to live in a little luxury for a couple of days. Don't worry about the cost. I took all my money out of Tod Harding's bank in Sommers Station before I left. I wanted him to think I was leaving town for good now that he's taken over my saloon."

Gabe stopped at the hotel entrance. "Sommers Station has a saloon?"

Bret grinned. "Just wait till you see how Faith's little town has grown. I have a lot to tell you. And, by the way, I know what you're thinking, Gabe, and you're right. I'm exactly the kind of woman you think I am, but I didn't deal in prostitution at Sommers Station. Me and Ben"—her smile faded, and she looked away—"we ran a legitimate saloon, just drinks and cards, that kind of thing. Come on. We'll get you checked in and meet in one of our rooms. I have a lot to tell you." She looked back up at him. "Including the fact that Faith most certainly does still love you and wants you to come home. She said to tell you she did feel your presence often, especially in the night, so that thing about your trying to be with her spiritually worked, I guess. I don't know much about Indians and spirits and all that kind of thing, but it's a sure thing she felt you with her. Maybe it's the kid that did it."

Gabe frowned. "Johnny?"

Bret smiled through tears. "No. Her *second* child, a son named Alex, after his grandfather Beaumont."

Gabe stared at the woman before him. The street noises around them, the people walking by, suddenly vanished from his consciousness. He was aware only of the words Bret Flowers had just spoken, and a mixture of joy and shock rushed through his blood. "I have a son?"

Bret nodded. "Looks just like his pa, too. He'll be four next month." She saw the tears in his eyes, and her heart ached for him. More than that, she was worried that he might be doubly revengeful against the men who had robbed him of so much. She touched his arm. "You need to think about this, Gabe. The last thing you want to do is go charging into Sommers Station and getting yourself shot because you didn't plan this right. Faith needs you more than ever. After all this waiting, don't go and get yourself killed."

He closed his eyes, now shaking with rage. A son! Faith had given birth to his son all alone, raised him without a father. He'd missed out on the boy's first four years, and Johnny must be seven or eight by now. He couldn't even remember how old the boy had been when he'd been hauled away unconscious from Cheyenne. Tod Harding and Joe Keller had robbed him and Faith and the children of so much. Someone had to pay for this!

He followed Bret inside, his mind reeling with confusion, joy, sorrow, hatred, vengeance. He was hardly aware of anything around him as he climbed the stairs with Bret and followed her to her second-floor room. He ignored the condemning looks of other patrons who saw them together, a painted woman and an Indian. He did not know that Bret had paid the man at the desk extra money to allow him to stay there. Management normally would not allow an Indian in a place like this—the newest, fanciest hotel in Denver.

Gabe found himself in Bret's room. The door closed, and he removed his hat and duster and threw them onto a chair. He did not even notice the fancy room as he walked to a window, looking out on the street. He scanned the city, just another example of how settled the West was becoming, filling with whites. He had no idea what was happening with the Sioux now. Charlie Jefferson had said that new trouble had broken out over whites wanting the Sioux to give up even more land. Red Cloud supposedly lived on one of the reservations now. The biggest trouble-makers were Sitting Bull, and the warrior Crazy Horse. Charlie had said there was some new officer out west making a lot of news, and a lot of trouble for the Indians. He was called George Custer.

But for the moment the Sioux were not his problem. He was sorry for what was happening to them, but he felt far removed from that life now. His focus had to be on Faith and Johnny . . . and on his son.

Alex! She'd named him Alex. He loved her all the more for being so thoughtful. How he ached to set eyes on her again, touch her again, be inside her again. "Tell me all of it," he said to Bret, not even turning around to look at her. "Faith, my son, Sommers Station, what's happened there. I want to know about Tod Harding, how many businesses he has there, what he's done to Faith. How Joe Keller got to be sheriff." He heard the rustle of her taffeta dress and many petticoats as she removed her cape and walked over to hang it on a hook.

"That's what I'm here for," she answered. "But suppose you tell me first what happened to you—how a trip to Cheyenne ended up with you in prison clear down in Indian Territory."

Gabe turned to see he'd been right about what lay under the cape. She was a shapely woman who filled out the bodice of a dress quite attractively—but that painted face, that bleached hair. "How did someone like Faith get to be close friends with someone like you?" he asked.

Bret laughed. "The better question is how did *I* end up befriending a woman like Faith! She's got me thinking like a proper woman. This is the first high-necked dress I've worn in years."

Gabe finally grinned. "Something tells me you are not so changed down deep inside."

"Damn, you have a handsome smile," Bret replied with more laughter. "And you're right. It's too bad you're my best friend's husband. But—" She shrugged. "That's life, I guess." She put her hands on her hips and sauntered a little closer. "You answer my questions first, and then I'll explain everything about Faith and Sommers Station—and how Faith and I got to be friends. Don't worry—Faith is as virtuous and hardworking and beautiful and determined as ever. She hasn't fallen into my way of life, if that's what you're thinking."

He smiled, his love for his wife obvious in his eyes. "I would never think that of Faith." He walked over and sat down in a chair, his frame seeming almost too big for the room. "I had just sold my horses and was headed out to do some shopping for Faith when Joe Keller and someone else, probably Tod Harding, grabbed me and smashed my ribs and skull before I knew what hit me," he told her, beginning his story. "There was a bad sandstorm that day, and I could hardly see two feet in front of me. That's the only reason they got the better of me."

Bret sat down on the bed and listened, her own hatred for Harding and Keller growing deeper as he talked. She did her own explaining when he was through, and one thing was clear and certain by the time they both had finished.

"Joe Keller and his men have to die," Gabe said matter-of-factly. "And Tod Harding must also pay, not just for having me falsely thrown into prison, but for forcing Faith to sell her land to him. I promised Judge Parker I would not kill him, but that does not mean I will not find my vengeance."

Bret got up and began pacing. "Like I said before, you need a plan, Gabe. Keller's men are nothing more than hired guns, and they know how to use them."

"So do I." Gabe also rose. "And I have a couple of things on my side—a hatred like nothing they have ever known—and surprise. They think I am dead."

Bret slowly nodded. "Won't they be shocked when they find out different?"

Gabe calmly considered the truth of what she said. "How many are there?" he asked coolly.

"Keller and six deputies. Can you imagine a little place like Sommers Station needing seven lawmen?" She smiled in a derisive sneer. "They came to take over the town, and they're doing it. Poor Faith's dream is falling into ruins. No one in town knows quite how to get rid of the man. Anyone who speaks against him ends up being burned out or thrown into jail for no good reason."

Gabe stepped closer. "Tell me something. If I was to go there and find a way to kill all those men, would the townspeople support me? Would they agree it is the right thing to do? Or would they say I should be hanged?"

Bret chuckled. "They would probably give you a medal and make *you* sheriff of Sommers Station. Actually, that wouldn't be a bad idea." She rubbed a hand over her forehead in thought. "How do you propose to take on seven men?"

He shrugged. "It's like I said. I have the element of surprise. All I need is a couple of men who would back me up. Is there anyone at Sommers Station who would do that? Is Buck Jones still around?"

"He sure is. He's been wanting to go after Keller himself, but Faith won't let him. She's afraid he'd get himself killed. But Buck is a rugged, brave son-of-a-gun, and damned experienced already in going up against outlaws and In—" She hesitated.

"Indians," Gabe finished for her. "Do not be afraid to say it. I am just glad Buck stayed on. I know he did it out of respect for Faith, and I know he is a man I can rely on. I want you to go back and talk to him, have him pick a couple more men who can be counted on to help. There is no other way to do this but to call Joe Keller out and have it over with. I am going to take that town back for Faith, and Tod Harding will find that out the next time he comes back to Sommers Station, the men who backed him will be gone, and he will have *me* to deal with!"

The cold fire in his eyes made even Bret uncomfortable. "All right. I'll talk to Buck, tell him you're alive and need his help. We'll both take the train to Cheyenne, and then you take the back pathways to Sommers Station. Come in at night. Take your horses into the livery. Buck still runs it. He'll be watching for you. Faith's house is behind the rooming house."

"I know. We were having it built when I left for Cheyenne."

"Do everything after dark and stay out of sight. Once you're inside the house, you'll have to stay there until Faith can gather Buck and whoever else wants to help. They can come after dark to a secret meeting, and you can tell them your plans." She shivered with apprehension. "I'll be praying you don't get hurt or killed. Faith would be so devastated."

"Do not worry. I am not the one who will die."

Bret studied his size, realized this man had once been a Sioux warrior, had made war against soldiers and settlers, had ridden with outlaws. Yes, he could handle himself, and God help the man or men whom Gabriel Beaumont hated.

She slowly nodded. "I hope you're right. Are you sure you want to do it this way? We could get a U.S. marshal there, or maybe soldiers—"

"No. *I* have to do it!"

Bret nodded. "Sure you do."

"I am sorry about your friend who was killed."

Bret's eyes teared. "Ben and I looked out for each other since we were kids. We were never lovers, just friends, but I cared about him more than anyone else in my life."

Gabe walked over and picked up his coat and hat. "You should go back there and take over your saloon again. Do not let Tod Harding defeat you. We will get it back."

He said it so matter-of-factly, Bret almost laughed. "Just like that?"

Gabe nodded. "Just like that." He walked closer, leaned down, and kissed her cheek. "Can you leave in the morning?"

Bret could not help wishing she could invite this man to stay in her room that night. "Yes. But I thought you would want to rest a little more first."

He shook his head. "I want nothing more than to see Faith again. The first night I come, I do not want any meetings. I want to be alone with her."

Bret grinned. "Of course you do, you devil. She'd want the same." She put her hands on her hips. "You know, I really think you *can* take back Sommers Station. I can't wait until Harding returns to discover his henchmen are all buried."

The frightening gleam of hatred came back into Gabe's eyes, and Bret thought how terrifying it would be to be the man's captive. Everyone had heard stories about the ways the Sioux had of torturing a man, or a woman. "How do you plan to get even with Harding without killing him?"

Gabe grinned wickedly, and Bret could almost picture him wearing nothing but a breechcloth and war paint. "You do not want to know," he answered. He turned to the door. "What is my room number? I was too lost in thought to pay attention at the desk."

Bret walked to a small table and picked up a key, handing it to him. "Three doors down, two-sixteen."

Gabe took the key, squeezing her hand as he did so. "You are a good woman."

Bret's eyebrows rose at the irony of the statement. "Well, I've never heard that one before. Thanks."

"It is I who thanks you." Gabe turned and left, wondering how he was going to sleep that night for thinking of what Faith had been through, the cruel way Harding had plotted to overtake Sommers Station. That town belonged to Faith Sommers Beaumont, and he would get back whatever part of it she had lost, even if he had to die doing it.

Chapter Thirty-one

Faith checked on Johnny and Alex, throwing another quilt over each of them. She walked back into the kitchen to build a fire in the cast-iron cookstove, which also served as a heating stove. She turned down the draft in the chimney. When Henry Baker had built the house, he had wisely installed two doors in each of the two rooms closest to the kitchen, which was the biggest room at the end of the house. One door in each of the two adjoining rooms opened into the hallway; the other door of each room opened to the kitchen, so in winter the two rooms could easily be heated. If she left open the door to her library, next to the boys' bedroom, it was a reasonably bearable place in winter to serve as her office, and she could heat the parlor with its brick fireplace.

Tonight she had only the cookstove going in the kitchen, keeping things pleasantly warm in spite of a cold wind outside. April had been a month of almost daily changing weather—warm one day, very cold the next. She kept a kettle of water constantly heated on the stove, and she used it now to fix herself some tea. Sleep was impossible, not just because Gabe could show up any night now, but because of his plans to take on Joe Keller. Would she have him back for one or two nights only to lose him to a bullet in the back? It sickened her to think of what he'd been through, the story Bret had told her. It was bad enough he'd been falsely arrested and forced to live in a rat-infested prison for over four years, but to think Keller had shot him and he'd been left untreated for weeks . . . She couldn't blame Gabe for wanting to seek his own revenge, but the danger he would be in left her restless and shaken.

At least he would have help. She smiled at the thought of the tears in Buck's eyes when he'd heard Gabe was alive. He'd said he would find a couple of men who could be trusted and who would not be afraid to help Gabe go up against Keller—and Buck himself was more than ready. That made her rest a little easier.

She filled the little metal tea strainer with tea leaves and dunked it into a mug of hot water, sitting down with it and staring blankly at the water as it slowly turned dark. There was so much to think about, so much to talk about with Gabe. Every night she washed and powdered herself, brushed out her hair . . . waited. What would he be like? Would they be strangers to each other now? Nearly five years had passed. Did he look any different? Would she look different to him?

Thank God Bret had been able to intercept his return and explain the situation so Gabe would not walk into disaster. Keller seemed to have no suspicion about why she had returned, her story about missing her friends apparently satisfying him. She had taken a job serving drinks at what was now Tod Harding's saloon. Bret had sold out to him through his banker before leaving, and now she worked for low wages in the saloon she had once owned, its name changed to the Whistle Stop.

"It's going to be mine again," she'd sworn to Faith, "soon as that wild Indian of yours takes care of Keller and his bunch."

Faith shivered at the thought of a confrontation. She pulled up the collar of the quilted housecoat she wore over her flannel nightgown, feeling a chill when the wind outside made the house creak. She drank some tea, thinking how she'd become so used to the Wyoming winds that she hardly noticed them anymore. She closed her eyes and savored the hot steam off the tea, lost in thought, when she heard the light tap at the back door.

Immediately all senses came alert, her heart pounding as she set down the cup of tea. It all seemed so unreal, the fact that Gabe could be on the other side of the door. She reminded herself it could also be Keller or one of his men, come to do to her what they had done to Bret. They wanted to break her, and she had been terrified ever since Bret's rape that they might. She rose on shaking legs, reaching up to take a pistol from the top of a tall cupboard, where the boys couldn't see or reach it.

"Who is it?" she called.

"Me. Gabe," came the reply.

Faith felt faint. There was no mistaking the deep voice. Still, could it be a trick? She opened the door just a crack, keeping the pistol ready. The reality he was still alive finally hit her. "Gabe!" she whimpered. "My God!" She stepped back as he quickly came inside and closed the door, snow on his hat and shoulders, and on the saddlebags and carpetbag he tossed to the floor. They stood staring at each other as he slowly removed his hat and set it on the table, then removed his heavy canvas duster, laying it over a chair.

"I . . . couldn't quite believe this was real," Faith told him, still clinging to the gun. She looked him over. Thinner. Yes, he was thinner, but he actually looked a little harder, stronger. She stood frozen as he came closer and pulled the gun out of her hand. He started to lay it on the table.

"The cupboard," she said, nodding toward the cupboard behind him. "On top, away from the children."

Gabe turned and set the pistol back where it belonged. Children. She'd said "children." He turned back to look her over . . . so beautiful in the soft lamplight. She hadn't changed at all. She was still his lovely, brave, determined, gentle, but fiery Faith Sommers Beaumont. And now she was mother to his own son. "I am so sorry for the hell you have been through," he told her.

"Sorry? My God, Gabe, you couldn't help it." Why did this meeting, dreamed of for so many years, feel so odd? Those years had taken so much from both of them.

"I can't help thinking maybe I could have kept it from happening. I should have been more alert. I should have known what Tod Harding was really after."

"Stop blaming yourself. That's ridiculous. *I'm* so sorry for *you*. I also should have seen the writing on the wall. What you have been through, it must have been so horrible!"

The wind rattled a window.

"I would like to see my son."

Faith nodded. She picked up the lantern from the kitchen table and carried it into the adjoining bedroom, holding the light over Alex's bed. Her heart ached when she heard a sudden gasp from Gabe, followed by a sob. He knelt beside the bed, lightly touched Alex's chubby little arm. He remained there, his shoulders shaking, and Faith quietly waited. Finally he wiped at his eyes and rose.

"He is beautiful," he whispered.

"Of course he is. He looks just like his father."

Gabe said nothing in reply. He walked over to Johnny's bed, shaking his head as he studied him. "He is so big. He has lost his baby features."

"He's eight years old. Hardly a day went by that he didn't ask about you. I told him you had to go on a long trip, that you loved him and would come back someday. He hasn't forgotten you, Gabe."

Gabe took a deep breath and walked out of the room. They stood in the hallway then, both feeling a little awkward. "I'll show you the rest of the house. There isn't much." Faith turned and carried the lantern down the hall to her library, then the parlor. She shivered. That end of the house was cold, as she did not keep a fire in the parlor fireplace at night. She led him back to the only room she had not shown him yet. "This is my . . . our . . . bedroom." She set the lamp on a dresser and turned, meeting his eyes. "This has been the loneliest room in the house."

They just stood there looking at each other for several seconds. He reached out then, and she took his hand. The moment they touched, each knew nothing had changed. Those five years had not made them strangers. All that time vanished as though it had been only five hours. In the next moment she was in his arms, his strong, sure arms. Her face rested against his broad chest, and she was pressed tight against him. His lips caressed her hair, and he stroked her back.

"Faith. My beautiful Faith."

"Oh, Gabe. I knew you wouldn't have just run out on me. I knew it! It was so awful not knowing what had happened to you." She looked up at him, and in the next moment their lips met. All awkwardness was gone. There was only this deep, burning, aching need to feel her man inside her again, and Gabe had been so long without a woman.

He lifted her in his arms and laid her on the bed, moving on top of her in desperate need. They could not touch enough, kiss enough, press their bodies together tightly enough. Clothes came off in eager desire, hurriedly, to do what must be done quickly, savagely. Only his boots and pants, then with those, his long johns. Only her housecoat and drawers. He pushed up her gown, and she opened herself in aching need, gasping when he shoved his hard shaft inside her. He buried his face in her hair and groaned, ramming deep and hard, reclaiming her, proving to himself and to her that this was real. He was alive and they were together again.

It was over quickly the first time, but both knew that would not be the only time. Not tonight. Amid hot kisses he removed her flannel gown, and suddenly the room seemed too hot instead of too chilly. Gabe removed his shirt, pushed the bed blankets aside, met her mouth again, tracing his tongue inside her lips. How wonderful it felt being with a woman again, and having that woman be Faith. He wanted to touch and taste every inch of her. He moved his lips down her neck, took a breast into his mouth in groaning hunger. She had fed his son with these breasts.

This was the beloved mother of his child. He had a family again.

Faith cried out with the pleasure of being touched this way again. She arched herself against him, and he moved to taste her other breast, licking and pulling at it in ways that made her wild with desire. She wrapped her fingers into his dark hair as he traveled down her belly, kissed her thighs, the hairs of her lovenest. His tongue flicked lightly at that secret place that set her on fire, and quickly his lips traveled back up over her breasts and he was inside of her again, rubbing at her in a way that built the fire bigger until she felt the glorious climax she had not experienced in years. She pulsated against him, groaning his name as he pounded into her, this time for much longer, each of them reveling in enjoying long-neglected needs, glorying in uniting bodies again in love, celebrating the fact that Gabe Beaumont was alive and very real . . . and as much a man as ever.

The night became like a dream for Faith. Her man was home. She was safe now. Somehow God would help Gabe do what he must do. God would not have brought him back to her only to take him away in death. She thought how she would have to write her father and tell him she finally believed in the true miracle of prayer. They made love three more times, unable to get enough of each other. She reveled in the strength of his arms, the peace of lying beside him, the ecstasy of being made love to by a man of such virility, of such gentleness. They tossed and rolled in heated passion, groping, tasting, unable to satiate their need for one another.

Finally, in the wee hours of dawn, they fell asleep in an exhaustion unlike any they had known before, a pleasant, exotic sort of exhaustion. When they awoke again, it was to sunshine, and to two little boys who were standing by the bed staring at Gabe. It was their voices that woke them.

"I think it's him," Johnny was saying to Alex. "Our daddy."

"Daddy?" Alex stared at the big, dark man who lay in bed with his mommy. His lips puckered as he watched the man thoughtfully, trying to decide if he liked him or not.

He'd always had his mommy to himself, and the man he saw beside her now was a stranger, kind of scary because of the strong look to his arms.

"You'll like him," Johnny was telling him. "He can teach you to ride a horse, and—" He stopped talking when Gabe opened his eyes.

Gabe sat up, nudging Faith awake. Gabe kept a blanket around himself as he moved his feet over the edge of the bed and studied both boys. "Hello," he said, seeing they were both skeptical and a little bit afraid. "I would like to hold you in my arms. I have missed my sons."

"Are you really my daddy?" Alex asked.

Gabe felt a lump forming in his throat. What a handsome, sturdy boy he was. "Yes, I am. I am sorry I have been gone so long, but it was not my fault. Some bad men took me away and put me in a place where I could not get out."

"Why?" Johnny asked.

"Because they wanted to steal something from your mommy, and they did not want me around to help her. But I am free now, and I am home." He held out his hands. "I love you, and I wish I could hug you."

Johnny grinned, and Gabe thought how the boy was growing more handsome as he got older. Being the outgoing, accepting child that he was, he threw his arms around Gabe's neck. "We love you, too, Daddy. Mommy said you'd come back."

Alex stood back a little, still watching Gabe thoughtfully. Faith wrapped herself in a blanket and got up, walking around to kneel beside the boy. "It's all right, Alex. He really is your daddy, and he loves you so much. It isn't his fault he couldn't be here until now. He needs very much to hug you. Won't you give your daddy a hug?"

Alex blinked, stepping a little closer. Gabe kissed Johnny's cheek and set him on the bed, then reached out for Alex. The boy still hesitated.

"Will you really teach me to ride a horse?" he asked.

"I will teach you many things," Gabe answered. "Anything you want to learn. But first I need that hug, or I will be very sad."

Alex looked at his mother.

"You don't want your daddy to be sad, do you?" she asked.

The boy shook his head, looked back at Gabe. "She's my mommy. You won't take her away from me, will you?"

Gabe grinned. "No, Alex, I will not take her away. We will all live together. Your mommy will always be here for you, and I will let you hug her and be with her as much as you want."

"Will you be nice to her?"

Gabe was touched at the child's sense of protectiveness for his mother.

"Of course I will be nice to her. I love her. I am here to take care of her now, take care of all of you, protect you."

The boy reached out and touched Gabe's big hand. "Okay. You can hug me."

Gabe struggled not to laugh at the authoritative way the child had spoken the words. His heart burst with love as he drew his son into his arms. He had not expected when he was first released that his homecoming would be quite this wonderful, and his hatred for Joe Keller and Tod Harding burned deeper at the thought of the years he had missed with this precious son. He held him tightly, fighting tears, until finally Alex decided he'd given this stranger enough for the moment and wiggled out of his arms.

"You boys go get dressed. Daddy and I have to wash and change," Faith told them. "And stay inside. It's very cold out today."

"Isn't it a school day?" Johnny asked.

Faith looked at Gabe, realizing then that if the boys went out, they would probably tell everyone they saw that their daddy was back. It must be kept a secret. "No," she lied. "There won't be any school for a few days, and I want you to stay in the house."

"Oh, heck. I want to play in the snow with Daddy. I want him to show Alex how to ride."

"We will get to all of that," Gabe told him. "Right now there is something else I have to do. It will only take a couple of days."

The boys went out pouting, and Faith closed the door, facing Gabe. "Gabe, I'm so scared."

All the softness he'd shown until now vanished, and a cold hatred moved into his green eyes. "Don't be. By tomorrow you will have control of this town again. I want you to go get Buck later and bring him over. We have to talk. Is Tod Harding in town?"

"No. I never know when he'll be around. He comes just long enough to collect rent and to check on his businesses, then leaves again."

He nodded. "Good. The first thing we have to do is put trustworthy guards at the telegraph station to make sure that no men who work for Harding at his bank and other businesses try to send him a wire, warning him not to come here. After I take care of Keller and his men, one of them might try to let Harding know what has happened. We will find out where he is and send him a fake wire, telling him there has been an emergency here and that he had better come back quick." His eyes frightened even Faith. "*I* will be waiting for him!"

Buck positioned himself on a roof across the street from the Whistle Stop Saloon. Stu Herron, a gunsmith who also knew how to handle guns, stood inside his shop, also across from the saloon. He watched out the window, rifle ready. Jack Delaney, the town blacksmith, was on the roof of Tod Harding's fancy hotel, his perch giving him a good view of the street. In their secret meeting the night before, Gabe had told them this would not take long. It was impossible to let the whole town in on what was going to happen that day. Word might get out to Keller. This had to be a surprise. The word had been whispered to a few people on the street to get inside. There was going to be trouble.

It was three o'clock in the afternoon, and a stiff wind blew sand down the street, but no more snow had fallen. Only a dusting of snow covered the streets, and the sun was shining, but the wind was bitterly cold. Buck hoped it did not affect his aim.

Gabe finally showed up, walking into the saloon. A moment later David Kuzak walked out. Gabe had given him the message to fetch Joe Keller. Gabe soon emerged from the saloon and stood leaning against a support post. Minutes later Keller came out of the sheriff's office up the street, Dave Kuzak and another deputy walking beside him. Buck kept an eye on a third deputy who stood farther down the street, watching curiously. He drew a bead on the man and waited. *That makes four, includin' Keller,* Buck thought. The other three deputies worked nights. They would be sleeping in the bunkhouse Keller had built for their housing. Buck and Gabe would take care of those three when they had finished with Keller.

Keller came closer to the saloon, then stopped. The street was empty, but Buck could see a few people watching out windows. Bret Flowers was looking through the glass of the front doors, kept closed today because of the cold. Keller's hat blew away as Gabe stepped off the boardwalk in front of the saloon. Buck couldn't hear the conversation, but he had a pretty good idea how it would go.

Gabe himself felt the beginnings of sweet victory at the look on Keller's face. "Hello, Joe."

Keller literally paled. "What the hell—"

"You surprised I am still alive? They did not hang me, after all, Joe. You have been found out, you and Harding both. I could go to higher authorities and let them take care of this, have you sent to prison—but I decided I would rather kill you. You ready to die today, Joe?"

The two deputies on either side of Keller stiffened, spreading their legs slightly. One wore a long duster, and he pushed it behind his gun. Kuzak also wore a long coat, but he carried a rifle. Joe Keller wore a short sheepskin jacket, leaving his six-guns free. In spite of the cold, Gabe had worn only winter underwear under a heavy wool shirt, so that his hands would be completely free.

"How the hell—when did you get into town?"

"Does it really matter?"

"How did you get out of prison?"

"A judge came along who discovered there were no legal papers to keep me there. He also discovered that Lieutenant Nathan Balen was not dead, and there had never been any charges against me. I have planned this moment from the day you arrested me in Cheyenne, beat and shot me and sent me off to Indian Territory to be hanged. Today *true* justice will be served. I know what you have been up to here in Sommers Station, and it is going to end. You are giving this town back to Faith Beaumont."

Keller swallowed, one hand resting nervously on one of his six-guns. "She don't own anything anymore except her boardinghouse and the house she lives in, and even those are on Harding property now."

"Not for long."

"You half-breed bastard! What makes you think you can go up against somebody like Tod Harding and his money? Killing me won't change anything. He'll bring in a whole army of his own men!"

"Not when I get through with him."

Keller grinned, but his own nervous apprehension was obvious. Gabe stood there calmly, looking very sure of himself. "I've got two men with me, and a third man behind you. Do you really think you can take down all four of us?"

"I will take my chances. The only thing I know for sure is you will be first, and you are the one who really counts. I will even let you draw first."

Keller looked around, aware people were watching. "Beaumont, you're going up against the law. If you lose this, you'll go to prison for real this time, and if you kill one of my men, you'll hang!"

This time Gabe grinned. "I hardly think there is anyone in this town who would hang me for killing one of your thugs. They would all like to get rid of you. If your men just want to get out of town, they are welcome to get on their horses and leave."

"You pompous ass! I've got another three men at the bunkhouse."

"We will take care of them."

"We?"

"You underestimate the people of this town, Keller, and their respect for Faith."

Keller was actually sweating now, in spite of the cold. Gabe Beaumont was out for blood, and the look in his eyes was indeed terrifyingly calm. Were there really others among the cowards of this town willing to help the man?

He glanced at Gabe's gun, figured if he had been in prison all this time, he was surely rusty. The man didn't have a chance. If Keller could keep him talking, distract him . . .

"How was prison, Beaumont? Give this up now, or you'll be dead or right back behind bars."

Gabe watched his eyes, only his eyes. "It will be worth it if you have also died. Make no mistake—"

Keller went for his gun, but Gabe didn't miss a beat. In that split second before Keller died, the man realized Gabe Beaumont was not off guard at all. He saw Gabe's gun drawn, saw the flash, felt the hard blow to his chest, then nothing.

Those watching from inside buildings and from rooftops saw, too, and everything happened in only seconds. Keller went down, and at the same time Gabe flattened himself on the street and rolled away from the bullets that Keller's two deputies shot at him. He fired again, bringing down Kuzak. The second man fell then from a bullet that ripped through his face from above, not from Gabe's gun. Gabe rolled onto his back, waving to Buck, who stood up holding his rifle in the air. The old man let out a war whoop. Just then Gabe noticed the third deputy aiming at Buck. He aimed and fired, and at nearly the same time another gunshot was heard, this one from the front of the gunsmith's store. Stu Herron stepped forward, his gun still smoking. Both Stu's and Gabe's bullets had hit the third deputy.

"Look out, Gabe!" Jack Delaney shouted then. Kuzak was getting up again. He had the rifle aimed at Gabe, and he got off a shot just as Gabe turned and shot again. This time Kuzak crumpled in death, but his bullet had skimmed across Gabe's left cheek, causing Gabe to whirl and hit the dirt. He lay there a moment, wondering if he was alive or dead, but he could hear people's voices. He supposed he must still be alive, and he could already taste blood running into his mouth.

Back at the house Faith stood at the doorway, waiting,

listening. Gabe had given her strict orders to remain there with the boys. Maude was with her, as was the schoolteacher, Sandra Bellings. The gunshots made them all jump. Faith lost track of how many shots there were. She knew only that, suddenly, it was silent. "I have to go see!" she told the other women. "Keep the boys here!"

She grabbed her woolen cape and ran out, terrified of what she might find. She and Gabe had made love again last night, such sweet, tender, passionate lovemaking, both knowing Gabe could die today. "Please, God, don't let him be dead or hurt," she murmured. She ran around the side of the rooming house and on up the street. A crowd had gathered, many of them buzzing with elation. Faith saw one deputy lying dead near the gunsmith's shop, and she breathed a sigh of relief. But the biggest crowd was farther up the street, and she couldn't see Gabe.

She ran ahead to find Joe Keller, David Kuzak, and another deputy lying dead in the street. She jumped when she heard more gunfire in the area of the deputy bunkhouse. She ran in that direction to see Gabe coming her way with Buck and the other three deputies, one of them holding a bleeding arm. All three deputies wore only their long johns and were barefoot, all shivering and cussing, begging to be allowed at least to put on coats.

Faith hardly noticed the cold, or the fact that the sky was growing darker to the west. A spring snowstorm was coming, but it didn't matter, as long as she could lie in Gabe's arms tonight and know that the town was free of Joe Keller and his men. The crowd seemed jubilant, and they began to gather around the remaining three deputies, some talking of a hanging.

Faith noticed blood on Gabe's face and all over the front of his shirt. "My God!" She stood frozen as Bret ran to him and handed him a towel, which he pressed to the wound across his left cheek.

"I'm all right," he told Faith when he reached her. He holstered his gun and put an arm around her. "It's just a flesh wound."

"Half an inch, and the bullet would have been in your brain," Bret said. She put her arms around both of them.

"He's all right, Faith, and Keller is dead. So is Kuzak. Thank God."

The crowd began to get over their shock and loosen up, some actually cheering.

"Hang the bastards!" someone shouted. More people gathered around the other three deputies, and Faith let go of Gabe, suddenly concerned, turning to stop the angry crowd. Finally Gabe shot his gun in the air to get their attention. He stood behind Faith, who looked pleadingly at the once peaceful group of people who had suddenly become vigilantes.

"Don't do this!" she begged. "Gabe has helped rid us of the corruption in this town. We wanted Keller gone because we wanted peace. We hardly needed a sheriff before Keller came here, because we are Christian, civilized people. If you hang these men, you're no better than Joe Keller!"

"Well, what the heck are we supposed to do with them?" one man asked.

Gabe faced them, all three men standing there barefoot and shivering as much from fear as from the cold. "You men don't mind getting out of town and never coming back, do you?"

"N-n-no," one replied, rubbing briskly at his arms.

"We've got no reason to be here now, not with Keller gone," another spoke up.

Gabe turned to Bret. "Any of these three harm you when they took you off to jail?" he asked her.

To Faith's surprise Bret actually reddened. "No," she answered, looking down at Kuzak. "It was that one." She looked back at Gabe. "Thank you. Ben would have been proud to know you."

Gabe nodded, understanding her deeper pain. Faith had told him about the rape.

Buck walked over and put an arm around Bret. "Come on back inside the saloon, Bret. You'll catch sick out here."

Bret scowled at him. "Listen, you, I never get sick."

Buck laughed in the peculiar cackle familiar to everyone in town. He took Bret's arm and led her back into the saloon, and Gabe addressed the remaining crowd. "Let these three get dressed and then take them over to the jail. We will keep them there until I settle with Tod Harding. If we let them go now, they might try to warn him. Once I get things straight with Harding, they can leave." Several men with guns goaded the three men back to the bunkhouse, others in the crowd beginning to feel braver now that someone had come along to rid them of their hated sheriff. Faith hoped she could continue to convince them it would be wrong to lynch the remaining deputies.

Gabe turned to Jack Delaney. "Let's go send that telegram to Tod Harding to come to Sommers Station."

"Gabe, your face. You should see a doctor," Faith told him.

"Not yet. I want to send that telegram first." He watched the crowd. "The rest of you keep an eye on anyone in town who works for Harding. Do not let any of them leave. I want to surprise Harding. He might not come at all if he knows what has happened here."

"Who the hell are you, mister?" one man asked.

Faith realized then that a lot of these people had no idea what had been planned here today, who Gabe was. "This is Gabe Beaumont, my husband. I've known for several days that he was still alive. Tod Harding and Joe Keller had him falsely arrested over five years ago and sent off to prison in Indian Territory."

Murmurs and whispers moved through the crowd.

"I'll be damned," someone said.

"He really is Indian!" said one woman.

"You've all seen what my husband did here today," Faith told them. "He did it for Sommers Station. We have our town back, and Gabe is going to try to help me convince Tod Harding to turn the deeds to the railroad property back over to me. But first we have to get him here, and he can't know that Gabe is still alive. It's all a very long story, and when we get that newspaper going that I have planned, I will tell it to all of you in the paper. A man who works for the *Rocky Mountain News* has written me about coming here to start a newspaper of his own, so Sommers Station will soon have its own special news. I want all your help in deciding what we should call it. We'll have a town meeting soon, and there will be many things to decide and also to celebrate."

People smiled then, some coming up to thank Gabe while the town undertaker ordered others to help him carry Keller and the deputies' bodies to the morgue. Faith walked with Gabe to the telegraph office, clinging to his arm, still reassuring herself he was all right.

It was over—almost. Gabe still had Harding to contend with. "You know you can't kill Harding, don't you?" she reminded him. "He's too powerful a man. The law would come after you for certain. Everyone in town will back you up for what happened here today. But Harding is another story. He has a lot of people behind him who can pull strings."

"Don't worry about Harding. I promised Judge Parker I wouldn't kill him. There are other ways of getting what you want out of a man."

"Oh? Like what?"

"You don't want to know. Don't forget I'm half–Sioux Indian."

Faith could almost hear the beating of drums, the cry of a warrior. She suspected he was right. She didn't want to know how he would get what he needed out of Harding, but she did enjoy the thought of Gabe making the man sweat. Harding had always been so pompous and arrogant, always the man in charge. Facing Gabe Beaumont would be something quite different for him.

Chapter Thirty-two

Faith waited at the depot, her heart pounding. If things didn't go right, Gabe could end up in a lot of trouble at the hands of Tod Harding. He did not want to meet the man there in public. Everyone knew he had some kind of plan, but he did not want to be seen riding off with Harding.

The train came steaming into the station, bell clanging, steam hissing, cars rumbling. The engine chugged past the station and came to a halt, and Faith watched as passengers began to disembark. Finally she spotted Harding, dressed dapper as ever, carrying a fancy new carpetbag as well as a briefcase. She hurried over to greet him, pretending friendliness and concern. "Mr. Harding."

The skirts of her deep-brown velvet dress made swirls in the snow as she approached him, and she kept the hood of her cream-colored woolen cloak pulled up over her head, wondering if spring would ever truly arrive this year.

Harding turned, scanning her curiously, wondering why on earth Faith Beaumont had come to greet him. He supposed there was truly a town emergency for Faith to be the one to come for him. He nodded to her. "Faith. What on earth is going on?" he asked. "I received a wire in Omaha from my bank cashier that there had been an emergency and I should come right away and bring the deeds to my railroad property. Has the bank been robbed? Why are my deeds needed?"

"Did you bring them?"

"Yes, but—"

"I'll explain at the house. Please come with me." She led him to a buggy, climbing in and taking up the reins herself. She drove around the back side of the depot, a block past the rooming house. Harding thought it a little strange that she didn't take the main street, but he supposed this strange emergency had something to do with their unusual route. She drove along the back street, past her house, past a few stores, the saloon, the blacksmith's, to the livery.

"Wait a minute. You said we were going to your house," he told her.

"We will soon. There is someone you must talk to first."

"Look, Faith—"

"You will understand soon."

"Look, if you've brought in someone willing to lend you money to buy back your property, it will do you no good. I do not intend to sell."

"We shall see, Mr. Harding."

Faith drove the buggy to the livery, and the door at the back of the building opened. Buck stepped out and held it open while she drove inside. Then Buck closed the door.

"What the hell is going on?" Harding asked.

Faith turned to him, leveling a pistol at him. "Get down, Mr. Harding."

He looked at the gun, his eyes wide with surprise. "What in God's name are you trying to pull?"

"I have killed men before, Mr. Harding, Indians and outlaws. As far as I am concerned, you are no better than an outlaw yourself. You are a thief and a liar. Now, please get down."

He gave her a scathing look before climbing down. "I think it's time I made sure you left town."

Faith threw down his briefcase, and Buck opened the front door to the livery. Faith snapped the reins to the sleek roan mare that pulled the buggy, then drove it outside. Buck closed the door, and Harding stood in bewilderment.

"Will you please tell me what is going on?" he asked Buck.

"I won't. But somebody else here will."

Harding looked around, his eyes taking a moment to adjust to the semidarkness inside the closed livery. He wrinkled his nose at the smell of horse manure and hay. "This is crazy. I don't see—"

Gabe stepped out from the back room, where Buck usually slept. He wore a wolfskin coat that came to his hips, and he held a rifle in his hands, pointed at Harding. "Well. We meet again, Mr. Harding."

Harding's mouth fell open, and he felt suddenly lightheaded. "Gabe Beaumont!" he said in a near whisper. Everything was beginning to fall into place now. "Look, Beaumont, I did find a soldier who said you'd killed that lieutenant. I don't even remember his name, but those were legitimate charges. You deserved—"

"Shut up, Harding!" Gabe cocked the rifle. "Just shut up. We both know the truth, and it is taking all the willpower I can muster not to pull this trigger and open up your belly! That judge you paid off never hanged me, and the judge who came after him was honest and fair. He saw right through it all and let me out."

"And if you murder me, you'll be right *back* in prison or feel a rope around your neck!"

"Oh, I don't intend to murder you, Harding. I intend only to make you *wish* you were dead!"

Harding felt pinpricks of fear rushing through his blood. "What are you talking about?"

"We are going for a little ride. I have a horse all saddled for you. You can go out sitting on it, or I can slam this rifle across your skull and take you out hanging over the horse's back. Which way do you want to go?"

"Go where?"

"None of your business."

Buck brought up the horses. "Climb up," he told Harding.

Harding kept his eyes on Gabe. "Do you have any idea how cold it is out there? Where are we going?"

"I know how cold it is, and I told you it's none of your business where we're going." Gabe came closer, handing the man a clean bandanna. "Put this in your mouth."

"What?"

Gabe rammed the barrel of his gun against the man's neck. "Put it in your mouth!"

Harding began to sweat in spite of the cold. "Where are Joe Keller and his men? They'll have your hide for this!"

"Keller's dead, and so are three of his deputies," Buck answered. "The other three was run out of town. Now, put the goddamn bandanna in your mouth."

Harding felt sick to his stomach. Keller dead! The whole town must have planned this! He looked into Gabe's eyes, and he knew that Gabe was the one who had killed Keller. "What is it you want?"

"You messed with my woman and shattered her dream," Gabe answered. "You stole five years from me and Faith, kept me from the son I did not even know I had. If your orders had been followed, I would be dead, and you would eventually have taken everything from Faith. Now, put that bandanna in your mouth. When we are away from town, I will tell you what I want."

Harding realized he had no choice but to cooperate. He shoved the bandanna into his mouth, and Buck tied another bandanna around him from behind so that he was soundly gagged. "That ought to keep your mouth from blabbin'," he told Harding. "Now, put your hands in front of you."

Harding obeyed, feeling more terror by the moment. The look in Gabe's eyes was devastating. Surely he meant to kill him. Buck snapped handcuffs around his wrists, then ordered him onto the horse. Harding barely managed to get his foot in the stirrup, he was so shaken. Finally he sat astride the horse, and Gabe climbed onto his own black gelding. Buck handed him the reins to Harding's horse, then handed up the man's briefcase. He opened the back door to the stables, and Gabe rode out, leading Harding's horse behind him, headed for the distant hills.

• • •

"Please don't do this! You have no right!" Harding begged. He stumbled, falling into snow, and cried out when a rock struck his knee. "Please, Beaumont, I'm freezing!" He was barefoot, and he wore only his long johns. Gabe had un-cuffed him and removed the rest of his clothes, which they'd left at the place they'd made camp, in a cave cut out of a canyon wall. When Harding had resisted, Gabe had landed a hard fist into his middle. Between the two men there was no contest. Gabe was bigger, stronger, certainly more skilled—and he was full of hatred and vengeance. The Indian in him almost enjoyed the man's abject terror. Tod Harding represented all that Gabriel hated about white men, and this one had messed with his woman.

Now Harding's wrists were cuffed again, and a rope was attached to the cuffs. Gabe had led him outside and forced him to walk behind his horse for close to two miles. The calm day had turned ugly, a bitter wind coming down off the mountains, bringing with it snow and sleet. Harding's long johns were wet.

"There is a nice warm fire back there in the cave," Gabe reminded Harding, yelling above the wind. "You could be sitting beside it. All you have to do is go back there and sign all those deeds over to Faith."

"I bought that property fair and square! I paid the railroad thirty dollars a lot, and I even paid Faith three dollars a lot for the work she had put into improvements."

"You knew all along she'd never pay two-fifty a lot. You let her put all her hopes and dreams into that land, and then you stole it from her! That would not have been so bad if you had not brought in Keller and his men and tried to take over the whole town!"

"Help!" Harding screamed. "Somebody help me!"

"Yell all you want, Harding. No one will hear you out here, especially with this wind." He rode a little faster, forcing Harding to run or fall and be dragged. "Agree to sign over the deeds and bring us no trouble, and you can be sitting by the fire in that cave with a blanket wrapped around you," he shouted to Harding. "You are lucky it is spring and only twenty degrees. If it was winter, it might be twenty below zero. Perhaps you would like me to remove your wool underwear and let you run naked in the wind. I have seen Indians do it. I have done it myself. It makes a man strong. But, then, you are not used to such things. Perhaps to make you cooperate, I will have to cut the bottoms of your feet and make you keep walking on them. The cuts will freeze. Soon your feet will freeze and perhaps you will have to have them cut off."

"All right! All right! Take me back to the cave! Please! I'll sign the goddamn deeds!"

Gabe halted his horse. He was plenty warm, in his winter moccasins and heavy wolfskin coat. He turned to look at Harding, enjoying the sight of him with great pleasure. "I would not change my mind if I were you."

"I won't!"

"And if you send someone after me, I will tell everyone the truth about you, what you have already done to me, how you swindled Faith out of that land, how you tried to take over the whole town, falsely sent me to prison. I'm sure Judge Parker will back up the charges against you."

"I didn't know Keller would go that far!" Harding answered. "I swear it! I just gave him the job of sheriff because he got voted out in Cheyenne and he'd done me some favors there."

"How well I know."

"It's the truth! I didn't know Keller was harassing people, killing people, threatening others. He took advantage of a favor. That's the God's truth! All I did wrong was buy that land out from under Faith."

"And get me out of the way first so I could not help her! What else did you plan for her, Harding? Did you plan to try to get into her bed? Faith Beaumont would never let the likes of you touch her!"

"You're right," Harding answered, frantically hoping to calm the man down. "She never let me get near her. She's a fine woman, Beaumont. And smart. She's smart. Somehow she knew I had something to do with what happened to you. She accused me of it. She's a hell of a woman, Beaumont. A hell of a woman. That's what attracted me to her, but she's not for somebody like me. She's not a woman who wants to be pampered and live in a castle. She likes to do things on her own. I never touched her wrongly, Beaumont. I hope you know that."

Gabe grinned in a sneer. "I know what you *wanted* to do. And I know what Keller and his men were *planning* to do! Do you know one of them raped Bret Flowers when they put her in jail? They shot her good friend Ben for no reason and killed a young boy who was unarmed—shot him in the *back*!"

Harding shook his head. "I didn't know they were doing those things. I swear."

Gabe turned his horse and rode closer to the man. "How many others have built up railroad land, brought in people to make more money for the railroad, only to get swindled by men like you, Harding? How many men like you have lined their pockets richly by cheating the government and the people alike?"

Harding was beginning to cry. "I . . . I don't know. I did a stupid thing. I know that now. Just . . . please take me back to the cave. Don't cut my feet. I'll sign over the deeds and I'll leave Sommers Station and never come back. You have my word."

"And how good *is* your word?" Gabe sneered.

Harding sniffed, his hair filling with sleet that was freezing in place. "It's good, Beaumont. You can have witnesses if you want. When we go back to town, you can call a meeting. I'll announce in public I have signed the land back over to Faith, and that I will leave Sommers Station and cause no more trouble for any of you. I'll keep men there to run my businesses, but I'll stay away, and I'll pay whatever rent Faith asks for the businesses." He shivered violently, and his body jerked in a sob.

Gabe reached back and untied the rawhide laces that held a blanket and another pair of winter moccasins. "You are lucky that I promised Judge Isaac Parker that I would not kill you," he told Harding. He threw down the items, then climbed down and unlocked the man's handcuffs, taking them off and removing the rope. "Put those moccasins on your feet and wrap the blanket around you. You can get on the horse. I will walk it back to the cave."

Harding broke down in sobs as he eagerly pulled on the moccasins. He wrapped himself in the blanket and stumbled over to the horse. Gabe gave him a boost, and he climbed on. Gabe took hold of the reins and led the animal back to camp. After nearly an hour of walking they reached the cave, and once inside, Gabe built up the fire. Harding sat close to it, still shivering and crying.

"Lie down and put your feet out," Gabe told him. "I will put hot rocks around them."

Harding obeyed, hoping the man didn't mean to whip out his knife and cut into his feet instead. Had he done such things to others? At the moment it was difficult to believe Gabe Beaumont could be a gentle father and husband, but surely he was, or Faith would not have waited for him the way she had. Here was a man who represented the real West. Harding hated this land, hated its wildness, its lawlessness, the Indians, half-breeds like Gabe Beaumont, men who were half-tame and half-animal. He would be glad to go back to Omaha. In fact, he would go all the way back to Chicago, where true civilization existed. He wondered sometimes if it would ever exist in places like this. Hell, there was still a lot of Indian trouble out there, soldiers and forts all over the place, Indians still raiding and killing.

He would gladly sign over the damn deeds and get the hell out of there. Let men like Gabe Beaumont and women like Faith Sommers have their damned West. As far as he was concerned, it was good only for making money. Let the poor prospectors come there and look for gold. Men like himself came after them and bought them out, then mined the gold the right way and made millions. Let the settlers come and build up the land, build their little towns. Men like himself came after them with the railroad and land grants and businesses and found ways to make money off all the hard work the stupid settlers put into the land. There was timber out there, and men like himself had the money to send loggers out and cut that timber. Let the ranchers fight the Indians and the elements to build their cattle ranches. Men like himself came after them and bought the cattle, making millions selling beef back east, owning their own slaughterhouses in Chicago and Omaha, owning the railroad that hauled the cattle. The settlers and ranchers needed loans. Men like himself owned the banks.

Yes, that's all this West was good for—so that men like himself could get rich off its minerals and timber and rich land. The only trouble was, there were a few, like Faith Sommers Beaumont, who rose above men like himself and stuck it out, finding ways to make their own riches without anyone's help. People like Faith were too damned independent and stubborn. They came out there with big dreams, and they were willing to risk everything for those dreams. Then there were men like Gabe Beaumont. What Harding could do through legal channels, men like Gabe accomplished with brute force. In that respect they were not so different. Gabe was in his element out here in the West. Now they were dealing on Gabe Beaumont's terms. He was completely dependent on the man for survival, and Gabe damn well knew it.

Harding shivered again, letting Gabe pack warm rocks around his feet and legs.

"You will sleep," Gabe told him. "And come morning you will sign the deeds. Then I will take you back. You will get on a train and leave."

It was an order—not a request, not a suggestion. "Gladly," Harding mumbled. "Gladly."

Fireworks filled the night sky with wild colors, and eleven-year-old Johnny and seven-year-old Alex watched with excited delight, along with their new brother and sister, two-year-old Sadie, named after her grandma Kelley, and six-month-old Matthew, who had his older brother's middle name. Faith had decided to give her third son his grandpa Kelley's first name.

To her deepest delight her father had come to visit Sommers Station with her brother, Benny, and his wife and three children. They had all come to town on the Union Pacific, which now made three stops a day at the ever-growing town of Sommers Station, two of them from the east, one from the west.

Faith had never known such happiness. She stood beside Gabe on the bandstand, holding little Matthew in her arms. It was July 1877. This Fourth of July celebration was made happier by the fact that Gabe had just been reelected for another three-year term as sheriff of Sommers Station.

In spite of his being half-Indian, he was well liked by everyone, an honest man who was fair in his dealings with troublemakers, but swift and sure, a man most would not want to go up against. He had foiled a bank robbery just last year, took a bullet in the back of his left shoulder.

So many wounds he'd suffered, but Gabe was tough. He had survived four horrible years in prison and had come back to her. There was no doubt in anyone's mind of his bravery and skill, and the fact that he had rid the town of Joe Keller and his bunch, as well as having somehow managed to get the railroad land back from Tod Harding, was all the people there needed to keep supporting Gabriel Beaumont for sheriff. Everyone gladly paid a little extra in town taxes to meet his wages.

Buck was one of Gabe's deputies, and to everyone's surprise and no little amusement, Buck Jones had not married the schoolteacher but instead had married Bret Flowers two years ago—a comical pair indeed, but Bret seemed happy. Buck was fifty, but still hard as nails, and, according to Bret, "a whole lot younger in bed." Faith smiled at the thought of the woman's brash remarks.

It hardly seemed possible she was thirty years old herself now. Gabe was forty, but like Buck, he was not a man who showed his age physically. Their lovemaking was as beautiful and vigorous as it had ever been, and their resulting family was the greatest joy in both their lives. Faith could not help feeling proud, not just of her family, but of the dream she had managed to realize, the dream Gabe had helped her hang on to.

How strange that the Indian who had helped her find her way there twelve years ago, then ridden out of her life, had become such an important part of her life now . . . this man who had once ridden with the Sioux and attacked settlers . . . who had ridden with outlaws and attacked the stage station . . . who had once had a Sioux wife and son. She'd heard the news last year of the terrible massacre

at the Little Bighorn up in Montana. She knew that the
deaths of General George Armstrong Custer and over two
hundred soldiers at the hands of the Sioux were a big blow
to Gabe. The news had jolted him into realizing just how
far removed he was from that life, and his heart was heavy
at the thought that the massacre was only the beginning of
the end for the Sioux. That way of life was over for him.
This was his new life—a husband, father, sheriff of Sommers Station—but he still often wore the bear-claw necklace.

Alex and Johnny squealed when another firecracker ex-
ploded in a shower of red and green stars. Johnny was
holding his grandfather's hand, and Benny was holding
little Sadie. Her brother and his wife and children all were
enjoying the celebrations.

Faith turned to Gabe, putting an arm around him.
"Congratulations, Sheriff Beaumont."

He smiled, rubbing her shoulder. "You got me into all
of this, you know. If I had never met you on the trail all
those years ago . . ."

"You might be running from soldiers right now," she
finished for him. "Don't forget you're as much white as
Indian, Gabe, whether or not you like to admit it. There is
nothing wrong with that."

"This is not just a celebration of the Fourth and of my
election. This is for you. It is a celebration of Sommers
Station. This place is all thanks to you, your determination,
your bravery. You suffered through a lot to have this.
There are not many men out here who are as brave as you
are."

Faith smiled. "I'm not so sure how brave I am. I came
out here because of a rather wild heart, Gabe, a determination to have my own way. I guess we're a lot alike that
way, a bit of wildness in both of us, a carelessness that
makes us appear brave when we're really just determined
to do things our own way."

He pulled her away from the others and held her close,
little Matthew between them. "Well, this wild heart is
wildly in love with you, and this is one of those nights that
I am anxious to get the kids into bed and glad your rela-

tives are staying at the boardinghouse so they will not hear us in the night."

"Hear us? Will we be making a lot of noise?"

He kissed her softly. "You will be making the most noise."

A rush of desire swept through her blood. This man never ceased to bring out the wantonness in her soul. "I will, will I?" She ran her hands along his muscular arms. "Well, maybe you're the one who will be making the most noise."

He laughed lightly. "We will see." He kissed her again, a long, sweet, deep kiss that suggested things to come. Faith could not imagine her life turning out any more wonderful than this. A parade moved through town, people dressed in silly costumes, a stagecoach decorated with flowers and banners. Faith turned to watch it, shaking her head.

"You know what is really strange, Gabe?"

"What's that?"

"All these years I've been here, determined to build Sommers Station into a town, working for Wells Fargo, greeting hundreds of stagecoaches, welcoming the coming of the railroad . . . all these years, and never once did I ride in a stagecoach myself. I came here and never left."

Matthew reached out for his father, and Gabe took the baby into his arms. "It's almost time for your speech, Mayor Beaumont," he told Faith.

Faith left him and walked to the edge of the bandstand, where a banner hung that said CHEERS TO FAITH BEAUMONT, MAYOR OF SOMMERS STATION. Nearby was a banner that read REELECT GABE BEAUMONT FOR SHERIFF. People were beginning to gather around the podium to listen to Faith talk about the future of Sommers Station, and it warmed her heart to think her own father was watching proudly. She had never dreamed that running away from Pennsylvania would come to this, and when she thought of poor young Johnny lying in that lost grave somewhere, her heart ached with the memory.

God led me here, and here I stayed, she thought. This surely was what God had meant for her, and she realized he had been with her all the time, through all the hardships, all the danger, all the tears, all the joy. The parade and fireworks ended, and the podium was lit with several hanging lanterns. Townspeople gathered for the final speech before heading home, and Faith's eyes teared as she scanned the crowd, many of whom had come in answer to her ads to build a new life there. So many familiar faces, including Bret and Buck, who stood at the front of the crowd. Maude and her husband were there; the schoolteacher, Sandra Bellings; Preacher Ames; Stu Herron, the gunsmith; Jack Delaney, the blacksmith; Calvin Malone, who ran the town newspaper called the *Station News;* Harold Williams, the town's new doctor was there; so many others—store owners, bankers, lawyers, hotel owners, restaurant owners, farmers, ranchers.

She loved them all, and they knew it. She opened her arms, smiling through tears. "Welcome everyone. Welcome to Sommers Station."

ABOUT THE AUTHOR

An award-winning romance writer, *Rosanne Bittner* has been acclaimed for both her thrilling love stories and the true-to-the-past authenticity of her novels. Specializing in the history of the American Indians and the early settlers, her books span the West from Canada to Mexico, Missouri to California, and are based on Rosanne's visits to almost every setting chosen for her novels, extensive research, and membership in the Western Outlaw-Lawman History Association, the Oregon-California Trails Association, the Council on America's Military Past, and the Nebraska State Historical Society.

She has won awards for Best Indian Novel and Best Western Series from *Romantic Times* and is a Silver Pen, Golden Certificate, Golden Heart and Reviewer's Choice for Excellence Award winner from *Affaire de Coeur*. She has also won several Reader's Choice awards and is a member of Romance Writers of America.

Rosanne and her husband have two grown sons and live in a small town in southwest Michigan.

From the author . . .

I hope you have enjoyed my story. To learn more about me and other books I have written, please send a self-addressed, stamped, letter-size envelope to me at 6013 North Coloma Road, Coloma, Michigan, 49038. Or contact my home page on the internet at http://www.Parrett.net/~bittner Thank you!

DON'T MISS THESE FABULOUS
BANTAM WOMEN'S FICTION TITLES

On Sale in September

TAME THE WILD WIND
by ROSANNE BITTNER
the mistress of romantic frontier fiction

Here is the sweeping romance
of a determined woman who runs a stagecoach inn
and the half-breed who changes worlds to
claim the woman he loves.

_____ 56996-1 $5.99/$7.99 in Canada

BETROTHED
by ELIZABETH ELLIOTT
"An exciting find for romance readers everywhere!"
—AMANDA QUICK,
New York Times bestselling author

Guy of Montague rides into Lonsdale Castle to
reclaim Halford Hall, only to be forced into a
betrothal with the baron's beautiful niece.

_____ 57566-X $5.50/$7.50 in Canada